ALL'S FAIR IN RUTS AND HEATS

A Dark Omegaverse Novel

NICHOL GOLDSTEIN

ALL'S FAIR IN RUTS AND HEATS
Published by NixComix Publishing
nixcomix.com

NixComix Publishing™ is a registered trademark, all rights reserved.

ISBN (print): 979-8-9870103-1-0
ISBN (e-book): 979-8-9870103-0-3

An application to register this book for cataloguing has been submitted to the Library of Congress, registration number: TX 9-190-907

First Edition: October 2022

Cover design by Fiona Jayde Media
Editing, print & e-book production by Jim Spivey / Working Vacation Studios

To Sarah. Without you, I never would have had the courage to write something like this. Thank you for inspiring me the way you do.

To Tristen. When I was rabidly throwing chapters at you like, "READ THIS!", you humored me and even set your own work aside to help make this story the best it could be. I love you.

To my husband, who encourages all my creative outlets, even when they come paired with dirty words. Very. Dirty. Words.

And to all my brave readers. I hope I light your panties on fire; there's no greater compliment an erotica writer can ask for. (Other than your tears, of course. They are delicious, decadent, and keep me young.)

CONTENT WARNINGS

This book is intended for an adult audience and contains content that may be upsetting for some readers. Please be aware that the following contains:

Inappropriate Language

Rape/Non-consensual elements

Alpha/Beta/Omega dynamics

Emotional Manipulation

Breeding Kink

Stalking

Suicide

Violence

And has a Bittersweet Ending

If you find this content triggering, please ensure you are in the right frame of mind before reading, knowing that difficult times may be in store for our characters.

WHOA-HO! A/B/O?

WHAT YOU NEED TO UNDERSTAND ABOUT THE ALPHA/BETA/OMEGA GENRE

Realizing that not everyone is familiar, I want to give a brief A/B/O primer to help ease you into the story. There is some terminology that might seem like strange word choices unless you understand the trope. If you are an A/B/O geek, hop, skip, and jump away! If you've never read it before, you'll benefit from this.

THINGS TO KNOW:

A/B/O is often very smut focused, no matter the author. In speaking to many women, people find the way this genre explores sex to be very liberating. Not only is it natural to go into heat and be insatiable during sex, but it's 100% desirable. Additionally, it's expected to have your partner take care of you afterward; anything else is cruel. In a way, the whole trope comes with a very sexually charged style of romance, where it's natural to be sexually active, and you're revered when you are. It's then expected for you to show your vulnerability, and you are given permission to allow yourself to be cared for/catered to during your times of need.

The social dynamic between the three secondary genders varies per story. Sometimes Alphas and Omegas are suppressed as arcane by Betas; sometimes Betas can be considered a slave class. It's up to the world the writer creates. In general, though:

- Alphas are exactly what you'd think. Powerful. Aggressive. They can be male or female.
- Omegas, which can also be male or female, are submissive, though often only during their heat cycles, whereas Alphas tend to keep their tendencies as intrinsic to their personalities.
- Consider Betas to be like regular people.

There are special quirks to the bodies of Alphas and Omegas. In many cases, this "species" is derived from the idea of werewolves, though often A/B/O doesn't use shapeshifting. It's more of an evolution where the animalistic traits stick, but the transformation goes away. Every author handles this differently. Mine do not shapeshift.

Here is a glossary of some standard terms:

- **Scent glands:** Think of them as at the pulse points and between the legs. Some are more platonic than others. The most intimate are on the neck — this is where the "mating glands" are. An Alpha usually bites an Omega, just once, to "claim" their partner. At that point, their scents are supposed to mix together, making them a blend. Others will then be able to identify someone as "mated," and often who they're mated to.
- **Presenting:** Imagine puberty on steroids. That's when their "secondary sexes"/"designations" are revealed. Alphas become large and more muscular, Omegas have hips that flare — "child bearing." Yes, Male Omegas give birth. Don't ask.

- **Suppressants:** Medicine that helps Alphas and Omegas stave off their ruts and heats. Prescribed.
- **Blockers:** Something like reverse perfume. Helps mask the scent of an Alpha or Omega to help them blend into society better.
- **Scents:** Everyone has their own scent, and it can change based on emotions. Alphas and Omegas have the keenest senses of smell and can "read the emotion of the room," so to speak.
- **Alphas** and **Omegas** often refer to themselves as "Alpha" and "Omega" when they are speaking from their instinct's point of view. They also refer to one another in this way. It's not derogatory...until it is.
- **An Alpha's command:** When an Alpha is mated with an Omega, they can command the Omega to make them obedient. This is a special tone of voice and is not every time they speak.

About sex:

- An Alpha's best pairing is with an Omega, whose nature it is to mold around the tendencies of their Alpha. Though Beta pairings work with either secondary sex, Alpha/Omega pairings are the most likely to breed successfully.
- Ruts and heats are exactly what they sound like — periods of being uncontrollably sexual. Voracious. It literally hurts if they're not having sex, more so for the Omegas than the Alphas. These last for about four to five days, normally. You should have at least two a year to be healthy.
- Omegas make "slick." Imagine a woman getting wet to the nth degree. It's supposed to be sweet smelling, delicious, and absolutely enticing.

- Alphas have "knots" at the bottom of their phalluses. Think of an inner tube that inflates just before they orgasm. It's meant to lock the Alpha and Omega together to keep their semen inside, making them more likely to breed successfully. It also gives the pair a bit of post-coital cuddle time, locked together until the knot releases.
- The Alpha must feed and take care of their Omega during their heats. Lost in a kind of delirium, they become mindless and can get weak over days of not thinking to eat.

Anything else should be fairly understandable in context. Enjoy and good luck!

CHAPTER 1

TRICKY, TRICKY, TRICKY

"IF THERE WAS SUCH a thing as a male *cunt*, it would be you." Caleb's teeth are bared as he looms, casting a shadow over the pale man before him. "Nice to know you've managed to be both the youngest judge on the circuit and the biggest moron."

Hayes looks unmoved. As an Alpha himself, he's uncowed by Caleb's insults. Always has been.

Leaning against his desk in absolute nonchalance, not bothering to look up, Hayes picks some lint off his austere judge's robes—a piece of white fluff easily spotted when lying on top of the deep, respectable black. "Angry, are we? You smell like it. Just be sure not to throw one of your mindless fits in my office, Reed, or we may have a significant problem. You know I made the right ruling, even if your ego is trying to tell you otherwise."

Caleb points at the door in a harsh gesture. "She had no case!"

Deigning to look Caleb in the eyes, Hayes says, "She had an excellent case. And she outwitted you quite masterfully if I do say so myself."

"She didn't outwit me! I clearly said —"

"Yes, yes. You already lawyered your point to death on the floor, don't you think? Did you find me so enthralled I'd want a repeat performance?" Hayes crosses his arms, regarding Caleb with narrowed, pale blue eyes. "This is the first case you've lost since high school debate. It happens to everyone eventually, even sniveling man-children like yourself. Accept that you were beaten, put on your adult diapers, and go cry elsewhere."

The rumble of Caleb's low growl would put a tremor of fear into most men, yet his once-rival stares him down without flinching.

"And if you don't leave now"—Hayes jerks his chin toward the exit—"I'll throw out all your cases as mistrials just to irritate you. See how well you'll do in Hart's district instead."

Asshole, Caleb thinks, clenching his back teeth and feeling the tendons in his jaw pulse. If he'd known he'd have this much weight to throw around, Caleb would have gone the judges' route in university, too. Hindsight.

Dismissing him with a more obvious nod this time, Hayes refuses to lower his eyes and his scent fills Caleb's nostrils with its silent threat. Though he doesn't dignify it with a response, Caleb takes the other Alpha's warning with the grace of a teenager, grunting with a sneer as he turns on his heels to storm out the door.

It's dark in his office at this point, everyone having gone home for the day. That doesn't mean they're done working—that's not what being a defense attorney is all about—it just means they've moved their base of operations to somewhere they can loosen their ties and take off their pointy shoes. That gives Caleb carte blanche to behave like the petulant maniac he is as he thrusts things off his desk, one thick arm swiping to take out innocent paperweights, folders, and his desktop keyboard. Anything that remains, he picks off one by one, *thwack* after cathartic *thwack.*

A fucking pro bono Omega. Caleb's nostrils flare at the thought. He scours his hands through his longish, black hair and tugs at it slightly, trying to ground himself in the land of non-assholes. It's not his forte.

He's not so archaic as to say the only place this Omega belongs is in his bed, ankles by her ears, screaming his name as he knots her… but he's not *not* saying it.

He throws some more things around, toppling his chair for good measure. Hayes was right; Caleb is absolutely pitching one of his famous fits, though the other male hadn't realized the special reason. Caleb is close to his rut—suddenly, unexpectedly—though that isn't necessarily the problem. The real problem is that it's clearly this pro bono Omega's fault. The way she riled him up in court was, in part, due to her catching him with a small piece of evidence he hadn't designed a rebuttal for—hadn't seen the need to. Another mistake in hindsight. Throwing him off his game, she made his cross-examination come off as halting, unsure, and unthought through. A pup on his first case. And so, Caleb lost with a jury vote of four against five. So close, but that only counts in horseshoes and hand grenades.

That's not what haunts him, though. The memory that twirls a spiral pattern across his brain is singular: He was lost in the smell of her, distracted to no end, sweating his desire and tasting her in the air. Even now, her maple syrup flavor sticks to his skin, just as intense it was in the courtroom. Judge, jury, defendant, plaintiff, observants, everyone was on suppressants and doused with pheromone blockers as required, which means there's no way Caleb could have smelled her so clearly…unless she was supposed to be his fucking mate. That mousey, little, brown-haired, hazel-eyed Mary Sue is someone he'd normally rip to shreds, going back for seconds. Thirds. Now he still wants to, but for an entirely different reason.

Mate, his brain screams.

Caleb's never smelled a suppressed female so strongly before. His dead mother told him daily that she could scent his father from miles away as if it was destiny, and he can't stand that this random woman who trounced him so thoroughly—and in such a humiliating way—is supposed to be The One.

Mate, mate, mate.

He huffs and puffs and tries not to blow the office down. This is getting him nowhere. Caleb needs to calm himself before he has an aneurysm, which would only serve to piss off his remaining clients, never mind his abhorrent boss. Not that he's thinking about them much just now.

Already obsessed, he needs to know more about her. Every specification and specialization. Every measurement and mistrial. Every freckle and flaw. Her pedigree and her preferences. Caleb never does anything in half measures, and what do lawyers do when they need to know something? They research.

"Well, Miss Ari Jacobson, there's a little bit of research headed your way."

And this time, he'll make sure that not a single fact slips through his fingers. This Alpha is going on the hunt for the most important treasure there is.

Mate.

Ari Jacobson, twenty-five years young, is comically, frantically pointing to the windshield, flailing with her mouth agape as her best friend drives her to work on a sunny summer day.

"MERGING! He's MERGING! *ON THE LEFT!*"

"As. I. Can. Clearly. See." Niles white-knuckles the steering wheel, trying to keep a death grip on his patience. "Again, I do this every day."

"Not with me in the car you don't!!" Ari is riding the imaginary brake on the passenger-side floor, her calf tense to the point of trembling while her toes splay in her cheap high-heeled shoes.

Niles's frown is glorious as he hunches over and puts on his blinker. "Next time I'll let you spend hours in your couch cushions looking for subway fare. Why not? Sounds like a great way to spend an afternoon."

He drives them around the maze of city streets in the haphazard, jerky way that comes par for the course with uncoordinated traffic lights. It's followed abruptly by the stomach-swooping zoom required to make it onto Storrow Drive without dying in the process, going from zero-to-zebra miles per hour in point-two seconds.

Ari grits her teeth in panic.

Why can't everything be laid out in a grid, like New York City?

But no. Here in Boston, it's all nonsensical alley shortcuts, random mini-highways, and one-ways with no double backs. The buildings are huge mirrors that block out the GPS's signal half the time, so you either have to already know where you're going or just point your car in the right direction, blare your horn, and pray.

Clutching her messenger bag to her chest, Ari squeals, "Too fast! Too fast!"

"We're doing thirty!" Niles cries, gearing up into a snit.

Ari claps back in terror more than anger, her tan skin fading to white. "Yeah, and my parents were doing a whopping thirty-five just before they died!"

That cuts into Niles's budding tirade. He swallows his frustration and says, "Seatbelts for safety," snapping his own and watching Ari snag hers in solidarity. "We're good. It's not snow or ice outside right now. Summer, Ari. Look out the window and smell the melted tarmac, yeah? It's gonna be fine."

Ari presses her lips in a flat line, trying not to annoy her best friend any further. He's doing her a favor. She lost her train pass and didn't have time to scrounge up cash for the daily fare. Plus, after what she did yesterday...oof. That stunt in court is having repercussions, and one of them is her smelling way stronger than any respectable Omega should in the cramped quarters of a subway car.

"You need to refill your prescription," Niles says, giving her the side-eye. He's just as tired of her reek as she is.

"The doctor said not to start taking them again yet." Ari groans as a car passes them, still refusing to let go of the seatbelt strap clutched in her iron fists. "Plus, they're expensive! I'm poor!"

She hates it sometimes. Pro bono work does not pay a lot.

Though it's still well above minimum wage, Boston prices are so stupidly expensive, it's more than easy to get sucked dry—which is exactly why Ari does what she does. Every time she can afford a pizza or some box wine, she remembers that most of her clients can't. Some of them are out there struggling to eat and work, food stamps and hope the only things making their ends meet, but then they get saddled with some false accusation that will destroy what little of their lives they have. No. Ari will not let those who are disadvantaged get snapped up by the maws of the flawed judicial system. Not when she can save them, especially from the proverbial Big Bad Wolf that is Caleb Reed.

That's why she weaned down her dose of suppressants to nil, hadn't worn blockers for days, and didn't shower that morning after masturbating three times in a row. She was a pheromone rage storm in that courtroom. He's not the only one who's willing to do anything to win. If he's more than happy to play dirty, then so is she.

Niles rolls up outside her office building, double parked as usual. Grabbing onto her hand before she gets out, he grins at her with those handsome white teeth. "Make sure they treat you good today. You're sacrificing a lot to be such a badass."

Ari scoffs. "If my boss knew, he'd report me, and they'd take my license away."

"Still!" Niles says, always in awe of her desire to put others before herself. Rubbing his warm, dark brown thumbs over her knuckles, he quirks an eyebrow with a swell of pride. "Aaaaand guess what? Like a good, not-so-poor best friend, I left you some cash for lunch in your bento box today."

"Bento?" she asks. "You made me a bento?"

"Breakfast bento," he says, stretching into the back and holding up a cute little froggy set complete with google eyes. He hands it over like a mom, knowing Ari barely feeds herself on a good day. "I'll be back around five thirty so I can get you home."

She sputters, cringing. "No way! I'll walk!"

"Pffft. Now there's an hour of your life spent blistering in high heels that you'll never get back."

Ari rolls her eyes at him, realizing he means well. The best actually. She's just terrified of cars. Tugging one of his long, tight braids, woven with blonde this time and making a pretty pattern, she says, "Love you," and rubs her wrist against his to take some of his calming scent with her. Ari does this with all her friends. It's a bit old-fashioned, but she likes being able to smell the people she's met during the day. It makes her feel less lonely at night.

"Love you, too. We Omegas have to stick together." Niles blows big, wet smooch sounds her way and puts the car back into gear, making Ari jump out faster than possible with an "EEP!" that rends the sky.

"Kudos to you for beating that sadistic bastard!" Paul says, clapping Ari on the back a bit, making her skin sting in a way that's far too pleasant. She tries to ignore it, instead flashing her colleague a grin.

"I know, right? It feels like I just vanquished an enemy! That man has no morals. He'll fight for anyone with a fist full of cash, guilty or not. Stupid Alphas."

Paul staggers back in jest, covering his chest as if she stabbed him. "Ouch!"

"Present company excluded," she corrects.

It's not that Ari hates Alphas on principle—and, as Alphas go, Caleb Reed is actually quite the stunning specimen, one worth stripping down and studying—but she can't be bothered with anyone so corrupt, especially now when she's about to be so vulnerable. After lessening her dose of suppressants, Ari can feel that ancient ache beginning. Though unfamiliar, she knows it's her oncoming heat. Her first one. She'd suppressed herself immediately after she presented, just like every Omega in foster care has to, and then her future always had bigger plans for her than Mother Nature did. Her doctor said it was time, though. She can do damage to her body if she doesn't let herself go into heat at least twice a year. Still, Ari wants to ensure no sex-crazed state of mind will make her lower her standards enough to dally with the dark devils of this world. Ones like Caleb Reed.

Besides, his smell was too strong. Something like leather mixed with cinnamon and ash. It permeated the whole courtroom, and it took all of her grit just to stay on task. Though she'd never admit it to anyone, her Omega was prodding her, echoing the words *Provide, Entice, Protect*—each word meant to pair with the individual undertones of his complex scent. But no thank you, arcane inner demon.

The other Alphas in the courtroom smelled like nothing and behaved well in the face of her pheromones, yet he was near frothing. She could see every single moment of his distress and it made her feel powerful to be so obviously wanted. Even now, it gives her a kind of smug satisfaction.

"So how did you win anyway?" Paul asks, eyeing her strangely.

"We 'object'-ed over each other so many times, he got himself worked up. I was able to clip his logic with a single snip." She sighs at the happy memory. "There was a piece of evidence he didn't look over closely enough—just one—but apparently that was enough. It flustered him. He had no rebuttal, and his client completely sank in their chair when the jury votes were read. Justice has been served." Ari flips her hair back over her shoulder in an overblown show of pride.

"I can smell you, you know," Paul says into his coffee cup.

Ari's eyes fly wide open, and she covers the sides of her neck in shock. How blunt! And rude! And...embarrassing...

"You wouldn't have happened to try to *distract* our mutual nemesis, would you?"

He's on to her! Not only that; it's likely that her face now is a dead giveaway.

Paul lifts an eyebrow, the edges of his lips curling up slightly. "You know that's unethical, right? You could be disbarred."

Ari makes a little noise, but he just laughs at her, his eyes squinting a bit. Cheeky bastard.

She's not worried about him telling on her at least. Pro bono lawyers are few and far between, doing what they can to get by. A scrappy bunch who works hard to beat the bad guys. She knows she looks down on Reed for the same sort of touch-and-go relationship with the rules, but she does it for the side of good instead of the side of whoever has the highest bankroll. That absolves her, in her humble opinion.

Paul's smile becomes a smirk in short order. "Seems like you're going to pay the price for that. Your little trick is putting you into heat, isn't it?"

He can smell it on her. Damnit.

She tries to act as prim as possible, pulling her hair over her shoulders to try and stifle her scent, though the mere mention of her impending affliction makes her slick begin to trickle. She hates that feeling. Cold as it dries on her inner thighs.

"Hush," she mutters. "Not so loud."

Paul makes a little humming sound as if he won a fight they weren't even having. "You're 'loud' enough on your own. Any Alpha here can smell it. I'm just up close and personal. It's going to happen soon, I can tell."

Ari doesn't like his tone. Still, he's her work buddy, so she may as well confess. "Yeah, I think so, too. My doctor told me this time it will come on strong and probably last longer than normal." She grimaces, lost in her own irritation. "I'm going to have to make sure whatever man I beckon to my bed will be worth it. I have a best friend who might see me through if I ask nicely enough."

The scent of Caleb Reed pulses, unwanted, in her mind. *Provide, Entice, Protect.*

Paul lifts his eyebrows. "Isn't your friend an Omega?"

"Not ideal, I know. For more than a few reasons," she admits, shrugging. "But I'd rather that than an agonizing dry heat, or a complete and total stranger."

Not only that, but Ari can't imagine being in the arms of an Alpha for days on end and then going back to her lonely apartment afterward. The very thought hurts, and that ache in her heart is way stronger than the increasing ache in her belly. Stupid as she is, she'd want it to mean something. How it could possibly "mean something" to anyone with only a day-or-so's notice is beyond her. This is what she gets for being too focused on her work to bother with a social life.

"I could do it for you," Paul says. He cocks his hips, tucking a hand into his pocket and scuffing the toe of his shoe across the floor. He at least has the sense to look sheepish as he sets down his coffee cup and tousles his hair. He almost seems shy before daring to look her in the face.

Ari can't help it. She really can't. She bursts into a belly laugh, smacking him on the arm probably rougher than she means to. "Yeah, right! And then who's gonna take over all my cases?" Ari is nothing if not practical even as she wipes a tear of mirth from her eye. "Besides, you don't smell right. Vanilla and dryer sheets. You remind me of when I do my laundry."

Too smarmy to look offended, instead Paul reviews her in a way she can't comprehend. "And you, my dear friend, smell like a mix of innocence and naiveté."

It makes her snort. "Noted. Now, excuse me, *dear friend;* I have no time for this. There's a breakfast bento calling my name." She fluffs her hair one more time, trying to be amusing and probably failing miserably. Out of habit more than anything else, she rubs her and Paul's wrists together quickly before walking away, making her verbal goodbyes over her shoulder.

In all honesty, she was being kind. Vanilla is the scent she sprays in her bathroom after a night of bad Chinese food has ruined her. No one wants to be reminded of their bathroom's scent when it's under complete lockdown...especially not during sex. The dryer sheet smell is stronger, though, and that's the one that tends to linger when they touch. It makes Ari remember that she has to do her chores when she gets home.

Caleb is about to crack the table from the grip he has on it. He's watching his mate through a foggy window just across the street from her office, where a convenient café gives him a great view of her conversation. She stands with a short-haired, tanned-skinned male in the first-floor foyer of a cheap-looking, skinny building. Skyscrapers made completely out of glass and steel have their benefits—one of them being that it makes stalking her so much easier. With the building so narrow, he could likely see her no matter where she was inside. An extra tick in his favor is that Caleb's eyesight has sharpened, another sign that his rut is coming. This goddamned woman has thrown his body into chaos.

Caleb glares at the man she's speaking to.

Threat.

The stranger is looking at Caleb's mate in a way that no other Omega or Beta would dare. Narrowing his eyes, Caleb can see the glint on the sonofabitch's teeth, never mind the way his nostrils flare every time Ari slides her hair around, revealing the glands on her neck and letting the other man breathe her in. She's being a tease and she doesn't even know it, judging by the look on her face, obviously oblivious to the other man's blatant want.

Protect.

She's so skinny. He noticed it yesterday in court, but he was too busy being on the losing side of a battle to really take it in. Her hips are wide, but she cinches quickly, too thin for his normal tastes. He is overwhelmed with the need to buy something high calorie at the café counter, run over to her building, and fucking force-feed it to her with his fingers before licking her mouth dry.

Provide.

His body begins to ache as he stares at the way her wrists are out and open. To say goodbye, she and the Threat touch those minor glands together platonically, marking each other in a friendly way. Old-fashioned. It would be cute if he didn't want to kill the stranger across the street. Caleb has half a mind to storm in, pin her down, and rub the man's stink off her, replacing it with his own.

Mine.

With Ari moving on, he looks down at his laptop. So far, he's got her address, her university records, and is currently scouring her social media accounts. Not very many pictures but lots of interesting details about her life. She seems to post at all hours, complaining about vague, innocuous details of this case or that, sharing random memes, or social justice warrior-ing. Nothing that indicates a man is taking up her time in the evenings.

Caleb has now learned some of her favorite things. Books. Movies. Romance tropes. He had to google most of them. She's always sharing her favorite novels and giving them little (what he learned to be) "tags," stating that it has a lot of Praise-kink, or Alpha dynamics, or whatever else it was that made her enjoy herself. Seems she has a thing for possessive, greedy behavior and is longing for that kind of attention.

Kitten, you have no idea.

Her screen names across all platforms are similar, as if once she decided, she'd swooped onto every site imaginable to snag the name that was rightfully hers. All have numerical endings, no doubt to ensure her wording of choice. JaffreyJunk1. JaffreyJunk3337. Jaffrey-Junk2187. It's adorable. It's clear that they're all her, though. Sometimes she copy/pastes the same post from one area to another, obviously a glutton for more likes. It makes Caleb smile to himself. Looking at her university transcripts, seems she lived in the town of Jaffrey, New Hampshire once upon a time. Perhaps she has a hard time letting things go.

That makes two of us.

Using pen and paper, old school style, Caleb starts adding more to his gathered list of her list of likes and dislikes, her nows and her thens...and that's when he sees it in one of her feeds. She complains that her doctor said she has to "just get it over with and have her first heat already."

Her first.

His eyes hover over that *F* word, seeing it pixel for pixel.

Her first fucking heat.

He's going to burst into flames. It doesn't matter how many angry, swearing, red-faced emojis she threw all over the post or how many Omegas commiserated in solidarity. What matters is that his mate is going to have some very specialized needs soon. Some unexpected, unexperienced, insatiable needs. And he's going to cater to every single one...apparently sooner than he planned. Whether she wants him now or not, she's going to. He'll make damn sure of it. Until then, Caleb just has to stave off his rut—though just thinking about her sweet slick makes him hard. He crosses his legs and sneaks in a quick adjustment, making his erection less obvious, and switching immediately to an upcoming client's rap sheet to cool himself down. He's going to have to transfer his caseload to his colleague Gwen for now. He's about to be very busy for the next few days. He has to seduce the woman he was apparently born for.

CHAPTER 2

CONSEQUENCES

THERE ARE a few twittering birds hopping around, but mostly it's fat, cooing pigeons. In cities, pigeons are everywhere. Ubiquitous. The sad thing is that people tend to think of them as vermin. Dirty. But aren't all animals dirty when you get right down to it? Pigeons are no different than white-necked swans in Caleb's opinion. He likes birds of all kinds, robins to ravens. To him, it's chipmunks that are disgusting. Fat cheeks, looking as though they're about to choke on their own greediness. Maybe they just remind him too much of himself.

Caleb is sitting on a bench outside his mate's apartment building and has been since five a.m. He's a bit stiff but his laptop keeps him busy. At least it's summer, so the temperature was reasonable enough in the pale light of dawn. At this point, though, his suit jacket is warmer than he'd like it to be. His…situation…is making him run hot, prickling him in the climbing heat.

He's on edge. His skin tingles. Like the hoarding chipmunks, Caleb feels greedy. Still, he types away, studying Ari's recent cases and looking for any patterns in her defense arguments, all happily accessible via the online records of her public proceedings. It's not so he can beat her in some hypothetical rematch. It's so he can dig deeper into that—no doubt—beautiful brain of hers.

When they left the district building after their showdown, he saw her turn toward the underground subway—smug satisfaction written all over her face—whereas he beelined back into the vestibule, needing to avoid her at all costs before he acted according to the will of the animal inside. Instead, he held his breath for as long as he could and decided to ream out Judge Hayes for his idiocy. Caleb survives by leveraging his anger more than anything else, after all.

Using public transportation makes sense for her. Parking garages are hellishly expensive, and on her salary, he's guessing the cheap, tin can trains are probably the best means of getting from point A to point B without going into hock. It suits her personality, somehow. Well, what parts he's come to understand, anyway.

He can see the subway entrance from here, just to the left of her building. If she starts work at about eight thirty, which is when everyone in the legal world seems to, Caleb imagines she'd leave her apartment around now. He's tucked away on the other corner of her complex near an obligatory and thin-ish tree, a splash of green in an otherwise sea of beige brick. If she turns directly toward the underground entrance, she shouldn't see him. He doesn't want her to see him. Yet.

His nostrils flare when she comes out, smelling her immediately in an eerie, preternatural way. Maple syrup. Something you want to lick off anything it touches. Sticky and sexy and sweet. More than that, her heat is coming soon. He can tell. Everything about her is riper and more real. He grunts a little, sitting straighter and trying to hide the desire that blooms when he tastes her scent in the air.

Jesus. Is this what my parents felt like?

He hates them, always has, and he'd hated their vapid, asinine, gross-more-often-than-not love story as well, but to experience this feeling himself makes it all a bit more understandable. It makes sense that his parents would have abandoned the world for each other. Paid any price. Caleb suddenly feels the same way. It's immediate, unquestionable, and undeniable. Within mere moments, she became his world.

Thanks, Mom and Dad. It sounds sarcastic even in his own mind, but it may just be the only worthwhile lesson they taught him. When you mate, you mate for life.

He had expected her hair to be tied up in the extra messy bun she'd had before, and he is not disappointed. It's borderline unprofessional. Unique. Cute. What he *hadn't* expected was a car to immediately rev forward from a parking spot along the curb, making her squeal with fright. Caleb's hackles rise and he immediately tucks his things into his bag, slinging it over his chest in short order, gripping the strap with a tense urge to act. To *Protect.*

He should leave. He should leave right now...but...

Ari's voice carries over too loudly. "No, no, no! There's no way I'm doing that again!" The next thing Caleb hears is a man's irritated voice. "Come on, Ari! Don't be such a brat!"

And he's done. One hundred percent done.

Standing up faster than anything, nearly toppling over himself in the process, Caleb stomps over, his scent ripe with the warning to *BACK THE FUCK OFF,* though Ari seems to be the only one to sense him. She wheels around quickly, eyes going wide as Caleb streaks toward her. Snaking a hand around her waist, he tugs her directly behind him and stares down the dark man in the car who gapes at him in surprise.

"And what the fuck do you want exactly?" Caleb says, eyes narrowed and teeth clenched.

The other man's scent is off. The stranger backs down immediately, his round, chocolate eyes embedding their stare into the steering wheel as he deflates by instinct. Another Omega. Caleb's temper begins to cool as Ari grabs his arm and shoves him back a step.

"What the hell are you doing?!" she yells.

He's sweating and trembling and ready to kill, that's what. Still, his voice comes out silken. "Hush, Omega."

And, wonder of wonders, she does. Her trap snaps shut with a click and her eyes lower in submission. That's not the feisty, valiant woman he battled against. That's her budding heat talking, making her soft and obedient for her Alpha. She's breathing him in, he knows it. Her chest rises and falls in quick rhythm as she pulls her gaze up his body—ankles to bulge, cufflinks to tie—finally locking eyes with him as her cheeks flush red and she licks her lips.

Oh, he wants her. He wants her right here in front of the whole world.

She whispers, "You're not. You can't be. Are...are you...?"

"Going into rut?" he completes her thought. A rude thing to ask in normal circumstances, but nothing about this is normal. She's too close to him. She's oh-so-close and wearing one of those tight pencil skirts and he wants to lick her. Suck her. Fuck her.

"Soon," he admits. "But why don't I wait for your heat first? Seems like that's coming soon, too."

What the fuck is he doing? What. The fuck. Is he doing?

Her jaw goes slack with shock, and a thrill runs through him. He crowds her space, letting his scent tell her everything she needs to know about just how much he wants her. This isn't how he planned to do things. He's being too forward. Going too fast. Being too honest. Wanting too much. He's going to maul her if he stays this close. She's quaking, leaning back on the car for support.

"I'll wait for you, kitten. As soon as you start to burn up inside, come to me."

Her face is flushed and, fuck, he can smell her slick begin to gather. Sweet, just like the rest of her. He can't help the low growl that rumbles in his chest. This is crazy. Behaving like this in public is obscene.

He touches her jaw with the minor scent glands on his fingertips, marking her neck dangerously close to where it matters and watching her eyes flutter closed. "I'll be so good to you," he whispers. "I promise."

Now and forever.

Remembering where he is, he nods toward the inconsequential person inside the car. "You know him?"

Breathy, she agrees. "He's my friend."

Caleb lifts his brows. "And why wouldn't you want to go with your friend?"

The other man leans closer the tiniest bit, a teasing smile on his face. "Because she's terrified of cars." But when Ari shoots him a look, he sinks down in his seat again, muttering a meek, "This is me shutting up."

Caleb smiles at her, broad and predatory. "My kitten has a weakness." He lowers his voice an octave. "Too bad it's not on the courtroom floor."

Her scent kicks up a notch, laced with such pride.

Omega is happy.

Though not all the way. She's still tinged with something that smells discomforted; borderline upset. Well, that won't do.

"Excuse me for being...overprotective," Caleb says, stepping back and not actually sorry one bit. "You can imagine that I'm not at my best at the moment. Forgive me." Because isn't that what a white knight says? Just like her fairy-tale novels.

Ari looks back and forth up the street as if she's never seen it before. Her face is still pink, heated and perfect. "Why are you here? Do you live nearby?" Though she doesn't exactly sound pleased with the idea. Good thing he'd researched his answer in advance.

"Pastry shop," he tells her, fixing his tie and nodding past the subway entrance. "About two blocks down. I go there sometimes." Or never. He can't take his eyes off her and she fidgets under his stare. "Apologies if I'm coming on a bit strong."

"Just a bit?"

He huffs a soft laugh. "When I smelled you the other day, I knew you were something special. Finding you now, both of us ready like this..." He gestures between their bodies. "Maybe it's fate."

He steps forward one last time, making a lewd show of scenting her. He runs his thumb along the column of her throat in broad daylight, his other fingers alighting over the arch of her neck, brushing her mating gland ever so slightly, and she collapses in his fucking arms with the sexiest gasp he's ever heard. Lips close to hers, he says, "I bet you'd smell perfect mixed with me."

This is inappropriate. Sexual harassment at the very least, barbaric if you want to get technical. He literally does not care.

"I'm waiting for you, Omega," he whispers, a little too desperate for his liking, trying not to pant as he takes her in. "Come to me when you're ready. I'll see you through this heat...and so many more."

Keeping a dark hold on the thin thread of his sanity, Caleb pulls back, eyes hooded, and reminds himself to nod at the male Omega in parting. It's what a gentleman would do.

It takes everything in him to walk away.

Everything.

"I'm going to die, Ari, I'm literally going to die. My whole body is just going to gush, and I will shrivel up forever!" Niles leans back dramatically in his seat. "God, did you smell him?"

"Unfortunately." Ari grimaces, ramming the seatbelt into the clasp with a little *snick*. Her panties are soaked, and she positions herself unsafely on her hip to avoid slicking up Niles's seats. They may be leather, and he may also be an Omega, but it's still embarrassing. Her hands tremble, and she feels both flushed with heat and pale with terror as Niles shifts the car into gear.

"Be gentle with me," she says. "I don't want to die with dirty underwear on." He just laughs. Shaking her head, she tries to avoid looking at the road as it begins to move, her tummy doing a little clenching dance. "You don't understand, Niles. That's the bad guy. That's the foe I vanquished to save the damsel in distress."

"What? Like, two days ago foe?"

"Yes."

"Caleb Reed? Evil lawyer Caleb Reed?"

"Yes!"

"And you threw him into rut?"

Ari hisses, "Shut up!"

Her friend just whistles at her. "Look at you. Getting the villain's dirty Alpha all riled up!"

"Watch the road!" she squeaks, a yellow light approaching from a solid forty feet away. At this point Niles just ignores her.

"Seems like the perfect Alpha to see you through your heat," he says. "He definitely knows what he's doing."

The glare she tosses him could set him on fire.

"What?" Niles cries defensively. "He's sexy!"

Her Omega agrees, but her mouth gripes, "He has resting B face."

"The word is *bitch*, Ari."

"He was born with resting B face."

"Christ, you're an adult. Just say bitch."

"B!"

"—iiitch!"

She'd pinch him, but then he just might kill them both in this metallic chariot of death.

"Again. One heat! It's not like I'm suggesting you marry him," he continues.

They go over a bump and her whole body cringes. Through a tight jaw, she reminds, "He didn't sound like he wanted just one."

"Yeah, well." Niles waves her off. "That's just Alpha talk. They get that way. Feral. All 'My Omega. Mine, mine, mine!' They seem overwhelming, but they give as good as they get." He winks at her. "Once it's all over, their brains come back, and everyone goes on their merry way."

"Unless they think you're their mate."

"Pffft. Mate." Niles chuckles, steering effortlessly when Ari wishes he'd put in a little more goddamned effort. "Why would he think that?"

"Everyone in the courtroom is supposed to be suppressed, Niles. And wearing pheromone blockers."

"So?"

"I didn't!"

"We've established that. That's why we're glad you weren't fired."

Ari gestures behind her with a firm thumb. "He doesn't know it was a trick!"

Niles blinks at her as if he doesn't get it. He blinks. And blinks. And... "Oh shit, he thinks he can smell you anyway."

She nods faster than she should. Almost manic.

"Could you smell him, too?" Niles asks, feeling horrified...but not on her behalf. He's feeling sorry for the desperate Alpha who had her pinned against his car.

"Yeah, a little," she admits. "Leather and cinnamon and ash." She wrinkles her nose.

Niles stops at a red light, turning slowly to face her, eyes wide and jaw dropped. "Ari. Ari. Ohmigod, Ari, you're soulmated."

She gapes at him. "WHAT?! Shut up!"

"Nuh-uh! Nope! You smelled him back! In a suppressed courtroom, you smelled him back!"

"But I didn't like it!" she whines. When Niles starts driving again, his mouth still wide open, she's so distracted she forgets to complain. "He smells wrong! Not, like, Paul kind of wrong! But not what I imagine to be soulmate kind of right, either!"

"Oh, man. Poor resting B face." Niles shakes his head sadly. "You sent the man into rut for no reason."

The thought makes Ari clench her thighs and that low ache in her belly starts up again, making everything down there too sensitive. "I don't want to think about it."

"And say what you want, he most certainly is putting you into heat. Hell, watching him all over you almost put *me* into heat."

"Why do I have to suffer just because he can't control himself?"

They pull up outside her office. As much as she hates to admit it, this is so much faster in a car. Clicking the shift into park, Niles leans back and levels a rude expression at her.

"It's biology."

"That's his problem." She tips farther onto her hip to avoid wetting Niles's seat, refusing to see the irony of the situation.

"Look, Miss First-Timer"—Niles purses his lips at her in annoyance—"did you want to let him touch you when you were standing outside my car?"

"No! Ugh! Gag!"

"Did you want your knees to knock, like I saw they were?"

She sees where he's going and picks at her clothes. "No."

"Did you want to soak your undies—and, quite soon, my car—all because he scented you?"

Ashamed, she pouts. "No."

Niles nods at her firmly. "Biology."

Maybe it's her heat coming, but her eyes get wet with tears, making her sniffle.

"Come on, Ari," Niles says. "I know you've been fighting against this since—well, since you were a teenager—but it's natural. It's not like he locked you in a room, shoved open your legs, and started biting your thighs to throw you into heat."

She gasps like a doddery old woman listening to something scandalous. "That's a myth!"

"Nope! Been thrown into off-cycle heats twice, thank you."

Ari shudders. Her friend just shrugs, though, having had several successful heats with no issues. He pets her shoulder as she starts to undo her seatbelt, already exhausted though the day hasn't even begun.

"It's not something to be afraid of, you know." Niles catches her eyes, trying his best to reassure her. "In a way, it's proof that we're meant to be connected. Alphas are kind to us when we need them. It makes them feel good, just like it does for us. You think he's an asshole? Wait until you see him around your nest. He'll have hearts for eyes and follow you around like a puppy, being so sweet that you'll eat every goddamned grape he gives you, whether you want them or not."

"Grapes?"

"Grapes," Niles says with a smirk.

"I hate grapes."

"For some reason every Alpha I've ever been with has given me grapes. It's like they told them in health class, 'This is what you give to Omegas to ensure a healthy coupling.'"

Ari groans, leaning on the window and feeling the cool glass on her forehead. "I need to get birth control."

"Now that's a problem to solve immediately, evil mastermind lawyer or not. The last thing I want to see is pups as ugly as you running around."

This time, she does pinch him. They're parked though, so they survive.

There are very few things that Caleb is thankful for in his life, but one of them is that he doesn't have to be in court today. No client meetings, no excruciating, fury-inducing little chit-chats with the boss, either. No. He has this day all to himself, and it's perfect timing. Because otherwise he wouldn't be able to break into Ari's apartment.

Within the pastry shop—which he was absolutely not lying about—he practically bathes himself in blockers, hunkering down in the tiny restroom to do it. It's terrible. It's horrible. His rut is coming on too early, which hurts, but he just keeps reminding himself it's only because he found his mate. It makes sense. His body is telling him in no uncertain terms to make her his, just like hers is saying the same. It's fucking romantic, if such a thing exists. Still, for this next part he needs to smell as close to nothing as possible. He's already turning heads with his aggressive scent. Even Betas are giving him a wide berth, which means he's bad off. If he doesn't put himself on mute, he'll leave a blazing trail of his pheromones in her personal space, hammering a nice, thick nail into his coffin while he's at it. If he keeps it mild enough, she might just think she's smelling what he'd already left on her today. Unsurprisingly, none of the romantic tropes she shared with strangers had boasted "And this had a delightful bit of stalking in it!" To say he has to tread lightly is an understatement.

Around the corner from her building once more, Caleb reminisces about his childhood. He wasn't a great kid, which is exactly why he knows how to get through the locked outer door of an apartment complex with no issues.

Thank you, credit cards.

He slips one nonchalantly through the latch, levering it with a bland expression as if he were just a normal tenant using normal keys. Once inside, her scent is terrifyingly easy to follow. Like her JaffreyJunk3337 account says, getting cheap rent seems to mean living at the top floor of a too-old building with no elevators. Following her invisible trail, up the stairs he goes. Then up some more. Up, up, up. No wonder she's so damn skinny if she has to trek through this twice a day. Or more.

Provide.

His apartment is also high up but at least he has a decent elevator. Here, he wastes seven whole minutes, refusing to bolt up the rickety stairwell and draw attention to himself. Each step creaks as if it's a minute away from collapsing, which concerns him to say the least. He's a heavy man—a gym rat, honestly—and these stairs are all but begging for mercy. Though, that thought applied to other circumstances, specifically to a certain mate pinned beneath his body, is incredibly sexy. Otherwise, he's kind of fearing for his life.

His old set of lockpicks don't jingle. Instead, they slide in so easy, it's as though they belong.

Fuck, why is everything making me hot right now?

Ari's scent is so strong here, he's melting. He wants to rub on the door and moan. Unfortunately, that's the exact opposite of covert. Three tweaks of his instrument and her door unlocks with a satisfied *click*, slipping open much easier than he expected. She didn't put on her deadbolt.

Protect.

"Oh, kitten. Have to teach you better than that. You never know what's lurking in the shadows." He whispers it under a devilish smile, enjoying himself way too much.

Sneaking around her house is pure bliss. She's a pig, and it makes him chuckle. There's junk everywhere. Jaffrey junk, apparently, if the slightly crumpled vanity license plate nailed to her wall says anything.

Paperwork. Knickknacks. A random pizza box with one lonely piece left inside. An empty bottle of cheap white zinfandel on her coffee table with a single flower in it—more like a weed, really. It's strangely exhilarating. Caleb is neat and orderly, but it's only because he never does anything. This place happily shouts "Home," whereas his placidly states "Rental." His life consists of work, the gym, showers, and bed. Sadly, his apartment doesn't even have the lingering smell of strangers. He's been seeing himself through his own ruts for a while now, sad as it is, though it's still better than something meaningless he'll regret as soon as his knot goes down.

Not this time, though.

In her room, her laundry basket is overflowing, and he snatches a pair of her dirty panties. Cotton. Plain. Perfect. Little hearts on them. She's so innocent it hurts. Breathing them in makes him whimper, but that doesn't stop him. His trousers constrain him so tightly it's agonizing, but he sucks in the scent of her slick, flicking his tongue and nearly rending the fabric with his teeth out of instinct.

Instead, he tucks the blessed item into his pocket, panting, having made it all so much worse for himself. He fantasizes about rolling in her bed and feels the sting as he begins to salivate.

Despite being afraid to leave a fingerprint, he can't help but check her fridge. A half-eaten carton of blueberries and a litany of condiments greet him, but not much else. He *tsks* under his breath, knowing he wants to give her more. Wine and dine her. Not just when she's in heat, but long after. Forever.

Mate, mate, mate.

He huffs, body aching to be touched. He sizzles with electric energy but has to hold back or he'll hit the point of no return. There's no outlet for this. If he goes to the gym and tries to work it out, the exertion will push him over the edge. If he touches himself, he'll outright battering ram over it. He eyes her bathroom, wanting to use her toothbrush for possessive reasons and needing a cold shower. It would do him good, but it will also rinse off his blockers and she'll know he was here. She'll be scared away then, mate or not. Caleb is many things, but a good man is not one of them. He wouldn't want her to find that out too soon. He'd have to chase her if she ran, and he wants her to be willing.

Need you, sweetheart. Gonna knot you. Gonna breed you. Gonna put myself inside you and never let you escape.

His eyes roll back in his head as he leans against the countertop, facing the ceiling and exposing his throat to be bitten. He needs to go home, and he needs to do it right now. It's already too late to hold back.

Wherever you are, kitten, I hope you feel this.

Ari's heat is so close, she can't stave it off much longer. The workday is almost over, and Niles is coming to pick her up...much to her chagrin. She's decided to be brave and beg him to see her through. He's not an Alpha, but she knows he can ease the worst of it. She'll blame it on biology, like he said, and grovel if she has to. Get on her knees, soak herself, and plead.

Niles was right; he needs to drive her. She can't risk riding the subway in unventilated, tight quarters with a litany of strangers. It's dangerous to be out an about when she's like this.

It's Reed's fault. That bastard marked her with his scent. Her jaw, her neck, her mating gland. It did something to her. His smell isn't quite right, but it's definitely not wrong. Having it on her all day is like slow death. She needs, needs, needs. No matter how many blockers she puts on, her lust is palpable. Around the office, all heads turn and go immediately to the space between her legs, looking for the tell-tale sign of wetness as though there's a damp slick spot on her clothes that she can't see.

There's just one more step to transfer her cases. The documents are all prepared, everything is listed out, she just needs to debrief Paul quickly, then go home and writhe. Her doctor said this heat might last a whole week, maybe longer, but her cases can't hang open that long. Sometimes it's about getting a client's kid out of juvie before they get beat into a gang. Sometimes it's about getting a wrongful arrest expunged so someone can get their job back and avoid eviction. Sometimes it's about getting a restraining order in place to protect the vulnerable against deadly stalkers. Paul can help them, he *has to* help them, but his expression tells her that this conversation isn't going to go the way she thinks. His mouth draws into a scowl that she can see from the other end of the hall and his conversation with their colleague, Hui Yeng, trails off mid-sentence. Turning, he stomps over, grabs her arm, and yanks her into an alcove in the wall, cramming her between his body, white plaster, and a fake, pointy plant.

He starts to say something, then stops, sniffing the air without bothering to hide it. It makes Ari cringe. He accuses her with two words. "Caleb Reed."

Of course, he'd recognize the scent the other Alpha left behind. Paul's been near their arch-nemesis often enough during arbitrations. He lifts his lips in a half-hearted smile.

"I thought you said you didn't have anyone to see you through your heat."

"You have to be joking," is all she can say, forcing a short laugh.

Maybe Paul can help me. He's an Alpha. Alpha can help me. It burns, it hurts. Please, Alpha.

She's about to lower herself to ask when his expression sours. "See what happens when you break the rules, Ari? When you trick people?"

Taken aback, she narrows her eyes. "I needed to win."

"At what cost? He's all over you. What did he do? Chase you down?"

Shaking her head, she starts to get defensive. It's unlike her. She pants, "He said...there was a pastry shop... I..."

Paul scoffs. "Look at you. Going off your suppressants, putting yourself through all this, and for what? To win a case you would have won anyway?"

"I had to be sure! I had to save someone's future!"

"And now Caleb Reed has his stink all over you!"

Her mouth drops open. Offended, she wants to storm away. This man and his bathroom smell can go pound sand.

"You gonna let him see you through your heat, too? I think he'd like that very much. A sweet sort of revenge."

Ari shakes her head. "I don't even know him."

Paul offers up his wrist to her nose and she tries not to gag. "I can do it, Ari. Me. My caseload is light. Someone else can take on our work and we'll do this together. I know what to do. I can make it all better. I'll make you feel so good, I promise."

Instead of enticing her like Caleb, she feels sick. Everything about her folds in on itself, cowering. She doesn't want this. No part of her body wants this.

Paul's lip lifts and he bares his teeth, startling her. "You will *listen to me,* Omega."

"Like hell she will!" Niles snags her arm and tugs her from Paul's threatening closeness. He pulls her into a protective hug half behind him, a shield against the Alpha threat. With a low curse, her best friend glares at Paul. "Looks like she'd prefer a dry heat to a man like you."

It's an insult. A good one, if Paul's growl says anything about it.

As Niles drags her outside on trembling legs, all she can say is, "You're double-parked again."

He doesn't bother responding. Instead, he ushers her into the car, shutting the door gently, knowing that sound is too loud right now. Light is too bright. He hops in on the other side as quickly as he can and locks all the doors. Dragging out his phone, he starts thumbing it, typing so fast it's a blur.

"What...what are you?"

"Shh." He puts it on speaker and fiddles with his old school GPS, turning it on and futzing with its position on the dash. The phone rings and Ari winces, wanting to cover her ears but scared to move.

"Sloane Law Offices," says the disembodied voice via Bluetooth.

"No. Niles, no." It comes out like a whisper.

He ignores her. "I need to speak to Caleb Reed, please."

Ari immediately clenches and slick coats Niles's seat as she whimpers. He looks at her with sympathy.

The stranger replies, "He's not in the office at the moment."

Niles mouths the word *Sorry* before speaking to the woman on the other side of the line. "I need to get a message to him. His girlfriend just went into heat. She lost her phone and can't get ahold of him but she's in bad shape. Can you have him call me back at this number?"

Traitor, Ari thinks somewhere in the back of her mind as she shivers.

The stranger trips on her words, saying, "Y-yes. Yes, of course. I completely understand. I see your number here, don't worry," before hanging up.

Solidarity among Omegas, Ari thinks, another cramp clenching her belly. It hurts. It hurts so much. Niles rubs her arm, nothing but sympathy on his face.

"What am I supposed to do?" she says. "I don't even know him."

"Well, pumpkin, you're about to."

The phone rings almost immediately and the sound is shrill and blaring in her ears. Niles presses the green button on his center console to answer. "Reed?"

"Where is she?!" Caleb pants on the other side of the line, low and frantic. Hearing it makes Ari groan, her lust tripling as slick floods her.

"Alpha..."

He must hear because he purrs. "Ohhh, kitten. Hold on, sweetheart. I can already tell you're doing so well, aren't you? Such a good girl for me. Tell me where you are. I'm coming."

Niles shakes his head, unseen. "You don't sound like you should drive right now. We're coming to you. Give me your address."

The rest of the words are a blur as Niles punches it in and hangs up. Her best friend oozes calming pheromones, trying to help her as best he can. "Hold on, Ari. I'll get you there. Shh. Shh. Your Alpha will help you soon."

"Alpha," she agrees. *Leather, cinnamon, and ash.* Not perfect, but so close it hurts.

CHAPTER 3
IT BEGINS

CALEB IS THANKING existence for grocery delivery right about now. Sweating and shaking with a raging hard-on hadn't kept him from clicking buttons, adding things to the shopping cart, and thumbing the icon for deliver—even if the utter normalcy of it did inspire him to slam the phone on his kitchen island afterward. But hey, he managed to do it face up, so the screen lived to see another day. A miracle in all honesty. Tracking the order, it should be here any minute. At that point, he can lock himself away in his own personal hellhole and protect the world from his presence.

He's never been this bad-off before going into seclusion. For all his suave promises to hold back, he's going into a very hard rut and will be fucking his hand for days on end, completely unable to wait for the woman who belongs to him. It's pathetic. It's infuriating! Lashing out with one arm, Caleb overturns an end table, sending a lamp to its untimely demise. The phone may have lived, but the lamp died an honorable death. The Lord giveth and the Lord taketh away.

He did this to himself, really. Seeing her this morning—Ari, Ari, gorgeous, beautiful, sweet Ari—and watching her submit to his scent, letting him mark her, bathing in her essence in her rudimentary apartment. All of it made his Alpha scream to protect her. From her friend in the car. From life's wins and woes. From starvation of all things. Thinking of that bare refrigerator with almost nothing to eat is enough for him to fucking roar, his voice breaking on the last note.

Oh yes. This rut is going to be a rough one.

The doorbell rings and his whole body goes on high alert.

"LEAVE IT OUTSIDE!" he hollers to whatever delivery man gets paid extra to do rut-runs. Some Beta idiot Caleb can barely smell, even though he can practically smell Egypt at this point.

Through the door, he hears mutters of agreement, and the man is smart enough to turn tail, leaving Caleb's front door bereft of anyone except him. He's pressed flat against the wood, listening to the other side where retreating, rapid footfalls could be seen as prey. Caleb's head is pounding, and his heart drop-kicks his ribs. His fingers clench into a tight fist, the animal in him wanting to chase down the guy and beat him just for being where he shouldn't be. In Caleb's territory.

He needs to calm down. He needs to be soothed. He needs his fucking *mate*.

Pulling open the door, the scents are too much. The light is stabbing him. He needs to den down. This shouldn't be so upsetting. This should be no different than any other time. He's used to being alone, locked far away, but now he has someone to wonder about and long for, and his body screams *Mate, Mate, MATE!*

He wants to tear his skin off.

The bags are there, but he has no idea what's in them anymore… except for blueberries. He'd gotten blueberries just in case. Another stupid thing to do. He yanks in the groceries and slams the door shut but has no mind to put anything away. His brain only circles the drain around the thought of the tart, blue-black orbs he now owns for no reason.

In case Omega comes to me. Because she likes them. Because she needs them, and I need her, and it hurts.

He really is fucking pathetic. Ready to snap at any minute. One more day and he would have seduced her, he's sure of it. She would have called his name, let their lips touch, fallen into his arms, and…

He can't wait anymore.

He pulls her panties from his pocket and gropes himself through his clothes, groaning loud enough to startle people from the ground floor to the penthouse. He's raging hard and has been for hours.

Omega. Need you. Oh please.

For the first time since his ruts began, he feels like he's going to die. Resting his forehead on the kitchen island, he opens his pants and works himself slowly. He's sensitive and yearns for the warmth of her. It radiated when he had her pressed against the car. When he caressed her mating gland just the tiniest bit and she collapsed in his arms, eyes closed, and face flushed to the heavens.

"Fuck, kitten." He grunts, more than willing to pretend his hand is her. But there's no slick—not like what she could have given him. He'd smelled it gathering between her legs and wanted to dive his fingers into it. It would have been so wet and hot and perfect.

That's it. It's certain. He's going to die. He's going to ignite into a bonfire of lust, and self-destruct.

His blackened phone screen lights up then, inches from his face, a text from the office he will gladly ignore, but the words catch his eye.

> Sir, your girlfriend

The message cuts off into an ellipse, and then goes dark. He fumbles, barely able to work his shaking hand, and unlocks the screen.

> Sir, your girlfriend lost her phone and went into heat. Her friend asked that you call him at…

Girlfriend? He doesn't have a girlfriend. Never has—not really.

Who the f—

Ari?

What if it's Ari?

Trembling with need and hope, he presses the underlined number in the text message, his device reaching out into the ether, begging for mercy on his behalf. Someone immediately picks up.

"Reed?" The voice from this morning. The Omega male. Caleb grits his teeth in satisfaction as much as possessiveness.

"Where is she?" He can't breathe. He can't breathe and he's going to break his phone into pieces. And that's when he hears her sweet voice moan the word:

"Alpha..."

It's like a cool calm washes over him. The urge to rend himself into jagged edges fades, replaced by the need to do anything for the woman on the other side of the line. Her heat has come, and she reached out to him, just like he told her to. That means she feels this as deeply as he does.

Mates.

Soulmates.

His voice, rough from his rampage, reaches out to soothe her. "Ohhh, kitten. Hold on, sweetheart." His hand is still clamped around himself, rocking his erection seductively as he speaks to her. "I can already tell you're doing so well, aren't you? Such a good girl for me. Tell me where you are. I'm coming."

And then I'm fucking coming. On you. In you. All over you. I'll lick it off, clean you up, and do it all over again.

The man chimes in again, too smart for his own good. "You don't sound like you should drive right now." Which is utterly true, but that wouldn't stop him. "We're coming to you. Give me your address."

Faster words have never rolled off Caleb's tongue.

He smells her as soon as the elevator *dings* open despite it being down the hall and around the corner. Caleb's door hangs ajar, and he leans against it, chest rising and falling in erratic breaths he tries to take in through his nose. His black hair is stringy with sweat, hanging in his eyes, though he barely notices. There are more important things to care about now.

Mate is coming. Omega needs me.

Her whimper once she catches wind of him makes him want to run to her, but he stays pressed against the door frame hard enough to leave a mark on his back. If he seems too far gone, her friend—Niles—may not want to leave her with him...though Caleb will fucking kill him if he tries to walk away with his woman now.

His mate's friend carries her in his arms. Wrapped around his wrist is a plastic bag that rustles as they approach. Caleb can't help it; he holds out his hands and waves her toward him, eyebrows knit, as if beckoning her home. When Niles brushes by him into the apartment instead of handing her over as he should, Caleb has to bite his tongue and taste the tang of blood to stay grounded.

Ari gets set down on the floor at their feet, an inappropriate place for a woman of such importance, though seeing her kneel and hunch over her belly is truly a sight to see. He's amping up and ready to pounce, but her friend shoves a pill bottle in his face.

"She has to take these every morning."

"What for?" Caleb manages.

"So she won't get pregnant."

Those are going in the fucking trash. Caleb never knew he wanted pups until this very moment, but suddenly it's all he can think about.

"You will not knot her; she's too vulnerable right now and may do something she regrets. Get it?" Niles tells him, trying to keep an air of authority even though he can smell Caleb's mania. Trying to soothe him with his unfamiliar, unwanted Omega pheromones, the man repeats, "You. Will not. Knot her."

Which means he's knotting her immediately. Caleb feels a tug at his pant leg and a tiny mewl as Ari calls for him. "Alpha, please."

His eyes close in ecstasy at the sound, and he replies with a distant, "I hear you." Whether he's speaking to Niles's demands or to Ari's plea is unclear even in his own mind.

"You need to text me every day, it doesn't matter what time." Niles taps his phone as if Caleb is a moron and needs a visual aid. He might not be wrong at this point. "Just the words 'we're okay.' Copy and paste. GIFs. Thumbs-up. I don't care, but it needs to be every day."

Caleb nods again, hating her friend but also loving him. *Friend has taken care of my Omega. He has brought my mate home to me. But now, it's my turn. I will do anything and everything. I will be anything and everything.*

Provide.

Protect.

And love.

Ari can barely think as Niles carries her through a foreign apartment. Slick is tracing down her inner thighs and soaking her skirt, leaving cool trickles on her fevered skin. Even her underwear is a tantalizing presence, taut against her sex, and she buries her face in Niles's neck for lack of any other comfort, even though Alpha is here. He's right *here.*

She's set on the ground and hard wood lies under her palms. It's warm, like Alpha had been pacing and leaving his scented footprints. It's all she can do not to bow down on the floor and lick them...and then a cramp catches her, making her double over and grit her teeth. She's grabbing at the air, trying to find something to anchor herself. Sensing cloth, she winds her hand around it, bunching it into a whorl. Looking up, it's clothes that belong to Caleb Reed. Her enemy. But still...

"Alpha, please..."

It's like she can see him physically change. A tension that gripped him eases and his smell becomes...perfect. Exactly what she needs.

Everything she needs. *Leather. Cinnamon. Ash. Provide, Entice, Protect.* She rubs her cheek over his leg.

"—but it needs to be every day," Niles blathers above her but she barely hears him. "You have my best friend in your home, and neither of us really knows you. I'm begging you to be gentle. Be kind. Take care of her. Give her everything she needs."

Caleb's voice is a low rumble, and she can hear his smile. "Oh, believe me, I intend to do just that."

It's so perfect. She clenches unconsciously and a fresh gush of slick wets her skirt. It's sticky. She hates it. "Help. Please..."

She feels dirty, but Alpha nearly staggers as he breathes her in, the most perfect expression on his face. He looks so strong. She wants strong. She wants *him.* She's prepared to beg for any ounce of his attention, but he already seems to know exactly what she's silently asking for. Nostrils flaring, his eyes scald her as he goes to his knees and gathers her up like something precious. How could she have hated him? She needs him. She's never needed anything so badly in her life.

Niles looks at her with a small smile on his face, amused and adoring. Without a word, he slips out the door and latches it, but Caleb doesn't bother twirling the lock. He's too fixated on her. And she'd have it no other way.

"Hurts," she whines.

"It's your first heat, isn't it?" He says it as though he knows. Maybe Niles told him.

She nods. "I'm sorry." She wants to weep. She can't please Alpha like this. She's inexperienced. She's going to embarrass herself and frustrate him. "I'm sorry," she repeats, her lips pressed together and trembling.

His lips caress her forehead, just as feverish as she is. It's both soothing and erotic. "You're perfect. You're perfect just as you are. Alpha will take such good care of you, Ari."

The sound of her name on his lips makes her whimper, grasping at him. She slides her hands over his neck, caressing his mating gland by accident, and he shivers sweetly. Locking his arms tighter, he lifts her as if she weighs nothing, princess-carrying her, but not into a normal bedroom. It's a room like she's seen in magazines made especially for Alphas and Omegas. They're dim, warm places to go, soundproof with laminate flooring. A place to be wet and loud and natural without ruining everything in sight. Only rich people have these, which she supposes makes sense, given the way he collects money hand over fist.

He sets her down in the center of the room and the moment his contact leaves her body, she sobs. She can't help it. His fingers stroke through her hair and there's another kiss, the crown of her head this time, as he shushes her. So kind, so soothing. Pulling the tresses at the nape of her neck, he angles her face upward and kisses her for real, letting out a soft, high-pitched sound when he does. Like a sweet exhale. It's just the slow drag of skin against skin, but Ari has never been kissed on the lips before. A near miss in college, but she always had other things on her mind. Never mind just being seen through her first heat, "I'm a virgin," she whispers against him.

She's about to apologize again when he growls softly, releasing her hair to wrap around her back and pull her to her knees, rough and demanding, sliding his mouth against the curve where her jaw meets her throat.

"Kitten, if you say anything else, I'm going to explode right here."

She digs her nails into his shoulders and tilts her neck back. "I want…" But she can't articulate it. No matter how many blogs she's binged, none of them gave her enough words to describe the feeling. It's just a raw need.

"I know," he says with sympathy. "Oh, sweetheart, I know. I feel it, too. I'm just the same."

She's dizzy. She's going to faint. Yet the smell of him makes her want to stay here in this moment and never let him go. He nips along the underside of her chin, wrapping around and meeting her lips, slipping in his tongue this time, slow and lingering, taking his time and sending tingles through her. A French kiss… and she loves it. It steals her breath and flutters her heart.

"I'll be back, just wait, sweetheart. I'm going to take such good care of you."

She nods. What else can she do? When he releases her softly, she feels as though she cascades to the floor in a puddle, her palms landing with a slap as he darts away and out into the cold world where he comes from. A world that doesn't have her in it.

Unacceptable.

When he comes back, holding every blanket and towel he probably owns, she can't take it anymore. She bursts into tears. "Don't leave me."

I'm afraid. I don't know where I am. I don't know what to do with myself. I don't know who you are, but I need you so much.

Sliding to his knees, he pulls her close again, up and over his lap in a straddle with her skirt rucked up to her hips. She can feel his length, hard as a rock, and knows exactly what it is. What it means. Her body begs for it, and she gasps something filthy.

He's kissing her collarbone and licking her neck. He smells so good. But still, "I don't know you," she whispers. "I don't know you. Please…"

He pulls her forward and presses his hot, rough tongue on her mating gland and sucks.

"Trust me, kitten," he purrs into her ear. "You'll learn."

***

It's archaic. Barbaric. Why does her being a virgin make her a million times more perfect? Even he's not, despite how socially awkward and mildly sadistic he is. Corporate-ladder-climbers and Alpha-climbers had all taken their turns with him. It makes him feel dirty, suddenly. Defiled. Tainted. He wishes he was pure, too. At least these forgotten strangers taught him precious lessons; ones he'll be putting to good use for his woman. His Omega. The one meant for him.

Mate.

His body sings as he tastes her, and she wants him to. It's irrefutable. Someone like her wants someone like him. She makes the sexiest noises, and his trousers dampen as they soak up her slick. Just like he wanted. Just like he fantasized about. Yes, and yes, and please.

Mate.

"Touch me," she pleads.

"How?" he asks, wanting to be a better man for her. Wanting to be gentle. Wanting to be someone he's not.

"I–I don't know. But it hurts, Alpha. Please."

He's burning up and his cock bumps against her, making him grunt. "I'll make all that pain go away, pretty thing." He's kissing away tears now. They taste like salt and desperation, and he loves them. Each and every tiny droplet is his to savor. "But I need to take off our clothes first."

"Yes," leaves her mouth, and he bares his teeth, holding back his primal urge to grab her shirt and shred it. Instead, with her still on his lap, he removes his own one button at a time, agonizingly slow, and takes in every expression she feeds him. Frustration. Desire. Appreciation. Lust. Her breaths are coming too fast as she sees the expanse of his skin. If he's guessing her emotions right, it's desire and anxiety mixed together in an overwhelming cocktail. Taking her hands, he rests them on his chest, directly over his heart, feeling like she needs him to go slow. To show her he won't hurt her. And he won't. Not yet.

She caresses his chest delicately, tentatively brushing over a nipple, her fingernails making him hiss in air through his teeth. He presses up against her through his pants...which he needs to lose immediately. Set on fire, maybe. Launch to a black hole somewhere, never to return.

He slips his fingers under her camisole, slightly damp with heavenly sweat, and lifts it off her. He's gentle. He's soft. Dexterous, it takes only one hand behind her back to unhook her bra and slide it down her arms. He thought she might try to hide, instead she arches her back proudly, presenting herself like a goddess. It makes him smile with pride.

"That's right, kitten. No need to be shy here." He slides a hand over her thrumming heartbeat and puts her hand over his again. "This was always meant to be. We need each other, you and I."

No protests, no complaints, just a smell of satisfaction coming off her in waves.

Omega is happy. She feels safe.

That means it's time to play.

Tipping her back, he lays her on the pile of blankets and worships her breasts, scraping his teeth so slightly against their peaks and making her squirm beneath him. One hand props him above her while the other searches out her skirt's fastener, peeling that off her next. The panties can stay for a minute. Those he wants to take off with his teeth.

"Now me, Ari. Just like I did. I want my skin on yours. I want to swallow you whole. I'll teach you, kitten. I'll teach you exactly how to make me come for you."

In that moment, she looks feral, her eyes gleaming with want and mischief and the urge to please her Alpha. It's the moment he falls in love. His heart aches as he brings her hands down and lets her do as she pleases, assuming she'll go slow but surprised once again as she yanks hard and pops the button off his pants, letting it clatter somewhere across the room. He chuckles against her forehead as he kisses it, feeling her hands slip over the ridges of his hips, pushing his clothes down as far as she can, boxers and all. His length is caressed by cool air, followed quickly by the heat of her aura and the call of her core. Pulling back, he mouths his way down her body, drawing out her sweet sounds of innocence as he nips her needy skin.

"So good for me. So fucking sexy. You smell like heaven, sweetheart. You taste like candy. I've never wanted anything as bad as I want you. You're so special. So perfect."

Her eyes are clamped shut and her pink mouth is open. "Keep... keep talking, please."

He hums his happiness against her belly button before dipping his tongue inside and making her twitch. When he pulls off to finish what she started, baring himself completely, she looks at him with something like awe.

"Tell me I smell good, kitten."

She nods. "You do."

"Tell me you want me."

"God, yes."

"Good girl," he says, diving in and sucking her through her underwear, making her ramble in harsh whispers as he leaks precum all over their lovely blankets. Between his ministrations, he asks, "You'll make a nest for me, won't you?"

"Yes."

He takes the fabric gently in his teeth, making sure not to snag her, and pulls them down a little. "And you're going to soak it with your slick."

"Uh-huh."

He tugs it further, backing up and sliding his hands down the insides of her soft thighs, feeling the wetness she blessed them with. "And you're going to let me fuck you."

She moans and trembles.

"And lick you everywhere."

She nods frantically, and her panties are gone. Lurching up, he notches himself without preamble and she nearly screams with shock and want.

"And then I'll make love to you. Slow and sweet. I'll be anything you want me to be, Ari."

She whimpers as he takes himself in his hand and circles around her entrance. Teasing and dipping in the tiniest bit before pulling all the way out.

She's so wet. So wet and she's going to be so tight. A virgin, a virgin, a virgin.

"Say you're mine."

"Yes."

He nips her lips. "Not good enough, kitten. Be good for your Alpha. Make me proud."

"Yours. I'm yours." She moans as he rocks in a little deeper. God, he doesn't even need to be inside her, his knot is already swelling. This is going to be embarrassingly short. Good thing she doesn't know any better, and he has a lifetime to make it up to her.

"Again, pretty girl."

"Yours," she insists.

He presses deeper and lets out an obscene noise, rocking his forehead against hers. "One more time."

"Please," she begs, and that's what he needed.

He slams himself inside her, virgin or not, and hears her scream with pleasure-pain. He cries out with her but is otherwise unyielding. "So hot, so hot, so fucking tight, baby girl."

Intense. He's never felt anything like this, and she smells like home.

One pump of sheer bliss.

One more of ecstasy.

One more... and his knot swells inside her, locking him in as she cries out. It doesn't stop his thrusting, a deep penetration hitting the base of her as he ruts gently, feeling the pull of his knot against that sensitive part inside her as she claws at his back, begging for God knows what. More? Less? It doesn't matter. All that matters is the cum flooding her insides and filling her up.

"Yessss, sweet girl. Yes, Ari."

She bucks when he says her name, but her face looks cramped with discomfort. He can't do anything about it until his knot goes down...except...

Reaching a hand between them, he thumbs her clit, and her cries are scandalous. "There we go, sweetheart. That's right."

Oh yes. He's got this now. He knows how to solve this puzzle. She's so sensitive that all he needs to do is move in slow circles and she flutters around him, making his breath stutter.

"Pretty girl, that's right. Give it to me." Up and down now. Sliding his fingers along her, pivoting his hips to press deeply inside, achieving precise timing with every stroke. He's shaking. Her body is clenching and fucking milking him for everything he's worth. "Higher, baby girl. You can do it. Come on."

He goes faster. Harder. She's basically screaming, and he loves it. She can blow out his fucking eardrums and he doesn't care one bit. Her wrists are over her head, tearing at the sheets, and the scent glands at her pulse points are flushed a tantalizing rouge. Her head is tipped to the side and her mating gland is swelled to match, calling to him, begging to be bitten. Jesus, he wants to. It's taking everything in him to hold back, but by the time this is over, she won't have just one mark; he's going to scar up every gland on her body and revel in her blood. He'll forge their connection. He'll own every inch of her.

"Come for me, Ari. Come for me right now. Do it, sweetheart, and Alpha will be so proud of you. You can do it. Fuck, I know you can. In three. Two. One, baby girl. Come."

And she does. It's hard and writhing and perfectly obedient.

Omega did what she was told.

Good.

He likes getting his way.

And just like that, the pain has ebbed. If anything, it's the opposite. That throb still lives in her, but it feels good. Pleasurable. His chest is pressed against hers and he's looking at her like she's the only thing alive. It would normally be off-putting, make her uncomfortable or shy or want to run far away. Instead, she preens.

Alpha likes me. I made Alpha feel good. Just by existing, I made him happy.

His kisses fall on her like rain, and she smiles under his adoration, giggling a little and making him chuckle a sweet sound in return.

"You're like magic, kitten."

Her smile becomes a grin. Now she feels shy, turning her face to the side and biting her lip, though entirely pleased with herself. He catches her chin and brings her back, connecting their gazes once more.

"I mean it."

And with the look on his face, she believes him. Her eyes soften and her view of him fogs, shimmering behind her tears. Her chest aches in a way she's never felt before. His thumb swipes across the crest of her cheek, and he slips his tongue over the wetness he finds on his fingerprint, tasting her emotion. With another sweet kiss, he loosens from inside her, slipping out with a sigh, and she misses him already.

"Come back." She pouts, aiming for adorable for some stupid reason.

"Oh, I will." He nuzzles her. "Again, and again."

Her face hurts from grinning and he follows suit. How did she never notice that he had dimples? More than that, he has smile lines that carve all the way up his cheeks. His hair is longish, jet black and unruly as it hides his ears in waves. His eyelashes are long, framing dark, bourbon-tinted eyes. "You're beautiful," she tells him.

He stiffens a little and frowns, his scent changing slightly. "That's just your heat talking."

"No." She shakes her head, combing through his tresses and watching the strands slip through her fingers. "You've always been beautiful. You were just also someone I had to crush into the dirt."

And he outright breaks into laughter, resting his forehead in the crook of her neck. "Oh yeah?"

She wraps him in her arms, pressing her cheek against the crown of his head.

Alpha likes me.

"Mm-hmm. And I'll trounce you again should we ever meet on the battlefield."

His whole body shakes as he snorts his laughter. "I'll have to remember to wear my armor."

With that, he pushes himself up and off her. Her eyebrows immediately knit, and she sits up in worry.

Why are you leaving? Don't go. Stay, Alpha, please.

"Did I do something wrong?"

Naked and carved like carved marble, he just looks at her with those beautiful smile lines. "I'm just going to get you something to eat. It's part of taking care of you, kitten."

She gets shy again, pleasantly so, blushing and covering her face.

"I'll come back. One second."

She can't help but watch his flexing rear end as he pads away. She still aches, but it's a lovely thing now. It's a promise of more attention to come.

There are blankets and towels laid everywhere, haphazard and messy with their scent. His seed is trickling out of her, and she loves it. She'd lick it if she could get down there. Instead, she begins to roll around in the bedding with a grin on her face before scooting it just so. In the end, there's a lining below her and a surrounding wall to nestle into. It's comfy and warm and smells like them. A perfect place for this. A nest.

She giggles.

She made *a nest.*

Instinct.

When he comes in and sees, his smile is a slow, seductive thing. "You did it." He outright glows with pride, and she eats it up like ambrosia. She's happier in this moment than she was when she passed the bar exam. It's moronic. It's stupid. It's biology.

He's carrying a bag of goodies in his hands. More playful than she's ever been with strangers, she can't help but ask, "What? Did you get me grapes?" Niles was right. For this man? She'd eat them. Even if they had seeds.

His eyes go wide with concern. He looks behind him as if trying to remember the stock in his fridge. Sheepishly, he says, "No, I'm sorry." He looks ashamed. "I only have blueberries."

And she wants him again. Immediately. Now.

She sighs. "That's perfect. Absolutely perfect."

Expression relaxing, his scent takes on notes of relief. He's adorable. Every expression, every arch of his brow. She wants to kiss him so badly. Her entire chest aches with that longing.

"Come to me, Alpha." She reaches her arms out. "Please."

His eyes get hooded, and he sets down what's in his hands. There's no hesitation before he crawls to her on his hands and knees, close enough for her to feel his body heat. "Only if you call me by name."

Even remembering who she's with, someone she never wanted to be with, she doesn't hesitate. Instead, she sighs the word. "Caleb."

"I love the sound of that, sweetheart. I want you to scream it for me. Can you do that? Can you be a good girl? My sweet angel?"

She nods. She's never nodded faster in her life. He kisses her again, and her legs spread wide, welcoming him with her whole heart. His breath hitches as he enters her, making her want him harder and faster until her brain whites out.

Like a good girl, like a sweet angel, like his perfect Omega, she whimpers the only word that lives in her mind. "Caleb…"

CHAPTER 4
MATE

CALEB AWAKENS happier than he's been in his whole life. His seclusion room is a depressing, lonely torture chamber more often than not, but its dim lights and cool flooring mean something different to him now. Ari's nest is perfect, surrounding their combined shape in a way that nestles but doesn't entrap. Blankets curl around his back, shielding him from the outside world as he spoons her, wrapping her in a weave of heavy, sated limbs.

When he'd taken care of his ruts alone, he'd allowed himself one item of comfort, immediately discarding it once the ordeal was over. When he'd been with other Omegas, their scent was pleasant enough for a while, but after the hormones cooled down, their reek curdled in his nose, and he chucked anything and everything they touched. He won't do that to Ari's beautiful creation, made just for him. It's special. Sacred.

Mate.

He nuzzles in more firmly, her woodsy brown hair making a beautiful pillow as he caresses the arch of her neck with his nose, breathing her in.

Maple syrup. Home.

Perfect. So perfect for me.

She's deeply asleep. Limp and peaceful. Her eyelids flutter over the high crests of her cheeks as she dreams, and he wonders if she's dreaming about him—either as a lover, smothering her with pleasure, or as an adversary across the courtroom floor, trying in vain to best her. He may be both, but he's definitely enjoying one experience more than the other.

He smiles, his lips grazing her skin, wanting to wake her up but refusing himself the indulgence. She needs her rest, and he can wait. Never has he wanted to care for an Omega like this. He's ready to give her everything. He doesn't have many good traits—barely any, actually—but what he has is hers.

Her beloved blueberries are long gone. He fed them to her with his fingers at first, then with his mouth, rolling the cool orbs along his tongue before passing them to her with a kiss. At first, she was unsure about it. Then she was shy. Now she'll let him put almost anything in her mouth. Their bodies are still locked together, unrelenting despite him nodding off, and the memory of her lips wrapped around his length riles him up again, hardening his knot inside her. She murmurs his name, feeling his change even while living in dreamland, and a small smile curves her lips before she settles.

He loves her. Dear God, he loves her. Smart, sexy, funny, sassy, adorable. If he took every trait he's found pleasant in all of existence and created a goddess to worship, it would be his Ari.

He's built a small feeding shrine of sorts. It's coated with anything and everything that won't spoil. He wants to keep her strong and satiated in every way without having to leave her side. He's been in this room for three days straight now, achieving exactly that. He needs to keep her happy. He needs to be her fantasy come to life. If he can't do that, she'll leave. He doesn't want her to leave. Ever.

Ruts and heats shut off the general need for the bathroom, but even when all this is over and the urge resurfaces, he irrationally wants to avoid taking a shower. He feels a compulsion to keep the scent of his cum and her slick slathered all over him. This room, too. He won't wash it, not ever. This place smells like them. Like love. Like every dream he's ever held in the secret place in his heart. If he could, he'd paint the room white with his essence, except that keeping his seed inside her is so much fucking better. He imagines her belonging to him even more as she swells under his palms, making him a family he'll do right by. A family he'll care for better than his parents ever cared for him.

But can he, though? Is he capable?

He wipes the thought from his mind, but it's too late. His knot loosens and he slips from her, drawing a little whimper from her sweet mouth.

"Soon, kitten," he whispers, nearly silent. "You need your rest. But Alpha will take care of you again. I promise. We're not done, yet."

Not by a long shot.

Caleb has been feeding her Tylenol every morning, telling her they're her special pills. It's a simple enough trick. She's half out of it anyway and he needs to cover up the fact that he'd chucked the real pills almost immediately. He wants to breed her, after all. Can't do that if she's taking preventative measures.

There's a risk in getting her pregnant, though. Not just the risk of her reacting badly to the situation, but the possible consequence of her friend raining hellfire down on him. Innocent, there are things Ari doesn't know, but Caleb is willing to bet her friend does.

The male Omega, Niles, had told him not to even knot her. When she comes back claimed, filled with pups or not, Caleb's going to have some explaining to do. He's ready to humble himself and blame the early mating on the passion of their matched cycles and the strength of their connection. It makes complete sense and may be accepted over time once he proves himself. But if Niles thought Caleb had been forgetting her medicine, it would lose him respect as an Alpha. More than that, he'd be considered fucking negligent. An

Alpha's whole role revolves around Providing and Protecting. If Caleb unwittingly abandoned those little white doses in the whirlwind of it all, he'd have failed a test written in his very genes. And if they knew he'd withheld them purposefully, Caleb would then be pegged as cruel and manipulative. And though it's not wrong, what does it benefit anyone to know? It would just let Ari's friend turn her against him, saying Caleb took advantage of Ari's inexperience. Niles would take her away then, and Caleb feels as if he would die. Mated couples who are separated suffer terribly…until someone new claims them, anyway.

No. No, that's not going to happen. Caleb's going to razzle-dazzle his jury of one and plead his case in a way that's sure to hit all the right notes.

"I'm sorry it happened like this. I should have done it differently. But when you find your true mate, your soulmate, *you can't hold back. I needed her in that moment. I still need her now. More than that, I love her. I'll take care of everything she needs from now on; you don't have to worry about a thing."*

It will be a stage-worthy performance, earning him trust, glittering eyes, and throbbing hearts. And since she'll have claimed him back, adorning him with a beautiful bite mark all his own, what can her friend do but respect the sacred bond they'll have forged?

These faux morning pills are just meant to ensure any "unexpected" pregnancy that may be discovered a few weeks down the road won't be seen as Caleb's fault. He'll have done what he was supposed to after all. Instead, it will have been another brilliant stroke of fate. Meant to be. Unstoppable.

Caleb arches his back, pressing deeper inside her for the *n*th time during this session, letting his seed fill her belly and needing it to stay in there. His knot is so big, nothing drips out, and it's fucking perfect. He's a good Alpha. Made for this. Made for her.

"Yes, that's right gorgeous," he groans against her as she shatters in his arms, coming apart just after he does. It's synchronous. They're already connected, he just needs to make the final claim.

She's been coming down closer and closer to reality in between rounds, talking with him lucidly while they lay together, knotted and unable to separate. It's mostly superficial, silly things—favorite colors and favorite animals—but they're things he couldn't glean from scouring her online details, so he's more than happy to soak up the new information. She's obsessed with the color green in any and all shades and likes big-eyed bush babies and waddling penguins. She wants to crossbreed them and get a pet that only Darwin could love. In Caleb's mind, the thing would have looked like a monstrosity.

This time she asks, "Would you mind telling me more about yourself? Since we're like this…I guess I just want to know you better. Learn the things that make you *you*. Things that matter."

"You mean my favorite brand of cereal doesn't matter?" he teases, trying not to show how much the question fills his heart.

She smacks him lightly on the shoulder. "I doubt cornflakes have had any real impact on your life."

"Well, then you underestimate the true power of cornflakes."

Giving up all too quickly, smelling like rejection, she nuzzles into him instead of pressing the matter. He wonders if she can hear his heart speed up when he sees her so vulnerable. There is danger dancing around any responses he could give her, though. Certain secrets must be kept at all costs. Still, if she's to be his mate, there are also things he can't hide—doesn't want to hide. Not if he wants this to be real.

"My…" He hesitates. "My parents died when I was in my twenties —but before you say you're sorry, don't be. I hated them. The feeling was, unfortunately, very mutual."

"Oh," is all she says, splayed over his chest and squeezing him a little tighter.

"I have a brother, though. We took care of each other no matter what. God knows we needed someone to. We were always getting into fights and causing trouble. It was my fault as often as not. He never cared, though. He accepted me for exactly who I was."

He's probably the only person in this world I've ever loved. Until you.

"Everyone deserves to be accepted." She blinks up at him with accusatory humor in her eyes. "Even a jerk like you."

"Is that defamation of character I hear?"

"I plead the fifth."

He rolls his eyes with a smirk. "You don't seem to think I'm so bad when I'm locked inside you, kitten."

She twiddles her fingers along his pectoral muscle, feigning nonchalance. "Maybe you have some good qualities..."

"And what would those be?"

She blushes with a grin, burying her face against his breastbone. She looks like a giddy schoolgirl with a crush. Maybe more than a crush. The thought makes him pulse within her, and the sensation makes her gasp softly. She's so responsive, it makes him proud.

Omega needs me. Provide. Love, pleasure, everything.

"I'm not a jerk to you," he says.

She hums her agreement with a little smile. "What do you think is your best quality?"

Clutching her round rear with a smirk, he hikes her up against him, drawing pleasure from every inch of her. "Other than the obvious?" But it seems like his lady is done being charmed by sex just now. Like a good mate, he gives in to the whims of his Omega. "My loyalty, maybe. And my dedication to the things I care about."

An understatement. It's more than just dedication; he tends to dive in with obsessive abandon, forsaking all else. This situation with her is no different. In just a few euphoric days, Ari has been tenderly added to the very short list of things he lives for. And isn't that what she's always wanted? To be enveloped in a warm blanket of never-ending attention? Her online posts often sounded so lonely. It's something they share, a chink in their armored facades.

Still locked together, he tilts his hips, pushing even deeper inside her and earning a high-pitched, stuttered breath for his efforts.

"Would you like that, kitten?" he whispers. "Someone dedicated. Someone to see to your needs. Someone to keep you happy, just like this. Someone to make you feel good."

She chuckles against him, an airy, satisfied sound. "I definitely feel good."

He kisses the top of her head at least fifty times, making her giggle until he's following suit. "Then I'll be sure to keep you that way."

Because maybe I can.

Just maybe.

The medicine has a bitter, chalky flavor as she lets it rest on her tongue. It's been several days—as far as Ari can tell in this windowless room, anyway—and every morning is the same. A white pill in her mouth and a text to Niles, dictated by her, and typed in by her Alpha.

Caleb Reed.

The pills are supposed to keep her from getting pregnant, though several times during her heat she feels as though she's lost her sanity and begged for him to breed her. She wanted nothing more than to have him knot her and stay, stay, stay. He doesn't mind. He seems to prefer it, shoving that milky white honey back inside her, making her inner walls tingle from the power of his potency.

More and more as she settles between spikes of lust, she remembers who he really is, though. Some embarrassment leaks in as well as the reminder that he doesn't quite smell right. Now that she's no longer fixated on trying to conquer the exonerator of evildoers, she can admit that his scent is Good. When she's in the throes of passion, Unbearably Good. But it's not as perfect as he says she is for him. It must be more of that "Alpha talk" Niles told her about. The "mine, mine, mine" thing.

She'd feel bad for tricking him, except that they're both enjoying this way too much...plus, Niles said all those words will go away once his rut ends. For her, too, because she's been saying the exact same sort of crazy, absurd things.

Stupid biology.

Oh well. What's the harm in giving in to nature? For now, anyway. Like Niles said, it's only one heat. Apparently, she has a lifetime of them to suffer through...though this isn't really suffering at all. At this point, she's not sure why she fought it so hard.

"Drink up," he says, handing over the water glass, helping her ease down her medicine. "What would you like to say today?"

"Hmm." She considers, curled in their damp nest of beautiful scents, all mixed together like in a fairytale. "Tell him we should be done soon, and I need new underwear."

Caleb scoffs. "There's no way I'm sending him that."

"Tell him I want pizza."

He raises an eyebrow at her. "I'll get you pizza."

Alpha wants to provide.

She rolls on her back, putting her head in his lap as she pouts. "But I don't want you to put any clothes on."

"What does that have to do with it?"

"Don't tell me you're going to go to the door naked to get it."

"Why not? I've got nothing to be ashamed of."

She'd contradict him, except that he's so right.

He rolls his shoulders in a cocky shrug. "Of course, if you're worried that it might be a delivery lady instead of a delivery man that I'm showing off for..."

Her hackles rise, something possessive wrenching her heart. She must have made a face, because he's smiling down with that adoring look he gets. How is she ever going to face him in court again? She'll lose every case, getting lost in his eyes. Why is he so beautiful? Why did she get herself into this mess? What happens after all this is over?

Never mind. That's a problem for another day. Right now, the thought of some random person seeing his perfect body makes her unreasonably angry, and that feeling takes over all other rational thought. "How many women have you been with? And how many of them have been Omegas?"

The grin on his face couldn't grow wider if it tried. "Is my kitten jealous?"

"Your kitten wants to claw someone's eyes out right about now."

"There's my girl." He leans over and kisses her forehead. "Save me from the masses, my feisty warrior."

"Damn right, I will."

I'll ruin anyone who touches my Alpha.

It's irrational and moronic, but she thinks it anyway. He's hers at the moment. Hers, and she wants him again. Right now.

Your Omega wants to own her place in this nest. Our nest.

That ache in her body is starting again and he can smell it on her.

"Before you get any fun ideas," Caleb says, "tell me what to send Niles."

"Tell him he's never allowed to see you naked."

Caleb barks a laugh that's truly charming and his scent kicks up into one of pure happiness. Ari's nose can help her pinpoint his emotions down to an exact word every now and then—pride, concern—but mostly he's a sliding scale from incredibly happy to a cold and strange *something else*. That's when he tends to look at her as if he owns her, eyes narrowed and jaw set. In those moments, though, she wants him to. It must be the pheromones they're constantly feeding each other—their Alpha and Omega performing a sacred, ancient ritual—or perhaps it's just the magic of this space they've created. The precious time spent together in her very first nest. They say you never forget your first.

He's literally typing her words in, muttering each syllable along the way, "She. Says. You're. Not. A-llowed. To. See. Me. Na-ked."

He hovers the phone over Ari's face for confirmation as her hair trails over his thighs. She hits SEND before she thinks better of it and Niles's reply is an immediate bubble filled with wide-eyed emojis and cry-laughing faces. She buries her face in her hands, cheeks flushed with embarrassment.

Biting his lip, Caleb tries not to laugh at her. "You told me to."

"You owe me a pizza," she gripes.

He shuffles around to lie next to her instead of just cradling her head. "What kind?"

"Hawaiian," she says without even having to think about it.

"For you, I'll suffer through it." He starts kissing under her ear again and she sighs. Her cramps are low and threatening, but he lays a hand over her lower belly and presses lightly. The grounding sensation and the heat from his fingertips both soothe her and make her immediately wet, her slick soaking into the fabric beneath them.

"I have a challenge for you, kitten."

She doesn't want a challenge. She wants him inside her.

He nips her earlobe. "If I order something, you have to let me edge you until the doorbell rings."

"I don't know what that means." She tugs his hand over her breast, and he dutifully obliges, kneading it in ways that makes her breath come in sighs. He laps at the back of her neck, slow circles around one of her mating glands, and it makes her tremble.

"So innocent. There's so, so much to teach you, sweetheart."

"Well, you better teach me soon. This is almost over." She hums her pleasure and smiles a little, enjoying teasing him, but that smell of something else...that kind of darkness...ebbs from him suddenly. It heightens the undertone of ashes in his scent.

"We have all the time in the world, kitten," he corrects, his scent fading back into normalcy. Tilting up her chin, he kisses her. Soft caresses, but she opens for him, wanting more. And more. The cinnamon of his scent amps up then, calling to her in the most seductive way.

Entice.

"Caleb." She releases the word like a whisper. "Please."

Against her lips, he murmurs, "Not hungry anymore?"

She turns over and slings a leg over his hip, bumping her core against his hardening length. "I am. Just for something else."

"Insatiable girl," he says, nibbling her lip.

"For you." Because he likes when she talks like that.

She's rewarded by him going rock hard between her legs. Grabbing the back of her knee, he pulls her over him to ride on top. She's new at this...unsure...but the looks on his face make it worth it. Her slick is dripping down, and he runs his fingers through it before teasing her with her own wetness.

"Use me as you see fit, my lady." He gets that mischievous gleam in his eyes. It makes him look dangerous and playful all at once.

"Only if you ask nicely." She's getting better at this.

"Oh, kitten, I'm prepared to beg." He grabs her hips quickly, positions her, and pistons inside before she can blink, making her gasp at how full she is, impaled on him. "But I'm also ready to take what I want."

Sexy. Dammit. "And you want me..."

"Sweetheart, there's nothing I want the way I want you."

Her heat blooms again and her body tingles. He arcs his hips rough and hard, splitting her again and again, hitting the deepest parts and causing that electric pulse to shoot through her veins.

Alpha needs me.

"I want to be good for you. Please, Alpha."

He rolls her so he's on top, going slow, but going deep. This is making love to her, just like he said he'd do, so different to when he bounces her off him in sharp ricochets that white out her mind. Inch by inch, she can feel the thick ridge of him dragging against the most sensitive parts within her, and her sounds go from tiny squeaks to something much throatier. So much greedier.

"Omega," he says, killing her with pleasure. "Ari. I want you. I want you forever."

Pillow talk. Praise. Ari loves this play between them. It makes her want to cry with happiness. But soon life will come back, and she'll lose this tender moment. She'll lose this special place. Everything will be lonely nights and empty beds again. But for now, she wants to pretend with him.

"Take me, Alpha." She wraps her legs up over his ribs, letting him hit her just right. "I'm yours."

He's grinding against her, his knot swelling. His teeth are grit as he stares at her with dark, glittering eyes. "You absolutely are."

Lowering quickly onto his elbows, his chest presses against hers as he nudges her jaw to the side and sucks her mating gland sweetly. She clenches around him, feeling his thickness.

"Say it again," he says, lapping and driving her wild.

"Yours, Alpha."

"With. My. Name." He drags his teeth against her. Dangerous, this is so dangerous...but she's so close.

"I'm yours. Caleb, I'm yours."

"Yes, kitten. That's right. Forever."

Mouthing her gland, she's clenching again. She's going to come just from this feeling alone. Kissing her there is so agonizingly good. Primal. His teeth scrape over it and she's in rapture. She's building up to that precipice, chanting his name like a prayer. Caleb and Caleb and yes and please!

But then sharp pain takes over her senses as he bites her.

No. Not just bites.

He *mates* her.

The pain crawls through her skin like ice-water spiders, her eyes flying wide in horror.

No. No, no, no, please.

Yet the sweet agony makes her come around him with a high-pitched sob. She's bleeding. She's bleeding into his mouth as he sucks her, and sucks her, and she's dying. She can't stop coming undone around him, writhing and trying to push him off, but she can't control her body. She can't control anything. All she can do is gasp a guttural moan when he knots her and shoots his cum inside.

Please. Stop, please.

But the words won't come out...and it's already too late.

His mind is going numb, and he feels her. He fucking feels her. He feels surprise and fear, knowing it's not his own, but he just keeps licking her, sealing her wound with his saliva and basking in their connection.

She bucks and struggles, but since they're knotted, it only feels good, tugging him in the most delicious of ways. She feels it, too, pleasure blending with everything else running through her mind. Her fast-paced, spiraling mind.

This is what it feels like to be Ari.

He groans, loving the taste of her blood on his tongue and the sensations her emotions bring. He's never going to be alone again. Not after this. They're bonded now. She just needs to bite him back. Deep in the throes of passion, she shoves him with her arms, so he cages her. She tilts her hips, so he ruts into her.

"So good, kitten. So sweet."

She's coming around him, squeezing him, and she's not stopping, either. Her ecstasy is longer than it's ever been, and he comes again from the secondhand intensity of her inner howl as she scrabbles for purchase, only driving him deeper and deeper in the process.

"Stop!" she manages, but he can't. He won't.

And as her panic spirals, he slowly comes to realize her struggles...are real. She wants to get away. After all this time, after all they've shared, she wants to run. Her fear pulses through him with new weight. This isn't nerves about what the future holds. She feels...violated.

Fucking *violated.*

Betrayal burns his heart as he remembers every rejection that's ever threatened to destroy him. How stupid he is for thinking anyone would want to stay. She cries out and thrashes as though she didn't ask for every moment of this, and it turns his stomach. He'd made her say it. Over and over! She said she was his!

Well, then, if she's going to play the victim, he's more than willing to play the monster.

Wrapping her hair around his fist, he pulls hard, pinning her head to subdue her struggles as he licks her again. "You're mine now, Ari."

Whether you want to be or not.

"No!" she yelps, filling him with fury.

Bitter and angry, he tries to push her his emotions. "Do you feel this, kitten? Can't you feel your Alpha right now?" But she can't because she hasn't bitten him back. Not yet—but fucking soon, or they're about to have a real problem.

Pushing, she rakes her nails over him in a gouge that will stay, collarbone to chest, ending in a twirl and making him bleed.

Bitch. Ohhh, you little bitch. But two can play at that game.

He grabs at her with one hand, latching onto her forearm and bringing it to his mouth. He'd wanted to do this anyway, but under completely different circumstances. The gland on her wrist flickers with her pulse and he eyes it for only moments before driving his teeth into that, too. A scream tears from her this time, the worst sound he's ever heard though it doesn't to stop him. Out of whatever kindness is left in him, he laps at it, sealing it closed even as she weeps.

"No, no, no, kitten. Shhh. That's not how we're going to end this moment. We're mated now. For life."

Her terror ramps. He can feel it, but he can't stop. Pinning down her marked wrist and keeping her other hand trapped beside her body, he starts to pump inside her, punctuating his thrusts with words. "Keeping you full, Ari. Keeping you right here. With me. Dedicated, right? To you. Now and always."

Her body goes slack with unwanted pleasure he can feel burn through their bond. She's enraptured just as much as she's disgusted. He hates it. Ohhh, he fucking hates it.

Why do I ruin everything?

With her no longer fighting him off, he reaches between their bodies and starts strumming between her legs as she moans. Too sensitive, she jerks, and it just feels so fucking good.

"*Climb higher,* little one. Make me proud." He's compelling her, looking into her tear-streaked eyes with his Alpha's command. He's claimed her now. That means he has power over her. Control. Ownership. "Obey me, Omega. *Come for me.*"

And she does, letting loose around him with something guttural and wounded and heartbroken. Still, he kisses her. And kisses her and kisses her, wanting to salvage this, knowing he's unable. This is wrong. It all went so terribly wrong. He's broken something precious and tenuous and sacred with his greed.

But it doesn't matter. Caleb is ruthless when it comes to getting what he wants, making up for a lifetime of being denied everything that mattered. He may have lost this moment, but he still won overall. He has what he wanted since the minute he first saw her. She's his, for better or for worse.

Mate.

CHAPTER 5

IGNORANCE IS BLISS

ARI STRUGGLES TO escape his painful grip, but his knot has her. There's nowhere to go and nothing to do, but that doesn't stop her from trying. She pushes at him and cries out, trying to get away, but the smell of his blood…

He mated me, he mated me!

…is something that begs her to taste it. He tasted hers after all. She's going crazy. It hurts but it feels good, and she's afraid.

He commands her, *"Be still, Omega."*

And she goes limp; she can't help it. "We're…we're not mates," she sputters, covering her eyes. She can't bear to look at him or the deep red slice she put on his chest.

"Tell that to our bodies, kitten," he says, pressing her down firmer on the floor, making it hard to breathe under his weight.

"It's my fault! I stopped taking my suppressants before the trial! I went off my blockers. I tried to get your attention. I wanted to trick you!" Now that the words are coming out, they come in a gush of panic. "I needed to win, and I'm sorry. I'm so, so sorry!"

His scent becomes that deep darkness again. "Ohhh, Ari. You're going to wish you hadn't told me that."

Her blood runs cold. He wouldn't hurt her, would he? "I didn't want this to happen! I'm sorry. I take it back. You take it back now, too!"

It's irrational. Childish. It doesn't work like that. Their chemistry is mixed now; they need each other. Even in this situation, she wants to run hard and fast, but she also never wants to leave him.

This is so messed up.

"Take it back? Impossible." He breathes deep, running his nose in the crook of her neck and making her shudder. "Even if I could, I wouldn't. You're mine."

"I'm not." She tries to push again but he's still inside her, and it still feels good. Her heat isn't over. Even so, she keeps trying to get out from under his massive body, struggling again as sweat makes their skin stick together.

He speaks through his teeth. "I told you, *be still!*"

And her muscles release, giving her space to break into sobs— heavy tears he kisses from her eyes.

"You can't escape me, Ari. We're not leaving this room until you claim me back, and I don't mind keeping you here for a long time."

"I can't..." Her voice comes out broken.

"You can," he whispers over her eyelids, his scent soothing her against her will. "And if we're confessing things, I have a few secrets for you, too."

She looks at him. He has a slight smirk on his face and mischief in his eyes.

"That day in front of your apartment? I knew you would be there. I was following you, kitten. I know where your office is, I know where your home is, I know what subway routes you take."

"That's..." she starts, a dark rock sinking into the pit of her stomach.

"And those little pills you've been taking every morning? The ones that would keep you from doing what a good Omega should? They're fake, sweetheart."

Her mouth drops open and her eyes go wide.

"Wouldn't it be beautiful if I got you pregnant during your first heat?"

"That...that doesn't happen," she stutters. "I need a few cycles to—"

"I wonder." He peppers kisses on her face. "What's between us is unique. I wouldn't be surprised if we break convention. We're soulmated."

"We're not." She grits her teeth as he arcs his hips and pulses inside her. Why isn't his knot going down? Why isn't this tragedy making his body release her?

Because he likes it.

That's the only answer. Somewhere, deep down, a part of him likes it.

"I can feel your wheels turning, little one." He rubs his cheek on hers, marking her everywhere he can. "That's part of what mating does. I'm in your head, sweetheart. And I want you in mine."

"I can't!"

"I could make you." It's a seduction as much as a threat. "I'll make you want it, Ari. One way or another."

He flops to his side, dragging her on top of him, but she can't struggle anymore. He's made it so she can't. Instead, he runs his fingers through her hair and touches her wound—her mating mark —and she cries out a sound of pleasure in spite of herself. "Darling, you asked for this."

"I didn't," she chokes out.

He mimics her breathy voice. "'Take me, Alpha. I'm yours. Breed me, Alpha—I need you. Don't leave. Stay forever.'"

She shudders, humiliated. "It's heat talk! Omegas do that! Just like the things you said when your Alpha took over!"

He tugs her hair a little harder, making her face him. "You think that wasn't real? That I didn't mean it?" Looking in her eyes, he indulges her with a smile. "Oh, kitten. You don't know how special you are, do you? How deeply you affect me. Did you think I would react this way for just anyone? Did you think all it takes is an unsuppressed female to make me lose my mind?"

Her lips tremble.

"Did you think I've never fucked another Omega through their heat in this very room in their own dirty little nests?"

She can't help it, she growls.

He chuckles at her. "They never acted like you. Never wanted me like you. Never put me into rut, even when I was deep inside them. When they begged their Alpha, they only said pretty words like, 'Harder. Faster. I need you now.'"

She hates them. She hates all of them. If she could tear out their throats, she would.

"I smelled you and knew you were mine immediately, trick or not. And sweetheart? I *was* suppressed. I *was* on blockers. And you still smelled me anyway, didn't you? Enough to throw you into heat. And wasn't I the bad guy? The enemy? Yet here you are. Wasn't there anyone else who smelled good enough to you? Anyone else you could have chosen?"

No. The only one she trusted made her want to throw up.

"Sweetheart, you're just afraid. It's to be expected. This is new to you and to your body. You don't know what's right and wrong. But I do. I'm older, more experienced, and I know the difference between Mine and Mine-for-Now.

"Let me ask—has anyone ever smelled better than me? Did you want anyone else to run themselves all over you the way I did outside of your apartment? Touch you? Mark you up? Leave their scent on your special parts? Tell me."

She hesitates, trembling in his arms.

"Tell me, Omega."

She twitches this time, honesty pouring from her lips. "No. Just you. No one's ever smelled better than you. You're almost perfect."

"Almost? Hedging your bets, little one?" He kisses her head, and she can feel his chest rumble with a held back laugh. "You know I'm meant for you. The nose doesn't lie." He caresses her bite mark with a tenderness that brings back her tears. "This...well, this is just a physical reminder that you belong to me. I want one, too, Ari. I want to show the world I'm yours."

It's twisted that part of her thrills at that. He's not commanding her. He's convincing her.

This is all my fault. I'm as ruthless as he is, doing anything to win. I have no moral high ground. He's right. I didn't know any better and I begged him to do exactly this. He was putting his teeth on me, and it felt so good. It was a warning, wasn't it? A silent ask. And I...I told him "Please." It's not his fault. It's mine.

She hiccups in his arms. What has she done? She's not only ruined her own life, but his, too. She's a horrible Omega. A horrible person.

But then his knot finally goes down...

She's free...

And suddenly she doesn't give a damn what she's done.

———

As soon as her chance comes, Ari throws herself off him, her muscles coiled and ready to lunge.

But, no, we're not playing that way, sweetheart.

What do Alphas love? Not just their role, but the instinct to take what's theirs. To win. To chase. And it's so fucking sexy, he can't stand it.

Caleb swipes at her, latching on to her leg before she can get too far, knocking her down with a *thwump* that should rattle her teeth. Dragging her toward him, she snarls and bites, and he wants nothing more than to subdue her. Her nest is kicked to crumples and he literally gives no shits. She'll make it again. He'll make her make it again.

"Pretty baby can't get away from me," he says, like it's a game. To him, it is. Cat and fucking mouse.

Her claws are out again as she lashes at him, so he pulls her legs high, upending her onto her back. Without hesitation, he dives in and clamps his teeth on the gland on her inner thigh, close enough to nuzzle her slick. When she bucks, it only helps him break the skin, and she screams once more, scarring his eardrums with high-pitched whines and filling him with raw adrenaline. Though her heat had almost dampened into silence, his bite brings it back in full force, ripping up and down her body. He can feel the pain in her heart. The pain in her mind. She wants this feeling to stop. She needs it to stop.

But fuck her.

Turning his head quick, he takes the meat of her other thigh into his mouth and bites it into bloody dashes, making her wails turn into throaty groans, her agony turning to pleasure as that heat builds in her womb. When she calls out "Alpha," he knows she's got her right where he wants her. Trapped.

Lurching forward on his hands and knees, his cock raging between them, he takes her unmarked wrist and sinks in his teeth. Next, he grabs her head and tugs it to the side roughly, imagining that he could break her neck if he wanted. Instead, he licks her unmarked mating gland, and more slick pours from her than he's ever felt.

And she says she doesn't want this.

Instead of fighting him off, she's pulling him closer now, and he takes full advantage, biting her other side with abandon—the hardest bite yet, making his jaw ache—and this time, she doesn't fight it. This time, her brain screams *Submission* and *Pleasure* and *Need.*

Bitterness makes him not seal her wounds this time. Let these marks hurt. She deserves it.

"My turn, kitten. Make me yours." She's hooking her heels around his rear, trying to pull him inside. He wants to be there. He wants it so much, he's going insane. Still, he says, "Not until you claim me, Ari. Call my name and make me yours."

Her trembles ensnare his rational side as he notches himself against her. She's screaming "Please" as his inner Alpha rages against his actions, howling *PROTECT,* but it doesn't matter.

"Claim me, you little cunt. Come on." He thrusts his mating gland against her lips and prays. "Make me bleed, kitten. Make me bleed and I'll make you come so hard, it'll blow your fucking mind."

He doesn't command her. He refuses to command her. But her teeth clamp down anyway, ripping into his skin... And it's fucking bliss.

It's only then that Ari feels his manic desire pulse through her like poison. It's so good and so bad but he plunges into her, and she can feel his deep, roaring satisfaction. She's coming already, but he's not yet, thrusting into her even as she thinks she's going to break. He's hers and she's his and her psyche is melting away. She doesn't know where he stops and she begins. It makes her feral with want, and she topples him over, straddling him and grinding their sexes together. He grunts as she lifts his hands over his head, pinning them as best she can and taking his mouth the way she's taking his body.

This is what it feels like to be Caleb.

Using her cheek, she shoves his face aside to lap at the wound she made, her own mark throbbing in a mirrored ecstasy-agony. Without thinking, she shoves him the other way and bites down on that side, too, setting him off into a moan of "Yes" that has her coming again as he knots her once more. But she won't stop now. She can't. She's going to die from this feeling and love every moment of her demise.

She tries to ride him but gets almost nowhere. Still, the pull against her entrance and his throbbing heat inside her is everything. "Fuck me, Alpha." She spits filthy words just like he does. "Fill me up. If I'm yours, fucking prove it."

And he does. He sits up and wraps his arms around her, pulling her up and down, bouncing her like a rag doll. His wiry pubic hair is the perfect scrape over her most sensitive part, and she moans against him. Hands in his dark mane, she tugs hard, feeling the sting of it on her own scalp as his head tips back. She kisses him then, driving her tongue down his throat, uncaring if she chokes the son of a bitch. If she's his? He's going to fucking feel it.

They come again, still locked together, their timing matching to the second. It's only after their cries subside that they collapse to the floor, her on his chest, him with his arms wrapped around her in a vise grip. Unable to stop herself, unable to do anything else, Ari's mind drifts in a haze of heady exhaustion, one word on her lips.

"Caleb."

The man who mated me.

After a moment of panting, his arms loosen, and he nuzzles her hair slowly. "It will be better next time." His words are so quiet, she can tell his own land of Nod is calling. "I'll be sweet, Ari. I'll be anything you want. Just stay with me. Be mine. Don't leave." He sounds so soft. So sleepy. Too honest.

Feeling his emotions echo in her body, the sadness and loneliness that rolls off him in waves grabs at her empathy and pulls. "I won't leave," she promises in a ragged, abused whisper. "We're... we're mated...that means we're in this together."

For better or for worse.

"Yes, pretty girl, absolutely. Forever."

His fingers leave little, circular trails along her back, lulling her into silence, into stillness. His smell is a comfort that it shouldn't be, his breaths are a gift she never wanted. She mulls over what life will be like, mated to a monster...but then sleep takes her far, far, and away.

Ari's next period of waking is a quiet one. For both of them. He's spooning her from behind, asleep, and she'd be free to sneak away if she wanted to...but somehow, she doesn't...and she has no idea how to feel about that.

Her heat had come on strong in the moments when they struggled, but since their long hours of blissed-out unconsciousness, it feels as though it's ebbing again. Her tummy still aches with cramps, but it's bearable. She doesn't want to wake him. Not yet.

Her nest is a mess, which hurts her more than it should, given it's just a pile of blankets and towels. His arms aren't wrapped around her, but his knees are up in the crook of her own, and that's enough for now.

She puts her hand between her legs, finishes herself as quietly as possible, and goes to sleep again.

The next time she awakens, he's gone, and she panics. She sits up quick and whips around, finally catching him in the corner preparing food for her. It's dwindling at this point and he's going to have to leave the room soon. She doesn't want that.

Wordlessly, he shows her the text message he's typed to Niles. Nothing cute, nothing honest, just a thumbs-up. Ari hits SEND, just like she has for days.

Caleb holds up her pill, and it makes her huff a sardonic laugh. "What even is this?"

He shrugs, having the wherewithal to look ashamed. "Tylenol. It might not have been what you thought, but that doesn't mean I'm not taking care of you."

She stares at nothing for a moment, her feelings an uncomfortable mix.

Leaning forward to take the little white tablet, she winces, the teeth-shaped cuts inside her thighs rubbing together. His eyebrows knit as he watches her down her medicine with trembling hands, and she can feel his concern and remorse. Shaking his head slightly, he gets on his knees.

"I'll help you, sweetheart," he says, laying her back. "Be still."

She doesn't like those words. Her legs clamp shut, and she cringes. Something like heartbreak comes from his side of their new bond.

"I'm just going to lick them closed. I'll do it for all of them."

"You should have done it before."

He sighs through his nose. "You're right."

Ari lies still but is tense as he spreads her legs, leans in, and laps at her with his rough, wet tongue. The bites immediately feel so much better, but he *tsks* slightly.

"These are going to scar differently, I think. Redder, maybe." She's not sure he sounds contrite enough. Chastely, he moves to her unsealed wrist, French kissing her pain away, and finally to her last mating bite, cooling the marks he caused.

"Six of these. Is that normal, oh experienced one?" she asks.

He smirks for only a minute. "No. I think we can both say I wasn't at my best."

Looking at the open gouge on his chest, she says, "Neither was I."

She sits up slowly, moving to kiss it. To make it all better. He stops her just before she touches him, catching her hand and lacing their fingers together.

"You don't have to." His eyes are far away, and his lips are pressed tightly together.

"Does it hurt?"

He nods.

"Then let me fix it. We're supposed to take care of each other, right?"

His eyes close and a line of sadness appears between his eyebrows, a single tear slipping over his cheek. Suddenly all is forgiven.

"Oh, Alpha," she soothes, leaning in and pressing the flat of her tongue over his chest, tasting the rough scabbing and reopening the wound only to close it again with the magic of her mouth. When he holds her close, it's the gentlest thing he's ever done, as if he's afraid to break her. And maybe he is. He smells that way.

"Here. Drink more." He gives her the water again, making her attend to her parched throat. When he brings over food, instead of feeding her with his mouth as he has been, he feeds her by hand. It's still intimate, but not so...controlling. Bread. Pastries. Apples. He does lick the juice from around her mouth, though, and it makes her want him again—however neither of them are ready.

"Would you like to know more about me?" he offers. She looks at him as he smiles softly, afraid to meet her eyes. "It seemed important to you."

"Yeah. I'd like that."

He brings them down and curls around her once more, running his face over her healing wounds, marking her with his scent and making her tremble with pleasure. She's not sure why that happens, but it's one of the best feelings. Before this talk is over, she's going to need him again; she knows it for a fact.

"Ask me anything."

She mulls it over for a moment. "Your mother and father both died?"

He sighs behind her, tickling the nape of her neck. "Yeah. I was about twenty-four. My uncle died, too, though under different circumstances. Everyone in my family is gone."

"Even your brother?"

He nuzzles closer and she can feel his hurt. "For all intents and purposes."

She whispers her sympathies, grabbing his hand and bringing it over her heart. "Why did you hate your parents?"

He dips down so his forehead rests on the very top of her back. "Probably because they hated me first."

"Why?"

"They were so happy before they had kids. Their life was perfect as it was. We ruined their dreams of what they wanted to be, I guess. And the more they were cold to us, ignored us, left us behind while they went and did whatever, the more we started acting out to get attention. Any kind of attention. Being bad got them to actually look at us for once. It just spiraled from there.

"They sent us away. My uncle was a priest at a high-end parochial school, so that's who was saddled with us next. I hated him, too—yet another mutual experience. I think my uncle may have loved my brother in the beginning but after a while, it changed. Anyone who stood up for me was seen as a nuisance. Like they'd been led astray or tainted, somehow. In the end, people turned against me just so they could get back into my uncle's good graces. In a cold school filled with marbled saints, the only lesson I learned was that they don't practice what they preach."

Ari's eyes are wet with tears, feeling his every heartache. "It sounds very lonely."

"I always had my brother, though. Until I didn't. I decided to change everything about my life then. My name. My legacy. My trust fund would have carried me through until eternity, but I wanted none of it. Their money made me sick. They didn't give me a shred of affection, yet they left me a fortune. I didn't want a cent."

"What did you do?"

"Donated it."

"I would have expected you to take it out and burn it."

He chuckles darkly. "That would have felt fantastic. But no."

"What did you donate to?"

He pauses before he sighs. "Foster programs."

Ari startles at that, turning over her shoulder slightly. "Why?"

He doesn't connect eyes with her. Instead, he looks wistful. "Because I had always wished I was in one. Maybe then my brother and I could have found someone to love us."

Ari lifts his chin, looking at him and seeing why he is the way he is. Part of it, anyway. Nuzzling closer, she kisses him. Even though her body isn't screaming for it, even though she doesn't have to, she looks into his honey-brown eyes and says, "Make love to me, Caleb... Please."

And who is he to deny her?

Caleb thinks his favorite position is snuggled around her back, breathing in the mixed chemistry of her new scent, allowing himself to feel her feelings without having to see the hurt in her eyes. He still believes this went wrong, but he got what he wanted and feels satisfaction in that. The ends justify the means. He's willing to act as sorry as he needs to be to make her accept this. To quiet down and get over it. It's working. And maybe he actually feels the regret he pretends to.

A little.

Maybe.

He does love her after all.

They're not knotted now, but they had been for at least the past half hour. She didn't even complain, though he supposes there would be no point if she did. It's not like he could do anything about it once he was already inside her. Still, he'd felt an apprehension from her side that he didn't know what to do with. He's still trying to breed her, even now, it seems she just doesn't understand that's what knotting is for. She thinks it's only about pleasure.

Innocent little kitten.

This time, it's him who says, "Tell me about yourself." Though he might know what she has to say already.

She surprises him. "My family is gone, too."

Well, now. That's not something he'd seen in his research. Though, if given more time...

"Foster care isn't what you think it is. It's just as cold and lonely, but at least it's better than the streets." Ari sighs. "When you go from house to house, you have nothing, so you make...alliances, I suppose. The more alliances you have in a house, the more likely you are not to move around as much. Sometimes those alliances become friends. Best friends."

"Niles?"

He can smell love ooze from her. "Yeah. I guess he did for me what your brother did for you. He was always looking out for me. Protecting me."

And then her friend brought her here, knowing she needed her Alpha more than anyone else. All of a sudden, Caleb loves him, too... in his own way. A rare emotion.

"Were you given up when you were born?"

She sniffles and shakes her head. "My parents died just before Christmas when I was fourteen. I know they loved me with their whole hearts, though. At least I had that, even if I didn't have it forever.

"It was a crash on Storrow Drive, just off the highway. When the other car hit us, everything around me shattered all at once. I got... stuck, you know? The belt kind of held me upside down so I didn't hit my head when we rolled. But my parents..." She trails off for a moment. "The car that hit us had three people in it, too. Also one survivor. The driver."

Laser focused on the details she's relaying, Caleb's mind spirals, doing a bit of math based on her age.

Oh no. Please, please no...

"I don't know what happened, really. It never went to trial, so I never even saw his face. I wish I had, though. I needed someone to hate back then." She curls in on herself more tightly and he moves to follow, keeping them as close as possible.

His heart is in his throat. "Do you know the names of the people in the other car?"

"It was a family. Their last name was Allein."

His eyes cinch and he holds her tight. Almost too tight. Regret and sympathy fill him to the brim. "And you wanted..." How does he even ask this? "You wanted to confront the man who did it?"

She sniffles and something confusing echoes from her emotions over their bond. He wishes he could read her mind.

"Yes," she admits. "Even now. But not for the reasons you think. Now, I think I...I want to forgive him."

Caleb laughs softly, short and half-hearted. "That sounds like you." He snuggles in, unsure but resolved. "I'll help you, then. Once this is all over, I'll take you to him."

Looking over her shoulder once more, her expression is lost. "How can you do that?"

Caleb replies, "He's my brother... And now, in a way, I guess he's yours."

CHAPTER 6
COMING HOME

THE TILE IS black with red accents, giving the bathroom a sort of stylish-but-ominous look. The hot water is washing their combined fluids away and rinsing them down the drain. It's almost unbearable. Caleb sifts his hands through Ari's wet hair as she tries not to cry.

"I hate it, too," he says, scrubbing her scalp gently.

Feeling each other is an entirely new experience. Ari has always smelled people. She's an Omega. That's what Alphas and Omegas do. But this is different. She can tangibly feel his disappointment. When she takes the bar of soap and cloth from him to wash between her legs all by herself, his mood dips to sullen. Turning his back on her, he works the shampoo through his own raven hair, weaving suds in and out of it. The white fluff trickles down his back and over his shoulder blades, his mating bites showing like indented pink circles that scream *Claimed* while straddling the crooks of his neck. Is that what hers look like?

Peering down at her wrists, one has already gotten pale, his immediate care having healed it from the start. The other is bruised pock marks, redder by far than the bites she licked clean on him. Her thighs look worse. Ari doesn't know what to say. She doesn't know how this works. What happens now?

"You can wear some of my clothes," he offers, rinsing his face and scrubbing off their residue. "Yours haven't withstood the test of time."

She snorts. "Yeah, what's that going to look like? You're huge. I'll swim in them."

Moving around her to give her access to the hot stream, his emotions fall into rejection this time. "You've seen those movies where the girl ends up in a baggy T-shirt and enormous boxers the next day, haven't you? It's supposed to be a sure sign of a night well-spent."

She smiles to herself, tipping her face into the water.

He hums a low, satisfied sound. "Do you know I can actually feel it when your mood shifts?" His fingers curl around her hips and massage gently. It's not a seduction; it's a comfort.

"I feel yours, too," she admits.

"Don't go." It comes out so quiet, she's not sure that she heard it. Immediately her heart aches with his pain. Maybe her own, she can't tell. She doesn't want to go, but the further in the past her heat is, the worse she feels about her situation. What he did to her...what she did to him. It's not anything she ever read about. In the stories and the articles online, it's all about pleasure, romance, and the science of chemistry. This? What they did was animalistic. Rabid. Is this what it means to be soulmated? She admitted to both him and to herself that he smelled good. So good. The best she's ever tasted in the air. But he's still not right.

"Are you afraid?" he asks.

She feels the warmth of him come closer as he rests his forehead against the nape of her neck, letting the shower's painful rain destroy their moratorium. Unable to speak, her lips trembling, she just nods.

"Me, too." The large hands on her hips reach up and take her hands, sliding their slippery fingers together in a knit embrace. "I'm sorry if I hurt you."

And that breaks the dam. She turns into his arms and sobs as he hushes her, cradling her and swaying back and forth.

"I'm sorry!" she chokes out the words. "I'm so sorry! I've ruined—"

"No, no, no," he interrupts her with kindness. "Saved, kitten. You may have just saved me."

She looks at him with clouded eyes as he takes her by the cheeks and wipes her tears, his lips close to hers. "Didn't I save you, too? Weren't you lonely, just like me?"

Her throat is closing on itself. "I only meant to distract you..."

He smirks, though he feels dark and cold. "Ahh, and distract me you did." His expression fades into something flat and blank as he finishes brushing the suds off her, reaching around to tweak off the shower stream and leaving them in a hot cloud. Looking at the shower curtain, he laughs through his nose a little. "I just realized we don't have any towels."

She blushes, eyes wide, and basically squawks her embarrassment. "Do you—do you have a washing machine in the apartment? I'll do it, I—"

"Shh, don't you dare. Your nest is a collector's item. I doubt I'll ever wash that room again."

Rolling her eyes doesn't even describe it.

"I'll leave it for next time."

But then her stomach drops. *Next time...*

He holds out a hand. "Come on out. We'll use my won't-fit-you clothes to dry you off, and then stick you in another set with the same problem."

"What about you?" She takes his hand without question, and he grins at her.

"My tag says to let me drip dry."

That gets her to laugh. "All right then, oh experienced one. Get me dressed and show me where the cornflakes are."

He kisses her knuckles and pulls open the curtain. "I told you not to underestimate their power."

. . .

Ari clutches her phone, sitting on Caleb's couch while he spends a bit more time freshening up. Apparently keeping his hair that nice is a "process."

Her last messages to Niles were a short series of thumbs-up each day. By counting her texts backward, she's been locked up here with Caleb for eleven days. It's mind-boggling. Her body feels amazing...in all the places it doesn't hurt, such as her lesser-healed wrist, neck, and thighs.

With a groan, she starts to text her friend.

> Hey, I need a ride home—

Wait. What happens to "home" when you're mated? Do they live separately? That thought hurts but...

She deletes what she'd typed and tries again.

> Hey, I think we're all done over here.

She sends. After a few seconds, the bubbles appear.

> OMG! Is it really you texting me this time, or
> is it still your man-meat Alpha? What did I
> tell you? Did he blow your mind or what?

Oh, he definitely blew her mind. She pauses. Pauses more. Then decides to rip off the Band-Aid.

> I'm mated now.

The pause she gets is longer this time. Bubbles start. Then stop. Then start. Then stop.

And she can't do this.

With a sting in her eyes, she shuts off her phone and tosses it on the coffee table with a small clatter. Leaning back on Caleb's soft couch, black leather that smells like him, she covers her eyes. She can't cry anymore, but she doesn't know what to do, either. She's a person of action but there's no compass to guide her, no way to be sure she's following the right path.

She thinks, *Maybe I should just trust my Alpha...*

Her Alpha. It's surreal.

Running her fingers over her sealed marks, they actually feel good. Sexy to touch. She smells...not exactly like him but a blend of both of them. If she was maple syrup and he was just a dash of cinnamon, it would make something nice, but a tinge of his ash scent carries through, so she smells like burnt pancakes. It makes her snicker a little.

"So, I take it you told Niles?" Caleb says, coming into the room, still drying his body with a random T-shirt, sweatpants slug low and showing off that lovely line men get from the crest of their hips all the way to their groin. His is perfectly grabbable. Lickable.

God, he's pretty.

"How can you tell?" She sulks.

"The man is literally blowing up my phone." Caleb's lips curve at the edges. "I don't think he likes me anymore."

She slings her arm back over her eyes. "I guess he has words for you."

Caleb sighs. "I guess I have words for him, too."

His mood sours to match hers, but for different reasons. She can smell it in the air and feel it with her body. He sits next to her, gathering her in his arms. If a man ever treated her like this before, she would have thought he was too grabby and twisted off his fingers—now, she wants to fall asleep on top of this overlarge brute, as she's already been doing for days. The thought of going to bed alone after this is so sad. It's what she's the most afraid of, after all. Being loved, then being left behind.

"I have the rest of the week off for my leave of absence," he says. "You?"

She blinks, tucked in and resting her cheek on his skin. "I forgot to ask."

He gazes down at her with the softest look in his eyes and warmth is all she feels. It fills her body and makes her smile.

"I smell like you," she says, unsure if it's a complaint or not.

He traces her mating gland, the one he was kind to, and she closes her eyes, subdued and seduced. "I smell like you, too. It's perfect."

Even as she nuzzles him deeper, she says, "I need to go home."

I want to go home. Maybe if I get away from you, this neediness will go away.

His scent dips into that dark place, and she feels goosebumps trail over her arms. He takes her hand and kisses her fingers, lapping at her wounded wrist once more for good measure. "It's only paper-work at this point, but I want to marry you."

She startles and looks up at him. His expression is sardonic, brows raised, but eyes half-lidded as he gives her a hurt smile. "I can smell that you're not sold on me yet, but I suppose it's too late for that."

Standing up for herself, she says, "You stalked me. Tricked me. Bit me." But it comes out like a sullen teenager said it instead of a strong woman. His feelings tip into anger and it puts Ari's nerves on edge.

"I thought all women liked stories where an Alpha did anything to get the Omega he wanted." After a pause he adds, "Don't you?"

She did. Everything that she's read always had that flavor. A man obsessed whose sole focus was the woman who was his destiny. Is this a dream come true, then? A romance novel come to life? If so, suddenly Ari feels bad for all the Omega characters she's read about.

His voice turns cold as he plays with her hand idly, looking at her fingernails. "It seems like soulmated pairs will go to the extreme to be together. After all, you did something very illegal to get to me. I wonder if you'd still be able to practice law if that ever came out."

She freezes, breath stopping entirely as that sentence hangs in the air like a noose.

"But I'd never tell." He peppers kisses over her wrist, looking soft but feeling hard and mean. "I would never put my wife in that situation."

His assumption lies heavy in the air between them, and Ari feels that urge to run again. He only seems to like it, his body warmer as he rests her palm over the red wound on his chest—the one she also didn't heal fast enough. Again, she feels as though she's lost the moral high ground.

Leaning down, he gives her a tentative kiss before whispering against her lips, "I'll take you home on the subway."

She looks around at his modest-yet-posh apartment. "You don't have a car?"

He chuckles a sweet sound, helping her off his lap, but not out of his arms. "Seems my kitten is afraid of cars." He ducks in, running his tongue over her mating gland and making her cry out. "But you still smell way too wonderful to ride the train alone. Let's call it a 'post-heat perfume.'"

"That's not a thing." She tries to wave him off with a smile, but he just pouts at her a little. Cute. Charming.

It's confusing. Is he a bad man or is he a good man? Does having an immoral job and carrying it out with excruciating efficiency make you a villain? If you're overly violent during your rut, are you violent always? Is there a gray area? Is there a soft side to Caleb that no one gets to see? If so, this is it right here. Ari's job is to protect the vulnerable...and based on what she's learned, that's this man in a nutshell. Easy to hurt. Easy to please. His hopes aimed so high that she couldn't bear to crush him. People refuse their mates, but it's supposed to hurt—not only emotionally, but physically. Could the mighty Caleb Reed bear being rejected by her?

When did she become so powerful?

Alpha needs me.

Rejecting him becomes so much worse if she has pups. Her body would literally revolt against her, and he would go mindless with rage. Nature kicks in and whispers, *Would it truly be so bad to stay? To make a family with such a strong Alpha?*

With conflicted emotions, Ari slides her hand over her belly and his heavy palm follows immediately, his cheek on her shoulder.

"Wouldn't it be amazing if I made it work, first try?" He basically purrs against her, and it does something to her insides. "That would make me feel so good, kitten. So proud of my Omega."

Her heat may be over, but hormones threaten to take her away on a cloud of lust anyway. She starts to respond to him, her slick gathering, and he laughs a bit, lips pressed to her shoulder.

"Does that mean you'll marry me?"

He pushes softly, leaning her onto the sofa, the cool surface kissing her back as he hovers above her. Lifting her T-shirt and paying a delicious amount of attention to her breast, he makes her clench on nothing and never want to leave him, even though she probably should. Still, her mouth says, "Yes."

Was it due to his ministrations, like before? It doesn't matter. Her and her stupid mouth. Her stupid need. His stupidly almost-perfect smell. Releasing her, he rests his ear over her heart and listens to it thrum way too fast. He feels like nothing but happiness.

"Everyone at work is going to hate me," she whispers.

Still on her chest, Caleb comforts her. "Betas will never understand. Alphas will be angry with me, but Omegas will come around. As long as I'm able to make you happy, everyone will come around."

She smiles a bit. "And you're going to make me happy, are you? Lofty goals, Reed."

"Mm." He kisses her breastbone. "But if we're going to make this work, we have to follow one rule from now on."

She raises an eyebrow and looks down at him.

"You can never go up against me in court."

"Afraid to lose?" she teases.

"No, kitten." His eyes twinkle. "I'm afraid I'll fuck you in front of the jury."

And what is there to say to that?

Niles's lips are pursed. He hasn't said more than a few words since showing up with cardboard moving boxes, ones Ari didn't ask for, but he somehow decided she needed. In a way, it was the last straw that tipped the scales, making Ari's next steps come into focus. She'd been on the fence, unsure of whether or not to leave her own home to go live with a stranger—especially so immediately—but apparently her life has been decided for her by two males, one of which she trusts with her life, the other one she doesn't really trust at all. How very misogynistic. It's like the old-timey pack mentality all over again.

She doesn't know if it's because of what happened, or because her...mate...is away, or because her best friend is looking at her like *that,* but she feels like crying. With a sniffle, she rubs her nose as she stuffs her fluffy comfort pillows into a trash bag, wondering if she even gets to use them anymore.

"I'm sorry," Niles says, breaking the silence. "This is my fault. We didn't know him. And now..."

"No." She shakes her head. "It's my fault. I led him on from the very beginning."

Niles presses his mouth together, flattening his full lips into a straight line. "But did you ask him to claim you?"

She shrugs. "Not in so many words. But I didn't say no, that's for sure."

Not until it was too late.

She didn't say no, and her words sure sounded an awful lot like yes in hindsight. It's her fault. It's easier when it's her fault. Still, her eyes water and accusatory daggers fly from Niles's eyes toward her phone, the tangible representation of the man who mated her.

"He knotted you, didn't he?"

Ari blinks at her friend. "Of course, he did."

The curse Niles spits under his breath sounds like it came

straight from Caleb's mouth. "I told him not to. I told him you weren't ready to deal with that kind of intensity on your first time out." He shakes his head. "Never trust an Alpha in rut," the last word spoken through his teeth.

This was a risk from the beginning...?

Crushed. That's how she feels. Betrayed. Maybe she *should* blame Niles.

You brought me to him! I asked you NOT TO, and you brought me anyway!

But the anger cuts off immediately. She loves her friend too much. She swipes her hand over one of her mating bites and it feels somehow soothing. When Niles catches sight of her gesture, though, he gawks and snatches her wrist.

"He bit you here, too?" With nothing but concern, Niles starts tipping her this way and that, moving her hair back on the other side of her neck and hissing in a breath before checking her other wrist. "And he didn't even seal these!" He sounds disgusted, and maybe he should be. "This is not normal, just so you know. This is degrading! He's marked you everywhere!"

You should see my thighs, she thinks bitterly. All of a sudden a wave of sadness comes over her unexpectedly, making her chest ache. But it's not her. It's Caleb.

Alpha is hurt. Alpha needs me.

Her eyebrows knit and a tear slips down her cheek. Immediately, Niles pulls her close and wraps his arms around her.

"I'm sorry, Ari. I'm so sorry. He was the bad guy and I..."

"It's okay," she tells him, holding him and running her fingers down a few of his carefully woven braids to calm herself. They're her favorite thing in the world. Niles knows, and that's why he keeps them so beautifully long. How could she ever be mad at him? "Caleb reminded me of what you said. That I still smelled him, even though he was suppressed and on blockers. I might not have been, but he was. And when I smelled him, my body just...reacted."

In the strongest way possible.

Niles pulls back with wet eyes. "So, it wasn't just because you went off your meds? You really are soulmated?"

Absolutely not!

But... "Yeah, I think so," she lies. She can't bear to see her friend so upset, and what can she do to change the situation, anyway?

Niles still looks unsure. He probably smells her half-heartedness. "You can still reject him, Ari. You can walk away. It will be painful, but I'll be there for you. When you fall in love and want it, you can be reclaimed, and it won't hurt anymore. I'll be with you every step of the way if that's what you want, I promise!"

But then what happens to Caleb?

She thinks about how he fed her, looking at her with such adoration. She thinks about how he washed her hair in the shower, not wanting to be away from her even after everything was over. How he let her come home without making it an issue or pressing his authority. How he held her hand on the subway and kissed her goodbye so sweetly. He didn't pressure her to come live with him, leaving it open and only ensuring that she had his phone number. Though maybe it was just another assumption on his part—thinking that she would come eventually. That she'd have to. That she'd want to. He's not wrong; she misses him already.

Stupid biology.

And, unlike Niles, Caleb wouldn't make her feel bad about their situation. He'd reassure her. Praise her. He'd tell her how good she was. How proud he was. How much he wanted her. Specifically her.

"I won't leave him." It comes out colder than she wants it to. Her skin prickles as she stares her friend down. "I won't. I claimed him back. He's *mine.*" She may or may not have bared her teeth.

At first, Niles looks startled, but his expression fades into a soft smile easily enough. "Okay. All right. I won't say anything else." His expression gets a little more genuine. "You're a good Omega, Ari. Better than me."

And she's immediately mollified. "I think I can help him be a better person. Soothe him, like a good Omega should. He's had a rough life. It makes sense to me why he is the way he is. His parents and…and his brother…" Her words fade to nothing.

"Not good?"

The conversation she had while nestled in her Alpha's arms trickles in and takes over her thoughts. "His brother was the driver," she whispers, almost to herself. How did it slip her mind until now?

"What driver?"

She looks up with glassy eyes. "The one who killed my parents."

Niles's lips part and surprise is written all over his face. "You're kidding."

She shakes her head. "But…it sounded like he wasn't in Caleb's life anymore. He said his brother was gone 'for all intents and purposes.'"

"What the hell does that mean?"

"Maybe he's in prison?" she guesses.

"Wouldn't you have known?"

"I was a minor," she says. "Maybe they kept me out of it?"

Niles sags, hands resting in his lap. "Pumpkin, I'm so sorry."

Her resolve builds. "I'm not." She nods, firming up the idea in her own mind. "Maybe this was destiny. Now, I get to have closure. I get to look him in the face and tell him he took my family from me, that he broke my heart…and then tell him I'm fine. That he didn't ruin me."

"Good, shove it in his face."

"No, that's not what I mean. For all I know, he feels bad about it. It was an accident, after all…"

"If he went to jail, he deserves to be there and he deserves to feel bad."

"But what if he's sorry? His parents died, too. They were in his car. What if he's also suffering but even worse because of the consequences? His life is destroyed. The least I can do is show him that, even though it was a tragedy, I survived. One less person to mourn. To feel guilty for. I'm here and I have people who love me and a fantastic job that I care about. I'm happy."

Niles takes her hand and rubs his thumb over the inside of her bitten wrist, caressing the red lines of Caleb's teeth marks. "Are you?"

She smiles a little. "He said he'd make sure I would be. It seemed to be his top priority."

Niles smiles back, eyes crinkling. "Good. That's his job. If he slacks—he might be an Alpha, and I might die trying—but I'll kick his ass!"

Ari laughs, sending that feeling over to the man who mated her, trying to calm his loneliness with their connection. She feels something in return that she can only describe as shyness. Then gratefulness. That's what her life will be like now. Taming the beast inside the ruthless Caleb Reed. She can live with that.

Caleb throws his car into park in the garage, the muted *click-click* of the gearshift a mundane comfort. Caleb doesn't have a fancy car, not really, but it doesn't suck, either. He'd wanted a Tesla but settled for a hybrid when he realized he didn't want to give his left nut for the equivalent of an oversized gadget.

The elevator to his office is especially unwelcome today. His hormones are still unbalanced, and the scents are too strong. Suddenly it matters that none of them are *hers*. How strange life can be.

It makes him feel lonely. He's often lonely, but he's been able to distance himself from feeling it until today. Today hurts. This is part of being a soulmated pair, though. His parents were soulmated. Everything was extreme, from their love to their fights to their needy voracity for one another. For Caleb's entire life, he's been aching to belong to someone in the way his parents belonged to each other, and he's finally found his other half.

A tickle of amusement flows over from their connection. Ari is with Niles, he guesses—which makes sense—and Caleb is experiencing her emotions via their new bond. He feels...shy about it. Still, he breathes in his new scent, mixed with her, and finds himself grateful.

I'm never going to be alone again.

The thought is enough to make him want to cry and grin like an idiot at the same time. Shaking his head at himself, he gets into the elevator and jabs the button for the correct floor. Within minutes, he's knocking on the unnecessarily expensive mahogany door of his mentor and boss, the ominous and malignant Charles Sloane himself.

"Come in my boy," the smoker's voice crackles as Caleb walks in. "You still have two days plus the weekend, don't you?"

God, he hates this place. Especially now, with his senses on high alert. Caleb's nostrils flare as he tastes the stink of the rail-thin, pale-faced man behind the desk and forces himself not to gag. "Yeah, I do, but I wanted to chat with you about something sooner rather than later."

Leaning back in his chair, Sloane steeples his knobbed fingers. "You smell off. You're not ready to come back yet. Trust an older Alpha. Go home. Don't stink up my office."

Caleb sidesteps the comment. "How do you feel about opening up a pro-bono role in the firm?"

Sloane eyes him with one brow cocked at an angle, his muted blue irises accusing Caleb of losing his mind. "We are very much a for-profit firm."

"I know that. But we need—"

"Clients, not charity cases, boy."

"Look at the bigger picture. Our reputation on the circuit isn't doing us any favors lately. Judge Hayes has made it quite clear—"

"Judge Hayes is a witless, brainless cur." Sloane scoffs and Caleb does his best not to roll his eyes in frustration despite the accuracy of the statement.

Stepping closer, Caleb rests his heavy palms on the executive-style desk, ink blotter well placed despite Sloane being a digital-only kind of guy. His mentor never lets him get a word in edgewise until he starts throwing his weight around, but he's not in the mood today. Today he wants to go soft. Caleb sighs through his nose, trying again. "Hear me out. Taking on a pro-bono lawyer would—"

"Make us look weak. We are who we are so that people will pay us exorbitant amounts of money to win, no matter the odds. If we start caring about the mindless masses, millionaires would be hobnobbing in our lobby with the meth addict of the day. Is that the client experience you'd like to give birth to?"

Sloane's smirk makes Caleb want to punch a wall. Maybe he should. He usually gets away with it.

Pulling out his vowels into long sounds, Sloane says, "Iyyy know what this is all abouuut."

Caleb grinds his teeth. "And what's that?"

"Rumor has it that the woman who bested you threw you into rut. Are you looking to get her a job here? I'm guessing you want to woo yourself a nice piece of Omega ass while you're on the clock. That's new for you, my boy." His expression looks as though he's caught Caleb doing something childish and is more than happy to reprimand him, *tsk*ing like a grandmother. Meanwhile, Caleb's closer to killing his mentor than he ever has been.

"That Omega is my mate now, thank you very much."

Sloane's whole body locks in place and his eyes go nice and round. "Your what?"

Caleb doesn't know whether to smirk, grin, or growl. He does a bit of all three. "Turns out I'm soulmated." He pulls his collar to the side and shows off his marks—one, then the other.

"You...utter fool!" Sloane hisses. "And here I thought you'd just lost that case with your lackluster brain. No. You lost it with your knot!"

Standing up, Sloane twists his decrepit body around the desk and grabs at the throat of Caleb's shirt, popping a button. With an ugly sneer, he sniffs Caleb and everything in him bristles. He glares at Sloane, but the old Alpha pays him no mind as he sucks in Caleb's mated scent in short snuffles, making a face like he caught a whiff of something nasty in a public bathroom. After a moment of humiliation, Caleb's mentor shoves him away as if he was vile, snarling with yellowed teeth.

"I always knew you were stupid boy, but I didn't know you were *fucking* stupid! If I go call over to the 'Law Offices of No Ones and Nothings,' am I going to learn that this little Omega slut is out on heat leave?"

Caleb growls and hunches over, leaning in his mentor's face, nearly nose to nose. "I. Am. Soulmated. You know special rules come into play with that. You threaten my Omega, I tear off your fucking face, and no one would even arrest me for it. It's within my rights."

After a long, drawn-out pause, and in the most unsettling of ways, Sloane laughs at him. Open mouthed, head thrown back, eyes winced and wet. He has the fucking audacity to pat Caleb on the shoulder as he insults him with every raspy guffaw.

Once I get partner in this firm, old man, I'm murdering you in your fucking sleep.

"And let me guess." Sloane wipes his eyes. "You wanted your new mate to work with us because it hurts to be apart, yes?"

That, yes. Also because she said she was afraid of going back to her office. That Threat might be a problem for her, or she might even be ostracized by her colleagues for her sudden relationship with him. Ari thrives on people. She wouldn't be able to stand being looked down on. At least here, under his protection, no one would dare say a single negative thing to her. He could keep her safe and happy in his domain.

He'd also be in control of her bankroll. If she works here, it's harder to leave him because then she'd lose her job, too. Another nice lever to pull to get his own way. Once he merges their bank accounts, he'll control the finances, giving her credit cards and pocket change and making sure he changes the fucking ATM pin on the regular. Credit cards can be stopped, and pocket money will dry up quick if she runs from him. There's also the nice swinging axe of the fact that he could get her disbarred for misconduct.

Told you you'd wished you'd never confessed that little sin to me, baby.

And if she's pregnant... Well, then she'll never try to leave in the first place. He can tell. She has a strong, idealistic view of families. She'd be a perfect mother.

A sort of confusion bubbles from her side, followed by an almost meditative calm. She's soothing him from far away. She senses his maelstrom of emotions and wants to help her mate.

Sweet Omega. Perfect Omega.

He's so fucking in love it's mind-boggling.

Sloane's giggles dry up as quick as they started and he looks at Caleb, his gaze switching from one eye to another, bouncing back and forth as that grip on his shoulder tightens.

"Oh, Caleb, my boy. She's tamed you."

Caleb tosses his hair back slightly but refuses to wither under his mentor's regard. That grip tightens to almost painful...then outright painful, but Caleb doesn't flinch, and he doesn't look down. Sloane hasn't hurt him, really hurt him, in years. What's a little bruising compared to the agony Sloane has wrought in the past?

"You think so?" Caleb asks. He is steadier than he's ever been in situations like this, and his mentor's expression tightens.

Maybe you don't have as much control over me as you thought, old man.

"You only have one job here, my boy. You win cases. You don't give me business suggestions or come to me with the gripes of petty judges who can be ousted with a single scandal. A few false whispers from my friends in higher places and his career is over. All I have to do is crook my fingers, and I'll have this city by the throat."

You wish.

Maybe Caleb doesn't want to be partner. Maybe he doesn't want this fucked-up law firm. Maybe he'll build his own practice—Gwen will follow him, he's sure of it.

"What is your job, Caleb Reed?"

To slit you in two.

"Winning cases."

"Anything else?"

Caleb knows the correct answer is no, instead his eyes narrow as he grins. "And pleasing my fucking mate."

Sloane looks nonplussed for a minute before he bursts into laughter again. "Oh, my boy. Don't you dare come back here before your leave is done. I think you still have slick on the brain."

Caleb allows himself to be pawed at a little in congratulations as he tries to keep himself from ripping out the man's jugular.

If you won't hire her, I will. If you can't help me keep her, I WILL.

If Ari hasn't taken his seed yet, he'll funnel all his spare cash into his own practice. That might be an even better scenario. After all, there's a chance she might be willing to walk away from a regular job, but if she's one of the few people sustaining his newborn practice, it will put even more pressure on her to stay with him. After all, if she left then, she wouldn't just destroy his heart, but also his livelihood—one he created just to make her happy. It would wrack her with guilt every time she even thought of leaving. It would be perfect.

For the first time, Caleb hopes he failed to breed her. It will give him more time to set her snare nice and tight.

Caleb is soaking with sweat in the gym locker room, using one of their white fluffy towels to swipe at his forehead and keep the salt from his eyes. If flirting with emotion is something one can do, he's been practicing all day, pushing feelings of missing her and a few erotic trickles as he imagines her. She gets embarrassed but also pushes back a feeling of unfeigned interest. Still, she hasn't texted yet, which is concerning. He wants to talk to her so badly, but he needs her to message him first. Like a gentleman, he gave her his number, but didn't pressure her to give her own—though he already knows it by heart. Once she finally does reach out, he's going to begin a schedule of communications over the next few days. He's prepared a litany of things he knows she'll like. They're not his taste per se, but he doesn't mind them. He'd planned sixty-four messages so far, but when a few—more than a few— hours went by with no contact, the pulsing fear of her not giving in to their connection became so heartbreaking he had to work out his anxiety. Caleb being Caleb, decided to do so with enough barbell weights to crush a Beta. Everything in him now aches in that perfect "At least I did it to myself" kind of way. It's oddly soothing.

When he checks his phone before hitting the shower, he sees a text with a shy, face-covered-with-its-hands emoji. It reads:

> I didn't ask, I'm so sorry, but I spent the whole day packing to come over

> …

> To MOVE over

> But then I realized you never asked me for that.

> You might not even want that. If you don't, it's no problem.

> Don't worry

> It's probably still my hormones being all out of whack.

His heart fucking throbs. Pitter pats. Does a jig in his goddamned rib cage. She wants to come to him. He'd prayed to any and all possible deities for this. He hopes she feels his happiness. His elation. His downright joy. He texts back:

> Kitten, you may have just made me the
> happiest I've ever been in my entire life.

From her side of the bond, he feels nervousness and pride. This is happening. It's not a dream.

Provide for Omega, his mind pounds. *PROTECT Omega. Even if only from yourself.*

Which may be impossible. But he swears, chemistry or not, he's going to make her fall in love with him. He's going to do and say all the right things. He'll do it forever. Then, maybe he won't have to coerce her at all. Maybe she'll just want to stay on her own.

He thinks for a long, hard minute and thumbs the icons for his contacts, checking the time and listening to the phone ring. When the male voice picks up, Caleb wastes no time.

"Mr. Canady, good to talk to you."

"Caleb! Good to hear from you! What can I do for you today?"

"How is he?"

The smile doesn't drop from the other man's voice, even as he sighs. "Same as always. I'm sure he's been missing you. You didn't come last weekend."

For the best of reasons, Caleb thinks. "Well, I'll be coming to visit with my mate soon." Saying it out loud this time brings him a giddiness he's not prepared for.

"Oh! Caleb! You're mated?!! That's AMAZING! Congratulations!"

He grins and looks away at nothing. Even he thinks he's pathetically adorable. "Thank you. I appreciate it." Caleb clears his throat and lets gravity sink back in. "I...I may need to start preparing for a family soon, Mr. Canady. It might be...time."

"Time for what?"

Caleb swallows, eyes already getting wet. "Time to let go."

Another sigh comes over the line, but this one has no smile in it. "It's probably for the best."

"Yeah?" he asks.

"Yeah," Canady agrees.

For some reason, that one word really matters.

"Okay then," Caleb says, rubbing his eyes like he's suddenly exhausted. "We'll come see him soon."

"Of course. Take all the time you need. We'll be here whenever you're ready."

Caleb thanks him and says his farewells. Staring at Ari's text messages, he knows this is the right choice. He hasn't been strong enough to step away and let go, but now? Now he has someone in his corner. Someone to help ease the pain of separation. Someone to help him say a terribly painful goodbye.

One that's very, very long overdue.

CHAPTER 7
ROMANCED BY HIS LIES

ARI DOESN'T GET AS MUCH of a leave of absence as Caleb does, so as soon as her heat is declared "over," back to the daily grind she goes. She feels like outright sneaking into her office to avoid making eye contact with anyone who knows her, but with her luck of late, they may as well all be welcoming her with cake.

The subway train is packed but everyone smells mild and subtle, unlike Caleb, who had still taken over her senses when she saw him last, even though her heat was over. Not perfect, but better and better all the time. He'd kissed her goodbye outside her home and that was that. Only it wasn't.

Now she's moving in. Tonight. She'd texted with him ad nauseam yesterday about what to do with furniture and knickknacks and all matter of stupid things, anything and everything to stall. She keeps reminding herself that he never asked her to live with him (though he did say he wanted to marry her) and it was completely her and, well, Niles's—idea in the first place, yet here she is, shoving herself at him one minute and hemming and hawing the next.

Why?

Because she didn't want this, that's why. Now her mind is at odds with her goddamned body because their chemistry is all mixed! The Caleb in her mutters, *"Fucking biology,"* and an old woman next to Ari startles, gawking and making her want to fade into the metal pole she's grabbing on to. The train rumbles under her feet, normal and safe. Not a scary car. Not the scary-yet-wonderful arms of the man who mated her. Here, Ari's just a regular city commuter in an oversized vehicle that's more likely to break down than not. This is who she is. This is what the crux of her identity is hinged on. She is an underpaid warrior for Justice, protecting those even poorer than she is from the cruelty of a world that hasn't taken care of them the way it should have.

The thought puffs her up with pride and Caleb sends his amusement. It makes her blush. Even when traveling at the speed of subway, getting farther and farther away from him, she can feel him so clearly. Can she ever get used to this?

Though, it's already had its perks, she supposes. Lying in bed alone last night had never felt less lonely. She could feel him pining for her as she'd stared, well past midnight, at the blinding white of her phone, texting him stupid things like:

> But see, I got this coffee table as a really good deal on Craigslist and it's meaningful to me. First piece of furniture I ever bought on my own. I had it before I even had a bed!

And Caleb had replied with a quick:

> Then I'll toss mine and we'll use yours.

Her thumbs flew across the glass as her lips quirked up at the corners.

> But it doesn't match the black leather gothic emo thing you've got going on

She'd been half serious but wondered if she'd gone too far. People like what they like. Maybe that was a little mean.

> Well, then maybe I need a non-black leather gothic emo thing to liven up the place. Yin and yang, kitten. You can be the light side

It was as though she could feel his smile.

> And do you see yourself as the dark side, oh experienced one?

There'd been a pause. Then bubbles. Then:

> When you sprinkle your sunshine on the world, I can be there in all the shadows

She'd snorted.

> That's definitely emo

This time, there'd been a longer pause and a voice message had come over instead of just a text. He'd been low and sleepy sounding.

"Tell me what you need me to be, Ari. I just want you to be happy, whatever that means. I'll be a good Alpha, I promise."

And her whole body had flushed red, forehead to toes. She'd been sure he felt her embarrassment and, dare she say, giddiness, because adoration flowed over their bond.

He'd sent a voice message again. "Bring anything and everything you want. My home is yours. I don't need stuff, kitten. Just you."

She'd basically squirmed with a grin. She'd never even dated before, so all this—quite literal—pillow talk had her over the moon. Other than his stalker-ness, bitey-ness, and work-unscrupulousness, a woman could get used to a man who would bend over backward for her...

But that was last night, and this is now. In the bright fluorescent light of real life, she has no idea what to do with all this.

The stop for her office smells pretty standard: body odor, train car metal, gasoline, and a piquant hint of grime. The red line track of the subway never does her any favors. Looking up the escalator toward the street level, she mutters, "That way lies danger," knowing she's officially read too many fantasy novels. Probably too many novels in general. The angled ride up top while chest-to-back with strangers suddenly seems too short, and dread fills her belly. The five-block gallop she has to do in order to get to work on time just isn't long enough this morning. If only she drank coffee… That would delay her a few minutes.

Her phone buzzes the minute she gets out from the underground's reception blackout. It's from Caleb. It's a meme of a kitten putting out a dumpster fire with a little red fireman's hat. The text he sent under it says:

> Have a good day saving the masses, sweetheart

She smiles to herself. This man is hopeless.

If she let her guard down, would she be hopeless, too?

That's a thought for another day. In the meantime, she presses the little button to request a walk signal, takes a deep breath, and prepares for war.

It's like *Mission: Impossible*. That's all that comes to Ari's mind as she sneaks into her office building, taking unnecessary flights of stairs and peeking around corners to see if the coast is clear. She can almost hear the bass riff and the high pitched *dee-dee-dooooo, dee-dee-dooooo, DOOT-DOOT*.

Swallowing her fear, she goes over to Paul's desk. He had to have inherited all her cases, and she's ready to take them back. Ready to look her colleague in the eye, puff up her chest and tell him a great big, "THANK YOU VERY MUCH!" before running away as fast as possible.

She only trips over her own ankles once on the way there.

Prickles running under her skin as she edges closer, she holds her breath and takes one fatal step after another, working closer and closer, nearer and nearer, lips pressed together and eyes wide in terror...only to find an empty cube. With a huff, she deflates immediately—tension not gone, just put on the back-burner for a minute.

"Are you looking for your files, Ari?" Hui Yeng's voice calls out from the cube just behind, amiable and welcoming. She's an awesome Omega. Just a few years older, Hui Yeng has worked her way up from the bottom, too, facing obstacles Ari would never understand. Ari looks up to her quite a bit, using her as a model for what's possible down the road as long as Ari works hard and stays focused.

"I've got them over here," Hui Yeng says, rooting around in her file cabinet. "Seems you weren't the only one out on leave, if you know what I mean." She tosses Ari a wink that leaves her blinking in surprise, looking back and forth from Hui Yeng to Paul's empty desk.

"You're kidding! Him too?"

"Yup. He went into rut pretty much right after you went on your heat leave. You weren't together, were you?" she teases, leaning in and flapping a pile of heavy manila folders in Ari's direction. She takes them and plops them onto Paul's chair for a minute.

"God, no. Please, God no," Ari replies with a laugh. "Paul's a good buddy, but he's not—"

"Ohmigod, you're mated?!" Hui Yeng squeals suddenly, looking with wide eyes at Ari's collar. She stupidly tries to cover both sides of her neck in embarrassment...and more than a little disquiet. Her colleague smells it on her in an instant and her congratulations dies in her throat.

"Ari?" she asks, eyebrows knitting. "Are you okay?"

She's still holding her glands idiotically, red faced and tight lipped. Of course, everyone is going to know—if not by sight, then by smell. Ari and Caleb are mixed together now. Burnt pancakes for life.

Clearing her throat, Ari begins to lower her hands and Hui Yeng's eyes fly wide in shock.

"What's this?" Grabbing Ari's wrists and turning them both over simultaneously, she looks from one to the other with her mouth dropped wide. After a second, her nose wriggles and her voice drops in a dark accusation she tries to cover with a smirk. "Who's the lucky Alpha?"

Ari wants to pull away, hide her extra bites, but that would look worse somehow. "H-his name is Caleb."

Hui Yeng's face falls, her tight, fake smile completely disappearing. "Tell me it's not Caleb Reed."

Words try to come out, they really do, but what could Ari say, really? Her colleague drops her hands and Ari draws them in toward her chest.

"I know... It shocked me, too." She can't help it; her body starts to tremble, and her eyes mist up. She feels like she needs to explain. Needs her colleague not to hate her or think less of her. "It...it was my first heat and—"

Hui Yeng snatches her again, pulling her hands in until Ari's knuckles lay over the other woman's collarbone. "Did you bite him back? If you didn't and you didn't want him to mate you, then I can file a—"

"I did bite him," Ari admits quietly. She tries to smile, but she has no idea if it comes out right.

The look on her colleague's face turns icy. Stony. Everyone hates Caleb Reed. Everyone here has lost to him, some more than once, and it was never for the right reasons. He made sure the good guys always lost, sometimes painfully and with heavy countersuits that left the defendants penniless.

"I guess I'll just congratulate you and leave it at that, then."

Ari nods, dropping her eyes and collecting her files. They're thick and heavy and carry a new weight today. "Anything you need to brief me on?"

"No," Hui Yeng says quickly. "I take good notes. You'll see. You're not due in court until next Tuesday, so you've got time to prep." The almond-eyed woman squints in fake friendliness. "And don't worry. You won't be going up against your *mate.*"

Ari winces, clutching the folders closer to her chest. "That's good." She tries to laugh, but it comes out breathy and insincere. "See you."

She can't get out of there fast enough. This is what she was afraid of. Exactly this. She's young for a lawyer and it took a lot of grit and hard work to get where she is. Now she's just a stupid claimed Omega, mated to the office boogeyman.

She won't cry. She won't.

Putting her stuff on her desk with a loud *thwump,* she hits her seat hard and immediately puts her face in her hands. Under the sound of her self-loathing is a buzzing noise, and she pulls her phone out of her laptop bag, seeing another text from the devil himself.

> Are you okay? I can feel you. How can I
> make it better?

Grimacing at her screen, Ari mutters, "Go back in time," under her breath, but there's no point in saying it to him.

He randomly asks:

> Do you like meatballs?

She blinks, her eyes tearing up for real. Sniffling, she types:

> They're my favorite. My mom used to make
> them all the time

He sends:

> Swedish or Italian?

No contest.

Italian

With eight million smiley faces, he texts back:

Then that's what I'm making you for dinner.
Comfort food for my Omega

Wiping her eyes, she can't help but smile a little.

You cook?

Devilish emojis this time.

Ohhh, sweetheart, I can do a lot of things

And she giggles.

I'll bet

A voice message comes over this time, sweet and reassuring. "My above message stands, kitten. You're not there for anyone but your clients. Be my knight in shining armor, okay?"

Her smile becomes a grin, and she starts to feel a little better.

Okay

And she opens her first case file.

The sun is shining through the office window in the late afternoon and, at this point, not even the air conditioner can save Ari from her torture. The heat radiating through the glass is one thing, but the scalding looks from her colleagues, not to mention the ones of dire concern, are driving her to the brink of screaming at everyone to just GO AWAY!

Her only solace is the texts she's getting from Caleb. Funny memes. Off-beat poem quotes. All sorts of things that bring a smile to her face, just exactly her sense of humor. Maybe it won't be so bad after all. They seem to have a lot in common. Maybe she *is* soulmated.

She looks up from his most recent message, probably with some vague grin plastered on her face, and hears murmuring down the hall. As soon as she looks up, the other faces turn away and all conversation ceases, making it very obvious that the cluster of colleagues were talking about her behind her back. Judging her.

With a deep and petulant frown, she opens the next case file. A car accident, this one a DUI. The other party is absolutely at fault, based on the police reports, but she still needs to talk to her clients. Dig deeper. Get into the situation and see it from all angles.

Why the hell, in this day and age, would anyone drive drunk?

Was Caleb's brother drunk, too? Was he victim of the snow and ice or was he tipped a little too far off baseline? Probably the latter if he's in jail. Vehicular manslaughter. How ridiculous is it that both the Allein/Reed brothers have had a hand in destroying Ari's life? If not in one way, then another.

Still, Caleb said he gave all his money to the foster system. For all she knows, her warm jackets and Christmas presents had all been funded from his family coffers. Maybe his brother destroyed her, but had Caleb secretly, unknowingly, been saving her. It makes her heart flutter.

In the shower, he told her, "You may have just saved me." But what from? What kind of pain has he been suffering alone? At least Ari has Niles. After his brother was taken away, Caleb had no one.

She works in silence for a good length before another message pops up—an emoji with an angsty expression, flipping its dark hair to the side.

> Does homemade pasta become an emo
> goth thing if I food color it black?

She sputters. Especially when he sends her a picture of flour everywhere, deep, dark noodles, and droplets of dye all along the counter. His next message is:

I think I made a mess

And she honestly laughs out loud.

The voices start up again as well as low chuckles. As soon as Ari looks up, the others turn away again, this time with residual snickers. They're long timers in the for-profit part of the firm, so Ari doesn't know them well. Jones, maybe? Keisling? Weiss? Only one is an Alpha. The others are just your predictable group of Beta lackeys. Ari wants to throw weirdly dyed pasta on them and mess up their cheap suits.

All of a sudden, she hates her job. The case file in front of her blurs into squiggles of details she doesn't care about. Maybe she needs to leave this firm. She needs to go somewhere where no one will judge her for a scenario that wasn't entirely her fault—though it's not like she can take it back. Maybe she'll move out of Boston proper and work in the boonies where no one knows either her or Caleb. Maybe she'll move out, quit law entirely, and go live on a farm. Anything to get away from this place. One thing is clear, the Ari from last week is not the Ari of today.

Right then, she decides to stop mourning herself. If she needs to let go of that Ari, then fine. If she needs to let go of this job, then fine. She's mated to a man who seems ecstatic to have her, if his hourly texts say anything. Maybe it's worth letting go of that lonely girl she was to finally become the woman she was meant to be. One who can find happiness, even in the most unexpected places.

Caleb shuttles Ari's things to his apartment while, halfway across the city, she finishes packing her life into cardboard boxes. To be honest, it's only taken two trips to get nearly all of it; she doesn't have much. In the end, she decided to give away the furniture for free, which seemed very much in character, saying she was silly for making such a big deal out of it in the first place. Stuff is just stuff. Though, in truth, he would have displayed her pieces with pride. He would do anything to make her comfortable in his home. *Their* home.

He grins to himself, lugging another box up in the elevator. It's slow going, but not too bad. He wants more time with her stuff, anyway. He pretended traffic had caught him up so he could rifle through her things a little before going for the next run. A lot of it he just sniffed out, but her journal he eyed with great interest. That treasure trove is his as soon as she goes to work tomorrow. He's happy he has two days off that she doesn't.

The last trip is on the subway, and that's something Caleb hates. He's a big man in a small space that stinks like strangers, and his anxiety ramps in places like these. Nothing good ever happens to him in crowds.

Ari's got a few light bags in her lap, more on the open chair next to her, and sitting atop his crossed legs is a shoebox of fake, sentimental jewelry—one he's itching to paw through. This one smells a little bit like Niles, so either he helped pack it, touches the stuff all the time, or he was the one who bought most of it for her in the first place. It flares the possessive nature of Caleb's heart.

Threat.

He picks up her hand and kisses her knuckles absentmindedly, a million miles away. He's lost ruminating over everything he can wrap his mind around when she startles him out of his swirling vortex.

"It feels like you're upset..."

Such simple words, but so soothing. It makes his lips curve up subtly at the corners. "Is it strange that I'm happy you can tell? You are too, though. I could feel it all day."

Her voice gets small. "It's just very fast. Not just us—everything.

My home. My job turning on me as soon as they smelled me. You should have seen how Hui Yeng looked at me when she saw…" She trails off, looking at her unoccupied bitten wrist. In hindsight, that was a mistake.

He untwines his fingers from hers and twirls her hand slightly, just enough to see her other bite, this one unsealed and red with yellow bruising around it.

Yes, a big mistake. But he still can't say he's sorry he did it.

He kisses that, too. "I didn't mean for them to embarrass you." Mood souring, he looks out the window across from him, watching the underground tunnel stream by. "I'd hoped you'd be proud."

She looks at him, but he doesn't want to meet her stare. He knows his expression shows the deep ding in his pride even if she can't feel it outright via their connection. He still doesn't know how it works.

With kindness, his Omega leans her head on his shoulder. "Maybe I will someday. It can be a conversation starter about how our love story began, or something."

"I like that." Heart throbbing, he leans his head back onto hers. "Is there anything I can do about your job?"

Like build my own company around you?

She snorts. "Other than lose constantly? No, probably not."

"Maybe if I keep sending you stupid messages all day and making you laugh, they'll be able to tell I'm not a bad guy."

"Bad guy aside, you definitely make me laugh." She snuggles a bit closer.

Mate is happy. Omega likes me.

That means his hard work paid off. He'd been scouring her social media for anything and everything that would tip him off to her sense of humor. If he studies enough, he'll get a handle on it and be able to mimic it all on his own. Right now, he still has fifty-four text messages with memes he's planned, and a lot of them ripped from her own Twitter feed from a year or two ago. Not funny enough to remember, but funny enough to share.

"It doesn't stop me from being furious, though," she says, and he feels her irritation spike just as well as he can smell it. "People who have never even talked to me are staring from down the hallway like I'm just some replaceable Omega who's sleeping with the enemy. Horrible part is, they're not wrong."

He looks for something to say and comes up empty.

"But screw them," she growls. Peering up at him, they finally really look at each other. "You go to a gym, right? Do they have punching bags? Can you sneak me in? I feel like I need to wail on something."

She's so goddamn adorable.

He chuckles at her. "Sorry, kitten, no punching bags." His voice drops as he plays with her fingers, trying to insert the right amount of self-deprecating sadness into his tone. "I'll let you have a go at me if you want." He forces himself to get even quieter. "It's my fault after all."

Her eyes go round, and he feels her biological need to comfort him.

"No, we did this together." She looks to the front and harrumphs a bit, crinkling one of the bags on her lap for no reason while she puffs tendrils of hair off her forehead. Returning to him with a glare, she says, "I didn't mean for this to happen, but this is where we are. I accept it. I'm not going to run away from this. From you. Whatever you feel for me, I'm gonna meet you where you are and then beat you at your own game." Her lips quirk up in an obvious challenge.

Grinning doesn't describe it. Caleb is outright beaming. Even in her trying to reassure him, she's so feisty.

She adds, "But that doesn't mean I don't still want to kick someone."

He laughs at her. "You're pretty funny, sweetheart. Did anyone ever tell you that?"

She smirks a bit. "Niles. He's really the only other person I talk to like this."

"So, if I need advice on how to not get beaten up by you, he's the one to ask?"

"Oh, definitely. He'll also tell you my favorite kind of ice cream."

Pistachio.

He snorts, feigning ignorance. "You could tell me that right now."

She lifts her eyebrows, looking disconcerted at the floor. "Oh my god, I just realized he could probably even tell you what kind of underwear I buy."

Caleb gives her a side-eyed leer, immediately interested. "Now *that* I'd like to find out on my own." Though he'd already stolen one pair of her panties and stripped off another one during her heat, he hadn't taken a lot of time to truly appreciate them.

She ducks her head onto his arm, blushing the perfect pink with a small groan. "I can feel you, you know! Stop...like...emotionally hitting on me!"

"What? You want me to keep it to myself?" He pecks her on the top of the head. "Not sure I could if I tried, kitten."

"Why do you call me that?"

"Kitten?"

"And 'sweetheart' and... and all those other things."

Because that's what the men in your romance novels do.

"'Kitten,' because of the phrase *sex kitten*." She almost chokes on her own spit, and he loves her for it. Tipping her chin up and looking her straight in her hazel eyes, he does his best to be who she fantasizes about. "And 'sweetheart' because that's who I think you must be under all that grumpy gusto."

Her face is so red he wants to fucking lick it and feel how hot it is.

"G-grumpy?! ME, grumpy?! Pot calling the kettle, kind sir!"

He grins, loving this moment. "Oh, so now I'm a 'kind sir'?"

She pulls away with a frown, but he can feel her giddiness. This is flirting, apparently.

"It's a turn of phrase," she grumps, proving his point. "Nothing about you is nice."

"Nothing, kitten?" He turns her face back again, sliding a thumb slowly over her bottom lip and making her eyes get half lidded. "Not one thing?"

He brings her in for a kiss and she basically starts to hyperventilate.

Oh, sweetheart. I'm going to eat you up.

He keeps their touch brief and soft. Chaste. Very unlike him, though it's unlike him to kiss in the first place. "You're so new to this." He smiles at her. "I guess that means you're lucky."

Her mouth is still close to his and her eyes are nearly shut. He's about to go crazy in about five seconds.

"Lucky how?"

"Because your nickname for me is 'Oh experienced one.' Maybe I'm glad I am. Because now I can tease you like this." He brings her in again and touches his tongue delicately to the seam of her lips. At that, she pushes him away, a silly smile on her face. The train is almost empty, but she's shooting embarrassed glances at the two others on the far side of the car. Their noses are basically shoved into their phone screens, but tell that to Ari. Caleb half expects her to shout over an apology.

Instead, whacking his chest a little, she scolds him. "You make me do stupid things."

He leans over comically low to put his head on the curve of her shoulder, shifting the box on his lap to hide his blooming erection. "The feeling is very mutual, I promise you."

She hums in amusement.

He eyes the subway map placed over the door, feeling antsy. "When's our stop, anyway? I want to go home and finish up the concoction/delight I've made for you."

"You mean the emo pasta with meatballs?"

He grins like an idiot, tipping his face shyly against her. "Exactly."

It's a little overwhelming. Okay, more than a bit. Caleb's pristine, austere...well, to be honest, showroom-style-bland apartment is now covered in boxes of all sizes. Banana boxes, old Amazon boxes, the inevitable stolen-from-the-outdoor-recycling-bin-and-kinda-smells-like-trash kind of boxes, anything that Niles could get his hands on with such short notice. Not that Ari had asked for it, which still (more than) irks her, though it's too late for that kind of thinking now.

Caleb stands looking down on her cardboard garden as if they're all gifts, hands in his pockets as that beautiful smile draws lines up the side of his face. The stubble he'd been growing across the hollows of his cheeks during their...heat/rut ordeal...has been shaven clean and perfect.

"No unpacking," she reminds him. "Food first."

His grin widens. "Well, I've got some actual cooking to do before we can eat, but at least all the prep work is done."

She scoffs. "Prep work. How long did that take you?"

"I made the pasta from scratch, so"—he shrugs—"a couple hours? Why? How long does it take you to set up?"

"All of three minutes for water to boil and another three minutes for the Ramen noodles to soften."

It's not a lie.

"Well, that won't do." He takes her hand and kisses it like a prince before tugging her into his arms. "This Alpha will provide for his Omega."

She snorts against his chest, taking in the scent of him. "Isn't the Omega supposed to be the one cooking? Traditionally speaking?"

"Not if you're making Ramen noodles. That shit should be banned in all fifty states."

With another peck to her head, he moves into the kitchen just off the living room where she stands. A small island separates them with low stools on her side, giving a clear view of all his culinary witchcraft. She hops up onto one of them.

"So...why did you pre-ruin the pasta?"

He looks a bit embarrassed. "I heard that, in Italy, they dye the pasta with squid ink to make it a different color. I thought it would be...I don't know...fancy or something."

Resting her chin on her hands, she smirks. "I just use a box of noodles and red sauce from a jar."

He scoffs. "Yeah, I'll bet." After a pause, he admits, "So do I. But at least I usually put stuff in the sauce. Onions, tomatoes, red wine, and stuff."

She perks up. "You have wine?"

With a shy grin, he shakes his head at her, bringing out dishes and silverware. "If you're carrying our pups, you shouldn't drink, sweetheart."

The words hit her like a slap. Seeing her, maybe feeling her, his expression fades and his emotions go to that black place. That darkness within. Is that what his anger feels like? No. That's wrong. But something like it.

"It's just that I'm only twenty-five," she says.

"And I'm thirty-four. I don't have a biological clock, kitten, but if I did, I guess it feels like it's ticking." He tries to give her a tight smile, but he doesn't mean it. That blackness within him deepens and there is a long pause before he asks a quiet, "If you had them, could you love them?"

Her heart breaks wide open. "Of course, I'd love them! What kind of question is that?!"

"One someone should have asked my parents before it was too late."

His darkness turns to utter sadness, and she grabs his hand, distracting him from the work he's trying to lose himself in. As earnest as she can possibly be, she says, "I will love them more than life itself."

His soft expression comes back, just a little. He feels sullen but hopeful. "Yeah?"

She nods. "I swear. I will never let my children feel the way you did, and I will never send my children away."

His eyes water a little and he sniffs, returning to his duty. "Thank you."

What a sad thing to have to thank someone for.

He goes to the fridge and brings out a monstrous bowl of now-grey, puffy, distended noodles and blinks at them. And blinks at them. And blinks some more.

"What the fuck happened?"

It breaks all the tension, making her burst out laughing. "Oh my God, what even is that?!"

"Seriously! How the hell...?! It looks like... Ugh!" Even he doesn't have words, though it only makes her laugh harder. Groaning, he scrapes the whole mess into the trash while "Taps" plays in Ari's head. She salutes the pasta as rigidly as she can to say her pseudo-respectful goodbyes.

Lifting his eyebrows at her, he says, "Guess it's meatballs only tonight."

"With red sauce?"

Please, for the love of all that's holy...

"Yeah. At least there's that. Remind me to never try to impress you again." And she's off in gales this time, making him chuckle at his own expense. "All right, I think I've been humiliated enough for one night. Go into the wild and leave me to cook in peace."

"I'll go unpack a bit," she says, still snickering but allowing him a moment to regain his male-homemaker swagger. "You still have a chance to impress me with your mom-meatballs."

He flips his hands in her direction, shooing her. "Yeah, yeah. Go put up tchotchkes and whatever else. Make us a home, Omega." His eyes glitter at her, and she feels her heart throb a little. "I got you a present, too. See if you can find it in one of the boxes."

And her eyes legitimately become stars. "A treasure hunt?"

With his smug smile, he feels like pure triumph. "Go see."

She dives off the chair. Her parents used to do this leading up to Christmas—little prizes hidden in the house. If she could find them, she'd get them early. She'd always wanted to tear every room apart, but they were usually hidden in plain sight once she really looked. She'd be nose-deep in some obscure, dusty bookcase, shifting piles of yellowed novels left and right only to find a teddy bear sitting innocently right on the very top shelf, looking down at her.

Like a child, she sniffs at all the boxes, looking for one that smells like him. Trick is that he handled each of them, so they all carry his special moniker to some degree. She's already frustrated, grunting a little as she's torn between starting with something practical—like clothes—or diving into the boxes with the most junk where it would be easier to hide something random.

Staring at him for any and all reactions, she scoots to a box that's Sharpie labeled as KITCHEN STUFF and grabs the folded top. He looks up at her and gives nothing away. With a cluck of her tongue, she moves over to another, this one filled with clothes, and feels the slightest trickle of thrill come over him. When she opens it, that feeling doubles and she grins. He realizes his error all too fast.

"That's cheating, kitten."

But she only bites her lip with a grin, still staring at him when she lifts up the first raggedy T-shirt on the pajama pile she's unearthed. With excitement to match, he dusts off his hands and comes to join, folding his legs in crisscross to land next to her.

"I'd expected this to take a little longer." All she does is wiggle as if she had her ancestor's tail. He snickers, gesturing at the box. "Well go ahead. Have at it."

Without another word, she upends it into a mess all over the floor and he barks a short laugh as she squeals and starts to dig, pawing through old T-shirts, Goodwill pajama bottoms, and Haynes six pack–style underwear...until she happens upon it.

A little black box.

A little black jewelry box.

No, no, no   please don't be this. I'm not ready for this. Wearing this is like wearing a scarlet letter.

Either he ignores or misinterprets her feelings, because he takes it from her and opens it, showing off not just an engagement ring, but a matched set with a wedding ring. It's the perfect style. It's exactly her taste. Did Niles help him pick it?

Still.

I don't want this. Please don't make me take this.

His excitement drops immediately. For the second time in their short relationship, he quotes her, always damning her with her own words. "You'd said, on that very couch yesterday, that you'd marry me. I'm just making it official." He nods to the kitchen where a tiny dining set lives in the corner. "The paperwork is right there. Marriage license ready for you to sign."

He takes her hand, grasping her all too firm as she tries to pull away. With a sharp glare, he holds fast, almost painfully so, and quotes her once again. "Didn't you say you accept it? You're not going to run from it. Or from me."

She feels nauseous. Why does she keep doing this? To him? To herself? All this time, with every word, she's been digging her own grave.

"You told me you were going to beat me at my own game, Ari. Doesn't that mean you're going to fall for me even harder than I've fallen for you? Or are you going to give up so quickly, *Omega?*"

There's a hint of command in there and her whole body is poised to do whatever he wants as he leans in and licks one of her mating glands, then the other, making her moan a little as he pushes hard, pinning her down on the floor.

"You're my fucking mate, and I'm not going to let you deny it." He pulls up his knee, nestling it right up against her sex and pressing, making her quiver. She's not in heat but the things he does to her make her feel like it's coming on again. "Admit it, Ari. You want this. You want me. Stop fighting it or I'm going to lose my goddamn patience. And I don't have much of it on a good day."

He feels scary. It's so confusing. She wants to please her Alpha, even though she doesn't. Why does he do this to her? Why doesn't he see that he's gone too far and back off? "Caleb, please..." she tries, but his leg only presses against her harder, lighting her up from the inside as he drags his teeth over her gland.

"No, sweetheart. You're mine. I need you. You're like fucking air."

This is warped. Twisted. He needs too much. She's liked books about possessive, desperate men because she could read them for a day and then put them away again. But this is her life. The rest of her life.

He pulls back and looks at her then, takes in whatever expression she's wearing, and all she feels from him is cold. His jaw ticks to the side and his eyes are nearly black as his muscles tremble with unleashed energy. She's terrified.

Finally moving off, he pulls her up to sit in front of him. Still on his knees, he takes one ring only—the engagement ring—and slips it on her finger, eyes greedy. "I want you, Ari Jacobson. In my entire life, I've only ever wanted you. The minute I smelled you, I knew you were mine."

His cinnamon scent becomes overwhelming.

Entice.

She's going to be sick.

He takes the wedding ring and looks at it for a minute before staring at her long and hard...and then he slips it on his own finger. It doesn't fit, only sliding past the first knuckle, but he crooks it to hold the ring on tight. "Until you're ready for me, I'll keep this one. But I believe that someday you'll ask me for it. The ball is in your court. It always has been. You've made all the decisions from the beginning; you just like to blame me for them. You've asked for everything I've given you since the moment you met me. But this?" He looks at the glinting white gold ring. "I'm not giving you this until you ask for it. Not just 'yes.' Not just 'please.' Not just 'I'm yours.' Someday, you're going to open that gorgeous mouth, look me in the eyes, and ask me to marry you."

His eyes soften and shimmer as he kisses her with nothing but sweetness. "Please, Ari," he whispers against her lips. "Please ask me."

And, even now, she knows it's inevitable. For herself, she feels afraid, coerced, and sad—but for him, she feels brokenhearted. It's not just his feelings flowing through their bond. It's hers. He hasn't ruined her life, it's the other way around. She's ruined his. She sucked him in. She *has* asked for this; he just didn't second guess her naïveté. Swallowing, she looks at the kitchen, already feeling the hours wind down to the moment she'll sign her life over to her Alpha. Because she will. It's fate.

CHAPTER 8

MATE (REPRISE)

BY THE TIME Ari gets home to Caleb's apartment...their apartment...she feels like she's going to kill something. If the bites made her a social pariah, the engagement ring set her out to be burned at the stake. Now people were outright whispering and not looking away when she caught them. Instead, some shook their heads in disdain and others knit their eyebrows in sympathy. Ari, for her part, tried to puff up her chest and walk straight on, wanting to be proud of her mate. Her Alpha.

Instead, she cowered.

She's not sure what she's more ashamed of, getting mated to him or withering under the stares of her colleagues. When she'd first joined the firm after she graduated, they'd all looked at her as if she was pure orphan trash who'd only wheedled her way in by leveraging sympathies and scholarships. That is, until she stood toe-to-toe with them and proved she'd earned her 4.0 grade average. This should be no different. She just needs to remain steadfast. She's still a fantastic lawyer, worthy of respect, who's found herself an attractive, addictive, insanely strong Alpha. She should be on the cover of magazines talking about the power of being soulmated. Instead, she caught Weiss calling her a stupid Omega bitch and his lackeys all agreeing mindlessly like the cultlike followers they are. She heard Hui Yeng whispering to others that she thinks Ari was raped and bitten against her will. She even heard Lynn, the office matron, tutting over her in feigned pity, talking about how big her Alpha's mouth must be to have left marks on her like that. The older woman had downright fanned herself and Ari smelled her desire. Instead of self-pity, she felt self-fury—enraged with not only them, but herself for putting up with it.

Stomping into the apartment, Caleb looks at her from the couch, putting down what he was musing over and standing up to greet her in concern as she throws her bag, laptop and all, on the floor—more than happy to have a temper tantrum.

"Welcome home?" he tries, though he's only met with a withering stare.

Marching up, she points her finger at him. "I am not weak!"

Nonplussed, he holds up his hands in a defensive position, her feminine wedding ring still wrapped too high on his ring finger. "I never said you were!"

"I'm NOT someone for them to treat like I'm just some ORPHAN LOSER!"

"You're a fucking treasure, kitten. Anyone who doesn't act like it deserves the shit kicked out of them."

"And I AM NOT going to just stand by and take this anymore! This is...it's...it's just complete and utter BULLSHIT!"

He ticks his eyebrow up after hearing her curse. "So, who do I have to kill?"

She rolls her eyes in a huff, surprised that his threats actually make her feel a little better. "No. No, you know what? Let's go visit that brother of yours. If I'm just a parentless piece of garbage in their eyes, I want to finally go confront the bastard who made me one. I'll tear into him. Take out some of this overwhelming, stupid, horrible cesspool inside me...just... *Gahh!*" She balls her hands into fists and shakes them. If she could crumple paper into knots, rip it to snowflakes, and burn it up sacrificial style, she would.

Caleb's whole demeanor changes. "You said you wanted to forgive him."

Hands on her hips, she grunts. "Yeah, well, I can forgive him after I tell him how horrible he is."

"No," Caleb says, firm as anything. "No, I won't let you do that."

"I don't need you to protect my morality meter, Caleb Reed. I'll apologize after. Maybe I'll regret being so mean, but if I don't rant at someone, I feel like I'm going to explode!"

He turns his back on her, snatching whatever he was looking at —a case file maybe. "Go vent your explosion somewhere else."

She tastes him in the air, and he's both sad and angry. "He's in prison, Caleb. I'm sure he's quite used to getting yelled at by this point."

The man who mated her turns on his heels and hisses, "Prison? Who the fuck told you he was in prison?!"

His attitude change deflates her instantly. "I just assumed that—"

"Don't assume!" he yells, getting closer. "Don't you assume you know anything about my brother!"

She stands up straighter, indignant. "It's his fault my parents are dead. It's his fault *your*—"

"Shut your mouth, sweetheart, or this conversation is going to go downhill very fast."

His rage outright confuses her at first, but it makes sense after a moment's reflection. It's exactly who he said he was. Loyal. Dedicated to things he cares about. His brother remains one of those things, she realizes.

She takes a beat before responding with a sincere, "I'm sorry."

And those words make his whole body relax, then sag. He flops back onto the couch and puts his hands over his face. "I'm sorry, too. I get very...protective over Ben."

"Is that his name?"

He huffs a little, sliding his hands down his cheeks and hunching over, resting his elbows on his thighs. "Yeah. My baby brother. If you count the three whole minutes between us, anyway. We're twins." He hangs his head down just above his knees, his hair a curtain hiding his eyes. "He's not in prison. He has *never* been in prison."

She steps a little closer. Caleb's emotions feel like absolute defeat. "Where is he?"

He doesn't look at her. "Hospice."

"What?" Her heart sinks with his pain. Hospice is where people go to die.

Putting his face in his hands again, he says, "Ben's been in a coma since the accident."

Dropping to her knees in front of him, Ari is horrified. She pulls at his palms, resting his knuckles over heart. "But it's been eleven years!"

"And I've fought to keep him here for every minute of it." The look on Caleb's face is blank and his emotions are in that dark place. "You may have noticed I have trouble letting things go."

That she has.

He turns his palms over, twiddling her fingers like he seems to like to do, running his thumbs over her wrist bites gently, which seems to soothe him. Right now, she doesn't mind them at all. Right now, they have a purpose.

"I go every weekend. Every day I have off, too. Unless I'm sick or something unavoidable happens, I'm with him. I read to him; I tell him about shit that's pissing me off. Even like this, he's still my best friend," Caleb says, and Ari's eyes fill with tears.

"I don't go on vacation. I never leave town. I do anything and everything so I can be there when he opens his eyes." Caleb shakes his head. "But he's not going to. And now"—he slides his fingers through Ari's hair—"I might have a family I need to take care of. I can't afford to keep him like this forever. Ben wouldn't *want* me to keep him like this forever. I was hoping you would come with me, say your piece, I could say mine, and then I'd let him go. I was going to start looking forward, instead of back.

"But I won't let you be cruel to him. I refuse to let the last words he hears be that. I won't allow anyone to bring him more pain. If that's all you have to offer, if you dare hurt him like that"—Caleb's scowl is outright dangerous—"I'll never forgive you."

Alpha needs to be soothed. Be calm. Be sweet. Be a good Omega.

She sits up, nestling between his legs and sliding her hands around his neck, swirling her thumbs over his mating glands, leaving their combined scent behind as a reminder that she's here. He shudders a sigh and wraps his arms around her.

"I want vacations with you, Ari. I want a family. I want the life I imagine before I go to sleep. The one I've never had because I've been stuck in this place, wishing for miracles. Please, Ari…will you please help me say goodbye?"

She nods against him. "Yes, Alpha."

And he hugs her even tighter. "Thank you."

Again, she can't help but think, *What a terribly sad thing to be thankful for.*

It seems that's a lot of what his life is.

Ari holds Caleb's hand as they walk up the subway stairs. Surprisingly, the hospice center is really close to where she works. This is her same train stop.

She squeezes her grip a little. "You said you can't afford his care. Is that emotionally? Financially?"

He squeezes her back with sad affection flowing through their bond. "Both. I had power of attorney over his trust fund, too, so I dissolved both his and mine at the same time. My income is all we have. Probably the stupidest decision I've ever made."

"Is that why you work for the Sloane Law Firm?"

That money grubbing, evil organization.

"Partly." He tips his face to the sky, letting the summer sunlight kiss his pale skin. He really must never go outside. "I'm sure you've heard of its founder."

She grimaces. "He's a monster."

Caleb's voice drops low. "He absolutely is."

He purses his lips a little, guiding them forward since she's looking at him and not where they're walking. He really is a good Alpha, taking care of her whenever he can. The awaiting wedding ring on his finger presses a warm line against her, a sad promise, but one she knows she'll make. It obviously means the world to him.

"Sloane's my mentor. Has been since just after college. After my parents died..." Caleb sighs. "He helped make arrangements for Ben. I could never afford this facility, but Sloane's a key donor. My guess is he needed something to funnel money into to avoid certain tax implications."

He pulls her backward a little, stopping her from walking straight into the road and getting run over. It's wordless. Effortless. Sweet. He doesn't even scold her for not paying attention. Niles would have been all over her.

"Without his help, I could never have paid for Ben's care. It's...a lot."

Maybe that's why Caleb's apartment is so posh-yet-plain. Weirdly, his TV is small. Teeny tiny. Even Ari has a big TV, so hers won the epic battle for top of the entertainment center in a complete, first-round KO.

She leans on him while they wait for a walk signal, the street fairly empty this early on a Saturday. "Maybe it will all be easier...you know...after."

Another wave of sadness comes over from his side.

"I'll help you," she says, snuggling closer. He lets go of her hand and winds around her waist, bringing her in for a hug in broad daylight. Strangely, she doesn't want him to let her go.

"I love you, sweetheart."

Her heart melts. She wants to feel this way for him, truly and one hundred percent. She wants to be the one to lift him out of his darkness. Stepping on her tippy-toes, she kisses his mating gland. "You're not alone. I'm here. We'll do this together."

There is a bittersweetness to his scent and emotion, so she gives him a tentative lick even though they're out in public. He grips her tighter.

"Now, now. Don't start that with me, kitten. As much as I want to run away and lose myself in you, if I don't do this now, I don't think I ever will."

She pulls back to see that shy smile she adores so much trying to shine through a veil of hurt. Attempting cuteness, she says, "I'm disappointed in you, oh experienced one. Where did the curse word in that sentence disappear to?"

Nonplussed, he asks, "What?"

She lifts her eyebrows. "Shouldn't you say, 'Don't *effing* start that with me, kitten'? Where's my vulgar, crass, foul-mouthed Alpha?"

A smirk graces his face. "You like it when I swear?"

Grinning, she dares to wink at him, though it's probably over-exaggerated and obnoxious looking. "It's very you."

He gives her a funny kiss, smooshing their faces together and asking, "Just like me being 'experienced'?"

She giggles this time. "And emo."

This time, when the walk signal comes, Ari's the one to tug him gently forward, leading him across the street. Like a puppy, he follows her.

The whole place smells like antiseptic, though nothing else about it reminds her of a hospital. Probably because it's not. No real healing happens here. Just sustaining, pain management, and round-the-clock care. In the lobby, the carpet is plush, and the colors are a soft, muted salmon. The light is yellow and casts a warm glow over everything. Ari looks around, feeling unsure. She doesn't like hospitals, and though this isn't one, the smell reminds her of being stuck in a cold, sterile room with a broken arm, a concussion, and two dead parents locked in a metal refrigerator a few floors down.

She shivers.

Feeling her, Caleb slides his hand reassuringly over her back and guides her forward as he approaches the front desk. "Is Mr. Canady here, Sarah?"

"Oh! Mr. Reed! We missed you last week. Who's the lovely lady?"

Ari swallows and holds out her hand. "I'm his fiancée."

Caleb looks at her with nothing but love in his eyes.

The woman's smile is transcendent as she shakes Ari's hand, making a good show of checking out her ring in ogling oohs and ahhs. Looking at her and Caleb's necks, she adds, "Not just fiancée! I see some mating bites, you two!"

Ari blushes and even Caleb looks sheepish.

"I guess you know where I was last weekend, then," he admits, only to receive a pleasant smack on his shoulder from the receptionist.

"Good for you, honey," Sarah says. "Good. For. You."

The woman smells so happy for Caleb, it's overwhelming, and Ari can't help but smile. At least there are some people in his life that cared enough to notice he was lonely.

Clearing his throat, he says, "I think Mr. Canady is expecting us."

The receptionist's mood sobers. "Yes, he is." She slides her hand over his arm in comfort this time. "You're doing the right thing. I know it's hard, but you are."

His lips press into a line, nodding while his eyes glisten. Ari squeezes his hand, but this time he doesn't squeeze back.

"Go on." Sarah nods at the door. "I'll send Mr. Canady."

With a nod, he tugs Ari along, knowing the way by rote. She can't help but wonder if the well-trod line in the carpet from lobby to the doorway was worn down by Caleb himself. Past the reception area, the hospital part of their setting becomes more obvious. Stretching for what looks like miles, the linoleum flooring's decorative flecks hide the daily wear and tear of footsteps and gurney wheels. Caleb's brother seems to be the very first door on the right once they get past the nurses' station. The stern woman behind it just tips her chin up at Caleb in a perfunctory way. He doesn't return the gesture and she doesn't bother to notice.

Ari hangs behind the threshold as Caleb steps in, his hands immediately moving to his pockets and his posture changing to one of resignation and sorrow. She tries to soothe him through their bond, but there's little she can do right now.

Peering in, Benjamin Stephen Allein lies still. He's also stunningly beautiful, which makes sense, given he and Caleb are twins. His hair seems to be kept shorter and it shows these enormously round ears—ones that Caleb clearly hides very well under his mane of hair. They're adorable. Ben's face is cleanly shaven, so they must take good care of him here. Or maybe they just set him up nicely for Caleb's final goodbye. Despite their hard work, Ben looks frail and thin, hooked up with IVs and one of those things looped under his nose to force in canned oxygen. There are tubes everywhere, mostly coming out from under the blankets, but he's tucked in nicely and they're arranged just so.

"Excuse me, dear," a gentle voice comes from behind her. Turning around, a plump older man smiles softly.

"Oh! Sorry!" Ari squeaks.

"Not a worry." He pets her kindly and scoots around, going to the bedside and bringing in Caleb for a hug, one he accepts with one arm only, keeping his face pointed directly at his brother. "I'm here, kiddo. I'll be ready for whenever it's time. Take as long as you need, okay?"

Caleb nods and Ari wishes she could see his expression. She's basically cringing outside the door, afraid to enter into this sacred moment. She doesn't belong here. The man who must be Mr. Canady scoots past her with another smile, leaving her alone to share in the pain that is to come. It's silent except for the blipping of machines and the hum of the central air conditioning. Everything feels like glass about to shatter.

"Hey, Ben." Caleb's voice is raspy. "I know...I know I've been keeping you here for a while. Too long, maybe. I'm not sure you would have wanted that...but..." Caleb's gaze drops to the floor in sorrow. "I've wanted you to wake up more than anything...but you can't. No matter how long I wait, you're never coming back. I know. I understand. Maybe I have for a long time. I just couldn't bear to lose you any more than I already had, so I made you stay the only way I knew how."

His sniffle breaks Ari's heart. His emotions are already in pieces, and hers are following fast.

"Maybe I'm still being selfish even now, letting you go for the reasons I am. I'm not sure. But I think you'd be happy for me. I found someone. A soulmate, just like we always dreamed of when we were kids. But we're not gonna be like mom and dad, Benny, I promise. I'm going to learn from their mistakes and be better than them.

"She's beautiful. I wish you could see her." He huffs a wet laugh and sniffles again. "No, wait, maybe I don't. You'd love her on sight, I know. She's funny, like you, and fucking feisty. I'm sorry I haven't mentioned her before, but it kind of happened fast.

"You won't believe it, but she's...connected to us in a way you wouldn't expect. She's got something important to say to you, too. I hope that, when she says it, it might give you some peace before... before you go."

Caleb looks over his shoulder toward her, his face so wet with tears Ari chokes up on his behalf. Holding up his hand, he invites her to join him, and she knows it's time to forgive and forget. Looking at her own personal boogieman now, resting in more than a decade of repercussions, how could she possibly do anything else? He's suffered enough for his crimes.

Snuffing back and unclogging her nose, Ari walks in, taking in the scent of the room...

And her heart stops.

Caleb's eyebrows knit as he looks at her, but she can't breathe... even though she must breathe.

She can smell Ben. Leather, just like Caleb. The one that whispers *Provide*. Ash, that scent of pain and destruction that growls *Protect*. Instead of cinnamon, though, Benjamin Allein smells like sugar. It's not the familiar pull to *Entice*, no. It's *Indulge*.

This is why Caleb always smelled wrong.

Trembling uncontrollably, Ari puts her hand over her heart and whispers the word, "Mate."

Caleb stands between his woman and his brother, watching the tears roll down her face and standing stock-still as that word falls from her lips in a heavy, unintentional sigh. *Almost perfect,* she had told him. He smelled *almost* perfect.

And Caleb goes cold.

"I assume you're talking to me?"

Her eyes, locked on Ben, flit to his for only a moment before darting back, her hands clutching at each other as she visibly shrinks from him.

"No." He draws out the vowel. "You aren't, are you?"

"Caleb...I—"

"Don't talk." He cuts her off. Ben is forgotten behind him as Caleb steps closer to his Omega. The woman who will someday be his wife. He takes up her hands, too fast and too hard, and shows her her own wrists. "He didn't do this to you, kitten. I did. He's brain-dead. He can't smell you, speak to you, hold you. I've mated you, Ari. I have. *Me.*"

But she won't take her eyes off Ben, and she won't stop crying. And she's not crying for Caleb's sake anymore.

Unacceptable.

Caleb pulls back and plays with his cufflinks, opening them to give his pulse space to hammer while his teeth grind painfully. Hurt doesn't describe it. Terror doesn't describe it. But then betrayal kicks in when she whimpers, "Don't kill him."

He turns to her faster than he ever thought possible. "*What* did you just say?"

She looks at him with eyes like glass balls and streaming tears like little waterfalls. It's like she's begging him, the way her hands are locked in prayer.

"Please. Please don't kill him!"

You filthy bitch, ohhh how the fuck could you say that to me?

Caleb's lips tremble and he doesn't know what to do with himself. "I'm not...I'm not killing him! I'm letting him go!"

Take it back. Oh please, for the love of God, take it back.

"It's not the same!" he insists, ruined by her words.

"Please, Caleb," she weeps at him. "Please don't kill him! I'll help you pay for his care. I'll do whatever I can, but please!"

Everything in him downshifts to nothingness. This isn't cold. This is numb. His heart slows to frozen. "Ben rammed into your parent's car on purpose, you know."

And it's not even a lie. She looks at him as if he gut-punched her.

"He did it for me—for both of us. He left me a letter saying he was going to save us from our parents. From all the pain they brought us. He was supposed to survive but he left that note, saying it was 'just in case something went wrong.'" Caleb gestures at the living corpse behind him. "As you can see, things went very, very wrong. And yet you're standing here, in front of me, calling *him* your mate."

He steps up to her, getting in her space, feeling her emotion as her heart wrenches into halves. "And he'll never even wake up to see you cry." Grabbing her face, he tilts up her chin, nearly grazing her lips with his own. "How sad for you."

He links their hands together as she quakes with overwhelming loss. It makes him squeeze her until she gasps, though it doesn't loosen his grip.

"Ben never asked what I wanted. I've thought so many times about what I would have said if he did. I would have told him that he was more important to me than anything in this world—but with you here now, standing by my side—for the first time, I'm glad he's like this. It's the only way you'd be mine."

She sobs hard, and he kisses her tears. "You are mine, aren't you, Ari?"

He can't help it. He's oozing some kind of menace. Perhaps that's why she nods against him, her wet cheek sliding over his.

"That's a good girl." He stands up taller. "Mr. Canady!" he calls, and the man pops in his head a few moments later. Caleb knows he'd given them privacy; he'd never snoop. Canady doesn't seem to mind Ari's emotional bloodletting and, as a Beta, he can't smell the danger in the room.

Instead, he asks, "Is it time?" with sympathy dripping like candle wax.

Ari wails, but Caleb only grips her tighter, wrapping his arms around and squeezing, giving her only just enough space to breathe. Still. It's Ben. He loves Ben so much. His whole life has revolved around this one sun. Caleb tries to blink back his sorrow, which has returned like a deadly tidal wave.

"Has he had any brain activity?"

"No," Canady answers.

"Has he shown any signs that he'll ever wake up?"

Canady shakes his head. "I'm sorry, but no."

Caleb threads his fingers through Ari's hair as she loses herself. "Then, please. Help him go."

Caleb's crumbling. He's dying inside. She said he's killing the person he's loved from the moment he was born, and he can't bear it.

The sweet man who's watched over Ben for so long is now flipping off his switches and Caleb wants to scream. The heart rate monitor, the one that's lulled Caleb to sleep on more than a few occasions, shuts off. The IV that's kept Ben hydrated is gone. The little stickies that go on his chest are removed. And lastly, that little tube gets taken from his nose, and Ben will have to get oxygen entirely on his own...which means he won't get any at all.

"There's so much I want to say to you," he tells his brother. "But I can never say enough."

Ari's body lets go and she sags against him. Instead of vice versa, he's somehow comforting her. Her scent is everywhere with panic and acrid fear. He's going to lose his mind. His Alpha is screaming to *Protect,* but there's nothing to protect her from.

And then Ben's breath hitches. One gasp, two.

God, please don't make me watch this. Go peaceful, Ben. Please don't suffer.

But his breath evens out into a steady rhythm, and then his...his eyebrows knit. His mouth pulls into a tiny frown. He's making...an expression.

"Benny?" Caleb's voice is high like a child as he begs someone to tell him, "What's happening?"

With a sigh, Canady again hooks up the diodes on Ben's chest and turns on the monitors to see that steady rhythm pumping. "I'm sorry, Caleb, this may not go as quickly as I'd thought."

"Is he going to get better?" Hope is all he feels.

Bring him back to me, please, please bring him back!

But Canady only shakes his head. "I don't think so. I don't want to give you false hope." He looks at Caleb's twin and smiles softly. "Maybe he just wasn't ready to say goodbye yet."

Offhand words to explain the unexplainable.

But then it clicks. It clicks like a heavy, rusted lock that will never be opened again. Caleb tugs on Ari's hair a little too hard and looks at her scrunched-up, red, and blotchy face, then he turns his eyes to his brother who is pained but breathing steadily, nostrils flaring in his thin face.

It's because Ben smells her.

Hilarious.

Twins in everything, meant to be mated to the same woman. Yet in one instant, she chose the one she can never have.

Of course she did.

The Lord giveth and the Lord taketh away.

But it isn't over yet. His poor Ari has had a hard, hard life, and Caleb will do anything to save her from wasting away, mourning a man who never even existed for her in the first place. After all, Ben was supposed to become a memory today. A beautiful, painful memory. Today was supposed to be a kindness, setting Ben free. Today was supposed to be the day Caleb's mate soothed him and helped him finally let go, stepping into the role of taking care of him just like Ben always had.

It seems that idea has turned sour.

He wants to throw up.

Instead, Caleb rocks Ari and shushes her, needing to step up his game and keep her where she belongs—in his arms. She's his soulmate, even if he's not hers. Hers is going to die, and it's going to hurt because she knows it.

"It's going to be okay," he whispers, as much to her as to himself. "I promise, it will be okay."

Because it has to be. There's no other option.

CHAPTER 9

THE PAINFUL PAST

CALEB'S MIND wades in and out of memories. The stuttering images remind him of a child's flipbook, but one that creates unexpectedly beautiful animation. The pages are made of pain but there's still so much love and effort to be found in each carefully drawn frame that it's become a masterpiece in its own right—as much as any one person's life can be, anyway. Its flickering moments have shaped everything that Caleb is, heart, mind, body, and soul.

Why is it the things people remember most clearly are always the things that hurt them? Perhaps all minds are simply a series of invisible scars.

———

Ben and Caleb are holding hands. They're sweating and it shows, but that doesn't mean they're going to stand down. It's too late for that. Ben is rigid and puffed up while Caleb is trembling and ready to pounce, lips pulled into a sneer.

"Take it back," Ben says through gritted teeth.

"Why should I?" the pompous, arrogant, ugly Bradley Hayes

taunts. "Feral Alphas, the both of you. No wonder your parents gave you away."

Caleb wants to lunge, but his brother just tightens his grip on him. It's a silent message to keep still and not prove these idiots right.

The church courtyard is sprinkled with the marble statues of dead saints who watch over this juvenile confrontation, used to schoolboys smashing their egos against one another as they sort out their pecking order. They frame the area in gray, neutral non-referees that couldn't, and wouldn't, call a time-out, even if you needed one. The rest of the small square is made of manicured bushes and benches for one to sit on while contemplating the divine. Instead, the three opposing forces—Hayes included—are standing on the one straight ahead, owning the high ground. At least they're out of rocks to chuck at this point. Caleb's head is already bleeding.

His clothes are too restrictive, the school uniform buttoned too tightly around his throat. Even though Caleb's Adam's apple has been growing more prominent every day since he presented, Uncle Matthew...*Father* Matthew...won't get him larger clothes. The pain is supposed to remind Caleb of the collar he must keep around his inner Alpha at all times. It keeps him unable to breathe well, both figuratively and literally, putting him at a disadvantage. He can't help but notice that, even though Hayes has only recently presented, he already has a new shirt and vest. They sag a tiny bit with room to grow into, something Caleb envies very much. Perhaps it's because Hayes's parents love him.

Ben's hand grips painfully. A vein bulges in Caleb's temple as he clenches his jaw. Meanwhile Hayes laughs at them, though Caleb knows it's pointed mostly in his direction.

"Shut your damned mouth," Caleb growls.

The other teen just *tsks*. "Language, Caleb. My, my. Such behavior doesn't suit you. Aren't you the prince of the academy?"

If by prince, you mean prisoner.

Hayes looks haughty and full of himself, his English accent

sticking out like a devil's horn. "Isn't that why your uncle gives you such special attention?"

You mean the hours of prayer to beg for forgiveness for just being alive?

Ben smirks, but it's dangerous. "Aww, look Caleb, he's jealous. Just fact-checking, though, didn't your parents abandon you here, too, Hayes? At least ours are still on the same continent. Same state even. Yours had to toss you all the way over the big pond. Can't imagine why. Maybe, before you start throwing your stupidity around, you should look in a mirror. Or is your pimply face too much to bear?"

"Oh, it absolutely is," Caleb matches Ben's expression, albeit with more menace. "I can barely look at those whiteheads on white-heads on whiteheads. It makes me scared to even punch him. I'd be too skeeved out when he pops all over my fist."

Bradley Hayes's crew grosses out as they give their pubescent master a collective look. The bully's wide eyes show his unexpected shock at their verbal comebacks. Normally, the Allein twins stay quiet until they start breaking arms.

"Caleb?" Ben asks, not needing to look at him. "Do you think our good friend here repents for his sins?"

"That's between him and God, I suppose. But Father Matthew would be very disappointed if he didn't." Caleb grins maliciously. "Better get on your knees and apologize, Bradley. Open that bumpy mouth of yours and finger your rosary beads. If Father Matthew has favorites, I'll bet God does, too. I'm guessing you're not one of them, though..."

Hayes looks hurt this time. Unlike Caleb and Ben, who think God either doesn't exist or can go fuck himself, most of the kids here are absolutely indoctrinated. Too bad Christians don't seem to practice what they preach, or else maybe they'd be decent people.

"Gonna cry again, Bradley?" Ben goads. "Aren't you supposed to be an Alpha? If this was a pack, we'd oust you in a second."

Caleb adds, "And if you didn't leave on your own, we're strong enough to make you."

He's not lying. The twins win every time they step in the ring, fighting dirty. Kicks and scratches, mud in their opponent's faces. Caleb's not even afraid to bite when the mood suits him. Once he bit someone on the face, just hard enough to leave a white, shiny scar for life.

"Come on," one of Hayes's Betas says. "It's not worth it."

Go on. Be good little boys and run.

The fact that Hayes wasn't the one to make the call for his group is telling. He doesn't even try to end the moment with a flimsy insult. It's the most satisfying experience of Caleb's life to date, beating someone with words. Words still bruise, but no one can point to them, cry, and tattle on you.

Ben squeezes his hand before letting go and clapping him on the back. "We did it, Cay."

Caleb nods, sighing out the last of his fury. "Finally."

"We graduate next year," Caleb tries to reason. "Only the younger grades have to do this, why us? We're too old."

Father Matthew eyes him and Ben with familiar disdain. "You wouldn't have to if you acted your age, Caleb. You wouldn't have to if you learned from your sins. And if you'd stop dragging your brother along for your joyride to hell, maybe Ben wouldn't have to do it, either."

It hits Caleb right in the chest, reminding him that people like Ben better. When Caleb's not around, Ben can almost fit in.

His brother's eyes narrow as he steps forward, far taller than their uncle and letting of a scent that's pure malice. "He doesn't drag me anywhere."

"You can fool yourself, Ben, but you can't fool the Lord." Matthew gestures at the vaulted ceiling.

"And you know what God wants?" Ben asks, walking closer toward their uncle and making him step back. Ben's voice is quiet, but it still echoes off the empty stairwell where they're happily having their family confrontation. Uncle Matthew seems to like to put on a show, always having their little tête-à-têtes in public spaces and putting the boys at risk for further social fall out among their peers, the only consequences that pious priest can't inflict himself.

"You act like you're a prophet," Caleb says. "Doesn't pride goeth before the fall, Father Morden?"

Their uncle scowls. He hates his last name. A reminder that his father was a mass murderer—someone their uncle only pretends to forgive in order to look pious at Sunday mass. The Morden name is an albatross tied around all their necks. Something people point to as soon as you step out of line, as if they never expected any better from one of *his* children in the first place. It's done nothing but breed a litter of spawn who hate both themselves and everything around them; they just all show it in their own flavorful ways.

Ben steps forward again, fury wafting dangerously from every pore and making Father Matthew pull back. "For someone who reads the Bible all the time, it's funny that you skip all the parts that don't work for you. 'Judge not, lest ye be judged.' 'Let those without sin cast the first stone.' 'As I have loved you, love one another.' Do you know what the word *hypocrisy* means, Father Morden?"

It seems their uncle is done with Ben's intimidation. With a growl, the beloved Father Matthew slaps him roughly upside the head, harder than normal this time, making a sharp sound echo in the empty air around them. Caleb snarls and lurches forward, but Ben holds out a hand to keep his brother at bay. Turning back toward their uncle, Ben sports a nice red welt.

"Is that what God wanted, Father Matthew? Or what you wanted?"

Their uncle's eyes drop then. He knows he's imperfect. That he faces the darkness just as much as everyone else in their family. He steps back a bit too close to the lip of the stairs, reeking of shame.

One step.

Two steps.

Three.

Ben says nothing, Caleb says nothing, though they both hope for the same thing.

With a single misplaced footfall, Matthew teeters on the top step, looking at the boys with wide eyes, but no matter how many times his fingers rake the air, it's too late. Unable to get his balance, unable to get a grip on anything around him, Matthew Morden lurches backward down the vaulted, marble staircase. The young men gape as their uncle topples, the first impact resulting in a *crunch* that will echo in their minds for years to come.

It seems God has had His say.

Ben backs Caleb away immediately as the *thuds* pound down in cartwheels. "Run."

Which is exactly what they do. They manage to turn a corner before the first set of students walk through the hall—middle schoolers holding their books and hearing the sounds of their Headmaster stuttering to the ground, head over feet, until he finally lands at the bottom and bleeds. It happened too fast, but all too slow at the same time. When the kids cry out, Ben pulls Caleb back, ensuring they won't be seen as the aftermath unfolds.

"It wasn't our fault," Ben whispers immediately.

"He did it to himself," Caleb agrees. "And it happened too fast to save him."

Ben nods. "...And he deserved it."

That's what he says anyway, but he's shaking. Caleb takes hold of his hand as both of them stay stuck in the moment, breathing hard and filled with dread.

"We can never say anything," Ben says, his voice catching. "They'll blame us."

And he's absolutely right.

Sneaking as fast as they can, Caleb and his brother make it to their dorm room unseen, locked away in a far part of the school where not many people come. They get in the same bed and spoon each other, Caleb crying softly while Ben wraps his arms around, stroking Caleb's chest to slow his heart.

When someone finds them to tell them the news, they're going to think they're gay. Incestuous. They're not—never have been, and never will be—but that doesn't stop the rumors. They're too close, but Caleb still wouldn't change it for the world. He doesn't care about what the others think anymore, anyway.

Caleb's going to suffocate. Sloane has his face pressed so hard into the wall, his nose feels as though it's going to break—if it hasn't broken already. All he can smell is blood. Despite the clenched fist in his hair, Caleb manages to rock onto his cheek and take a sobbing breath.

"Please," he begs. "Please stop..." But he's met with nothing but grunts.

Sloane is behind him, punishing his words by thrusting up Caleb's shirt and ripping his fingernails down Caleb's skin, lighting his nerves on fire as he feels one rivulet of blood trickle over his back. The only other sensation is Sloane pivoting his hips, hitting Caleb's ass as he thrusts between his legs over and over again—not inside him, but pushing between his upper thighs like a piston. Caleb's trousers are shoved down to his knees so he can't run, and even if he tries, Sloane is stronger than him. He always has been. Caleb is frozen and can do nothing but mewl like the weakling he is. He focuses on his hand, pressed flat against the wooden paneling, seeing his fingertips turn white as they claw into the surface.

Please stop, please stop, please stop!

Sloane reaches around and grabs Caleb's erection painfully, his low voice chuckling. "And you say you don't want this..."

Caleb yelps, "I can't help it!" and he truly can't. He's horrified and terrified and wants to escape, but he's also powerless. Still, the merciless strokes are hitting him in such a way, and he can't make his body stop. He hates this, he hates this, *he hates this!*

When the monster behind him bursts with a groan, it leaves a mess between Caleb's thighs and Sloane wrenches his head back one more time, leveraging the roots of Caleb's hair until he feels as if his neck is going to snap.

"Don't you say a word," Sloane says.

He then shoves Caleb so hard against the wall his teeth clack, and by the time he slides to the carpeted floor, Sloane has already put himself together again.

The male hunkers down in front of him. "And before you get any *R* words embedded in your filthy mind, remember this. I didn't use your mouth. I didn't use your backside. I didn't use anything that comes with the word *sex* attached to it." Sloane just regards him without expression. "Can you guess why I did this?"

Caleb doesn't talk. He was told not to talk. He just sucks back snot and blood while he cowers, his body still exposed to the private world of Sloane's office.

"Because I'm the stronger Alpha. Because you need to know your place, my boy, and it will always be beneath me." With a cruel smile, Sloane leans closer. "And this will never happen again. Do you know why?"

He leans even closer, and Caleb is terrified he's going to kiss him. He whips his face to the side with a whimper as Sloane's cigarette breath whispers over the shell of his ear.

"Because you disgust me."

And with that, he's gone, leaving Caleb a mess on the floor, panting, unable to move, only to sob like the man-child he is. He's only an intern with a bachelor's degree, not a passing mark for the bar exam. Why did he try to stand up for those people? They might have been innocent, and Sloane's client may have been guilty, but the plaintiffs are the enemy always! It wasn't his place. He's weak, weak, *weak!*

He doesn't know how much time passes as his mind circles like this; he only knows that the sky has moved to sunset when Ben walks into the private office.

"Cay, you never showed up to..."

And Caleb curls on himself, more ashamed than he's ever been in his life. He shrinks against the wall and lets out a pained gasp. That must be when Ben sees his back.

"What the fuck, Cay?"

I'm dirty, don't touch me. Please don't touch me.

But touch him Ben does, and Caleb is too spent to do anything about it. When his brother turns him over, Caleb is still out, flaccid and ruined with another man's seed. It would look like his own if it was on his belly or his hands, but it's impossible for him to have done this to himself and Ben knows it.

"Sloane," his brother whispers and Caleb dies inside, bursting into another bout of sobs as Ben gathers him up and gets him on his knees, fixing him back into his pants and pulling his shirt down gently over his back.

"I'll kill him," Ben says. "I'll fucking kill him."

"You can't." Uncle Matthew was an accident; this would be on purpose. He can't let Ben be that person. "And you can't tell. Promise me you won't tell!"

He can feel Ben's hands in his hair as he holds him. "We need to!"

"Please," Caleb begs. "If I'm not b-back tomorrow, he said he'd tell about Mom and Dad."

"Fuck Mom and Dad," Ben growls. "You're not coming here ever again. Their secrets aren't worth this."

"Don't!" Caleb whimpers, too desperate for his own good.

"Even if I don't say anything...what did he do to your face, Cay? Mom and Dad are gonna see this!"

Caleb whispers. "I don't want them to know. Benny, please, I don't even want *you* to know..."

Ben starts rocking him back and forth. Caleb is limp in his arms but that doesn't stop his brother from keeping his dead weight held tight. "I'll convince them you can't come back here. I'll protect you."

"H-he said he'd never do it again," Caleb tries.

Because I disgust him. I'm disgusting.

"That's not good enough. Ripping him to shreds won't be good enough." Ben's scent ramps into dangerous territory. "Hey. We're

gonna sneak you out of here, okay? We're gonna wait until the receptionist leaves and there's only the over-achievers with their heads
down, yeah?"

"Yeah..." he agrees pathetically.

"And then I'm gonna get you out of here."

"Yeah?"

"And then I'm gonna make sure you never come back."

"—why it makes sense for Caleb to intern with me at Powell's firm.
He'd be a perfect fit." Ben finishes, confident and authoritative, his
closing statement perfectly delivered.

Their mom, a senator, scoffs. "You boys are too close already. It's
unhealthy. A little separation would do you good."

"She's not wrong," their father chimes in, leaning over the island
in the center of the kitchen and giving one of those too-charming-to-
be-real grins. "How are you guys gonna find your mates if you're too
busy being in each other's business all the time? I doubt Cay over
here would be a good wingman. He'd scare off all the good ones. Or
maybe they'll think he looks cute with a broken nose and a pair of
black eyes."

"You're horrible, Hank." Their father is met with a kind tug on
the ear as their mother nuzzles into him. It's only a minute before
she turns a cold eye on the twins again. "You know what's at stake
here. Sloane's only stipulation was that Caleb work for him. I know
he's an ass   "

"Putting it mildly, sweetheart," their dad points out, cheering
with his coffee cup.

"—but Caleb needs someone with Sloane's prestige once law
school is over. A recommendation from a man in his position would
make a big statement and potential firms might overlook Caleb's...
lesser qualities when they make their hiring decisions. It might be
the only way someone will take a risk on someone like him. This isn't
a game."

Ben tries to be reasonable; he really does. "Caleb and I have the exact same background and the exact same tendencies, so if I can work for someone else and still get the contacts I need—the guidance, the opportunities—he can, too. Besides, we're adults now. Sink or swim, it should be up to us."

"Tell that to the bills I pay for your apartment," their mother gripes. "You think the fourteenth floor is cheap?"

"We'll move," Caleb says, voice husky and nasal. It's the first time he's spoken in this whole ordeal. He wishes he was anywhere else... except near Charles Sloane...and that's the only reason he's letting this conversation happen. His back throbs while he sits with his elbows on the dining room table, lips pressed against his clasped hands. His nose is braced and throbs like a motherfucker, making his brain turn into muck. "We'll go somewhere we can afford."

"And what?" their mother asks. "Commute in? Do you know how that will make me look? Never mind the dirt Sloane has on us, a senator's son living in some hovel and schlepping it in a train car will make you look—"

"Like the people who vote for you?" Ben says. "Like the people who don't live in your bubble? Maybe it would help you in the midterms, Mom, think of it that way."

She waves a finger at him. "Don't you counter me, Benjamin. I made you and I can unmake you just as easily."

"*Fucking try it,*" Caleb growls out loud.

"See?" Their father has the audacity to laugh. "You're too close. Cay's over here about to jump in and defend your honor." He turns his gaze over to Caleb, dull eyed and half not-caring. "It's like you don't believe your brother can fight his own battles." He turns back to Ben. "The same goes for you."

"I don't care that he hit you, Caleb," his mother says, fingers pressing into the ridge of her eyebrow in frustration. "I don't. You know why? Number one, because I know you earned it. Number two, because that will heal in a few days, but the damage he'll do to me is irreparable! Once people know I'm connected to the underground movement, the smear campaigns will be unstoppable! Not to mention all the crap your father got himself into when he was younger coming back to bite us! We contend with your grandfather's history every day, but what Sloane knows would make more juicy headlines than this family can survive. The media vultures will swarm us! I refuse to give up everything I've worked for because my Alpha son can't take a little discipline when he earns it!"

Ben eyes Caleb, silently begging him to say something. His head-shake is infinitesimal, but his brother sees it anyway.

You can't tell her how disgusting I am. How weak. How ruined.

I'll never live it down.

His mother jabs a finger at him with bared teeth. "Get with the program, Caleb. Protect this family. Your grandfather was a monster, your grandmother died of grief, your uncle was killed in his own church—we can't take another scandal. This is my livelihood!"

Isn't it supposed to be your passion for those you serve?

"I hate it there. Doesn't that matter?" Caleb asks.

"Because it absolutely should." Ben glares at them.

"So help me, Caleb, you will leave that practice over my dead body!" their mother vows.

"Mine too, apparently." Their father kisses her temple, quieting her down and chuckling as if she was outright precious. "If we're gambling, let's make it double or nothing."

Ben sits down heavily at the table next to Caleb, his eyes locked on their father. "High stakes and bad odds. So, I lose the fight, then?"

Their father shrugs. "Honestly, kid, it wasn't your fight in the first place."

"You're right," Caleb agrees. "It was mine. But I'm tired of talking about it. I'll do what you want, I don't care anymore."

He gets up to walk out, but not without hearing one last barb. "Some Alpha," his mother mocks. Caleb can't help but pray they're the last words he ever hears from her.

Ben follows in his wake and Caleb knows well enough to leave the front door open so his brother can slam it himself. Settling into the car, the one that the Sloane's firm provides, Caleb's tears come again, but quietly this time. He doesn't have much left in him. All he wants at this point is to disappear. He lets Ben wrap around him even though he knows they're too old for this. He knows, but he needs it. He needs it because no one else loves him.

Caleb's voice is small as it lets out a terrible truth. "I don't want to be alive anymore."

Ben holds him all too tight, pulling him as close as he can past the center gearshift. The twist of his body rips open some of the marks on his back, but they're shallow. They'll heal. Unless Caleb stops healing all together.

"Don't say that," Ben whispers into his hair. "Don't ever say that. I need you, Cay. We have no one but each other. If I don't have you, I'm lost. Do you want me to be lost?"

Caleb's lips tremble. "No..."

"Then don't go," Ben says, rough and mean. "Don't you ever fucking go, do you hear me? Promise."

Caleb curls into himself and shudders. "I promise."

But with those two words, he knows he's just damned himself to a life of unending pain. This made-in-the-moment vow will haunt him. But Ben is Ben, and Caleb would do anything for him. Even suffer.

In the present, Caleb silently collects the memories of his brother and tucks them deeper into their little box in his heart. They're his secrets and no one else's. Not now. Not ever.

He and Ari sit together on the floor at the foot of the bedroom dresser. She has Ben's letter in her hands, but Caleb already knows it by heart. Some of the ink is smeared into blots with Ben's tear stains, but the paper itself is brittle and crinkled with his own. He recites it to her, completely detached. It says:

Cay,

I'm not going to let them do this to you anymore. To us. There's so much in life that wasn't our fault, but we were blamed anyway. So many things we were hated for. And it all started with them.

Needing their approval is our biggest weakness and I'm sick of it. They're not family, they're just the people who sired us. They don't even love us enough to make one simple compromise. I don't care what they say, I refuse to let them keep you under that man's thumb even one more minute.

I'm only writing you this letter in case something goes wrong. If it doesn't work, it doesn't work, but I'm sure as hell going to try. They don't buckle their belts, Cay, never have. "Click it or ticket." Their fault, not mine. Remember that. Besides, it's icy. I have an excuse. I just have to go fast enough. Maybe flip. Maybe ram into something. I'll figure it out.

If I come back, we'll start over. It will be alright, Cay. But, no matter what, remember our promise. Never forget, no matter what.

"Love, Benny," Caleb finishes.

Ari looks stunned. Shellshocked, maybe. Today has been hard for both of them, but he's not sure who was hit harder. Still, one thing remains the truth. Benjamin Allein is a murderer and Caleb Reed is not. Ari's trying hard not to believe it, but the confession lies in her hands.

Out of all the things to do, Ari makes fun of him. "Caleb Elijah Allein. You sound like a millionaire playboy in a romance novel."

He has no idea what to do with that comment. "And which do you prefer? Ari Allein or Ari Reed?"

She makes a face. "Ugh. Don't call me either. They both sound stupid. I'm keeping my maiden name."

Something in him, some knot he knew was there but couldn't process yet, releases. She's not rejecting him outright. Not yet. If she wants to keep her name, he'll gladly give her that. "For professional reasons, I'm guessing."

She hums her agreement. "Who's the man he's talking about?"

Caleb sighs. "Sloane."

She blinks at him, face blotched with broken capillaries. "But..." And then it dawns on her. "But you needed to pay for Ben."

"I needed to pay for Ben," he echoes. "He waited until I blew my money and screwed myself. Then he taught me what an idiot I am. I had no choice. To save my brother, I sold my soul to the devil."

He wishes that she'd hold his hand, but she doesn't. After a pause, she asks a wistful, "Did your parents love each other up until the very end?"

"Oh yes. It was quite romantic. If ever two people were on the same page about their life together, it was them. They wanted to blow the standard dream of most people out of the water. They wanted to be something like heroes, I guess. The kind of people that others make plaques for. The kind of couple where, if one dies, the other follows right away because they can't bear to be without each other. Ben and I just got in the way. They resented us for taking away their superpowers and making them mundane."

Ari touches her belly, and he can feel her trepidation. "I'm surprised you want pups at all after the life you've lived."

"Me too," he admits. "But I do. Would it be so bad to be a regular person? To do it right?"

She laughs at him, and it's mean spirited. "I can't imagine someone like you being a good father."

And it stings. More than stings. It's like a hammer. He looks at the ceiling and asks, "Why am I always getting rejected, do you think? Not just you now, but everyone always."

It's because I am who I am. Disgusting. Cold. Calculating. A man who's absolutely willing to sully himself to get what he wants.

It's an utterly valid question and it was utterly vulnerable of him to ask it, but it was easier to say out loud because he knows it will tickle her protective bone—to see him as someone to be saved. If he smells her right through his clogged nose, he's hit the mark. Pity opens doorways.

He asks, "Since biting you, have I done anything really wrong?"

"Define wrong," she says, cold and unlike herself. "Besides, it's only been a few days."

"But have I?"

She thinks about it. He hopes that all the times he's told her that she's "asked for this" have sunk in. He knows they did when she replies: "No, you haven't."

He smiles a little. "I'm sorry for falling in love so quickly." She is his soulmate after all. He's just not hers. "I've been so alone but, seeing you, I really felt it. I thought I could have a future and I couldn't let it pass me by. You hated me, I could smell it in court, but everything in me wanted you from the moment I saw you. And no matter what you might say, hate me or not, you wanted me back."

"I was going into heat," she says through her teeth.

"But you still smelled me. Unlike you, I was playing by the rules. Suppressed, doused with blockers, being a model citizen. If you can smell someone so well when they're like that, they say it means you're meant to be."

Harsh, she says, "It's probably only because you smell like..." But she realizes her cruelty all too late and catches the end of that sentence between her teeth, though Caleb hears it anyway.

"Like Ben?" He works his jaw, the ache in his chest unimaginable. The rejection is so overwhelming he can't breathe, and he hopes she feels every stab of his pain. Shaking his head, he says, "Maybe it's better to be alone."

He gets up to leave her behind. "I'll let you have the bed tonight."

She looks afraid. Good for her.

"Are you sleeping on the couch?"

"No, sweetheart. In your nest. Maybe I'll be able to lay there, smell the scent of us together, and have pretty dreams where this is real."

With that, he walks away, locking himself wordlessly in the room where he suffers the most.

The door slams and Ari's muscles jerk with the sound, guilt rolling in her belly. She's being selfish, she knows, but she's been rationalizing this whole situation by shoving the word *soulmated* down her own throat.

They're not soulmated.

She and Ben are.

Her heart wrenches. Ben is dying. She's only just smelled him and it's already too late. But should she even want him after that letter? It was no accident. Everything he did, he did on purpose.

Until that moment in Ben's room, she'd been prepared to be with Caleb. She'd been enjoying him. Very few people in this world are soulmated, most are just love matches. Can't they make that work? Couldn't that be enough? Except for the fact that Ari wants to crawl into the hospital bed and die alongside the man she knows she belongs to.

Not for the first time, she says, "Fucking biology."

This morning she was tentatively happy. With reservations to the moon and back, but she's had such wonderful moments. Felt such amazing feelings. Laughed so much. Caleb is romantic, adorable, funny, and considerate. He's also too intense, manipulative, and has a darkness it will take a lifetime to heal. As broken as she might feel over Ben today, Caleb has been lost for so much longer. He needs her. No one has ever needed Ari before, not like this.

Her back pocket buzzes, and she takes out her phone, looking at it as if it's an anomaly in her current state of mind. It's Niles, of course, with winky faces punctuating every word.

> Are you having fun over there?

Oh, God. How does she even begin this conversation? What parts does she even want to say? *"Dear Niles, I'm actually soulmated to the man who killed my parents (on purpose) but—plot twist—he's dying! I called him my mate out loud and broke my fiancé's heart because—oh yeah, I'm ENGAGED NOW—and I hate everything about my life!"*

No. No, she will absolutely not be saying that. Instead, she texts back:

> This is hard. I don't think I like this.

But it's not like she can just leave. Then she'd never see Ben again.

Caleb. She'd meant Caleb.

Niles calls her and she picks up, whispering a "Hold on..." before edging out of the bedroom, too close to where Caleb lies in pain, and goes out into the building's hallway, lined with other wooden apartment doors. "Okay, I can talk now."

"You freaked me out for a second. What, did you have to, like, escape him to have this conversation?"

"Well, I don't exactly want him to be in earshot."

"Point taken. Did something happen?"

So much. Too much.

"Remember how I kept saying that I don't know him? Well, that keeps coming back to bite me. Not only that, but I don't know enough about relationships. I keep saying the wrong things and it gets me in trouble. I don't know if I'm infatuated like a teenager or really falling in love or..."

Trying to run away? Wishing I'd met his brother first?

Niles clucks his tongue against the roof of his mouth. "Maybe you're putting too much pressure on yourself. Maybe you should just let whatever you guys have grow naturally over time."

She pfffts. "Yeah, tell that to the guy who mated me after knowing me for about a full minute, and who has also already stuck an unexpected engagement ring on my finger. Thanks for the heads-up on that, by the way."

"Engagement what?! And heads-up for...?"

"For the ring. You picked perfectly."

"Whoa, whoa, hold on. First of all...A RING? And second of all, I didn't know anything about it, as indicated by my previous sentences."

She sinks to the floor and presses her back against the wall. "Well, it's amazing. Beautiful. Exactly what I've always wanted."

"You don't really have that 'squee' sound you probably should."

No, I absolutely do not.

He continues. "Look, Ari, my offer still stands, if you need to reject him —"

"I'm never doing that," she says. "Never."

He'll break.

Niles sighs heavily into the phone. "So, get to know him better. If that's what's getting to you, fix the problem." His tone takes on something mischievous. "Snoop."

"What, like, Doggie-Dog?"

"No!" He sputters a laugh. "No, like snoop around his house. Poke in the cabinets and drawers. See what lives in all his hidey-holes. Check out his DVDs and Netflix history and judge him for his transgressions."

She chuckles. "That's mean. It's an invasion of privacy."

"Yeah, well, he kind of threw that out the window when he knotted you."

And didn't give me my medicine.

Suddenly she doesn't care about his personal boundaries.

"Niles, do you think I could be pregnant?"

"No, pumpkin. Not with the cocktail of meds I got you. That stuff is Alpha seed killer, right there."

She swallows. "What if it didn't work?"

Niles pauses. "I think you'll know within the week."

"Why?"

"You're an Omega, Ari. Now that your heat is over, you'll have your bleed in the next few days."

"Oh. That. Yet another thing I haven't experienced. Joy."

"Plus, they say you can feel it if you are. Something in your hormones changes and you feel overly lovey."

"Yeah, that doesn't exactly describe my mood at the present moment."

"You're just being paranoid." Niles blows air out of his mouth in a puff. "So…"

"So?"

"You gonna snoop?"

She smirks, feeling sneaky and in need of something to do. "Yeah. I think I will."

"Good girl! I've taught you well!"

"You mean in the last two minutes?"

"It still counts as teaching. If you didn't think of it and I did, I've imparted wisdom unto you."

She rubs her face, not wanting to deal with another "experienced one" right now. Her eyes are puffy and all she wants to do is sleep, but when is she going to get another chance like this? "All right. Take your sage wisdom somewhere else. I've got some work to do."

"Text me everything!"

She snorts. "No way!"

He whines. "Don't be so mean!"

"Just because I'm willing to learn about the man who mated me doesn't mean that you're privy to all his dirty secrets."

"Like pornography? Think he has Alpha-to-Alpha stuff?"

"Niles!"

Her friend bursts out laughing. "Okay, okay. You go dig. Have fun, but only use your mystical findings for the sake of good, otherwise you'll turn into a bat or something."

"Noted."

He smooches her goodbye kisses, but she's not in the mood. Still, she gives him one just to get him off the phone. There's a limit to how much she's willing to sulk.

She shuts the door to the apartment so softly there's no way Caleb could have heard her. The apartment does seem like a strange, eclectic mix of them both at this point, their belongings converging in...ways. Caleb called it "chaotic good." Basically, she'd stuck something of hers on every surface that exists. Even her wine bottle flower vase is there with a new handful of dandelions. They don't last for long, but they're everywhere and free, so they're easy to get a hold of.

She decides to start with the entertainment center. There are still a good number of not-quite-unpacked boxes looming around, but she shuffles them to the side to take a look at what he's got on display. A few Marvel movies—to be expected in this day and age. Old time movies. *Star Wars* of all things. And then she spots *The Notebook*. Probably one of the most tragic romances she's ever watched in her entire life. She'd wept until her nose bled. Scouring his collection with new interest, she finds quite a few rom-coms and serious love-love stuff throughout. Not to mention a few of her fantasy favorites.

They do have things in common.

By way of books, it's mostly lawyer-y things, which makes absolute sense—she's already read a good deal of it, too—but there's still a raggedy paperback novel to be found from time to time. Some of them are horror, some of them are more romances—bodice rippers, this time—ones she knows quite well and likes very much.

Caleb, Caleb. You surprise me at every turn.

His romantic soul has been seduced by all the smutty goodness she herself has been trapped in for years. She smiles to herself a little. Sliding her fingers along another row of spines, she happens on something irregularly sized, an outright tome, and pulls it out. A photo album.

Oh, now this should be adorable.

She's greeted by two chubby baby boys, held by their father. The stranger is handsome in a sort of cowboy way, and his crooked smirk and a large nose are two traits Caleb seems to have inherited directly. The next picture has...his mother, Ari supposes...with big round eyes just as expressive as the ones she's gotten to know so well over the last few days.

There's not one single picture of just the twins. Their parents are in all of them. Ari feels confused. This isn't what she'd pictured when she imagined his supposedly cold family...but then it comes together. The pictures aren't about the boys. The boys are a prop. As they age, they move to the background of photos, running around happily together. The camera lenses don't focus on them, though. Not even once. And as the twins get older, those sweet smiles seem to fade, their appearances fewer and fewer, until they're no longer in the pictures at all. The album goes on, though. Snapshots of Caleb's mother and father on top of the Eiffel Tower. Near waterfalls. On beaches. At parties. But no little boys run in the background anymore. It's as if they'd died, but no one got sad.

It's official. Ari's been more heartbroken in these past few days than she has in the past five years combined.

Flipping through quickly, Caleb's parents age bit by bit, and the boys don't reappear until closer to the end of the thick volume of pages. Graduation caps and gowns...only the parents don't really look happy this time. Their smiles are strained. Fake. And the twins look downright upset to be touched by these people, these strangers, whose arms are wrapped around them in a good show for the camera. Which one is Ben, and which one is Caleb? Which is her soulmate, and which is the man who mated her?

They disappear from the albums again after that one picture, and it stops when Caleb's parents look middle-aged. There are still empty pages in the back of the book, leaving it incomplete, but that makes sense, considering. The Allein family never had a chance to fill it all the way.

Ari has a new understanding of the poor, abandoned boys. She may have been in foster care, but no one had ever held her while looking like all they wanted to do was push her away. Not only that, but she knows that her parents loved her from her very beginning to their very end. But Ben's...*Caleb's* parents didn't.

What would the twins have been like if these selfish people hadn't broken them? She wants to know the answer to that more than anything else in the world. To that end, Ari's just going to have to keep soothing Caleb, helping to quell his darkness, and give them both a chance at finding out.

Looking at her ring, she knows she's in this for life. For better or for worse, it's time to give in.

***

Caleb couldn't get more tangled in her broken nest if he tried. It smells like dried slick, cum, and hope. He wraps himself in it as if he's cold, even though he's anything but. Still, he's more than happy to add more sweat and tears to this heady mix of them.

He's on the verge of sleep when a knock on the door startles him. He doesn't know whether to be annoyed or elated. He chooses confusion. Rubbing his eyes, groggy, he fumbles his way to the door in the windowless dark and flips on the light, pressing the handle to open up and invite her into his cave.

She looks unsure and has the tiniest smile on her face, holding up her phone and moving it in little twiddles. "Take a picture with me?"

He scoffs. There's nothing else to do. "Forgive me, but you look like you've been crying for days, and I doubt I look much better."

Her face falls and he feels her disappointment. She's looking at the ground when she says, "Maybe tomorrow?"

He raises his eyebrow at her.

She adds, "And I'd like you to come sleep in the bed with me."

Something like a pleasant pain hurts and heals him all at once. He's amazed. But he's in no mood for her generosity.

"Are you sure that's what you want? Or is this another thing you'll resent me for? You say things you don't mean all the time, don't you? Or do you expect me to read your mind and know when to say no?"

She looks wounded. Smells wounded. It hurts him in a different way.

Protect your Omega. Even from yourself.

"I'm sorry. I..." He looks around, searching for words. Voice husky with pain, he admits, "I don't want you to leave me, but I don't know how to fix this. I don't know what to do."

She steps in close, wrapping her arms around his waist and he grabs her immediately, trying to stay gentle though he knows he feels like nothing but fear.

"Marry me, Caleb," she says. Pushing him back, she looks into his eyes, firm with resolve. "I know what I'm asking, and I know what you're afraid of. We don't have to be soulmated to love each other." Reaching up, she cups his face in her hand. "You don't have to be perfect to be special. And you don't have to be afraid because I'm never leaving you. It's okay to get your hopes up. Build your dreams with me. And whether now or later, I'll make you a family, Caleb, I promise. And I will love all of you with everything I am. We're going to be like *my* parents. We're going to love our kids so much that it will keep them happy, even long after we're gone."

He tucks his cheek into her palm and lets the tears come. It's natural. He has gallons of them.

Intimately aware of the lamentations in her diary at this point, he knows that being abandoned is her greatest fear, yet he'd left her by herself to fester in her regret. Somehow, it made her open her heart to him. It's so, so soon, but she already asked him that precious question...and she asked him in a way he can't be blamed for. Maybe he can win this battle after all.

Standing on her tippy-toes, she guides him down to her lips, kissing him so soft and sweet that he loses himself in her. And when her tongue touches his of her own volition, it feels like nothing but victory. He loves her. He loves her so damn much. Today, he has lost, lost, lost—but maybe he's also won.

"Of course, I'll marry you." Nuzzling her, he feels her satisfaction and a deep thrill of her hope. Into her hair, he whispers, "Thank you, sweetheart. I'll be a good Alpha, a strong Alpha, you'll see."

Maybe this can be another part of their love story, the pain and the angst and the moments of imperfection are new memories to collect, day by day, with his Omega by his side.

He can't help it. It's not the same, and will never be the same again, but still his heart calls out:

Mate.

And also, *Wife.*

"CALEB," Canady says with a sigh. "I promise, I will call you if there's any change in Ben. It's a summer Sunday. Go out. Do something with that pretty mate of yours."

Caleb sits hunched over on the couch while Ari is still passed out in his bed. Their bed. "I can't. Not when he's like this."

"I told you, it may take a while. As soon as he proved he could breathe on his own..." Canady trails off. "Do you want me to stop his intravenous drips? Take out the feeding tube?"

The thought makes Caleb's whole brain revolt. "No. No, you can't do that. You want me to starve my brother to death? I'm not going t—"

"Caleb." Canady sounds like a father he never had. "I know it's hard. I know. I'll do anything you want me to do, but his vitals don't show any other changes. I don't want you to let this drag out forever."

"Just..." Caleb squeezes his eyes shut and presses his fingers into the ridge of his brow. "Just continue treatment as you normally would."

"Okay. For now, business as usual."

"Thank you."

"Now, I order you to go play."

"Play?"

"Play. *P-L-A-Y*. If anyone deserves a day of rest, it's you."

Caleb doesn't feel like he deserves much of anything. Still, he mutters his agreements and his goodbyes before deciding to pop onto his e-mail for a bit, a distraction as much as anything else. He goes back to work tomorrow, though he doesn't feel in the right frame of mind for it. Not that it matters.

There's an e-mail from Gwen, briefing him on what he's taking back when he gets in. Court on fucking Wednesday...and for a case he's never touched before. That's a shitty move. There's another message, from Sloane this time; subject: "For the mated Alpha." When he opens it, he smiles in spite of everything.

Ari chooses that minute to stumble out of bed, hair a bit of a mess and rubbing her tired eyes. "What's up with you? You're sad, then you're angry, then you're happy. I can't keep up."

He bites his bottom lip, stifling a grin. Having someone know how he feels is the most precious gift in the entire world. "What's your opinion on boats?"

"Huh?" Her eyes close out of sync as she works to pry herself out of walking REM sleep.

Tapping his phone, Caleb says, "Seems my boss got us tickets for a sunset cruise this evening. A sort of congratulations."

She stands straight and feels like pure excitement. "Oh? OH! Can Niles come? We've never been on a boat!"

Ah, well, damnit.

But she looks like she'd wag her tail if she had one. "I'm sure I can spring for an extra ticket, kitten. Is the hour decent enough to ping him?"

"What's the hour?"

He looks at his screen. "Nine twenty-two and fourteen seconds. Fifteen. Sixteen."

Giggling, she says, "Yeah, give me a minute."

"Sixty seconds on the clock. One...two..."

She about-faces back into their bedroom, and he's more than happy to watch her pajamaed ass as she goes. Even in some frumpy thing that hangs off her, he can still imagine those tight muscles under her clothes.

"I feel that!"

Caught again.

He chuckles. "Sorry, not sorry."

Grumbling from the other room, the moments tick by. He feels her disappointment before she calls back. "He says he can't!"

Caleb thinks for a second. What would make his Omega happy? "Can he come for dinner tomorrow night instead?"

"Emo pasta?"

"God, no!"

Another moment passes and happiness flows through their bond. "He says yes!"

Well, hoo-fucking-ray.

Caleb would prefer it if Niles abandoned her entirely, leaving Caleb as the only one she can rely on now and forever. She'd get over it after a while. Plus, he likes to kiss her tears away.

"Ask him what he wants, and I'll shop for it."

She pokes her head out of the door and blinks at him. "Can I come?"

His heart swells. "Absolutely."

She looks so cute he wants to eat her up. "I'll...I'll get ready, then."

"Take your time."

I'll just be here watching every video I can about slow dancing. Sunset cruises are places for romance. If your Alpha is going to play, he's going to do it just right.

Ari's chin tips up when she stands outside her office building, physically willing herself to face today with fresh eyes. For whatever reasons, good or bad, she has chosen her Alpha and she's not going to let herself regret it. Yes, he does bad things, but there's more to him than that. Things that make her smile. Like the fact that he fast dances like an idiot and slow dances like a dream. He eats like a debutante and actually calorie counts. It's not that he hogs the bed, it's that he wants her to lay basically on top of him so he can play with her fingers and nuzzle her hair. He's too big, nearly busting out of his clothes, but she is *not* upset about it. She can feel how pleased he is when he catches her staring, too, and so she's decided not to bother toning down her ogling anymore. God knows he doesn't.

Toward the end of the evening on their harbor cruise, the color of the sunset had reflected off his black hair as he looked into the sea-stained depths, his mouth and brow entirely too serious. Ari felt like she could stare at him forever in that moment, counting his freckles and braiding his hair. She may not be in love, but she's satisfied. Pleasantly so. He'd done his best to make that night as perfect as it could be, carrying them both away from the pain in their hearts and letting them forget for a while. He really is just like one of her stories, sometimes.

She draws more eyes than she had on Friday when she walks into the reception area. Stupid gossip. Seems her current situation has spread to anyone and everyone at this point—as indicated when she sees Paul in the corridor and his expression darkens immediately. She doesn't even have a second before he grabs her by the arm and yanks her into a conference room with a scowl.

She squeaks, "What the heck are you doing?" but is outright ignored.

Her colleague, newly returned from his rut, shuts the door much harder than he needs to, making Ari flinch. She grabs onto the strap of her laptop bag with white knuckles and immediately feels the complete attention of her Alpha flow over from Caleb's side of their bond. He must have sensed her discomfort. He didn't want her to go to work today. *She* didn't want her to go to work today. The blackness in Paul's eyes just solidifies their mutual, fatalistic prediction.

Grabbing her and turning her this way and that, Paul looks at her neck, her wrists, and sneers at her. "Your Omega friend do that?"

His sarcasm does nothing but irritate her. "Of course not!"

"You've got to be kidding me, Ari. How did this happen?"

His paws are still on her as he inspects and rubs his scent on her with his fingertips. It makes her feel dirty. She squirms, trying to get out of his grip, but he holds her tight.

"Be still, Omega!"

How she loathes those words. "You can't boss me around like that anymore, Paul. I'm mated now."

"You didn't want this," he states. "I know it for a fact. What he did is illegal!"

Ari sees Caleb's sad face in her mind and lies through her teeth. "I did want it. I asked for it."

Paul just glares at her. With Caleb's scent masking hers, Ari prays he can't smell her lie outright. Besides, she's started her pills and blockers again this morning. After a while no one will smell her much at all... But these damn wrist bites put everyone on edge.

He's just concerned and angry on her behalf, that's all. He's her work friend. She wants to trust him. "Everyone hates me now. No one's even trying to be understanding. Do you...do you think I should quit?"

"I think you should run," Paul says. "My offer's still open. I'll help you, Ari. I'll take you away from here."

The thought makes her stomach roll. Not this again. "Didn't you just have your rut with someone?"

Sardonically, he smirks. "No. I did it alone. Seems there was someone specific on my mind."

She winces and makes a sour face. What is she? Alpha bait?

Paul continues, "If he mated you, being away from him will—"

"Hurt." She knows quite well. It hurts now.

Alpha, come save me.

Immediately, her phone starts buzzing, and she looks for any excuse to answer it. Before she can, Paul says, "But if someone bites over his marks at your next heat, they'll reclaim you. It will make it feel better. It might not ever go away, and I'm not saying I'm going to mate you, but I am saying you have the right to choose someone."

Ben. I choose Ben.

Ari's heart aches and her eyes well with tears.

She wants Ben to bite her. That feeling is immediate and instinctual and real, but it will never be possible. Perhaps that's why, without even thinking about it, she decided to fall into the arms of the next best thing. The one who she can save, as opposed to the one she can't.

She's a horrible, deceitful person.

Poor Caleb.

"I already chose."

Paul pushes a heavy sigh through his nose. "Then maybe you should quit. If not...maybe I will."

She's talking to Niles in the living room—now dotted with her decor—while Caleb finishes cooking. She's jabbering on about their little cruise, showing Niles the millions of pictures she took of them while zealously downing the wine she's been yearning for. A little cheap Zinfandel is all it takes to make his Omega relax into her new home.

Caleb clatters pots and pans around a bit, more annoyed than he should be. Ari came home and her bleeds had started. No pups for him. Not yet anyway. Though he looks forward to trying again. And again. Not for a little while, though. She's grumpy and he has a phantom pain he wasn't expecting. Feeling her emotions is one thing, feeling her body is another. Once he realized he wasn't dying of some internal medical problem, he looked it up. It's another soul-mated thing, proving that, at the very least, she is definitely his perfect match. It makes him want to ram his hand in a drawer and smash all his fingers just to see if it makes her gasp. If Ben is her true soulmate, but Caleb's mated to her, how does it work? Will she feel any of his pain at all? Does she not feel Ben's pain because they're not mated?

And never fucking will be.

He feels a natural sort of curiosity. Ticking up his eyebrows, he takes the edge of a straight bladed knife and presses it against the pad of his thumb, increasing the pressure as he stares at Ari out of the corner of his eye. When he slits through the skin, trying to keep his hiss as quiet as possible, she actually looks at her hand in confusion for a moment before continuing her conversation, absentmindedly rubbing her fingers together while her feelings are tinged with a sudden unease.

Ah. Success.

That's not a trait for normal mated pairs. He is special, just like she said. Not perfect, but he still matters. Suddenly, he can't wait to fuck her. Can they share pleasure, too?

Taking his thumb into his mouth, he sucks the blood off the little slice he carved, minding his own business for a bit. Dinner is done, he just has to plate it. He likes going out of his way to make fancy things, which amuses Ari. His Alpha is screaming *Provide* while her Omega happily shouts *Ramen Noodles*. Sometimes he cooks to perfection and other times he screws it up on purpose just to seem vulnerable. She wrote in her journal that she found it endearing. Tonight is not that kind of night, however. Tonight, he'll make his Omega proud.

"Don't do that," Niles scolds Ari as they join him at the dinner table.

"Do what?" she asks.

"That. That drool thing you're doing."

Caleb preens silently, setting down the last dish. Would it be weird to tell Niles to fuck off because his Omega can drool whenever she wants?

Probably.

To say that his mate eats like an animal isn't a lie. Her cheeks are all filled out and she makes nothing but smacky, slurping sounds.

Caleb's glad he cut up her meat really small. He'll have to add "learning the Heimlich maneuver" to his growing list of things to do to keep up with Ari's needs.

Niles looks at Caleb with sympathy as she runs a finger over the plate to gather some sauce, sucking it outright. "I'm sorry she's like this. I never house-trained her."

"Hush, interloper. I'm smitten."

Niles rolls his eyes. "You say that now but take this thing out in public and your opinion will change."

Ari gives her friend the side-eye but can't fight verbally with her mouth as full as it is. Instead, she kicks him under the table and Niles rams his knee in the process.

Caleb laughs a little. "I don't give a shit about other people. But if they thought she was anything other than perfect, I think I'd have a problem with that." He lifts his eyebrows in Niles's direction with meaning.

Ari swallows, loud and crude on purpose, and gives her friend a triumphant grin before taking a nice swig of wine, her cheeks pinking up in a perfect blush. If Caleb and Ari weren't both having period cramps, he'd try to seduce her tonight. Instead, he's going to feed them both chocolate.

"Ari could learn a little from you; she's always got something to prove." Niles sighs. He gives her sad eyes. "Are they still giving you trouble at work?"

She puts down the huge bite she'd stabbed onto her fork, her mouth hanging open for a split second too long. "I don't want to talk about that."

Niles gives her a sarcastic, patronizing look. One he's likely honed during his years of service.

"Okay, I do want to talk about it." Faster than should be possible, she says, "IThinkIWannaQuit!"

Niles grabs her wrists and Caleb prickles when she grunts. Her friend must have grabbed the bruised one too hard. He's really starting to regret those marks—but he's also in love with them.

Mine.

They'll finish healing soon, anyway, if people would just stop fucking grabbing them.

"But you love your job," Niles says.

"I love the work I do. I don't have to do it there. I don't technically have to do it at all!"

"So, what? You gonna be a housewife? No offense, pumpkin, but you'd suck at being a housewife."

Both Ari and Caleb reply, "Hey!" at the same time in different octaves.

Niles looks at Caleb with wide eyes. "Can she get a job with you?"

Caleb looks at his beautiful bride, trying to push her all the warmth he feels. "Interestingly enough, I already pitched the idea to my boss. I like having her around." He touches her fingers, and the smallest curve of a smile graces her lips. He'll take it. His kitten needs love like plants need water.

"And...?" Niles waves him on, twirling his fingers impatiently.

"An unequivocal no." Caleb sighs, trying to catch Ari's gaze. "Which is why I'm thinking of starting a new practice—one with a pro-bono partner."

Both Ari's emotion and her eyes scream something Caleb can only vaguely translate as the sensation of sunlight.

"What do you think, kitten? Join me and fight for the right?"

"Does that mean you'll only take on cases for the innocent?" she asks, awestruck.

He laughs, a staccato blatt of a thing. "Not if we want to afford to keep the doors open. Besides, innocence is for the court to decide. I'm just there to make sure my client is seen in the best possible light."

"And the other side is seen in the worst," she gripes.

He snorts. "So, you and I are doing the same thing, then. Good to know law school works for everybody."

Caleb waits for his turn to get kicked from under the table. Ari feels pissed enough to give him a good bruise. Hell, half of him wants it, to see if she can feel it, too.

Be a good Alpha, he reminds himself.

Trying a less snarky route this time, he says, "If it makes you feel any better, even the innocent are guilty of something. Just like the guilty aren't without their redeeming moments."

Like me.

Surprisingly, Niles jumps in on Caleb's side. "Things aren't always so black-and-white, Ari. You've got to learn to let the waters get a little muddy once and a while."

"I hate moral ambiguity." She breathes in deeply through her nose and holds it for a minute before letting it out. "It might be possible. MIGHT! I'll think about it. It might just be the wine talking."

"Yes, no more agreements unless you mean them." Caleb leans in and takes her hand, kissing every one of her fingers and placing a slow lick on her wrist, making her giggle while simultaneously freaking out her friend.

"What the hell did I just see?! Audience, people! You have an audience! Mated pairs! Honestly!"

Grinning, Caleb thinks, *I'd have it no other way.*

"I hate moral ambiguity," Ari mutters to herself, clutching a bouquet of roses in her lap. "I hate it, I hate it...so why am I living it?"

"I'm sorry?" the receptionist asks.

Ari sits up straighter than ever, nearly smashing the flowers into her chest. The salmon pink lobby is laughing at her, she knows it is. "Sorry, don't mind me."

It's the same woman from the other day and she gives Ari a sympathetic smile. "Nervous?"

Oh yes. If Caleb knew I was here...

She won't complete that thought. This week has been hard on

him. He lost his first case out of the gate once he got back to work—only his second loss ever, his first being to her—and he'd been filled with fury and self-loathing. At least yesterday he won two back-to-back. His mood skyrocketed then. Not into happiness, but a sort of heady satisfaction. Now he's back to texting her lots of funny things and trying to make plans for the weekend. It makes her guilt spike, but she'd cleared her afternoon for this. She won at court yesterday, too, and this is her reward to herself. If you can call such a thing a reward.

She nods. "I've never met Ben on my own."

The other woman nods sagely. "Just take it at your own pace, dear. We know it's hard to say goodbye."

A creaking hinge startles Ari to the point where she jerks to attention, brain screaming, *The Jig is Up!* but it's only Mr. Canady opening the door and peeking at her.

"Ah, Mrs. Reed?"

"Ari," she corrects, standing up. "Ari Jacobson." When she's met with a confused stare, she clarifies. "I'm keeping my maiden name. I'm a liberal."

He chuckles a little and shakes his head. "Well, that's fine by me. If Caleb's happy, I'm happy."

That filthy guilt grabs Ari's throat and throttles her again. Still, she smiles back. "I'm going to try my very best to be everything he needs."

Because she absolutely is. She's only here because she never got to say her piece to the man who killed her parents. She won't be mean to him—she couldn't, even if she tried—but if she forces herself to acknowledge that no matter how this man smells, he's not for her, it might help her let go of the fantasy she's continually building in her mind. The one where he wakes up.

"Come on, then," Canady waves her in. "We just finished up his calisthenics." When she looks at him funny, he adds, "We have to keep his muscles in use. We do it a few times a day."

"Even now?"

Canady just smiles at her. "Caleb has always wanted the best care for his brother, no matter the cost. It seems that won't change."

It's heartwarming in the most terrible way. Caleb really does love him.

A thorn pokes her as she brings the flowers right up under her chin. Their scent is overpowering, and that is absolutely the point. She's going to hold them the whole time so she can look at Ben as just a man, nothing else. She needs to stave off her urge to breathe him in; things will only go horribly if she does. Clearing her throat, she nods again and follows.

For the second time, she's afraid to step over the threshold, but Mr. Canady enters ahead of her and smiles that gentle, reassuring smile, gesturing to her in welcome and giving her the courage to step in, nearly shivering behind her shield of roses.

The male nurse tries to calm her. "For better or worse, dear, he won't bite you." Which only makes her want to sob.

But I want him to bite me. Mate me. Love me. Alpha, please wake up.

"Just have a seat. You're welcome for as long as you'd like. Will you be able to see yourself out when you're ready?"

She nods, silken petals caressing her nose. "Yeah. Thank you."

"Not a worry. Call if you need anything. We're right outside."

Which is a comfort until Mr. Canady shuts the door behind him, leaving her to deal with whatever comes next all on her own. At first, she just focuses on the red blooms in her hands. She'd been saving up all week for these, skipping lunches. She doesn't mind. Caleb makes her breakfast every day—the seductive power of cornflakes— which is more than she used to eat before. Her lunch money has always been repurposed for other things, anyway. To be able to afford takeout, to be able to get the fancier razors to shave her legs. This bouquet is extravagant. A waste of money.

Except it's not.

It's protection.

Ari doesn't sit. She stares at the man who lays there silently, just as beautiful as she remembers—though how could she have forgotten? He's a slender version of the man she sleeps beside at night. He's still clean-shaven and has the same pattern of moles and freckles. His nose is a little different, though. Caleb has a ridge along the top of his, as if he'd broken it once or something.

Eleven years. Ben has been like this for eleven years. How much money has that cost? Is that why Caleb does what he does, representing anyone and everyone just to be able to keep his brother alive? If so, does that mean Caleb should be forgiven for all the suffering he's caused? The same sort of question applies to his brother. If Ben killed their parents to save Caleb, should he be forgiven, too? But why did he have to hit another car? Why did he have to choose another family to die? Her family. And even with that truth, why does Ari have this deep, aching feeling that she can't live in a world without this man?

She stares at her soulmate, just sitting in this throb of pain—embracing it—and she can feel Caleb's sympathy through their connection, reminding her that he exists. He probably thinks it's another incident at her work. They do blindside her sometimes. Maybe he won't be suspicious, then. She feels him, feels his care, but doesn't want to.

If Caleb was the one who was too weak to deal with his family and too weak to get out from under Sloane's thumb in the first place, forcing Ben to do what he did, can she shift the blame for all this onto him instead?

The fact that it crossed her mind disgusts her. No. Caleb is a victim, doing the best he can to take care of the people he loves, meanwhile Ari's taking advantage, indulging in her sudden obsession. And she'd been so angry at Caleb for coming on too strong when he smelled her. Yet here she stands, willing to give up her morals for a man she's never even truly met. She's a hypocrite.

Enough is enough.

Clutching her flowers tight, refusing to breathe in even an atom of his scent, Ari steps closer—close enough that the crest of her hip touches the rail on the side of Ben's bed. It's all she can do not to put her head on his chest to listen to his heartbeat.

"I can't hate you. I don't know why, I just can't. But this is wrong. I'm not this person. I *refuse* to be this person."

I already belong to someone, and I need to remember that.

Ben's lashes flutter as if he's lost in a dream. His chest fills and his head tips in her direction, letting his black hair spill over the pillow.

Ari's muscles seize. She's frozen.

He moved... Is that supposed to happen?

He breathes in deeply through his nose. Again and again, thick eyebrows knitting together. His plush lips part, starting to form shapes...sighing one deep, resonating word.

"Mate."

Then another.

"*...Mine.*"

He settles back into silence as Ari's knees go weak. A smile curves his lips...a sign that he smells her. He knows her. He belongs to her.

He's waking up for her.

Pulse skyrocketing, terror and hope warring in her chest like beasts, her thoughts consist of one, pounding word.

Run.

So that's exactly what she does. Turning tail, Ari wrenches open the handle and darts out of the room, not minding the looks of any of the others as she bolts, slamming into door after door after door to escape, leaving red rose petals trailing behind her in drips and drops on the carpeted floor.

CHAPTER 11

THE ELEVATOR GOES DOWN

ARI NEEDS TO ESCAPE. She needs to go home. Not Caleb's home. *Her* home. Far and away from any shared space where she'd have to put on a smile and pretend not to feel this. It's all she can do to ride the train and not shatter, but as soon as she huffs up those stairs to her old apartment and lurches into the empty space, she gives in and loses it entirely.

Going into a corner that smells like no one but her, Ari curls up into a ball and lets herself cry. It's as if everything is being pulled from her chest with a rusted chain, leaving a bloodless wound that seeps its poison onto the lonely floor.

Ben called her *Mate*. He whispered, *Mine*.

She'd almost melted into sea glass at his bedside. But Caleb and Mr. Canady said he hadn't even moved in years—over a decade—so how is this possible?! What is she supposed to do? What if her fantasies come true and Ben wakes up? Gets stronger? Yearns for her the way she does him? What if he's only getting better because he smells her and knows they're meant to be? It's so romantic, it's tragic.

If Caleb truly loves his brother, would he allow him to steal Ari away? Or would he chase her until the end of the time, making sure she kept every word of her hastily made promises?

The latter is likely the truth.

She feels an unfortunate loyalty to Caleb. Maybe it's just because he bit her. No, it's definitely because he bit her. But now that she's gotten to know him, she feels a deep affection for the man who mated her, something she may have felt even if she just met him as a human being instead of "her Alpha."

But...is it really affection? Or is it pity?

She cries harder, for Caleb's sake this time. He deserves better than an Omega like her. He deserves to be soulmated. He deserves to be loved. Adored. And she should be grateful to know someone like him. As strong, steadfast, and loyal as him. After all, if not for Caleb's dedication, she'd have never met Ben. She'd have gone through life never having known his scent, and he would have withered away.

Ari snuggles into her dirty carpet. Her apartment is empty. Everything that didn't migrate to Caleb's was either sold or given away, college students sucking up her inventory like living straws and leaving her with nothing by the way of comfort. The lease isn't up yet, so there's two more months of wasting her money here, but right now, she's grateful. This place is another shield, protecting her from the emotional onslaught that comes with being tangled up with the Allein twins.

Her phone dings, and it's only then that she realizes it's been doing so for quite some time. Looking at her home screen, she realizes that she's missed messages from both Caleb and Niles. When she looks at her best friend's texts first—the safer of the two, by far —he's grumpy, telling her that her mate is blowing up his phone looking for her. Caleb has probably been feeling her emotions all day, and here she is, too self-absorbed to bother feeling any of his. Checking in, she feels a sort of anxiousness that she knows she's absolutely responsible for.

With a deep breath, she opens up Caleb's message thread, watching it escalate as she scrolls down, starting with innocuous things like "Are you alright?" to "What can I do?" to "Who do I have to kill?" with not too many shades in between.

Alpha cares about me. Worries about me. He shouldn't be so kind. Not when I'm here, thinking the things I am and doing the things I'm doing.

It occurs to her that she'd never gone back to the office. She has cases she needs to be working on, yet here she is, focused on anything but. Between today, two weeks of heat leave, and constant distractions from her coworkers' malice, she's been completely phoning it in. Her clients deserve better than that. If she can't perform, their whole lives might be ruined. When did she lose her way?

When I decided I would do anything to win against the unstoppable Caleb Reed.

Her fault from the very beginning.

She texts them both back, copy-pasting the message:

> Sorry, working late. I've been slacking and it shows

After a moment, Niles texts back a GIF. One cat, adorable and beady-eyed, spanks another while calling it a Bad Kitten. The manhandled cat squirms and Ari just about doubles over in laughter. The unexpectedness of it hurls her from one extreme to the other, like a pendulum swinging from tick to tock. Leave it to him—though she wouldn't be surprised if Caleb texted her the exact same thing. She'll show it to him later. He'll get a kick out of it.

Instead of meme-ing her, her Alpha sends:

> Good girl. I hope you work this hard when we start our practice together. Though I might be distracted and have you up on my desk more often than not. I don't have to be in rut to want you…and I love the way you taste

She blushes furiously and clamps her legs together. Her bleeds had started and took control of two days of her life with a vengeance while she loudly thanked medical science for the invention of painkillers, but they were blessedly short, ending just as fast as they came. With her body back to normal, Caleb's attention thrills her in the way it always has, though it probably shouldn't anymore.

Alpha wants me. I want my Alpha. Biology.

She feels lonely suddenly. It's sad to be in a space that only smells like her. She misses that rich, leather part of the Allein scent that never mixed into her chemistry. Here, everything smells like the Old Her. Uncomplicated. Boring. Now, for better or for worse, she is...more.

All the corners are dusty and filled with the crumbs of her previous life whereas Caleb's apartment is showroom clean. She can almost picture him with his eyes narrowed and his face pulled into a frown as he tidies up, annoyed that dust bunnies are a thing. She thought all bachelors were supposed to be pigs. After all, Niles is a pig. So is she, if it counts.

After growing up in cold, impersonal foster homes, transactional at best, Ari finds she likes being taken care of. Great apartment, (mostly) amazing food, more attention than she could ever ask for, a warm body to hold her at night, nicknames that belong to her and her alone, and a nest she made all by herself; one her Alpha rolls in periodically with a grin on his face and a twinkle in his eye.

Suddenly, she wants to go home to her...not mate...but close enough to ache for. Close enough to be irreplaceable. To make her heart swell with tenderness. And when she goes to him, she will try to be a good Omega.

First, though, she has a job to do.

It's a ratty kind of book. The kind that's been loved for too long with crinkly pages from either silently shed tears, spilled water, or her unfortunate attempts at watercolor paintings. The journal's hard cover is stained with this or that or God knows what. Still, it's perfect

just the way it is and smells like Ari when Caleb first met her. Intoxicating.

He flips the journal pages back and forth, scouring Ari's private
little dreamworld. She hadn't bothered to give this gem a new home
yet, leaving it in her leftover boxes after use, but it's only a matter of
time until Caleb's pawing embeds his scent, leaving it very obvious
he's been misbehaving. He'll probably need to put some of her other
things away "just to help out and be nice" before she comes home.
That should explain away his stink. For it to be convincing, he'll have
to fucking scrub himself over each and every trinket, leaving as many
traces behind as he possibly can. It will be tedious, skin-scraping
work, but it's a sacrifice he's more than willing to make for access to
this holy grail of information.

Caleb can only read Ari's emotions, not her actual thoughts, so
his curiosity over her inner workings remains unsated. This small,
unfinished novel of her mind's wanderings goes a long way to fill
that greedy void, though he knows he'll never get enough.

He gleans what he can from every mark and musing. Her watercolors are always unintentionally drippy flowers with colors that
blend together wrong, muddy and undefinable. Some pages sport
little dried circles where her tears blurred the ink, dappling the para-
graphs where she confesses her insecurities, fears, and loneliness.
Perhaps unsurprisingly, most of her angry rants tend to be pointed at
men. Her attitude toward those who even dare to flirt with her is
perfectly stubborn and prudish...yet Caleb is still irrationally
aggrieved that she'd ever even known any men before she met him.

Mine.

The passages he's narrowed in on now are about her fantasies.
Ones where she isn't lonely. Ones where she has a loved one...or the
perfect lover. She even tried writing her own sex scene just like the
smutty books he's been weaving his way through, skimming for the
good parts. He reads aloud to no one, still holding on to a paranoid
fear of silence, and wishes she could hear the needy tone in his voice
as he shares her seductive imaginings with the crows on his small

balcony outside. Maybe this weekend he'll recite some of the racier parts of one of her favorite romances to her. And then, of course, act it out, word for word for thrusting word.

Ari's cute, bubbly writing enthralls Caleb as he reads. "...and my dark-haired knight would kneel like he worshiped me. Like I was his queen. Like I was a goddess.'"

Ohhh, kitten, you absolutely are. All that and more.

He flips to the next page, able to smell her desire on every ivory line. "'He would lick me... not in just the sacred places. In the ones nobody ever touches. My ankles. The backs of my knees. Just above the curve of my rear where those two sacral indents lie.'"

Sweetheart, I'll lick you anywhere you want.

His computer pings and he tears himself away from her wet dreams. Looking at the screen, her social media profiles pages are up, side-by-side. She copy-pastes the same message across platforms, whining. "I hate being a lawyer sometimes! Why do I have to work so late!"

Ping, ping, ping. Facebook then Twitter then Tumblr, searching for the attention of the masses and little, meaningless red hearts.

He snorts. "Working, my ass, kitten. Do your job and come home."

None of her accounts are locked down and that makes haunting her nice and easy. For a moment, he toys with the idea of making a fake account and friending/following her to interact in another way. Maybe he'd learn even more secrets if he was a faceless, electronic friend. Maybe she'd complain to this unknown e-person about her life. About him. It would help him self-correct without her ever having to know.

She seems to only post pictures of flowers or birds on Instagram. Things you find around the city. Dandelions and skrag grass poking up through concrete sidewalks. Pigeons and sparrows. She has a few pictures aimed at the sky, accidentally capturing bats instead of birds, though it's adorable that she can't tell the difference. Maybe he'll have to teach her how to tell a predator from a scavenger. He is, after all, the "experienced one."

Another *ping* goes out, Twitter only. A GIF that has a heavy man slamming his fists on a desk, screaming, "I NEED SLEEP" in fat, white letters. Caleb smirks.

"All right. That one's funny."

He's exhausted, too...but also something else. Aroused. The thought of licking her, just like in her story, has woken his body up and made every inch of his skin pay attention. He's gone without sex for years at a time, but lately he feels like a teenager, constantly palming his pants for any thrill he can get. He'd give up eons of sleep to be touched by her again. He and Ari haven't done anything but share a few kisses since her heat ended, but his Alpha is losing its patience. His mind hammers for him to *Breed*. To fill her flat belly with his pups. Little babies he can dote on together with the love of his life.

Work keeps them apart during the day and it makes his heart ache. Especially with how she suffers. He wants to run to her office and prowl around her desk, snarling at anyone who dares approach. When she comes home at night, it's like a knot in his chest relaxes, but she's away longer than normal tonight and he's reaching his limit.

Does she miss him, too? Can she feel this? Or has Ben fucked it all up?

He doesn't want to think about Ben.

Instead, he focuses on missing her. His glands throb as bad as his loins do. He knows she senses him when he's like this at least, and a mischievous thought comes over him.

What would she do if she caught me at home with my hand between my legs, pumping my fist, and sighing her name? I could make my voice low and heavy and perfect, I know I could. Just the right amount of desperate.

That seems like something out of one of her books. Though often it's vice versa and the girl is caught panting and moaning her high-pitched want as she slicks up her bed with sweetness.

God, if I found her like that, I'd pounce so fucking hard her head would spin.

"Come home, kitten," he groans. "Your mate is hungry for you."

Ari is leaning over her case files when her glands begin to throb. It feels distant, but it's there. Not just her mating bites, either. The ones at her pulse points and between her legs are also clambering for attention. Desire warms her belly, and she has to try hard to gather the threads of her thoughts, which are being dragged away and spooled for safekeeping.

She's alone in the building. Her desk light is on, but the rest of the office is semi-dark, waiting for her to leave and set the security alarm on her way out. The moon hangs bright tonight and Ari wonders if it's pulling at her somehow. Does Caleb feel this?

As if on command, her phone lights up with a message.

> Can I touch myself while I think about you?

Her mouth drops open, and she looks around, back and forth, blushing from collar to crown. Somehow this is more shocking than when he'd teased about putting her on his desk earlier. More scandalous. Another comes through.

> Will you touch yourself while you think of me?

Her slick starts to gather. She can't help it. She's no stranger to masturbation, but this wouldn't be just that. It would be the start of something with meaning instead of a means to an end.

> I want to feel you again, kitten. I want to be
> inside you

Biting her lip, she groans, her body thrumming as she feels the lust of the man who mated her.

> You felt so good wrapped around me,
> sweetheart. And I made you feel good, too. I
> still can. Again, and again

She can't do this. Never mind her conflict, she's at work. She has to put a stop to this. Taking a deep breath, she dares to type back:

> If you're really touching yourself, you
> shouldn't be able to type so fast

There.

She adds a winky face for good measure.

That should cool things off. Feeling his amusement, silence follows, and she considers it a job well done...but then that ache grows deeper. Hungrier. She's wet. So very wet. She'll have to wipe down her leather seat—standard issue for Omegas because of times like these. Everyone was tired of replacing the ruined office chairs.

A voice message pops up this time. One she's dying to click on, though simultaneously afraid of. Making sure she's alone once more, she clicks the PLAY button and presses the phone up to her ear.

Caleb's voice is deep. Dark. Resonant. It's like he's right next to her, whispering. "How about like this, then? I only need one hand, sweetheart. I can show you someday if you want. Show you how I pretend you're on top of me..."

He gasps softly and Ari's eyes slip closed. She can hear a sound. Something like skin slapping skin. He really is touching himself. "God," she says out loud, listening to a moment of nothing but his heavy breathing and his fisting.

"If you were here, kitten, I'd want you to kneel over my face. I'd do this while I tasted you. You're so...*so* sweet."

He's outright moaning little sounds now. Drip and drops of sighs and ahs and something that sounds like her name.

"I swear, Alpha will be so good to you. Keep you happy. Keep you satisfied. Come home, baby girl. Come home and let me fuck you."

The audio file ends, and her brain begs her to play it again from the beginning, that space between her legs hot and messy with desire. Her nipples are tightly furled under her silky camisole and her light bra does nothing to shield them from its casual caress. Her slick has ruined her. There's no way she can ride the subway like this. She wants to go home, but she can't. Embarrassed but honest, she texts back the filthiest thing.

> I can't. I've soaked through my skirt, so I can't ride the train

It's a long walk, and they'll be calmed down by the time she gets home, she's sure of it. Maybe that's for the best. But another voice message pops up.

"You're wet for me, kitten? Hmm... My Omega likes noises, doesn't she? Stay there. I'm coming. And then, Ari, I'm *coming*. In front of you. Whether you participate or not."

Frantic, she texts him back.

> But I'm at the office!

Another voice message pops up in short order. "Stay, Omega. Alpha's coming for you. I'll make all the noises you want."

Caleb's never driven so haphazardly in his entire life. Stop signs? What stop signs? It's dark enough that he'll see any headlights coming his way, though it would be ironic if another car accident robbed his Ari of something she wants. That's the only thought keeping him driving like a sane person.

He made her wet. Wet for him. Even now, after everything. She can't claim "heat" this time; all she can do is be honest. Even if she just watches him come into his hand, it will be enough to see that sexy face of hers, the one he remembers so well from such a short time ago. If she's nice, maybe she'll let him come on her belly. Her tits. Maybe in her mouth.

"Fuck." He palms his erection through his jeans, too stiff and uncomfortable for his size, constricting him like a scratchy weight over his cock.

When he hits a red light, he unbuttons himself for comfort, though the heat of his blood keeps him pumped up to a mostly concealed half-mast. As soon as the light turns green, his car peels out, leaving stuttered tire tracks on the asphalt. Caleb, in his current state of mind, thinks the road fucking deserved it, and decides to repeat the action as often as possible, so long as it gets him to her faster.

He's never been more pleased about his stalking than he is right now, knowing exactly where her office is and screeching to a halt outside. No need to finagle his way through parallel parking; it's too late at night and the streets are all but empty, which is a relief, because right now he'd happily park in the fire lane.

Like a good girl, she's waiting in the vestibule behind glass doors with wide eyes, blinking at him. She looks so innocent. He wants to strip off every scrap of his clothing and rub himself all over her, fingers shoved deep inside while he made sure she still smelled like him. He'd bite her all over again, and in even more places this time. All those places she said she was untouched.

When she opens up the door, she stammers, "You...you'd need a badge to get in, so I just—"

And he's on her in a moment, holding her cheeks and tilting her head up, forcing her mouth open with his tongue. The noises she makes are like sweet death and all he knows is that he needs her.

Mine, he begs the universe. *Please let her stay mine.*

He stumbles them backward, holding her up so they don't

outright cascade to the floor. Right around the time he hears the heavy latch of the front security lock, she hits the wall behind her with a small *thump*. Nuzzling in to suck her mating gland, he makes her cry out in pleasure before seeing elevator doors to either side of them.

Perfect.

He rams the call button and cages her, owning her mouth and swallowing her cries as he fists her hair. When the car dings open, all he needs to do is pivot them inside, bumping himself up against the elevator's interior as she spins around him, balancing herself with one leg straddling each side of his left thigh. As soon as the door slips shut in its innocence, Caleb rucks up her skirt halfway and pulls her hips down, grinding her sweet sex over him and listening to her gasp against his mouth. He shifts her back and forth, making her ride against him with cute squeaks while his jeans soak through immediately with her slick.

"So pretty," he whispers against her. "So wet for me, sweetheart. I wanna put my mouth on you and suck you dry."

He can actually feel her fucking clench, and the damp spot on his pants widens considerably. "Fuck, fuck, fuck, pretty kitten. Watch me. Watch me touch myself for you."

He licks her gland again, sending shivers through her as he wrenches his pants down just enough to unearth himself. He runs the tips of his fingers over his length and leans back from her, looking down and silently begging her to follow his gaze. Precum has gathered on his head, and he swipes it around with the pad of his thumb. Lifting it, he wants to smear himself along her pretty mouth but decides to take it himself at the last minute, wrapping his lips around and sucking on his own salty tang. When she bares her teeth in what can only be jealousy, wanting his taste by instinct, he knows he has her full attention. Still he whispers, "Watch me."

He closes his eyes and feels his own pleasure, letting his head sink back against the mirrored wall of the elevator with a well-staged hum of desire, pumping his hand. He can't get all the way to the bottom as he likes, but that will make it take longer. Maybe it will entice her to help him.

He wants to command her. He wants to fucking force her again. He wants to be rough and mean, press her against the reflective glass and rail her from behind while still watching her face as she falls apart. He wants to put handprints and scratches on her, knowing he'd lap up her blood like sugar off a strawberry. Instead, he's a good Alpha. He becomes what she imagines in her wildest dreams.

"God, I want to feel you, Ari. Can I pretend my hand is you? Only" —he lets his words stutter—"th-that will never be good enough. Nothing feels like you. You were so warm, wrapped around me like you were made for me."

And you were, kitten. You absolutely were.

She whimpers and presses down on his thigh of her own volition, rocking her hips and grinding her panty-covered clit over his tensed muscle. He feels her slick run around to the back of his knee in heated drips and hisses in a breath.

"Fuck, I want you, pretty girl." She's half-lidded, lips red like cherries, and she hangs on his every word. "You and your maple syrup scent. Everything wholesome and sweet in life. I can get lost in your smell. Your taste."

She kisses him all on her own and he releases himself to tangle his hands in her hair once more, pulling her close as he lifts his leg to make her ride harder. She whimpers, and his lust is molten.

"Omega, I want you to love me." The utter truth. "I want it so bad. I need you, sweetheart." He's going to melt. Combust. Glow incandescent. Nibbling her lip just a tad too hard, he growls his inner Alpha's words.

"Mate..." and *"...Mine."*

She comes with a sharp cry, her pleasure rocketing through him in a wave that tips him over the edge. Just as he'd hoped, they're sharing their pleasure...and it's overwhelming. The ecstasy of it ricochets back and forth between them until it becomes too much to bear and her emotions tip into something else, tears sliding over her cheeks as her breath stutters in sounds of rapture—just like she did during her heat. He remembers her heat. He wants that again and again, forever.

He's taken over by adoration as he shushes her, holding her tightly while the sense of satisfaction floats him above it all, euphoria owning all his senses as he revels in the slippery slide between them.

It smells like home.

This is progress. This is a step in the right direction. He can make this happen again, he's sure of it. After all, all he has to do is plan carefully, learn her fantasies...and be anything other than his true self.

CHAPTER 12
THE SCENT OF YOU

GOD HELP HER, Ari had actually almost screamed "Ben" when she came.

Caleb kisses her tears and licks her glands over and over, as though he loves them. Correcting herself, she whispers his name into the crook of his neck, smelling his shampoo and lapping at his mating bites, one then the other, reminding herself that she made them. His pleasure is enthralling. It makes her feel powerful. Special. Singular. He pushes his happiness to her in a sweet caress against her mind and she lets herself just feel it.

Wrapping her arms around his shoulders, she shifts, feeling the sticky mess they left between them. They need to get cleaned up, but... "I don't want to go home in the car." It comes out pathetic and childish and he chuckles at her.

"I'll do ten miles an hour if that's what you want. I'll stop at yellow lights. I'll slow down at all the crosswalks."

She scoffs against his collarbone, her head leaning down as the aftershocks still thrum between her legs. "That will take forever."

He cinches his arms around her waist and nuzzles. "Worth it." Pulling away, he looks at her with a reverence she wouldn't have thought possible, the amber brown of his irises warm in the yellow light above them. "Let me take you home, gorgeous."

She wants to fall in love with him. In this moment, she truly does.

Nodding, she steps away, but when the cool air hits her soggy wetness—"Eeeeyuck!" It's everywhere! She should be ashamed of herself...for so many reasons.

Caleb gets on his knees and licks a rivulet of slick from her leg with a groan, still hungry for her. Her breath hitches as he moves his way up slowly, his plush mouth a perfect pink against her skin. "It's a shame I can't clean you properly," he murmurs.

"In the shower?" she asks, breathy and amused.

He looks devilish. "With my tongue."

Her body clenches once more around nothing and she hates that empty feeling. Feeling brave, she says, "No one said we had to leave yet."

"No, they didn't." His smile is bliss. "This place already smells like us. Let's claim it as our own. Our private little world, locked away, gilded with gold and mirrors." He pushes her skirt up over her hips and suckles at her ruined underwear, making her vision white out as his purr vibrates along her seam. "Tell me what you need. I'll take you any way you want. I'll fucking worship you, kitten."

It sends a hot wave up her body, seducing her. It's like a dream come true. How is he so perfect?

This time, she's a good girl. This time, she makes herself whisper:

"Caleb..."

***

"Another case lost, my boy. How the mighty have fallen."

Sloane is pissed, no matter how flat his expression is. His pale blue eyes focus in, and the old man's pupils become slits of anger.

Caleb defends himself with an angry growl. "I came off my rut and immediately took back all my cases. I even took on something I'd never touched before at your request."

"Yes. Another spectacular loss."

Standing, Caleb hunches forward to lean on the dark leather chair that sits across from Sloane's desk, his shoulder blades reared back in a tangible threat. "I've only been back for six days, and I've won two out of four. That's not nothi—"

"Tell that to your suffering clients. I'm sure they'll be very understanding."

"We already made bail and filed an appeal in both cases, and I'm not charging for the extra time. Take it from my pay."

Sloane hmms. "Perhaps I should lessen your caseload?"

It's not out of kindness. It's an insult. And it's absolutely intended to be.

Caleb prickles. He's been banking money for years, anything that doesn't go to Ben's care, but with his brother holding on for an indefinite amount of time and Caleb unwilling to force a goodbye, he can't afford to lighten his load.

Ari is a distraction.

Ari is *the best* distraction.

"I'll do better." Caleb's hands clench and he watches his knuckles turn white, reminding him of another time Sloane had humiliated him in this very room.

I need that money to build my own practice. I need that practice to make Ari work for me. I need her to work for me, so I control every cent she earns. If I control her money, she can't leave. And she can't leave because I'll go insane.

"I may be mated now, but that doesn't mean I'm incompe—"

"Yes, you are. The woman who bested you put you into rut, you lost control, and you bit her. A woman you barely know. And yet you say *soulmated.* I didn't know you believed in such stupid things."

Caleb wants to throw the chair through the wall. Through the window. Through this fucking wraith's face.

"Look at you," Sloane continues. "You're losing cases and more than willing to lose interest in your work. The receptionist tells me you go home at six now, is that right? Where's your commitment?"

I save it for my wife.

Marriage certificate is signed and sealed. She's his on paper as much as she is in teeth marks.

Sloane's evil lips tip up into the hint of a smile. "With your enthusiasm for your home life, it would be no surprise if she was already taken with pups."

Not yet, but soon.

It'll be nice to breed her when she's willing. Maybe it will make better babies. Let her stand in the courtroom, her womb a perfect curve as she defends the self-proclaimed innocent. It's an intoxicating thought. One that makes Caleb thrilled, until the face of his mentor sinks into disdain.

"You smell domesticated. A simpering Alpha instead of the man I molded into greatness. Are you capable of anything, child? Or will you be a disappointment your entire life?"

It hurts more than it should. Still, Caleb needs to be strong—now more than ever. He grins in a dangerous way. "I suppose only time will tell."

Sloane's voice rumbles in thought for a moment before he returns Caleb's expression, tooth by vicious tooth. "Partnership is off the table."

Caleb's eyes go wide with shock. He's made other plans now, but he's been fucking groomed for this! Withstood horrible, terrible, evil things for this!

"Any male who's expecting, even a Beta, can only become more and more distracted as their female grows wide."

For the umpteenth time in his life, Sloane has turned something sacred into something he can use to punish him. If Caleb wants his wife's neck in a noose, it's only because he's been strangled so long, he knows nothing else.

Suddenly, stubbornly, Caleb refuses to give him this. "I'd imagine so. The thought of her doting on our family as I keep her filled with my seed is delicious. God knows she likes taking it."

Let his fucking mentor eat that sentiment.

Sloane's scent transitions from anger to disgust. The best part is that Caleb would have normally pitched a fit about now. Tossed shit around. Raised his voice and pointed. Made useless threats to anyone who wasn't his mentor. Sloane had loved that behavior in him, yet here he is—furious, but reigning it in. His Omega has worked wonders on him.

"Perhaps I should castrate you to keep you focused," Sloane challenges, raising an eyebrow.

Caleb only smirks at the taunt. "Try it and I'll cut you in fucking half."

I hope you have cancer. Caleb throws that thought at his mentor with all his might. *I want you to suffer and cough and shrink into hollow skin. I want them to have to take out pieces of you that will never grow back.*

Sloane's nostrils flare, catching his malicious scent no doubt, and finally smiles honestly. "At least you still have some fire in your belly." He juts his chin toward the door. "Out. And Reed? I have no use for tamed Alphas. One more loss, and you can keep walking."

Fair enough.

Ari's hands are folded in her lap as she stares at them, hunched over and already completely, preemptively chastised, making herself small. Tension frazzles her nerves so hard, even her hair hurts, pulled into a severe ponytail to hide the fact that she hadn't washed it last night.

Udesh Patnaik's office faces other glass buildings versus the general staff's view of the street. Ari's never been sure which is better. All she knows is the open floor gets the midday summer sun, which the AC can't always handle, whereas the offices tend to freeze in the winter. Out of the two options, she'd rather fry.

Patnaik is an off-putting man on most days, but he tends to see the bigger picture. How all the pieces fit together. People's motivations and personal levers. From that perspective, he's good at his job. He'll toss Ari scraps—less than she's worth by far—but enough to keep her fed and make her stay. He looks out the window with his thick, almost hairless arms crossed behind him, his back expanding and contracting in slow breaths as the moment drags.

"HR told me to speak with you. Seems your scent...and your Alpha's...had all but ruined the elevator this morning. I guess working on the weekend has its perks."

Actually, it was Friday, but who's counting?

Me. I'm counting.

My orgasms specifically.

"I'm sure you noticed that it was bleached out before you rode up today. Made some fond memories, did you?"

Ari simmers with shame, knowing a good number of people now have a very clear idea of what she does with the man who mated her. And every single moment of it was intentional this time. He made her want it. Want *him*. She has no excuses anymore.

Patnaik sits down with a sigh. "Many here are concerned about you. They know how much you hated the very idea of Caleb Reed, yet you came back with as many bites as..."

A whore is what he doesn't say. Women of the night used to let their customers bite anything and everything that wasn't their neck, and the torn rings Caleb left on Ari's wrists are still doing their job and getting her into trouble. With the way he nuzzles those little circles, though, she can't help but have a soft spot for them. Even so, she pulls down her cuffs again, wearing long sleeves in summer if only to stave off the nasty looks.

"We all know he took advantage of you, Ari. Say the word and we'll do everything we can to stand by you."

She hates this. She hates every moment of this. Setting her jaw but refusing to look her boss in the eyes, she says, "You don't understand. I bit him. Twice. And I bit him first."

A little fib to sway the jury.

She finally gathers the courage to glare at her boss, but the man only looks back, an unreadable expression on his heavily jowled face. Ari presses on, putting herself in Caleb's shoes and letting his words fall from her mouth. "When you know, you know. What's the point of standing on ceremony if you want to be claimed? We're soulmated." She paints a grin on her face, knowing how untrue that statement is. "And you should see Caleb's bites. I promise you, they outnumber mine."

Patnaik seems to ease a bit. Picking up a pen, he taps it on his desk a little, snorting a laugh. "Listen to you protecting him. You're a good Omega, Ari... But you need to focus on your work. You haven't been performing poorly per se, so I'm not going to reprimand you for that, but normally I'd fire someone for this sort of inappropriate office behavior."

"Why aren't you?"

His face twists into something sardonic. "Paul de Santos just gave his notice this morning. I've got two weeks of him wrapping up files, and then I'm short-staffed. Seems the elevator thing was the last straw for him. You know how much he hates Reed. Sorry, *your Alpha.*"

"My soulmate," she corrects quietly, the lie feeling wrong on her tongue this time. She scrubs a hand over her face, trying to keep a hold on her composure.

"You don't have to hide it. I know it can be hard for pairs like you to be apart."

"Can it?" she asks. Is that why she lost herself in sex this weekend? Maybe she needed distractions to avoid thinking about Ben. The truth is she wants to see him right now. Wash these lies out of her mouth. See her true soulmate face-to-face one last time...before she lets him go.

Patnaik chuckles. "You haven't done your research, have you?

You might want to educate yourself. Things are more interesting than they are for regular mated pairs. Do you know anyone else who's soulmated?"

She shakes her head, shrugging as if it didn't matter. The closest thing she's aware of is the infamous Allein parents. You know, the ones who made Caleb so miserable Ben killed them.

She hates her life.

Patnaik tries to be kind. "It will be all right, Ari. I can be lenient so long as you stay professional. Do you think you caught his seed?"

Everything about her turns red. "I...I don't think so, sir. Not yet."

He nods. "Just so you know, we have a leave policy for new mothers no matter what their designation is—though it's a little longer for Omegas. Once you give birth, you take time off with a portion of your pay, just like heat-leave. It will give you time to bond with your pups."

That's an amazing workplace benefit, something Caleb could never offer if he started his own firm. Knowing how badly he wants children, how could she leave this place now?

She smiles softly. "Do you have your own?"

"Me?" Patnaik asks. "Of course! Don't let my looks fool you. I was a strong Alpha, too, once. My Omega just makes food that sticks to me like slabs."

"Well, it's good I can't cook then."

They share an honest chuckle. Dismissing her with pleasantries, her boss holds out his wrist, knowing she likes to casually mark those she meets. He doesn't flinch at her bites or look at her as if she's anything less than what she is: a strong woman who's been put in a rare circumstance. It makes her more eager to rub their minor glands together, and she nudges him with both wrists in amiable camaraderie. It will also mute Caleb's scent on her before she goes to see Ben. She needs to say her piece. Then say goodbye.

· · ·

Is it bad that everyone recognizes her? Will the receptionist tell Caleb that she came here? Will Mr. Canady? Ari wonders if Caleb still visits his brother after that initial fiasco...or more importantly, *when* he does it.

Please don't let it be during lunch breaks.

Her new husband had popped out for a few hours over the weekend; is this where he went? Is he telling his silent brother all about her quirks or is he avoiding the topic completely? She's not sure which she'd prefer. Both are upsetting for different reasons.

Ari is downright wary as she clutches a new bouquet of roses, shuffling down the now-familiar hallway by herself. Standing in the doorway, she shoves her flowers toward her face and walks in, immediately seeing Ben's chest fill as he takes a deep breath, perhaps tasting her in the air.

Alpha likes us. Alpha wants us. Alpha, please wake up.

No. No, that's not what she's here for.

"Hullo, Mrs. Ari!"

Ari squawks and literally jumps in the air, whipping around to find Mr. Canady, hands up in defense, but with a huge smile on his face. "Nice to see you, too."

Hoist by my own petard! Caught red-handed! You'll never take me alive! A million cliches go through Ari's mind at a rolling boil.

"I'm so glad to see you," the older man says with a grin, clapping his hands together. "I haven't called Caleb to tell him the improvements, as I didn't want to get his hopes up, but I think it needs to be said at this point!"

"What?"

Canady floats over to Ben's bed and shakes the metal safety rail a bit with a foolish giggle. "He's breathing well, keeping his oxygen level up on his own, aaaaaand his heartbeat is stronger. We're even getting some moderate hints of...wait for iiiiiiiit...*brain activity!*"

"What?" she repeats, breathless. It's like a snake just coiled tight around her chest.

"I think the visits from both of you must be keeping him strong.

Making sure he doesn't give up. Or maybe he's just a ladies' man." Canady ticks his eyebrows up suggestively.

"What?" Ari asks again, a blathering idiot at this point.

He laughs at her. "Just keep talking to him. They say people in a coma can hear you. Tell him about work. About the sky. Who knows! So long as he hears your voice."

Mr. Canady shuffles in a happy, dancing circle around her. "One sec and I'll give you your privacy." With a quick move, he ducks by Ben and adjusts the bag for his IV fluids, changing out for a new one. After that, he tosses her a wink. "I like your flowers, by the way. Pretty."

When he shuts the door behind himself, Ari stares at it for a minute, squinting as if it's the only way to hold in her eyeballs.

What am I supposed to say? "I fell immediately in love with you against my better judgment, I'm now painfully obsessed with you, so please for the love of God don't die, but also don't come anywhere near me."

Seems like a moot point, considering. Ari grinds her teeth, cursing herself in true Caleb-language, all the swears she has in her vocabulary plus the thesaurus for good measure. What the hell did she come here for again?

Oh. Right.

She spins on her heels, her bouquet a foolish defense as she wields it like a paper fan. If she accidentally flamencos, she may drop dead of shame. Firm, just as firm as she was with Patnaik, Ari says, "Your brother mated me."

She swears she can see Ben's nostrils flare but refuses to breathe him in to get a sense of his reaction. Wanting to hide behind the soft petals, she buries her face and keeps her mouth moving. "He showed me your letter. Did you know that...that you didn't just kill your parents? You killed mine, too."

Ben outright twitches this time. His fingers jerk and Ari's heart revs fast enough to get a ticket. Or a coronary. Maybe both.

She clears her throat, ignoring his tic and pressing on. "I don't really know if you should be forgiven for what you've done, but everyone deserves a chance. If you wake up, I...I won't pursue any legal action against you. At this point, the statute of limitations has run out anyway."

She needs to put herself back there. Back in that dark place where her world fell apart. Back in a place where Ben wasn't her soulmate. She's been waiting almost half her life to say this. "I was only fourteen when it happened. I lost everything. My family. My home. My friends. I expected an arrest. A confrontation. A trial. I wanted to meet you, look you in the eyes, and *spit* on you. None of that ever happened. I never knew who you were...

"You're the reason I studied law at first. I wanted to find you and help whoever my lawyer was put you away for good...but as I progressed, I met people who were sad about the mistakes they'd made. Or those who didn't mean to make a mistake in the first place. My heart went out to them, and with more than just sympathy. I wanted them to heal. I felt like I could save them if they were truly sorry. I could forgive them. Absolve them.

"Would you be sorry, too, Ben? Sorry for hurting me? I want to forgive you, then walk away...and never come back."

His chest rises and falls more quickly, his mouth pulling into a pained frown and his eyebrows drawing together. Equipment beeps erratically, setting off quiet alarms while Ari freezes. Did she do this?

Mr. Canady opens the door in a rush with his eyebrows knit as he flies to Ben's bedside. Confused, the male nurse fingers Ben's pulse and checks his chest monitors before snapping his gaze up at Ari. "You're an Omega, right?" When she stares at him, he gestures at himself curtly. "I'm a Beta. It's hard to tell. But if you're with Caleb, then I'm guessing you are."

She nods.

"With his recent progress, I don't want to use sedatives. I need you to calm him."

Ari's heart plummets. That means she has to rub her scent on him. Canady tips Ben's head to the side, revealing his mating gland, not seeing any problem with it. It's okay to soothe someone platonically that way, but only with your wrists and only between families. She's kind of his family...but...

"Ari, hurry."

She takes a deep breath, holds it, and puts down her roses on the little table at Ben's bedside. Despite the exposed gland on Ben's neck, she tries the easy way first. Picking up his wrist, she slides hers over his, slow and lingering—so much more than friendly. Ben gasps out loud, startling both of them and making Ari breathe again, taking him in.

Leather, ash, sugar.

Immediately she wants to cling to him. Lay beside him and stay, even if he can never speak to her.

Mate. Mine.

Both of their pulses double-time and Canady outright panics. Like a stupid Beta, he gestures at Ben's mating gland again, seeing her Omega influence as just an arcane parlor trick, not knowing this would be her first connection to her true mate. A betrayal to the man she'd spent all weekend making love to.

"Here, Ari. Mark him here!"

It's so intimate. She's going to burst into tears. Leaning over his bed rail, she wraps her arm around him and places her wrist against his neck. "Easy, Alpha," she says, voice trembling.

My Alpha.

"Shh. Be calm. Be still. Hush now, Ben. You can do it."

His face relaxes and turns toward her once more, his expression lost and searching behind closed eyes. His hand tries to lift, drops, and his vitals start to even out again.

Canady claps his hands in victory. "Did you see that?! Did you *see* that?!?" He jumps and practically clicks his heels while Ari still leans too close, inches away from kissing the man of her dreams. She's going to break her own rules. All of them, right here, right now.

Maybe he knows I'm his. Maybe he thinks I'm worth waking up for.

"Maybe Ben can smell his brother on you and knows you're his family," Canady says, cooling her ardor as if she'd been dipped in liquid nitrogen. Her chest hurts. She wants to breathe, needs to breathe, but can't breathe. She's going to faint, but the happy male in front of her is too elated to notice. His grin is eight million miles wide. "I'll go call Caleb right now! I know he—"

"No, it's all right. I'll tell him." Ari pulls back from Ben's bed, realizing that Caleb will find out she's been here, though she can't bring herself to care just now.

"Oh, I wish I could be there when he hears the news!" Canady squeals. "He's going to be so happy! If Ben wakes up, I'll call immediately! In the meantime, I'll order a neurologist. If Ben comes to, he'll need a litany of things, Mrs. Ari. You and Caleb will have to be prepared. Ben isn't strong, and we don't know what this dormant period has done to him. He may not be who he once was, and he may need a lot of care. Physical therapy. Occupational. Speech. He may not be able to eat on his own..."

Still, Canady's eyes are glittering, and a tear falls down. He swipes at it, his smile wobbly. "I'm sorry. It's just that I've watched over him for so many years, I'd lost all hope. Forgive me. As hard as it might be, I want to see him wake up!"

"Me too."

But does she? Yes. No. What's worse? A sleeping prince or an eternally broken one?

"It will be expensive, Mrs. Ari. You need to prepare Caleb. Perhaps Mr. Sloane can help, but this will be far above and beyond the cost of his current care."

That's it, then. It's decided. Caleb can't quit his job, and neither can she. This is no time to take a risk when the stakes are so high. People at her job will settle down so long as she stays professional and competent. If Caleb's dealt with that monster Sloane for this long, he can just keep dealing. More than anything, she just wants to see what happens when Ben wakes up. And not just for her sake. For Caleb's, too.

At least, that's what she tells herself.

CHAPTER 13

DON'T LIFT THE VEIL

"THANK YOU, Mr. Ciel, I think we have a good case."

Ari reaches out her hand to the older gentleman sitting across the conference table, who still seems wary and exhausted, rubbing his wet eyes. A thin, rattail braid hangs over his shoulder and he fiddles with it endlessly, already looking defeated. "We do?"

"We do. And thank you for coming to me. I know veterans often—"

"No," he interrupts her. "No, I've heard great things about you. I'm lucky to have you." When he stands and clasps onto her open palm, Ari reaches up to slide their wrists together.

The man's wife stands up to take her hand as well. "Thank you, Miss Jacobson."

"*Mrs.* Jacobson," she corrects with a smile, rubbing her minor scent gland against the woman as well. "Don't worry. I strongly believe the evidence is on our side."

A tentative smile ekes out on her new client's face, stretching his lips thin—maybe more polite than earnest, but Ari will make a believer out of him yet. Him and his wife. She feels good about this one. Escorting them out, she drops them at reception and introduces them to the receptionist, setting up their next conversation and rubbing her wrist casually on her colleague as well, thanking her for her hard work. This one earns Ari a look of confusion from all parties involved.

Damn it. Too obvious.

Ari has been rubbing herself on anyone and everyone she's come in contact with today, being way too friendly. It probably looks like she's overcompensating and trying to get back into everyone's good graces—which would be a little desperate of her—but Ari can't really care about that right now. What she does care about is dulling what's left of Ben's scent before she goes home to Caleb.

Getting back to her desk, she sees several of his to-be-expected text messages waiting for her. Her gut churns. It's not gurgling or making her run to the bathroom, so it's definitely not the Chinese food she snagged on the way back to the office (though maybe she is allergic to MSG...), it's the feeling that she's betrayed the man who mated her. Her husband. Her lover. The one who tries so hard and would be so wonderful if only he smelled just a little bit different.

More and more, she feels like a bad person. Part of it is for wanting Ben to stay asleep, and the other part is for wanting him to wake up...because she really does. She can't help it.

Mate.

She scrubs her face, but it only gets her a slight whiff of Ben's scent again, making her want to taste him. To pretend he can taste her. The longing she feels is echoed back at her, but from Caleb. He thinks they're feeling the same thing—and they are. Just not in the way he wants.

With a sigh, she puts on her big girl panties and looks at Caleb's text messages.

I've started to build a business plan over lunch. I think I can fall back on some recurring revenue streams like estate planning or family retainers, and we'll leverage your reputation to see if we can get the state to still sponsor your work within a new practice

The air feels like a sack of pokey, jagged rocks pressing on Ari's shoulders.

We can rent a shared office in several places around town. The rates are fair enough. We only have to get a space during client-meeting days, so that could save us some cash. I can probably float us for half a year, looking at our bank account and savings stash

"Our bank account," he said, because they already merged their finances. God, this man makes her move fast. He kept repeating, "Everything I have is yours" until Ari's eyes went starry, and she begrudgingly adjusted all her automatic billing—an exercise in self-inflicted torture.

Have you ever defended anyone with graphic arts skills? I have no idea who could make us a logo, and something laid out in Word with Comic Sans isn't going to get us anywhere

She chuckles halfheartedly.

I want us to be solid before we make a move, but I need out of here. I need to get away from Sloane. Plus, I can't seem to stay away from you

Ari deserves to be buried in sand up to her neck before they release the hungry crabs. She wonders how she'd look with a missing eye.

Caleb's trying to be open. Honest. He's treating her like a mate should, dropping his walls and trying to do what's best for their little family of two. But he's not thinking about the third person in the equation. The one who may just become so much more expensive. And animated. And heartbreaking. And potentially perfect.

Going home is a terrifying concept. This is a conversation she does not want to have for so, so many reasons, but it's a conversation that's coming, regardless. She can't even build a case in her own mind; how is she going to say this out loud in a way that doesn't fully incriminate her?

She grunts and thumps her forehead on the desk. Honesty is probably the best policy.

Ari is in the door for less than a minute before Caleb sweeps her into his arms and buries his nose in the crook of her neck with a heavy, long-suffering sigh.

"Hate it when you work late," he muffles.

Yeah, well, what can I say? I don't really want to be here.

He kisses loudly down her shoulder, taking hold of her hand and smooching toward her fingertips, grimacing a little. "You stink of people."

"What?" She tries to laugh him off. "If I didn't know any better, I'd say that all your romantic gestures are really just you trying to meet my colleagues vicariously."

Turning her hand over, he's about to run himself across her bite marks to wipe away all those other scents when his entire movement stops.

He already knows.

Ari tears off the Band-Aid, quick and painful. "I went to the hospital and saw Ben today."

Caleb's sweet emotions immediately go black. His gaze flicks up to hers, predatory, and her nerves tingle under the regard of his narrowing pupils. She's quick to explain as Caleb's grip on her gets firmer to the point of discomfort.

"It's not what you think! I never got to say my piece to him. We went there for closure, and I never got mine."

Caleb's grasp gets downright painful, and she squeaks.

"I wasn't mean to him! I promise! But...but you know how, when we were there together, he moved? How his vitals got stronger? It happened again. I asked Ben if he would be sorry about what he'd done and they...well...all the monitors went crazy."

"Liar," Caleb growls. "Why didn't Canady call me?"

"I..."—she tries to pull her hand back, wincing now—"I said I would tell you. When things went haywire, we panicked. Mr. Canady told me to calm him down as an Omega. I had to rub my wrist along the glands on his neck."

Caleb's lips pull back into a sneer and his scent becomes danger-ous. Ari's apprehension kicks straight up into fear.

"We didn't want to sedate him! Well, Mr. Canady said we shouldn't. He was doing so well, even brain activity! Oxygen! All good things, right? Mr. Canady thinks he might—"

Voice low, Caleb murmurs, "You want to replace me."

Yes.

"No!" Ari balks, trying to jerk her hand out of his grip but still unable as he steps forward and casts his heavy shadow over her. "I'm not going to leave you!"

"Liar." It's a whisper this time, and all the more menacing for it.

Ari's eyes drop immediately to the ground as she submits to her Alpha, drawn to his power even if she's the one locked in his deadly maw. "I can't help what he smells like to me, no more than I can help how I smell to you. But I will never cheat on you, and I won't leave!"

"It's not enough."

Suddenly, he shoves her, and her rear thumps against the wood of the apartment door, both of his meaty palms landing heavily to either side of her head, hard enough where she fears the door might crack. Her breath is so close to hyperventilation she can't think beyond it, other than to sense Caleb's feelings of rejection and rage.

"You spent the weekend in my arms, kitten. In our bed. In our shower. On our floor. You kissed me and touched me, and I loved every minute. I fed you and bathed you and fucked your pretty brains out. I made you come so many times you begged me to stop. It wasn't your heat; it wasn't my rut. So, what's your excuse? Boredom? A sense of duty? Playing house? Why do you lead me on like this, huh? Is it fun for you? Why do you do this to me? You said you were *mine!*" He pulls back, and his palm becomes a fist as it slams next to her head, making her cringe.

"Alpha, I'm afraid."

"Fuck you!" he spits. She feels the mist of his voice over her cheek as her tears come down.

"Don't you understand? I want to save him for you!"

"No one does *anything* for me!" He turns his back on her and upends the coffee table with a harsh grunt, shattering things all over the floor, pieces fanning out and getting lost in the thick threads of the carpet.

"Except Ben," she says. "And now me."

With something that sounds like a sob, he rakes his hand over the kitchen countertop this time, letting things break in crunches and clatters on the floor.

Ari's guilt rips into her with ragged claws. If she's going to get this out, she'll get it all out in one go. "But you can't leave your job."

He turns to look at her over his shoulder, his expression one of betrayal she's seen way too many times in the short month they've been together.

"Mr. Canady thinks we can wake him up, but he told me that, if that happens, his expenses will go through the roof. He said you should talk to Sloane. That he might help pay for some of it."

Caleb's hands go to his hips, and he shakes his head with the most unhappy grin Ari's ever seen in her life. He breathes in deep before leaning over the countertop and grabbing at his own hair, fisting it in clumps as his hands tremble. He feels like hate.

"I'm going to take a shower." Casting a glare in her direction, he adds, "I'd offer for you to join me, but you'd probably just stand there and imagine I'm someone else. I'm sure you could. You're good at pretending."

He starts to move away but Ari lunges forward, grabbing him by the elbow and pulling him back. "I'm not leaving you!"

His smile is terrible. "Maybe not here." He gestures at the apartment. "Maybe not here." He gestures to his temple. "But what about here, Ari?" He gestures to his heart this time. "I haven't earned it yet, but I wanted to believe that I could."

He pulls out of her grip. "Ben has always been the better of the two of us—except in one way. I'm not a murderer. I didn't kill my parents, Ari. Or yours. I didn't send you to an orphanage or abandon the only person who ever needed me. Why don't you think about *that* the next time you feel like rubbing yourself all over him."

She doesn't know what to say. Her jaw is dropped as she tries to make words that won't come. Her brain just isn't fast enough.

Maybe absolution is a gift she shouldn't grant. Perhaps some things aren't meant to be forgiven. Maybe some consequences are justly earned. There must be times when no amount of sorry is good enough.

Is it better for Ben to stay asleep?

But he spoke to her. He senses her. He belongs to her. She's lying when she says any of this is for Caleb. She's being nothing but selfish.

But her grit is going to be stronger than this needy impulse. Stronger than some stupid chemicals in her stupid brain. She's been putting off and pushing away her biology since she first presented. Heats, bleeds—none of it has ever been something she wanted to deal with. This is just another item on that checklist of things that suck about being an Omega.

She'll simply draw a line she won't cross. If she can wake up Ben and get him on his road to recovery, then perhaps she and Caleb could move away. Far away. Like China kind of away. Little by little, she could forget Ben's scent. Probably when Caleb fills her with pups. That would make her really his. Maybe, during her next heat, she should try to get pregnant. No matter who her biological soulmate is, she's Caleb's wife.

Nursing her sore hand and twirling her wedding ring, she thinks, *For better or for worse.*

The water is stinging cold, icing up Caleb's body and letting his fury sink down into a familiar self-hate while he listens to Ari clean up the glass and whatever other things he may have broken. How much of it was hers? Hopefully all of it.

Her guilt is all over him like a stink, but he doesn't know if he cares. His hurt is just too great. This weekend had been perfect. He'd done everything right. Every night when she fell asleep in his arms, he was planning the next thing to do. The next way to woo her. Why isn't it working?

The only answer is Ben.

Caleb curls his hands into fists that lay balled up on the freezing tile as he stands with his hair sagging over his forehead and into his eyes. He'd stepped out for a few hours over the weekend to see his brother just like always—a habit more than anything else—and Ben was the same, laying there placidly, just without a few of the tubes Caleb was used to.

His feelings about his brother have always been quite clear. They consisted of two words: WAKE. UP. Sometimes "wake *the fuck* up" if he was especially depressed. How is he supposed to feel now? What is he supposed to do about their shared soulmate? One thing's for sure: not what he just did. She didn't lie. She didn't try to hide it. She told him honestly.

But she didn't fucking *apologize,* and she didn't feel *sorry enough.*

He half wonders why she wouldn't have just told him she wanted to go again, but then laughs at himself. It's probably because she knew this reaction was the most likely. It becomes one of those "begging for forgiveness instead of asking for permission" kind of things. He's guilty of more than a few of those himself.

Outside the hammering water is the *crinkle-scrape-drag* sound of Ari brooming up the mess she made him make. She could have walked out. Gone to Niles's place. Gone back to Ben's bedside. But here she is, dealing with his aftermath.

He runs shampoo through his hair as fast as possible. Soap is a perfunctory swipe at best as he finishes up and towels off, slinging on only enough clothes to be decent before ducking out, hair slicked back completely and running rivers down his bare back. She's on her hands and knees with a dustpan, and when he comes closer, she cowers, fear spiking in both her emotion and her scent, but he can also feel her guilt rolling around underneath it. He can use that.

Getting down on his knees as well, he mirrors her contrite posture and touches her thigh gently. "I'll do it."

She shakes her head. "It was my fault."

Yes, it absolutely fucking was.

"I can pick up after myself. I...I used to do this a lot before you came. I've always been so angry. I can't take it out on people, so I take it out on things. But I'm not a kid anymore. It's childish and stupid and I need to grow up. If I'm going to be a good mate and a good father, I can't be like this anymore. I'll do better."

She curls into herself. "You scared me."

"I know."

"You hurt me."

Shit.

"And you even hurt the door," she adds. "What did Pedro ever do to you?"

His head twitches before his eyes go up and see a nice dent in the wooden surface. "Our door's name is Pedro now?"

"It's always been Pedro; you just never asked."

She looks at him with wide eyes that glisten with unshed tears, but she still tries to smile a little. The tension completely diffuses. He lets her in again, and through her wariness he can still feel her support and dedication.

Caleb looks at the door and flops his hands in his lap. "Pedro, I'm sorry. You're the best door I've ever known. I shouldn't have done that to you."

She huffs a little, amusement flowing over their bond. Scooping up her chin, he makes her look him in the eye. "Kitten, I'm sorry. You're the best woman I've ever known. I shouldn't have done that to you."

She gives him a watery smile. "Okay."

Tell me you're sorry, too, Ari. Say it. C'mon.

But she doesn't.

Not even once.

The wind is nice and cool up here, even if it's so high that it makes Ari dizzy. "Why didn't I know we had a balcony?"

"I have many secrets, sweetheart," Caleb teases.

She scoffs a little, eyeing the crow on the edge of the fourteenth-floor barrier wall, the only thing between their little table and falling to their dooms. Another one alights on the edge, eyeing her and cocking its head to the side. "Should I be worried? Is this, like, an Edgar Allen Poe kinda vibe?"

"Nevermore." He shrugs. "I feed them all the time, so they come back. I like them. I like all birds, really."

Ari tastes her dinner and moans her appreciation. "What is this mouth-gasm thou hast bestowed unto me?"

His chuckle is warm. "Chicken cordon bleu. It's a bitch to make, kitten. I expect a significant amount of affection for my hard work."

Sometimes he's so cute. And sometimes he's absolutely terrifying. Cute tends to win out, though. He always tries his best to make it up to her after something goes wrong. He's sorry, and that's good enough.

"You like birds?" Ari says, her mouth half full. "I like them, too. I take pictures for my Instagram account."

"You have Instagram?"

She rolls her eyes at herself. "I have everything. Except Pinterest. It just shows me hobbies I want to do but suck at."

"Like what?"

"Painting. I do horrible watercolors."

He leans in with his chin resting on his hands, fingers laced together. It's as if he's fascinated by her. "What do you paint?"

"Flowers. Well, they're supposed to be flowers anyway. They come out more like brown blobs when I get a little too enthusiastic. Do you have any hobbies?"

"Other than you?"

She snorts and takes another bite, eyeing the cawing thing that wants what's rightfully hers. "You are getting none of this, you hear me? This is too good for the likes of you."

Caleb throws them some scraps of meat and cheese from his plate, watching the little fight that ensues, black birds pecking the ground and flapping for dominance while screaming at each other. "I go to the gym, I work, and I visit my brother. That was my entire life before you, sweetheart."

She reaches over and squeezes his hand. "Well, now we'll do more. Do you like the beach?"

He pffts. "What, Revere Beach? You step in the sand wrong and find a hypodermic in your instep."

"Not anymore! They cleaned it up!"

"And Hampton is miserable with people. Nowhere to park, either, unless you get there at an ungodly hour of the morning."

She raises an eyebrow. "And you know this, how?"

He smirks. "I defend a lot of people who supposedly did bad things on Hampton Beach."

Her groan echoes off the clouds. They look like thumped pillows in the sky and seem to enjoy throwing her voice back at her. "The sad part is that I do, too. That place is a den of devils at the right time of night." With her mouth full, she tries again. "A lake?"

"You want me to drive you to a lake?"

"I retract my statement."

He pauses, taking a bite and cleaning his mouth out completely before he speaks again. "How about a museum? We can look at some not-so-horrible watercolors."

She cocks an eyebrow. "Now that's an idea. You may have to comfort me when I wail and lament over my lack of talent, though."

"That could be arranged."

They finish their meal in amicable silence and Ari cleans up. She figures it's only fair. He catches her waist as she tries to sneak by and kisses her hip. "Thank you, Omega."

"You're insatiable, you know that?"

"Hmm, you think?"

"I know."

He twists her around and kisses the crest of her rear, just where it curves into her back, making her sigh with tingles.

"If I am, it's only for you."

He gives her a few more for good measure, going from slow and open mouthed to something more like hard *mmmwahs*. She hip-chucks him playfully and he lets her go with a short laugh, allowing her to make a less than graceful exit as she trips a little over the threshold.

Smooth.

She hasn't gone to see Ben again for the past couple weeks, though she knows Caleb has. Ari has no idea what he tells his brother about, and she doesn't really want to think about it. All she knows is that Ben has shown no more progress. In fact, he's moved back to still-ness. Her stupid mind says that he's waiting for her...but he can't have her. She won't let him. Ari is nothing if not stubborn, her

Omega be damned. That's not to say she hasn't been tempted, though. She's wasted a ridiculous amount of money on flowers just to stand in front of the hospice center and look at its red brick face, warring with herself before turning around and walking away.

To keep her mind off it, she focuses on her work. It's bonus time at the end of the quarter, and she can finish up her apartment lease soon, too. It will be a nice influx of cash and can immediately be put toward helping pay for Ben's future. Even if she doesn't want to see him, she still wants him to wake up. For Caleb.

With her heat leave plus a few weeks of utter distraction, she's not hopeful that her bonus will be super large, but with her win rate, it should at least be something worthwhile. Caleb, for his part, is working just as hard. Without even talking to each other about it, they've both started bringing their work home instead of staying late at the office. Evenings consist of whatever heavenly morsels Caleb makes on their romantic, raven-filled balcony (he's getting better and better at cooking) and working from the couch. She sits on the floor, legs woven together in crisscross applesauce, with her laptop on the coffee table and her files in her lap. Caleb sits on the cushions with his computer over his thighs, a sterner expression than she's ever seen, and his files and notebooks strewn on the other side of the couch, making him have to lean over to get them. The space directly next to him is always devoid of anything in case Ari feels like jumping up, snuggling, and whining. She only did it once, but he's left space for her ever since. She'd question if she'd annoyed him when she'd squashed all his paperwork, except for that she knows better. Feeling his emotions, he'd melted a little. She knows that little place is carved out for her, just in case.

It's like working at the office in a way. They listen to each other's frustrated grunts, scoffs, and the incessant *tappa-tappa* of their keyboards. They bounce ideas off each other regarding rebuttal plans and have long since breached the attorney/client privilege to brainstorm viable paths toward success. If there's one thing she's learned, though, it's that he's a much better lawyer than she is. Her aptly named "oh experienced one" deserves his title. A nine-year age gap makes a real difference when it comes to practice, presence, and prestige.

Caleb handwrites notes, which is adorable. His penmanship is remarkable, too. Ari still writes little hearts over the *I*s in her journal, so she doesn't trust her professionalism when it comes to pen-to-paper. At least one of them is a grown up.

"Bathroom break," he says, closing his laptop, leaning backward, and groaning through a stretch.

"You don't have to announce it."

"You do."

"Don't pick up my bad habits."

He ruffles her hair, messing it up completely before pecking her on the head. "Want to know what number it is?"

"UGH!" She whaps him. Ari sneaks in her baser bodily functions before a shower, please and thank you. In all honesty, she thinks he does, too. They're not quite "there" yet. After a pause, she says, "I suppose the amount of time you spend will expose your secrets anyway."

"What if I'm just doing my hair?"

"Pfft. You're always doing your hair."

"It's my best trait."

"One of them." She smiles up at him, and he downright glows.

"And my muscles?"

"Oh, definitely."

"And my c—"

"I was going to say sweet side," she cuts him off. "But sure, that too."

He nuzzles into her, licking her mating gland and sighing his happiness over the crook of her neck, giving her goosebumps.

"Insatiable," she whispers, more distracted than she'd like.

"Absolutely."

With another slow lick that leaves her wanting more, he gets up and winds down the hallway, leaving her grinning like an idiot. As long as she doesn't see Ben, she knows she can make this work.

Biting her lip, she decides to sift through his case files. She likes seeing if he has anyone worth saving on his roster. Surprisingly, he does have a few, and it makes her forgive him a bit more. She grabs his notebook, thumbing through and admiring the cursive. His *F*s are really pretty. So are his *J*s. No lopsided hearts over his letters, just perfectly shaped little dots. Picking up the pad entirely, she decides to treat it like a flip book, fluttering the pages and taking in his writing without really looking at it.

Until she sees her name.

Her *screen* name.

...All of them.

Her throat tightens as she turns back, finding that section again, having passed by it all too quickly.

There's her Twitter. Facebook. Tumblr. Instagram. A stupid DeviantArt account she opened before she realized her art sucks. There are notes on romance novels and little quotes about them. She recognizes some of the reviews—her words, verbatim. Spinning on her hips, she looks at his bookshelf, knowing she's scanned by some of those titles mixed among everything else in his library.

Vitriol runs through her bloodstream as she reads words like *Possessive. Greedy. Devoted. Praise. Forward and blunt. Needs me to need her. Shared loneliness.*

Her address is underlined. Her work address is listed in smaller letters to the side. Her...her social security number is in the corner. Her student ID number. The license plate she hung on the wall of her apartment, the one she still hasn't unpacked here yet, is drawn in a little rectangle...

She sets down the notebook, her stomach somewhere behind her lungs, making it hard to breathe as her mouth fills with saliva and her belly churns. She knew he'd stalked her...but this... He's not a murderer, but he's not a good man.

He comes back in at a quick clip, his face the epitome of concern. "What's wrong? I can feel y—"

"Did you go into my house?"

He freezes. His skin tone goes from pale to white as he sets his jaw.

"Were you. In. My. House?!" Each word is punctuated with a finger stab at his notepad. His eye twitches a bit, and she can feel fear run through him.

"Yes."

"God damn you." She stands up, disgusted and on her way toward the door, uncaring about where the hell she ends up. In one quick move, he blocks her way, frantic and shaking his head.

"Hey! Hey, wait! I went too far, I know! I'm sorry! I needed to understand you! That's what we do, Ari. We research. Right? We vet things for accuracy. We strategize."

"Get away from me," she growls. "Who are you? Do you mean anything you say, or is this all a show you're putting on to lure me in? To make me like you? You and your *praise,* and your *devotedness,* and *possessiveness.*"

His expression darkens. "It was working until right now."

She pulls back her hand to slap him, but he grabs her wrist. Dragging her close, he stares her down.

"But those parts of me are real...I just learned that I could show them to you. That you'd like them. I'm trying to be everything you need me to be, but you see my flaws, too. I bit you too soon. I'm intense. I'm violent and moody." Then he softens. "But I also cook for you. I take care of you. I forgive you when you make mistakes. I waited for you to want me before I touched you again after your heat.

"Every relationship starts with someone trying to be what their partner wants, Ari, and then the curtain slowly lifts. I'm no different from any other person in that respect. The only thing that makes me unique is how ruthless I am when it comes to getting what I want. I wanted you. I *want* you. I have you, but I don't. The chase is never-ending, kitten, because even though you're mine, I will constantly have to fight for you, unlike any other mated Alpha in the world. But because I'm ruthless, unscrupulous, fucking obsessed, I can be that man. I *am* that man."

She sneers. "And what if I don't want that man?"

He caresses her mating gland, making her shiver even as she resists it. "Then how sad for you."

His longing is like a knife.

"Tell me who you want me to be, Ari. I'll do it as best I can. If the veil lifts too high and you don't like it, I'll slam it back down. No one loves me. Not really. No one ever has. But other than Ben, you're the first person I've ever loved. That's enough for me. I can live with that. I just need you to stay."

Ari shakes her head. "You don't even know me."

His eyes flit to the notebook that doomed him. "I know more than you think. Now I just get to experience it firsthand."

She couldn't glare harder if she tried.

His smile is sardonic. Wounded. "I take it I'm sleeping in the nest tonight."

Her teeth grind. "You mean the rut room?"

"Whatever you call it, it's the room that smells like us."

He hurts. It's so muddy. Why can't he just be bad? Why does she have to feel this pull toward him? This need to help him. Be with him. Save him from his sadness.

Alpha needs you. No one else. Just you.

She says, "You only want me because of how I smell. If I wasn't like this, I'd just be another person to be beaten in a courtroom."

"And without Ben's smell, he'd just be the man who killed your parents, lying in the bed like Sleeping Beauty. But now you want to be the prince who kisses him and wakes him up."

She flinches, her shame ramping, and he shushes her in that tender way only he can.

"I'm sorry, sweetheart. I really am. Everyone wants a fairy tale...but the truth is, no one ever gets them. Just ask me. I know that all the way down to the deepest part of me. No one ever loves the villain, do they? But unfortunately, that's all I'll ever be. No matter how hard I try…"

"No. I don't believe that," she says. He can become better than who he is now. With support and trust and kindness, he can change into the person he was meant to be.

Can't he?

She doesn't know. The conflict within her is overwhelming, making her burst into heavy tears that overflow with sorrow and pity. Caleb, being Caleb, just holds her through it all, hushing her like the pretend man of her dreams that he is. And despite the alarm bells in her mind, she is comforted. She lifts her arms slowly, making the decision to hold him too. He needs this. He needs acceptance. He needs forgiveness. He needs love.

And when her arms wrap around, sliding up his back and holding tight, he cries with her. Relief floods their bond until she's drowning in it. Care and regret and sorrow bounce between them, sticking to all their sensitive spots. In the most horrible, terrible way, they're not alone. And, mated as they are, they never will be. For better or for worse.

***

Caleb is grateful for a lot of things this morning. On the forefront of his mind, he's most happy about the fact that Ari didn't realize he followed her to work. That nice café right outside her office still has beautiful views through her company's wide windows. After their recent elevator tryst, she'd shyly given him a walkthrough, showing him enemy and patronizer cubes as well as the little four-by-four box she calls her own. Knowing exactly where she sits now, his hawklike eyes have free reign to stare.

So happy you don't drink coffee, kitten. Gives me my privacy.

He doesn't drink it, either. Instead, he sucks back black tea with honey, disgustingly strong because he'd been too distracted to take the bag out in time.

In the spaces between his loving looks up at her, he glances at his laptop, more than happy to "work from home" for the day. Sloane's had no more complaints about his performance, especially since Caleb's taken up the habit of e-mailing him around 9:00 p.m. with status updates again, proving he's both online and busy. Every time he clicks the magic paper airplane icon to send a message through the interwebs, he whispers a nice *Fuck you* under his breath, always when Ari is out of earshot.

His mate is rubbing her back in the most endearing way. He'd slept in her nest again, cuddled in her blankets, but in the middle of the night, she'd joined him, whispering, "You're trying. I know you are." After taking his arm and looping it over herself, she'd pressed her back against his chest, allowing him to immediately fold over her while holding back the urge to weep. To kiss her. To make love to her. To scratch her. Bite her more. Tear at her flesh until she bled. Instead, he'd just held her tenderly without sleeping as she rolled around, completely uncomfortable on the flat, hard floor. It was cute, just like her rubbing her back is cute now. Maybe he'll give her a massage tonight.

It's not quite lunchtime, but she stands up anyway, stretching backward and exchanging a few words with that pompous Threat from her damn office—though there are worse threats now. Their bond immediately flares with her annoyance, and he'd proud. He's glad that fucker's last day is today.

Burn in hell, you dick.

She bends over, flashing him the curve of her skirted ass, and grabs her bag...to leave. Caleb sits up straighter. He'd made her lunch today as an apology. Why would she have to go anywhere? Is she too sore to work?

Through the exposition of the glass, he watches her make her way to the elevators. Their elevator is the one that greets her, taking her down two floors to the main lobby. His eyes are locked on as she turns out of the building, but not in the direction of the subway. Why?

His laptop is crammed in his bag faster than anything and he's out the door, not even trashing his Styrofoam-clad, bitter, would-be-tea on the way. He keeps to the other side of the street and a bit behind her, ducking people and slamming shoulders with no issue. Some may turn to look at him in irritation, but when they see an Alpha of his size, they're smart enough to leave well enough a-fuck-ing-lone.

She comes up to a flower stand he knows well. He passes by it all the time. Pausing at a crosswalk light, he misses a few signals as she talks with the florist and buys a cheap bouquet of roses. He's been smelling those on her for a while now, every few days or so. Maybe she likes to keep them on her desk. Maybe she pretends they're from him to keep her colleagues at bay. But she doesn't turn back to her office. Instead, she does her thing of rubbing wrists with strangers and goes on her merry way, him following at a distance.

His stomach sinks.

Please, don't do this. Please don't do what I think you're doing.

But she does. The bitch goes to the fucking hospice. Every time she smelled like flowers, that meant she'd been with his brother.

Caleb staggers a bit under the weight of his shock. He wants to run. Toward her, away from her. He wants to throw up. He wants to kill something. He loves his brother, but more and more he's becoming convinced that thing isn't his brother. That thing is a living corpse for her to hang her hopes and dreams on.

He follows her inside, pissed that he ever brought her here. That he ever brought up Ben at all. He should have known better—though how could he?

The receptionist isn't at the front desk, and all the better for it. He sneaks to the doorway and opens it just slightly, enough to see Canady talking to his wife. His *mate*. He greets her with such familiar warmth that Caleb suddenly hates the man. Ari must feel Caleb, because she shrinks slightly, touching her chest in discomfort, but she should be used to the feeling of him loathing his workplace by now. It should be no surprise to feel this from him.

"Alas, he hasn't woken up," Canady tells her. "Still, I know he'll be happy to see you."

She clutches the flowers tight to her chest and smiles, tight-lipped and nervous. Probably afraid to get caught. She turns into Ben's room with only the slightest hesitation.

Luck is in his favor. Canady doesn't go back to the nurses' station; he goes to start rounds. The cunt who normally mans the desk back there ignores Caleb anyway, so he's not worried about her.

Keeping his steps silent, he hangs just outside Ben's door, staying out of sight and more than ready to confront Ari the moment she leaves. He'll show her who he really is. He'll lift the goddamn veil. He'll fucking throttle her in front of an audience.

There is a rustle sound and a creak of a chair. He can hear every word as she says, "Let me make this quite clear. Your brother mated me."

Not "he's my mate," but "he mated me." It's not a lie, but he hates her a little for saying it like that.

She sighs. "You did what you could for him when you were around, but you're not here anymore. Now it's my turn."

Caleb blinks, unsure of how to feel.

"He's struggling. I think he clings on to things too tight because you were taken away from him. He's afraid to be alone but he's been alone for so long he doesn't know how to be with people anymore. If I had to describe him in one word, it would be desperate. He's trying too hard to replace you. With me. And I'm going to try my hardest to be good enough.

"The world has hurt Caleb. You tried to protect him, I know you did, but in the end, you abandoned him, too. You're part of what broke him. But maybe I can help heal him."

Caleb's heart throbs.

"Maybe, if I can wake you up, then I'll have healed both of you.

Then Caleb and I can leave. He'll take care of me. Caleb...he needs me. Loves me. And I want to fall in love with him, too."

There is a silence at first...then a mumble. It's a deep and masculine word.

"...Threat."

Caleb's blood pressure drops. His head reels. Did Ben just speak? Elation fills him until that word sinks in.

Threat.

You're the fucking threat.

But the thought hurts him for the first time.

His brother is speaking. Ben has ruined his entire life for Caleb's sake, and no matter what Caleb did, he couldn't wake up Ben again. Yet here and now, Ari is coaxing his brother back into the world...but all Caleb wants to do is put him back to sleep.

What the fuck is he doing?

Something hurts Caleb's finger, and he winces in sync with Ari's gasp, probably having pricked herself on a thorn. Ari whispers the word, "Ben?" with audible tears in her voice and Caleb doesn't know what to do.

Ben's voice comes out again, that beloved, long dreamed of voice. He sighs one more word, heady with longing. "...Mate."

And Caleb shreds in two.

CHAPTER 14
THIS IS ME TRYING

"...THREAT," Ben mumbles, his voice deep and gruff with disuse.

Every nerve in Ari's body fires at once, drawing her in a straight line from toes to crown, rigid with shock and more than a tinge of fear. She gazes out past her bouquet, eyes so wide they bulge, and sees Ben turn his face toward her once again, that lovely black hair shifting and leaving trails along his uncreased pillowcase. His chest rises and falls a bit quickly, his heart rate monitor compressing its familiar pattern of blips and bleeps.

I'm going to have to mark him with my scent again, aren't I? Ari wonders in a panic. *Canady is going to come back and he's going to make me calm him again. And if I do it now, Caleb will never forgive me.*

But does that matter? Ari isn't Caleb's. She's Ben's. She always has been and forever will be Ben's.

It's not real. It's biology.

Still, she's going to choke on her desire, she knows. A thorn tears into her thumb and she gasps. Voice broken, she says, "Ben?"

His entire expression relaxes into one of bliss, turning it into the most kissable face in the world.

"...Mate."

He said it again.

Ari's hands release involuntarily, and she drops her roses, going immediately to her knees, assaulted with Ben's scent.

Leather, ash, sugar. Leather, ash, sugar.

No. She needs Caleb's cinnamon scent. Where is he? She needs Caleb! The heartbreak she feels is immediate, crushing her at the same time exhilaration grabs her lungs and squeezes. She can't breathe. He's too good. Her soulmate's aroma is like sin and seduction topped with a heavy dollop of greed.

She wants to be a better person than she is. She wants to stop being caught in this whirlwind that feels like home. Caleb's told her so many times that she was his home. She'd thought he was being sweet or exaggerating, but she finally understands. This is what she does to him. It's no wonder Caleb can't control himself. No wonder he can't stop from leaping over all boundaries. No wonder he—

But all thoughts fly out the window when Ben's eyes flutter open, staring blankly for only a moment before they lock on her. All of existence gets put on pause as Ari stares at her soulmate, seeing Caleb's eyes but more docile, somehow. Sweeter. Ben tries to lift his hand, but he can't. Still, his expression melts into something that can only be described as love. He's looking at her as though he knows her.

Because he does.

"Mate..." he whispers again, eyebrows knit as if it was a question.

Pressing her hand over her heart, she says, "Ari."

"Ari?" he repeats her name with the ghost of a smile, his heart rate spiking again on the monitors. "Beautiful... Perfect." He holds her gaze while his eyelids become heavier, his blinks coming more slowly until he eventually fades back into a peaceful sleep. Not something that will stretch on for painful decades. A dream-laden moment he will absolutely awaken from.

It's only when Canady runs in that Ari realizes that this entire exchange took a minute and not the years she'd been living in her mind. Ones where she was mated to Ben, alive and well, and filled with enough love to slather the world. The male nurse checks pulses, plays with tubing and talks at her, but Ari can't hear anything right now. All she can do is soak in the scent of Ben. The scent of her future. One she needs, even if she doesn't want to.

"Ari?" Canady taps her. "Are you all right, honey? Do you need some water? Do we need to call Caleb? What happened? Ben's going all haywire again!" It all comes out so fast, Ari's isn't sure what to address first.

"Ben spoke..."

"What?" The man grabs her shoulders, staring at her though Ari refuses to look anywhere else other than her true mate.

"And he opened his eyes. He...he talked to me. Understood me."

She's immediately scrunched into a warm chest that smells like nothing but soap as Mr. Canady holds her, elated, and starts to shout cheers to the sky. They're blunted by the insulation of this place, and to Ari, they're nothing more than white noise. Her mind is one loud hum.

There's no denying it. Ben is coming back to the world. It's a miracle. Sensational. Spectacular. But what's she going to do now?

Just like before.

Run.

Caleb left without confronting her. The minute his twin whispered the word *Mate,* Caleb fled. What else could he possibly do?

Ari did nothing wrong...other than say Ben's name in a way that tore out Caleb's stomach. And perhaps the fact that she went there in the first place, given the fight they'd just had. But she went there to tell Ben she belonged to Caleb. That matters, doesn't it?

It mattered until Ben spoke. Now the reset button has been pressed, and nothing Caleb has said or done will make an ounce of difference. Ben will steal her. Caleb's brother may have ruined Ari's life in the past, but he's paid a heavy price for it. Caleb is ruining it now and only reaps the benefits. If he really loved her, he wouldn't want her to stay; he'd just want her to be happy. Perhaps he doesn't love her at all, then. Perhaps he only requires her.

For the umpteenth time in his life, Caleb's heart is broken. Drowning in a sea of people on the city streets, he's more alone than he's ever been, because happiness is right there, so close he's tasted its sweetness, but he still can't make it his. He can't do anything.

No one loves me. No one ever has. Even my brother put his need to be a savior over my need to have him in my life. Every dream I've ever had is a lie I've fed myself. There's no such thing as a Happily Ever After.

When the elevator dings, Caleb realizes habit has led him to his office. One of his only safe spaces, though the irony of that sentiment isn't lost on him. Sloane's heavy door is mere feet away, and behind there, Caleb has suffered immensely. Unfortunately, nowhere he goes is much better. His home is a place where loneliness drowns him in dead air, hollow ruts, and unending emptiness. The gym is a space for posturing, where he looks in the mirror and realizes that he'll never be good enough. Strong enough. Attractive enough. He'll never best all the other Alphas who parade around, doing the work Caleb struggles with in a way that looks effortless. Graceful. Natural. Nothing about Caleb's life has ever been natural. He can always push for More and Better…but it's never good enough. It buys him neither favors nor forgiveness. His life is a series of "what have you done for me lately"s. What happens when he doesn't want to "do" anymore? Who will tolerate him then?

He's at his desk. When did he get to his desk?

Gwen looks at him with her thin eyebrows high and her blue eyes narrowed. "I thought you were working from home today."

What home?

"Couldn't concentrate."

"Hmm. We can't have that now, can we?"

"Not in the mood for your attitude right now, Gwen."

She clicks her pen and sighs. "I wasn't aware that I had one."

"You always have one." Caleb tosses down his laptop bag a bit harder than he needs to, changing her cold expression to one of concern that makes his skin crawl.

"You look rough. Maybe you don't need to work from home. Maybe you need to just *be* home."

She talks as if she's his superior. It makes him want to snap her neck. "Because you know me so well?" he says through his teeth.

Her concern deepens, laced with irritation. "Go home. And take whatever Alpha shit you have going on with you." She waves her hand at his whole body, indicating his worthlessness. "None of us can afford your distractions today."

Sloane exits his office with interest, leaning against the door with a smirk that puts razor blades against Caleb's throat.

"Well, then don't get distracted, Gwen," Caleb says. "I believe you spoke to me first and haven't shut the fuck up since."

Unfortunately, it seems Gwen isn't feeling tolerant today. An Amazon, she stands up to her full, intimidating height—another area in which he fails in comparison—and stares straight at him. Sloane's grin only widens. That sadist loves a show, and Caleb is absolutely in the mood to put one on.

She leans in. "I don't know who you think you are...or rather, I know exactly who you think you are, but it's in need of adjustment." She flicks her short, blonde hair out of her eyes and stares him down as if she matters. "You seem to have this leftover swagger from when you were a winner. Everyone put up with your shit because you were a legend. But your star is fading."

Without giving her space for another word, he counters, "Too bad yours never rose in the first place."

She raises a finger at him, trying to shake it like he's some child to be scolded, and he decides then and there to fucking verbally railroad her.

He plays with his cufflinks. "You can't succeed even when you have no distractions, can you? Freshly mated, I still won ninety-seven percent of my cases this quarter so far. Isn't yours at seventy? Consistently? Month over month, year over year? You can't blame that on me, no matter how many outbursts I may or may not have. No matter how many *distractions* I might have caused.

"It's just like you not to take accountability. No wonder your client list has more convicts than classists. Your cheap win rate is all they can afford. My retainer is double yours and I'm worth every fucking penny. Pfft, fading star. Tell that to my bank account. But you don't really need a big one, do you? You don't have a mate to go home to. You don't have a family. You couldn't even get a Beta to fuck you because your personality got hit by a Mack truck."

She backhands him. He saw it coming but decided to take it like a champ. Turning back toward her, he licks his split lip and smiles. "And you hit like a fucking girl."

Sloane outright laughs behind him, and Caleb feels that stinging thrill of pride he gets from the monster who made him. The look on Gwen's face could melt metal, but Caleb is a ghost.

Wordlessly, but with more bangs than required, she packs up her shit and decides to do her own "Work from Home" act, flipping him off along the way. He salutes her with a sideways quirk to his mouth and ticks his eyebrows at Sloane.

"There's my boy," the man grumbles in his ragged voice. "Get to work."

Caleb repeats the salute gesture, the same sort of "Fuck you," and turns back toward his desk, unpacking.

Well. So much for getting that blonde bitch to work for me, he thinks. *Not that it matters. Apparently, my mate...my wife...has already earmarked all my money for my brother's recovery.*

Caleb couldn't afford to start a business now if he tried. Trapped in an impossible situation, the only thing he can do is work. Thank goodness that's how he's been putting his little black heart in a box for years. Maybe he just needs to stop taking it out.

Lesson learned.

"He's late." Ari pouts at a cute egg timer she inherited: a chicken with a crank dial for a belly. "And he also hasn't been texting me like a maniac."

She leans over and tweaks the dial if for no other reason than to hear the sound of it counting down. Everything about Ari's emotions feel tattered and sore. There's no way Caleb can't feel this. Maybe he's giving her space. She doesn't want space. She wants to be smothered and reminded of who she belongs to.

Please, someone remind me.

A different timer goes off and Ari tries to pick up a pot lid, unceremoniously burning the crap out of her hand and dropping it again before she remembers that potholders exist and she now has some. New ones. Black kitten ones. They make her want to cry.

What would Ben call me? What would my next nickname be?

She wants to murder herself. She really does.

The dinner she's making is the first she's dealt with in over a month and probably the most intense Internet recipe she could handle. It looks...strange. If food could look floppy, this is it. It looks like one of her watercolor paintings. You know what it's supposed to be, but the execution...

Blowing on it for posterity, not actually caring if she blisters her mouth (why start now?), Ari gives the beef burgundy sauce a little lick. Then a little sip. Then a full mouthful.

Oh yeah. Definitely worth eating, no matter how it looks.

She's not overcompensating. She's not. She's just trying to be a good wife. She's new at this. Her first relationship is a doozy and she's trying her best to keep up. Last night, she told Caleb she knew he was trying. This is her trying.

Taking out her phone, she points it at her slop. It somehow manages to look even worse, but she snaps a picture anyway. Taking a breath, she sends it to Caleb.

Her glands throb with pain suddenly. Something like a fresh heartbreak. Is that Caleb? Is something wrong? She thought they ended last night on a good note. He'd even made her breakfast and lunch today.

Little bubbles start. Then stop. Start. And stop. Ari stares at her phone for much longer than she should, and finally a voice recording comes over. Dread is all she feels.

Please don't be something sexy. I can't bear it if you do that right now.

Biting her lip, she presses the ominous triangle button. Caleb's tone is cold and mean. "Why don't you bring it to Ben?"

Her heart drops. Her thumbs fly over the screen as she texts back:

The next voice message is bitter. "Why?"

She can feel his anger from miles away.

The next file *tsks* at her. "No, Ari. I'm just the man who mated you."

All the blood leaves her face. Pulling a chair out, she lands a bit too hard. Does he know where she was today? Did Mr. Canady say something?

No.

No, he was there. He's throwing her exact words back at her, like he always does. He goes to see Ben on weekends, so why would he...?

He followed her.

He *followed* her! Of course, he had! He hadn't trusted her—was right not to, maybe—but how dare he?!

Standing, Ari opens the trash and dumps in her whole vat of sauce, not caring if it leaks through the damn bag. Opening another pan that was waiting to steam vegetables, she tosses that down the drain. Why bother being a good wife to a man who refuses to be a good husband? A good mate. A good Alpha! Is this what taking care of her looks like? Well, who needs care like that?

Ari's going to stay at her own apartment. Never mind him giving her the big bed as if he's the better man for it. She doesn't need his bed, just like he doesn't deserve her nest.

The nest...

With a fury unlike she's ever known, Ari bursts into the room where he made her his. The blankets are strewn everywhere, muddled and mashed together in snuggle piles. The room reeks of them, which is exactly how he likes it. Piling it all onto itself, Ari picks up every lick of cloth and scrap of fabric. Every towel and sheet and pillow. Every cotton blend, shag, and silk.

And she bleaches it all fucking clean.

"I hate sleeping bags," Niles gripes. "It's eighty damn degrees out, and I feel like I'm a baking potato or something."

"*Baked* potato," Ari says, face pressed into her pillow. Her empty apartment echoes a little as they sit in darkness. A bit of light from the streetlamps finds its way through her window, but not much. "And no one said you had to lay in it."

Niles ignores her. "The floor is uncomfortable. People's backs are curved, Ari. *S*-curved. They were not meant for hard, unforgivingly flat surfaces." He lets out an irritated sigh. "Why are we even here? Why didn't you just come to my house?"

"You have that yap-yap dog now. He gives me hives."

"Say nothing about Bee-bee. Never slander my precious Bee-bee. Okay. Fine. Well, then why aren't we at your place?"

"You mean Caleb's place? Because it makes me sad." And that it does. Everything there makes her think of her husband. The kitchen where he'd make such nice meals. The raven-filled porch where they could see the corner of the sunset. The red and black bathroom where he's washed her hair more times than she can count. The space on the couch that he'd always left open for her when they'd work from home at night—the one she'd never really taken advantage of the way she could have…

She sniffles again.

"Dude." Niles rolls his eyes at her.

"Not a dude."

"Not-a-dude, I know he's your mate and separation anxiety is a thing and all, but he's just working late. You don't have to be this mopey! Weepy. Whatever-y."

"Yes, I know. I'm pathetic. But also…it's complicated."

"Pumpkin, nothing about you is complicated. You're the simplest person I've ever known."

She lifts her face and eyes him. "Is that a compliment?"

Niles just fluffs his sleeping bag. "You heard my words. It's up to you to interpret them as you see fit."

Her face hits the pillow again, muffling her voice. "God, I missed you."

"No one could ever love you like I do. That's why I'm the—"

"Besssst Friennnnnd!" they say in unison, fist bumping without having to look.

They fall into silence for a moment, before he says, "I want ice cream. And not your disgusting pistachio, either. I want something with chocolate and peanut butter."

She tries to avoid drooling. "And whipped cream."

"Cherries?" he asks.

Looking at each other for a brief minute, they scrunch their faces and jinx each other with a "Nahhh."

"Well, it's too late to do anything about it now," she says. "Just go to bed or we'll be ruined for work tomorrow."

"You'll be ruined. I'm going home soon."

Ari's jaw drops as if she'd just been run through. "Deserter!"

"It's after midnight!"

She pouts. "Have a sleepover with me?"

He looks at her as though she's the strangest thing he's ever seen. "What are we? Twelve?"

She sighs harshly and hides her face in her hands. "I didn't know you when I was twelve."

Sitting up, Niles looks concerned for the first time. "What's really going on, Ari? You smell wrong. And not like, mixed-with-an-Alpha wrong, I mean like... I don't even know how to say it."

Sliding her fingers over each other, toying with the tips of them the way that Caleb does, she admits. "I did something bad. Caleb and I...we both keep doing bad things. We can blame it on our biology, but maybe it just means there's something wrong with us deep down. Our Alpha/Omega brains are just giving voice to our...I dunno...inner evil."

Niles pets her hair. "There's no way your inner is anything evil."

She snorts. "You have no idea. But Caleb tries to take the bad things about me together with the good. Even when I upset him. I'm trying to do that for him, too... But he's..."

"He's what?"

"He's...a lot..."

"Yeah. I'll bet. And what bad things about you does he have to take in? Other than you being a sloppy eater?"

She groans. "You don't know the half of it! I'm a worse person than I ever thought I was."

There is a long pause as she reminds herself how much she trusts Niles. She needs to open up and talk to someone or she's going to self-destruct. This whole situation is too much for her. If anyone would be willing to catch her when she's falling, it's Niles.

"There's something I haven't told you," she says. "Told anyone, actually."

"Who would you tell, if not me?"

"Touché." She smiles a little. "Things have been much harder than I've said. Like, really, really hard. Do you remember when I told you about—"

Suddenly, she gasps in pain, her chest wrenching and sorrow flooding every piece of her. She cries out and Niles sits up straight, grabbing at her shoulders.

"What's going on? Ari? Ari, are you okay?"

She's clutching at herself, her eyes welling with tears. "It hurts." Every emotion in her turns to black, swallowing all hope and leaving a yawning void that will never be filled. Her happiness obliterates into explosions that rock her body to the side. She curls into a ball as the weight of her sorrow crushes her into grains of sand. But this pain…this suffering…it's not hers.

It's Caleb's.

"Niles, give me my phone," she chokes out, holding her hand up and flailing a little. It's shoved into her palm, and she immediately thumbprints the thing open. Caleb's text waits for her, just like she knew it would. Four little words break her heart again and again with each and every syllable.

What have you done?

The nest. She ruined the nest. Cradling the device to her chest, she sobs. "I'm sorry. I'm sorry."

Niles is all over her. "What's happening? Ari? C'mon, pumpkin, what's going on?"

"I hurt him, Niles! I hurt him and I can feel it!"

He lifts her face, eyes wide as he touches her everywhere, not sure what to do. "Is this a soulmate thing?"

"He's not my soulmate!" she cries out, trying to shove Niles away. Something is pulling glass shards through her chest, and she can't take it. But those pixel-black words are all she can think about. Such sad, terrible words.

What have you done?

How many times can she ruin this man's hopes and dreams before he's done with her? Before he gives up? Before he breaks?

"Take me home!"

"Pumpkin, the trains have stopped—"

"Drive."

"What? Why?"

"Drive!" she yells through gritted teeth.

With that, he takes her hand and pulls her to her feet, abandoning everything to the floor. Let it rot, for all she cares. Why did she do this? Why didn't she put herself in his shoes? Why doesn't she ever think?! Too young, too impulsive, too stupid!

Niles shuts the car door for her, and she clicks her buckle with trembling hands, already bracing herself on the dashboard. As soon as he's in on his side, she tells him, "Speed. Break all the rules. Get me to him."

Alpha, Alpha, Alpha, I'm sorry.

Her friend shakes his head back and forth a bit as he starts the ignition. "What did you do?" Just like Caleb's text. She can almost hear the words in her husband's voice. The heartbreak. The shock. He probably thinks she's going to leave him. But she won't. She can't! She promised!

"When he's sad...or when I reject him...he sleeps in the nest I made."

"Back from your heat?! Ari, it's been, like, a month and a half! Why do you still have that?"

"He doesn't want to lose it. When he feels insecure, he..." She can't breathe, there's not enough air in the world. "...He stays there. It makes him feel calm."

"Can't you calm your own Alpha?" Niles asks, incredulous.

It makes her lips tremble. "Do you know, I never really think to try."

Not since I met Ben.

Bad Omega. Such a worthless Omega.

"I was mad at him...even though it was my fault. I made a mistake, but I didn't want to take responsibility when I got caught. He did something wrong, too, so I turned it back on him, even though what he did should not have been a surprise.

"I...I washed the nest, Niles. I scrubbed out the whole room. I didn't leave any trace of our scent in there. There's nothing for him to soothe himself with. And he's hurt. So, so hurt."

Niles gapes at her. "Why would you do that?"

Because I'm petty and bitter and he's not my MATE!

Even though he is.

She sobs again, covering her mouth with the back of her hand. "Just drive. Just take me home."

The click of the gearshift doesn't even bother her. Nor does the rev of the engine. Right now, all Ari cares about is fixing what she broke.

Ari clutches her seatbelt even though the car is parked and off at this point. Niles opens her door, and she proceeds to almost fall out, vomiting when she leans over. Niles doesn't even say anything, he just walks her up to the apartment, her stomach clenching on nothing because Ari hadn't eaten dinner. Or the lunch Caleb made for her. She's running on empty and all the worse for it.

His door, their door, is locked and deadbolted but Ari is in no condition to do a damn thing about it. Niles knocks, soft at first, given the hour, but moving to a heavy pound when no one answers.

"Dammit," Niles mutters under his breath, patting Ari's bag down for her keychain, too large with a collection of inane objects that appeared over time. The jiggling in the lock is too loud and Ari's going to throw up again. Her mouth is wet and the back of her throat burns.

The door swings with a creak and Niles brings her in. It's dark, save the one overhead kitchen light. Caleb sits on his rear on the living room floor, nearly obscured. His back is against the glass of the hidden balcony door, the one covered with a drape that just looks like a long window shade. His button-up collar is wide open, and he looks haggard, sporting a short, wide glass of some kind of liquid. By the stink of the apartment, making Ari's belly churn all the more, it's alcohol. He sneers when he smells her.

"Seems like I wasn't the only one sick tonight. Where were you?"

Ari doesn't answer. She feels green.

Niles answers for her. "We were in her old apartment." He covers for her without being asked. "We hang out there sometimes. We even have sleeping blankets and ice cream. You should come." He manages to keep the sarcasm out of his voice, but his scent prickles with irritation.

It's because Alpha's not taking care of me.

Caleb eyes him. "How the hell did you get here so fast?"

Ari gasps out, "I told him to drive. I told him to get me here as fast as he could."

Eyes narrowing with dark humor, Caleb asks, "Why?"

She tells him, "Because I needed to be with you."

That gets him moving, though he stumbles a bit, drunker than he should be. He must have been well on his way before he even got home. "Come here, Omega," Caleb says quietly, taking her from Niles. Her friend barely gives her over.

"You gonna actually take care of her or are you gonna do"—Niles gestures—"whatever the hell you've been doing?"

Caleb doesn't answer with anything other than a "Thank you for bringing her home."

Ari is smothered in Caleb's embrace, just as she should be.

Leather, ash, cinnamon; *the most important part. The part I need to focus on. That part that makes him, him.*

Niles's lips purse in consideration before petting her back. "You got this, Ari?"

She doesn't bother to speak, she only nods against her Alpha's chest.

"All right. Call me in the morning, yeah?"

She nods again. As Niles walks himself out, Caleb leads her the few steps it takes to get to the kitchen table, sitting her down. He rocks on the balls of his feet as he takes a clean dish towel and wets it, swiping the cool damp over her forehead before handing it over.

"It was a mess in here. Pots everywhere. You even left out some of the concoction you made," he says.

"Did it look disgusting?"

His lips tip up a little. "It was like a rock."

"Well." She presses the cloth firmer over her temple. "It looked floppy before. Maybe it's an improvement."

"It was inedible." He leans against the counter. "I threw it away."

Please don't throw me away too, Alpha. Pretty please.

Still...

"You followed me." Not a question.

"Yes." So simple. Not defensive, not sorry. Just owning who he is.

Her eyes well with tears again. "So, you heard him talk?"

Caleb chuckles. "Heard my brother call me a threat and you his mate? No, I didn't hear a thing." He knocks back the rest of his drink, setting the glass down too hard and wiping his mouth on his sleeve.

"You should go by yourself next time," Ari says. "Maybe he'll talk to you, too."

Huffing shortly, Caleb levels his gaze at her. "I think he has other priorities." His emotions flash with anger again and Ari winces.

"I'm ruining something...but I don't mean to."

He rubs his eyes and slurs slightly. "Don't you?" Uncorking some rectangular bottle full of amber liquid, the color of his eyes—Ben's eyes—Caleb pours himself something else.

"Tell me not to go again, Alpha. Compel me. Make me obey."

His expression doesn't change but his emotions go black again. An unfathomable darkness. Shooting back the entire glass without a word, he rights himself and leaves, going to the nesting room and locking himself in. Ari knows it's barren of comfort and reeks of bleach. It will give him a headache at the best or nosebleed at the worst. It's not going to make him feel any better, only so much worse. It doesn't smell like them at all anymore. No trace that they'd ever shared anything as lovers. No sign that they'd seen out their needs with each other and come out mated on the other side. No hope for the future lies in that windowless, desolate hole.

After all, she'd made sure of it.

CHAPTER 15

THE ROAD TO RUIN

CALEB STANDS ACROSS FROM BEN. His brother lays there, just like always. Silent. He looks older. Skinnier. What would he even be like if he wakes up? What would his memory be like? What would his body work like? Could he even be a mate or a husband? Or will he be a talking marionette on medical devices and bed pans? It doesn't make Caleb depressed. It doesn't make him angry. In all honesty, he doesn't know how to feel. He doesn't know what to do. Say. Think.

He shuffles his feet. "Hey, Ben."

Nothing.

He tries to wake up his brother with any remaining scent of Ari's, but he'd washed that right the fuck off this morning alongside the reek of bleach. Ben's nostrils flare slightly—likely only due to her vestiges, now embedded forever into Caleb's natural scent—but he doesn't move otherwise.

Tugging over a chair, Caleb gripes, "Did I do something wrong specifically, or are you always this selective when it comes to what company you'll keep?"

He puts up his foot on Ben's bedside, nudging him with his shoe. Soft, then hard. Then harder, being as annoying as possible, like when they were kids. "Wake up, Ben! Wake up, wake up, wake-upwakeup!"

"Stop," Ben mutters, his voice whiny as he shoves at Caleb's foot a little. It's barely a caress, but it happens.

Jesus fucking Christ.

Caleb pulls back and is on his feet in a minute, the chair upending uselessly behind him as he grabs at his brother's face, tapping it. "Ben? Benny?"

His twin grimaces and tries to pull away. "Said stop, Cay." He humphs slightly and frowns.

Caleb's laugh is a burst of sound, his grin unending...until it fades. It becomes a grimace as he grits his teeth.

"Why?" he asks. "Why did you wake up? I wanted you to wake up for so long, why now?"

Those beloved eyes blink open, slow and heavy. Ben looks at him with something like surprise. "Cay?"

And the tears finally come. Caleb chokes on them a little, holding back by only the thinnest, most frayed of threads. This is real. It's not a dream. He feels like he's waited a lifetime for this moment.

"Yeah, Benny?"

"You look like shit."

And laughter bubbles up through the hurt. "Yeah, I do, don't I?"

Ben pats next to him. "C'mere."

Shaking his head with a grin, Caleb says, "We're too old for that."

A tiny snort pulls Ben's chest tight. "Do it at three, do it at twenty-three."

"Thirty-four," Caleb corrects. Ben's eyes fade into confusion. "We're thirty-four now. Thirty-five in a few months."

"No fucking way..." It comes out in a disbelieving gust of breath, making Caleb laugh again. A painful, wonderful thing.

"I know, right?"

When it sinks in that Caleb's not joking, Ben looks taken aback, and why the hell wouldn't he be? He blinks around at his room, seeming to register it for the first time. "Where? Ugh. No. Don't. Just c'mon." He weakly gestures once more, smoothing the blankets beside him.

Caleb's eyebrows knit. "You've...you've got tubes and shit, Benny, I don't wanna —"

"Figure it out."

And who is he to argue?

There's too much stuff and it all comes out of Ben at different angles, some over the thin comforter, some under. IV tubes and stomach tubes, fucking catheter and heart monitor wires. Caleb shuffles to the other side of the bed where there's less chaos and finagles down the metal side rail with more grunts than is proper before gingerly working his way onto the mattress. There are a good number of oofs, hisses, and curses from both parties, but they manage it. Soon, Caleb finds himself laying on Ben's shoulder with his arm locked around him. It's surreal. It's magical. It's a fucking miracle.

Caleb gives in...and cries. It comes on as just fogged vision at first, but it builds in momentum until he's sobbing low moans and clutching at fabric, a mess of shaking, too rigid limbs as his face pulls into agony. Ben's hospital gown is soaking under his thunderstorm, but Caleb barely registers it. He's too busy holding his brother, cursing and blessing him in the same sentences. Gratefulness, regret, sorrow, anger, loneliness, pain, it all roils like a hurricane about to tear cities down.

"Hey, hey, stop. Hey. Shh. S'gonna be okay," Ben says, swiping his hand through Caleb's hair, a ghost of a gesture, one Caleb both barely feels and also feels with his entire heart. He wants to crush his twin in his embrace until they become one person, just as they should have been from the very beginning.

Please don't go away. Stay with me. Please, Benny, please. I can't do it again. I can't, I can't, I can't!

Ben shushes him and hushes him, murmuring a soothing this or that, oddly lulling himself back into sleep as soon as Caleb's weeping tapers off into silence. Caleb almost doesn't realize until Ben's snores come in little snuffles, dreams fluttering his eyelids.

Refusing to move, anxiety gathers Caleb's insides into one slick knot in his chest.

What if he never wakes up again? What if that was my final moment, and I didn't do it right? What if Ben's last memories will be of his brother, who he killed for, being so disgustingly weak, pathetic, and selfish?

Caleb whimpers as he quakes. Ben *has to* wake up again. Ari's still silently calling to him. The question is, how long will Ben sleep? Another hour? Another day? Caleb will lay here forever if he has to. He's been waiting this long, he'll wait for as long as it takes. Days. Months. Millennia.

The analog clock on the wall says it only takes twelve minutes and forty-three seconds, but Caleb counted every tick with a terrifying urge to scream.

"Arm's numb," Ben complains, stretching his toes sleepily beneath the blanket.

Caleb tamps down on his flare of emotion, forcing tranquility to override it. Hiding his tidal wave of fear behind an exaggerated smile, he shifts off of his brother. "I'm surprised more of you isn't numb."

"Brain's numb."

"Yeah, well, when you haven't used it for eleven years…"

Ben blinks at the ceiling, still looking drowsy. "Mom and Dad…?"

Caleb's heart sinks. What is he supposed to say? "You did it, Benny. You did what you wanted to."

Ben fiddles with Caleb's fingers that lay across his chest, something they've always done for comfort. Something Caleb does to Ari now.

"I tried to stop."

Sitting up, Caleb stares at his brother. "What?"

"I tried to…" He squints his eyes as if it's hard to remember. "I was gonna hit a wall. Just under the overpass. But then I thought about it. About you. About Mom and Dad. About what I was really doing. And I realized...just how stupid I am."

Ben's eyes fill up this time, and it's Caleb's turn to pet his brother's hair. "You were just trying to save me."

Turning his head, Ben says, "I realized...the world is so big. We didn't have to stay with them. To listen. To obey. So, I tried to stop. I was going to turn the wheel, get back in the lane, but Mom panicked...screamed...and grabbed it. She yanked it to the side. Hard. I think the ice made it worse...and..." Ben shakes his head, dazed. There is a long moment before he says, "Now my brother is an old man."

Caleb sits, putting himself in that place at that moment. Of course, his mother would have tried to take control. And of course, it would have fucked them all. He pulls back a deep sniffle. "We're both old men."

"Say what you want, I'm still twenty-three."

Closer to Ari's age than mine.

Caleb's heart stops for a moment before sinking in his body, all the way to his gut. If Ben didn't mean to kill their parents, if Ben didn't purposefully ram the car into *Ari's* parents, then the moral high ground Caleb has stood on all this time is lost. This was the only way in which he won against Ben. Now it turns out that neither one of them is a murderer. But one is a stalker. And violent. And manipulative. And —

Ben looks at Caleb, his eyes pained. "Sloane...?"

Caleb just shakes his head. "Don't you worry about Sloane. Don't you worry about anything."

I'm the one who needs to be worried. My castle is being bombed from every angle. What the fuck am I supposed to do now? Where the hell do I belong?

Nowhere.

It's a terrible thought that hammers its chorus like death metal. Screaming and all.

Ben turns his face into Caleb's arms, and he holds his twin as gingerly as possible, trying to stray from anything and everything that could poke or pull. He buries his nose in his brother's hair, breathing him in. "I missed you, Benny. I missed you so much."

Don't leave again. Don't go anywhere. Stay. I'm so scared. I'm already afraid to lose you.

Caleb's shoulders start to tremble, and Ben wraps his frail arms around him. "Mm. I'm here, Cay. Still here."

I'm going to break. Please, somebody help me, I'm about to break. It's too much.

"There's a girl who comes..." Ben trails off.

Caleb's eyes cinch shut. "Ari."

"Yeah." It comes out dreamy, and he can hear Ben's smile. "Ari. She's —"

"My wife." He can't help it. He has to say it. "She's my soulmate, just like we used to dream about. I can feel her emotions, Benny. I can feel her body's pain. It's amazing."

His brother stops moving. "But—"

"She smells like maple syrup, doesn't she? She makes fun of our scents mixed together because she says we smell like burnt pancakes. I love it though. It's my favorite smell in the entire world."

"Cay?" Ben tries, but Caleb won't let him.

"She visits here sometimes when I can't, but I've been coming a lot. A couple times a week, all these years. I never left the area just in case I got a call that you woke up. I've never given up on you, Ben."

Except for when I did. When I thought you were replaceable. When I tried to fill the hole in my heart with a woman who never wanted me.

"She's funny, like you, but in a sort of innocent way. She doesn't even swear. Mostly. Unless something really pisses her off. I think I'm a bad influence, though. I catch her cursing at her cases under her breath. She's a lawyer. Pro-bono. Fighting for the unwashed masses and all that."

Why is he telling him about her?

"And I'm a defense attorney now, just like we always wanted. I'm sure we can pick up your credits where you left off and get you your degree, too. That is, if you're not brain damaged or anything."

"Fuck off," Ben says, pleasant enough, though it sounds distant.

Caleb forces a chuckle. "I'll help you study. I'm a good lawyer, I swear. I'm someone people respect now."

Or just put up with.

"Who do you work for?"

"Sloane Law Off..." his words trail off.

Ben looks up at him as if wounded. "No."

"Shh," Caleb tries again. "Not your problem. It's mine."

"But I..."

"I know, Benny. I know. It was my choice." *Because I fucked myself over. Because I blew all my money but needed to take care of you. I took a handout that came with a contract.*

"Sloane has been a good mentor to me," he continues. *When he's not physically hurting me. When he's not ruining everything I hold dear. When he's not holding my reins so tight, he's choking me with them.*

"And I might make partner soon." *Except that Sloane took it away. I was distracted and I was careless and he took it away.*

Ben whispers, "I'm so sorry, Cay."

"Never say that." *Not even if you steal my wife.* "You sacrificed everything for me. Don't you dare apologize to me now. You're waking up...that's all I ever needed. And if you can't forgive Sloane, we'll run away or something. Like we should have done in the first place."

"...With Ari?" It comes out small, pleading, and Caleb tears up again.

"Yeah, Benny. With Ari."

Because the Lord giveth, and the Lord taketh away. Never one without the other.

If there truly is a God, Caleb hates him. He hates everything.

Except his obligated wife.

And Ben.

.   .   .

"You disgust me," Sloane hisses. It's not for the first time, but every time he says it, Caleb dies a little inside. "Two p.m. and you finally decide to grace us with your presence. You missed three client meetings. You didn't answer your phone. Texts. E-mails. Are you truly that disinterested in what pays your bills or do you just want the attention? To be babied. To have everyone ask you, 'What's wrong? What happened?' even though you know quite well no one cares."

"Obviously you care." Which is the wrong thing to say.

"Fuck off, child. Did I ask you anything about where you've been? Did I ask you why you look like your face got held under water? No. Know why? Because it's fucking obvious."

Caleb glances up. *Does he know Ben is awake? Did Canady tell him? He seemed like he wanted to tell the entire goddamned world.*

"Your mate is a distraction. And you say 'soulmated.' Swollen, crying eyes do not a happy marriage make, my boy. Though I'm sure you know that. I'm surprised someone can stand you in close quarters for so long. She obviously seems to be realizing the error of her ways."

It hurts. Ohhh, it hurts...and Sloane knows it. His expression is one of triumph. Caleb should want to do something about it, wipe it off his face somehow, but he doesn't. It's vicious because it's true. If there's anything Caleb hates, it's that.

"Why do you do this?" Caleb asks. "Are you truly so weak that you need to constantly belittle me in order to feel stronger?"

Sloane's eyes go wide. Caleb had never dared say anything like this. He goes on, getting his words in before the shock wears off.

"You rutted me, you insult me, you break me down day-by-day-by-day, and yet you expect me to be this pillar of excellence."

"You fucking whelp."

"No. I'm seriously asking why." Caleb doesn't raise his voice. He doesn't need to. His words are louder than a thunderclap. "You've abused me in so many ways, you're either a sadist or you're terrified."

"Shut your—"

"And if you're terrified, what of? I think you're threatened by me, and always have been. I think that's why you try so hard to annihilate me."

"Threatened? What the did you just—?"

"I'm not young anymore and neither are you. And that's the key thing, isn't it? Look at you. You're dying. Who knew that Hades was mortal?"

Sloane stands now and Caleb doesn't even bother looking at him. "By all means, Charles, come at me. Look at me and look at you. Unless you have a fucking gun in your desk, I'll kill you. One of my hands can snap that saggy neck of yours and you know it. I used to think about it all the time."

Leaning forward on his desk, Sloane's lips tick up at the corners. "Yeah? And what would you do? You truly think you wouldn't get caught?"

Caleb smiles and meets Sloane's eyes. "You forget that I defend murderers all the time. I know exactly what kind of technicalities we use to get them off without a scratch. I don't need to not get caught, you dying bastard, I only need to make sure I don't get sentenced."

Sloane's face falls.

Caleb steps around his mentor's desk. "Didn't think of that, did you?"

Seeing the man stumble back should do something for him, make him feel powerful, but it doesn't. Caleb has dreamed about this moment and yet here he is, taking no pleasure in it. No sorrow, either. "There are soooo many ways I can kill you, Charles. Do you remember Phillip Wallen? Remember how you got him acquitted?"

Sloane's ass hits the wall.

"Do you remember how Donohue went after her own kids?" Caleb continues. "Kids. They convict anyone and everyone the minute pups come into the picture but she was white, and she was rich, and she wasn't anyone famous, so there were no good headlines to make off her. I got her arrest expunged, never mind making sure she didn't do jail time. Do you remember those crime scene photos? Remember how I showed them to you, and you shoved them back at me, just telling me to do my job? Well, what if I did my job? What if I did it so well, you died in the most painful ways, and I never saw the inside of a cell? What if I took all the money I made from you, posted bail, and spent the days awaiting my trial sipping brandy, knowing that I eviscerated you?"

Sloane is looking around for an implement of destruction, anything to stave off Caleb, but he looms closer and shoves Sloane so hard, it knocks the wind out of him, leaving him coughing up his smoker's lung.

"Should I rut you, too, you evil bastard? Should I 'not rape' you just to show you how weak and powerless you've fucking become? Should I show you that, if I'm disgusting, it's only because who you are rubbed off on me like a stain. Because that's what you are." *Shove.* "Who you are." *Slam.* "And all you'll ever be."

A sort of haze sets in. A delirium.

His mentor sneers. "You better kill me now, boy. If not, I'm raking you over the fucking coals."

Caleb grins. "And what? Show how vulnerable you are in front of an audience? Show how feeble the mighty Charles Sloane has become? How many Alphas will smell blood in the water and come for you then? No. You won't do that. Why don't you just let me go, instead? Bygones be bygones. I'll start my own practice and you'll just stay the fuck out of it."

"I'll ruin you. I'll drag your name through the mud across the entire city."

"And I'll sue you for defamation of character."

Sloane claps back, "And what? Your pretty pro-bono wife going to defend you? Perhaps that will be all you can afford. Damage will already be done, boy."

Caleb leans in, unable to help himself, and whispers over the shell of Sloane's ear, just as the man had done to him over a decade ago. "I quit."

With a growl, Sloane tries to shove him back, but he can't. He's too weak. "I won't let you."

Caleb digs in his nails, and Sloane cries out. "You don't have to let me do anything. The world is bigger than you."

Backing off, Caleb spits in his mentor's face and Sloane reels back so hard he hits the wall again.

"Know what, Charles? You're not just disgusting. You're pitiful. If I'm sure of anything, it's the fact that you're going to die alone, in pain, with no one but yourself to mourn you."

With that, Caleb walks away, leaving his mentor behind. Sloane screams that he'll destroy him—completely, utterly—but Caleb doesn't care. He's not sure he cares about anything right now. He already knows what he has to do...and it's not wasting one more minute in this terrible place.

***

She is a horrible person. That's what Ari thinks of herself, anyway. It doesn't stop her, though. Nothing could stop her. No amount of rationalization, no amount of self-hate—her feet are moving on her own. She even forgot to buy flowers.

No one does anything in reception other than glow and wave when they see her, gesturing to the back with utter joy. It seems Ben opening his eyes has really put everyone in high spirits. Mr. Canady catches her on her way in and wraps her in a warm embrace.

"Ariiii, my sweet Omega! How are you doing today?"

Ben. I need to get to Ben. Please, get out of my way, I have to go to him.

Instead, she nods with a smile as kind as she can make it.

"We're going to have to move him soon. I sent Caleb away with a handful of brochures on assisted living. None of them are sponsored by Mr. Sloane, but there are loans available for medical care. I'm sure he'll talk to you all about it."

Ari's eyebrows knit. "Ben can't stay here anymore?"

"No." But Canady says it with a grin. "Our job here is to help people at the end of their lives, Ari. Ben's just getting a second beginning!"

She grins. She can't help it. "You really think so?"

Just because he talked a little? Do a few words really matter so much?

Tightening her ponytail, she blathers on. "I can't believe it! That's amazing! Fantastic!"

And also terrible. Run again. Please run. Think of Caleb. Think of how he feels right now. He's numb. You're a horrible Omega. How dare you smile when your...mate...is so heartbroken?

"Go see. Caleb just left a bit ago. He was beside himself with surprise, it was wonderful!"

He was here? The thought only pangs her. That must have been what she felt earlier. With a little nod, she turns toward Ben's room, takes a deep breath, and peeks in.

He's...sitting up. It's at a steep incline, so he's still mostly leaned back, but it's something. He's trying to handle some kind of toy. It looks like an egg and he squeezes it with his hands, completely lucid. Her brain rings in a four-alarm fire.

He was supposed to be ASLEEP!

Run, run, run.

And —

Go closer. Hold him. Alpha. Alpha. Oh God, Alpha.

Ben's nostrils flare and he looks up at her. She has a feeling he could find her in a crowd of millions.

"Ari," he says, and everything in her tingles. She stays in the doorway, clutching the frame, terrified. Weakly, Ben gestures toward a chair at his bedside. "Sit with me?"

He seems shy. It's so adorable, Ari feels like she's melting. She doesn't sit, but steps in a little, her eyes flicking again to the thing in his hands.

Sheepish, he shrugs. Barely. "Trying to get stronger."

For me. Tell me it's for me.

She holds herself still and won't come closer. They stare at each other as if the world doesn't exist. With a mischievous glint in his eyes, he nods a little toward a water cup with a straw poking out of it. It's close enough to grab, but he says, "Can you help me? I'm thirsty, but it's a little…"—he looks shy again—"heavy."

He smells as though he's teasing her, and maybe he is, but her Alpha asked her for something, and Ari's body obeys immediately. Gratefully.

She picks it up, going to his bedside. His eyes twinkle still. "It will be easier if you sit."

"Oh? Oh…" she says, like an idiot. Barely placing her hip on the side of the bed, she leans in with trembling hands so Ben can take a drink. His pretty lips wrap around and suck, giving her intense, unforgettable ideas. He rests his cool palm over her knuckles, maybe to steady her, though it does absolutely no good. Both of them shiver when they touch, an involuntary reaction as Ari's skin prickles.

Alpha. Alpha. Please… oh, please.

She sets down the cup for him as he gazes at her, his scent screaming sugar. That irreplaceable *Indulge* feeling that's unique to him.

"I'll get better," he whispers. "I will."

She doesn't know what to say other than, "Caleb will be so happy."

But Ben's face falls into a frown. A soft sadness. "You're his soulmate?"

I'm yours.

"Yes." She can't stop looking at him. It's as if she's hypnotized.

Ben shakes his head, just a little. "No. No, I don't think so."

It should be blatantly offensive, but it's not. She trembles and he reaches out to her, sliding his hand over her wrist gently. He tries to lift it, but she is, indeed, too heavy, so she helps him, letting him simply guide her, instead.

"I shouldn't be doing this." He looks at her with pain in his expression. "There are so many reasons not to…but I can't stop. It's like the animal inside me is finally awake." He leads her up to his face and nuzzles her wrist gland, paying no mind to the bite mark there.

His eyes close and his gorgeous smile blooms. "So sweet. God, how are you so sweet?"

He nuzzles her and her whole body shakes. Her slick gathers, her panties immediately soaking through…and he knows it. His eyes snap up to hers, hooded, his face flushing with heat.

"Oh, Ari," he sighs. "You're not Caleb's. You're mine."

In a quick moment, he turns his face and licks her inner wrist, making her cry out in pleasure before pulling away from him.

She holds her arm to her chest defensively. "No. I can't be that person for you. I promised never to leave him. That means something to me. It doesn't matter whether or not he's my true mate." *But it does.* "What matters is that I care about him!"

"Care?" Ben asks, his eyebrows lifting. "Not love?"

In three words, he's ruined her.

"I'm not coming back," she says, shaking her head. "I can't do this."

Her brain finally kicks in and Ari runs away. She needs to go home. There's a horrible, empty ache within, just like Caleb has made her feel. But it happened so easily. No heat. No seduction. Just Ben's presence. His face. Her body felt him and just reacted.

She hates herself.

Horrible person. Horrible Omega. You shouldn't be here. You have no place in this family! You'll only destroy them both!

Which she believes with her whole heart.

Hustle and bustle. That's a concept Ari has only ever ascribed to the city outside, but the apartment has taken on that moniker for itself. There are strangers fluxing in and out, bringing in items that have all been stacked in the hallway or leaned against the wall just inside her door, which gapes wide open. Metal rods. Strange stands. Items that look like equipment. A mattress.

Her breath stops.

No.

Entering, everything is being brought into the rut room...the nest. The one that she ruined but promised herself she would make again. Two heavyset Betas push by her with a nod as they bring the mattress inside. Queen size.

No. No, please don't bring him here. I can't hold back if you bring him here.

Caleb comes out of the room, standing aside so that others can move in. Sounds echo in the room's emptiness. Clicks and thumps of things being set up.

"Caleb..." she says, trying to get his attention, though it comes out weak.

"Put it in the corner." He ignores her, pointing. "That way we only have to put the rail on one side. You can pin it down, so it doesn't roll, right?"

There are mutters of agreement.

"Caleb?" she tries again, stronger this time. He just stands at the doorway, mouth pursed as he stares at the work being done. "Caleb!"

"Shut up, Omega," he commands her, and she complies immediately, stepping back against the kitchen island and holding on to it for dear life. There she stays as he barks directions. He smells funny. She's never smelled this on anyone. She's never felt this emotion on anyone. It's way beyond the color black.

People leave and Caleb only nods at them as they walk out. Ari has no concept of time, she just watches them go with wide eyes, hating them all for being here. For doing whatever it is they did. For making whatever it is they just made.

Alone now, Caleb steps up, not looking at her. "I've hired a full-time nurse. She'll sleep on the pull-out sofa so she can help him at a moment's notice. You won't have to worry about that part."

Ari's mouth finally falls open again as tears drip down her face. "Why are you doing this? Why are you bringing him here?"

"Why do you smell like him?"

And fear sinks in. He looks disheveled again. Furious and sad and...something else. "Your scent is wrong," she says. "I don't know what's going on."

He grabs her wrist and pivots her a few steps, slamming her against the wall so hard it hurts. "You're my wife. Everything I have is yours, you know that, right?"

She nods frantically, his large hands wrapped around her wrists to pin her. "Caleb, you're hurting me..." But she doesn't think he's listening. His eyes are wild.

"You know the safe under the bed. You've tried to crack it for fun, but you can't."

She blinks at him, and he smiles at her...but it's wrong.

"Today, the passcode is your birthday. Say it back to me."

"M-my birthday."

"That's right, kitten. He's coming here, whether you want it or not. Before then, though..."

And he rushes in. His mouth is on hers and she can't help but open for him. He nips her lips, working frantically under her ear and lapping at her mating gland, dragging his teeth over it.

"Caleb," she moans.

"Dirty girl. Getting wet for someone that's not me."

She tries to pull away, but he just presses his chest against hers, pinning her harder. She struggles but gets nowhere; he's just too big. "I couldn't help it! I'm sorry! I left as soon as it happened! I didn't mean to! It's not my fault!"

"I know, sweetheart. I know it's not."

But that doesn't stop his violence. He drags her to the floor, yanking her hair until she's lying down beneath him, gripping both her arms and shoving them to her chest with one hand. The pressure is immense, and she can barely breathe. He pulls her skirt up over her hips.

"Time to put you into heat, little kitten."

She shakes her head as fast as she can. "It's too soon!"

She's writhing, kicking her legs, but he's between them, bracing them open. With his free hand, he caresses the bite marks on her inner thighs, making her moan.

"Not if I bite you here."

That's what Niles said. He's been forced into heat before. Maybe I was too...?

Ari doesn't remember. She can't think. She can only feel her womb clench as he pets her. "Please, Caleb. Please don't."

But she can't push him off. It's too late. Leaning down, he sucks her through her clothes, growling at her taste. "So fucking sexy. I want this, Ari. Give it to me. Just one more time." His teeth graze over the marks on the whitest parts of her skin and she shivers...

Then he bites her.

He bites her *hard.*

And her heat starts immediately.

CHAPTER 16
LEARNING TO FLY

LICKING INSTEAD of biting as he so desperately wants, Caleb tastes her. He wants her blood. He wants her slick, her spit, her tears, all of it, but he'll settle for the tang of sweat in the crook of her neck as he makes love to her from behind. They're still on the floor, right where he dropped them down, and the rough carpet is leaving burns over his hips and knees depending on their position, though he couldn't give a fuck if he tried. He's lost in her, mindless with plea-sure. If nothing else, he can still feel hers through their bond. It's just as fantastic as the first time. Perhaps more because it's laced with such bittersweet flecks of emotion.

"I love you," he whispers against her, bottoming out in a long stroke as she grips around his length. "I love you so much."

Say it back. Please, tell me you love me, too. Everything could change if you'd only say it.

"Alpha. You feel so good."

Unoriginal. Uninspiring. The same words as every other Omega he's ever fucked.

So he treats her like a stranger, going faster and grabbing her thigh as they lay on their side, swinging her leg over his hip as he thrusts into her, her slick making a mess below them. Good. He keeps his teeth on her. If he needs to bite down to hold her in place, he absolutely will, but there's no need. His Ari is ravenous.

"I want your knot, Alpha. Please. I'm burning up. I need it."

But like he's told her twice already, "No, sweetheart," no matter how much his inner animal fights against those words. Instead, he slides a hand over her belly and begins to toy with her, caressing that special bundle of nerves. Immediately her body bucks. "Gonna count you down again, Ari. You can't finish until I tell you to."

"Will you knot me if I'm a good girl?" she whines.

"Fuck, gorgeous, what a beautiful thing to say." He begins to strum her, even though his answer hasn't changed. She squeezes him inside, a quick pulse as his thrusts slow. He focuses on arching his back and staying shallow, sliding his thick head the length of her entrance where she seems to need him most. Higher up, his fingers rub clockwise, making her squirm, then counterclockwise to make her start panting. When her cunt seems to draw in like a vise, he whispers, "Five."

She whimpers, loving this as much as she hates it. She starts to flutter inside, and he licks her mating gland to keep her building that spark into a bonfire. Her moans are high pitched and breathy, and her fingernails rake the carpet as she tries to hold back from her peak.

"So good, kitten. I know. I feel it, too. Four."

"Caleb, please."

"Hush, Omega."

He can barely pull out anymore for as tight as she's grabbing him, and his knot threatens. Going deeper again, he thickens at the bottom, causing a lewd slap every time the bulge hits her. He's going to come soon, too. Probably exactly when she does.

"Three, sweetheart." His fingers move fast against her silken surface as she whimpers without end. "That's a good girl. That's right. Count to one with me, Ari." He moves fast again. The sound of their cores hitting is wet and perfect. "Say it, sweetheart."

"T-two," she stutters. "I can't..."

"Yes, you can, gorgeous." He smacks her on the hip a little, soothing the sting away before his hand starts its mischief again. She's not even moaning anymore. She's begging for release.

"Hold on. Hold on, sweetheart." He's going to die from her pleasure, and it would be the perfect way to go. Something inside him winds into a tight coil that's going to spring any minute. Gasping, he grits his teeth and growls in her ear. "Now!"

"One!" She comes with a wail as he ruts into her, pistoning as fast as he can, riding through it even as her ecstasy washes over him. He can't anymore. He just... he just...

Pulling from her, he wraps himself in his hand and pumps as fast as possible until his knot gets the better of him, spilling his seed all over the floor, mixing with her slick and marking this spot just for them. It's not a nest, it never will be, but at least it's theirs now. He'll take what he can get.

She whimpers. "Why won't you knot me? So empty. Alpha, it hurts..."

Out of kindness, he takes his clean hand and fingers her, curling three into a ball as he nudges in and out, tearing a guttural sound from her throat.

"Fill me up, Caleb, please."

"No, sweetheart."

"I want your pups. Make me yours."

You wouldn't have to say that if you were already mine.

She starts to calm down, but he still holds her close. She's raging hot and she'll need him again in only a few minutes. He's more than willing to go as many rounds as she wants. He'd shake the world down, if only she'd ask just right.

"Alpha, let me be a good Omega. Let me give you children. Let me make your dreams come true."

If only, sweetheart.

He nuzzles her from behind, rubbing his scent all over her. Everywhere he can reach. Neck. Shoulders. The top of her back. "You'd be such a wonderful mother. You'd be kind and fair. You'd show them the difference between right and wrong. You'd love them forever. You'd teach them how to paint horrible pictures and cook horrible meals."

She huffs a breathless laugh. "Rude."

He holds her closer, palming one of her breasts as his knot rests behind her legs, tucked up alongside her backside. "I mean it. If I'm ever reborn, I wish it could be to someone like you."

"Oedipal."

"Oh, absolutely." He grins, lips caressing her skin. "But you'd take care of me, wouldn't you?" A hand drifts between her legs again and she yelps in the best possible way.

"I'll take care of all of our children, Alpha."

Our.

Hope fills him again, but he kills it quickly. Ari is queen of heat-talk. She'll say anything to keep this tender moment alive. So, why not? He'll join her.

"How many shall I give you?"

"At least two. Maybe three."

He starts to stroke her again, letting her internal fire burn. "All at once, or can I take it slow, kitten? Give you one at a time..."

"Anything for you," she whimpers.

He licks her neck, suckles her, and her whole body shakes even as he pins her down. "Mine. Sweetheart, you're mine."

Lie to me. Or tell me the truth. You decide, Ari. It's now or never.

"Want you again, Alpha."

His heart hurts. She almost turns to look at him, but he keeps her trapped. Making a quick excuse, he says, "From now on, I only want you to say my name. 'Alpha' could be anyone. I want you to know that you're with me."

"Caleb," she sighs in agreement.

He stands up, lifting her with him and hiking her into a straddle over his hips. He teases her entrance as he hardens for her again, walking them backward out of the hall. Her face is flushed, cheeks like pink petals as she leans in for kiss after lovely kiss.

"Knot me, Caleb. I want it. I want it so much. I'll do anything."

Bringing her into the once-nest, he rests her on the edge of the bed—the new one meant for Ben—and her whole demeanor changes.

Eyes wide, she scrambles, trying to get away.

"No. Not here. Stop."

He leans forward, pushing his length into her hard and fast until he can go no deeper. Her eyes roll back in her pretty head as their combined fluids soak into the bedding. "Yes, here, sweetheart. I want him to fucking roll in it."

Because he's winning out in the end.

She fights him then, swearing in hisses, pushing at him, and trying to escape. Her hands slide off his sweat-stained skin, no purchase to be had while her sharp little nails graze the faded flourish of the scar she'd once given him. He silently begs her to tear it open again. Split him in two and suck him dry. Instead, she tries to shove at his face next, catching him by surprise as her claws dig in and pull from his eyebrow to the bottom of his jaw, missing his eye by kismet more than intent.

His harsh cry seems to stun her, and she stills immediately, mouth open wide as she gasps, feeling the flash of his pain. It's beautiful when he bleeds on her. Red spatters on white skin. He's panting as the wound leaves wet trails dripping along his face, but that doesn't stop him from fucking her. And it doesn't stop her from taking it, as she was made to. They don't speak anymore; they just grunt and groan, their breath sighing and hitching as they let the pain and pleasure mix between them. Every stroke hikes her farther and farther up onto the bed and she's too far gone to complain anymore. Her eyes slammed shut, she only winds her fingers in his hair and pulls him closer, daring to steal a kiss that tastes like blood.

He still won't knot her, even though this time the empty ache makes her weep.

Say you're mine, he begs silently. *Say you love me, and I'll do anything. Please.*

But she doesn't. And she never will. It's the last nail in the coffin as he kisses her down from their shared high. They exchange breaths, faces oh so close, and he's dizzy with the intensity of this moment. The longing. The unfulfilled wishes. He's afraid, but it's too late now. The die is cast.

Voice filled with sorrow, he commands, *"Sleep, my Omega."*

And that's exactly what she does.

Ari is groggy. She can't move. Every part of her is hot and sweating and her cramps are coming back, burning her in little clenches. She needs her husband. She needs him inside her and she needs it now.

"Caleb..." She reaches behind her on Ben's hospital bed, but he's nowhere to be found. "Caleb!" she tries again.

He doesn't come.

Panic seizes her just as another cramp does. His emotions are that 'beyond black' again.

"Caleb!" she yells, eyes wide as she looks around at what used to be her nest, now arranged with medical equipment. It makes her afraid. More afraid than she's ever been.

Another wave of pain comes over her and she curls into a little ball, sniveling until she hears his footsteps. Hope flares in her.

Alpha, Alpha, Alpha.

When he enters, all she feels is shock. He has a wound winding down his face, ragged with a dark scab. It looks as though it will leave a scar. Desperate, she reaches for him.

My fault.

"Let me soothe it, please! I'm so sorry! If I can —"

"No, sweetheart. Let me keep it." He holds up a glass of water to her lips and she drinks it greedily, drips and drops and streams running down her chin. For the first time, he doesn't lick them off.

He's wearing clothes. Why is he wearing clothes?

She clutches at his collar. "Hurts, Alph— Caleb. Please, help. I need you."

He scoops her up in his arms and brings her into the living room, opening the drapes and exposing her to the bright morning sun. They must have been at it all night, but she still needs more.

"Please," she whines again, no other words to convey her need.

Instead, he opens up the sliding glass door, letting the air kiss her sheen of sweat. Getting down on all fours, he looks at her with love —so much she doesn't know what to do with it all. He still smells wrong, especially now.

He kisses her forehead. "I'll be back soon."

Everything in her goes rigid with terror. Grasping at him, she cries. "Don't go! I'm begging you. Caleb, I need..." *Oh it hurts so much.* "I need you."

It's crazy how easily he pulls her off, the tiniest of smiles on his face. The saddest, most sorrowful smile. "Hush, Omega. Put those pretty fingers between your legs and hold it together. Just for a little while. Trust your Alpha."

But she can't trust him at all.

He stands and her whole body rejects the notion as she grabs at his ankles, only to be overpowered by the mere strength of his stride. "Caleb," she whines. "Please." She doubles over with pain and moans.

He pauses for a moment, his hand going to his lower belly. With sympathy, he says, "I won't take long."

She's shivering with desire when the door clicks shut behind him, her mind whirling. She can't put sentences together now, panting and whimpering through heavy tears. She's going to die from lust and emptiness.

Naked and alone, she tries to take care of herself, but it's not enough. Is Caleb punishing her? He made her slick up Ben's bed. He finished all over it, too. Is he going to torture them? Why? It's not their fault! It's fucking *biology!*

Even as she cries, she prays for him to come back. Through their connection she can feel his heartache. It's a never-ending chasm that's going to eat her alive.

She's going to implode.

No, she's going to burst.

No, she's going to light on fire.

She comes mindlessly, her hands working their pitiful magic, but it's not enough. Her fingers are too slim to fill her. Her orgasms are too weak to satisfy. She's weeping Caleb's name for what feels like hours until the door finally kicks open, and he returns.

With Ben in his arms.

"Don't just leave me in the car while you go do whatever," Ben gripes, holding his midsection just under his ribs. "I'm a delicate goddamn flower and this is *not* a comfortable place. That buddy of yours took out the feeding tube as soon as I ate a fucking cracker. I basically have a hole, you bastard." Though it's said with love. "I'm a blow-up doll. You want a blow-up doll for a brother?"

"If it's you? Absolutely."

Caleb reaches in and hikes Ben into his arms. It's not difficult at all. When did he become so light? He's not a feather by a long shot but he's light enough to carry for miles, never mind up an elevator and down the hall. Caleb wonders if his brother will be able to be the man he needs to be...but that's really up to him, isn't it?

"Slow down, you insensitive prick, or I'll mark up the other side of your face," Ben says, frowning even as he nuzzles Caleb's chest.

Caleb can feel Ari's searing agony all through his abdomen and it's all he can do to keep Ben above his accidental erection. He can't help it. He feels Ari's pleasure and pain, even now.

"This looks familiar," Ben murmurs, glancing around.

"I never left our apartment. I wanted to keep everything the same so when you came home, you'd know where you were."

"Is the bathroom still black and red?"

"Yep." Caleb hikes Ben a little higher so he can hit the elevator button for the fourteenth floor.

"Good. Best choice I ever made. My bedroom?"

"My room now, sorry about that. I took mine and converted it into...well, doesn't matter. I fixed it up and made it your room. Not perfect, but it'll do for now. Until you're stronger. Got you a queen-size bed, though."

"Pfft. And you said we were too old to cuddle."

Caleb chuckles a bit as the elevator dings open and he steps them inside.

Okay, maybe Ben's not so light after all. Caleb's arms tremble a bit, but he'll be damned if he lets go before he has to.

"Everything's going to be new and strange," Caleb says. "Technology is fucking crazy, but at least the people are still assholes."

"Good to know I can rely on something."

Caleb shrugs as best he can, hoisting up Ben again, making his brother grunt and grimace.

Please let this work, Caleb begs. *Please let him be strong enough.*

"You'll be okay," Caleb says. "You were always good at adapting. Unlike me."

"As indicated by the fact that you haven't moved in eleven years."

"Yeah, well..."

Ben wraps his arms tighter as the elevator opens again. Swallowing hard, Caleb turns toward his apartment, tension winding in his gut.

"You smell funny," Ben says.

"You smell funny, but at least I have the decency not to say anything about it."

"Prick."

"Yeah, prick."

"Another thing that hasn't changed." His brother grins at him, making him chuckle again.

"Love you, Benny. You know that, right? I love you so fucking much."

Ben hugs him tighter. "You pussy."

Caleb outright laughs, tears pricking his eyes. "Yeah, that too."

Ten feet away.

Seven feet away.

In the softest voice Caleb's ever heard, Ben asks, "...Is Ari there?"

Because of course he does. Caleb nods, a cold rock in his heart. "Yeah. You'll see her, too."

Three feet away.

Two feet.

One...

Caleb had left the door unlocked, a foolish choice given the treasure he left inside, but it makes it so much easier to twist the knob, placing Ben down and letting him brace himself on wobbly, trembling legs as he leans on Caleb for support.

Please be strong. Please, oh please be strong.

Opening the door, the scent of Ari's need is overwhelming, and Ben goes rigid with a gasp. He's not strong enough to stand alone, but Caleb leads him in while Ben tries to take steps, clutching Caleb way too hard. He reeks of panic suddenly, and that signal lets Caleb know everything's going to be okay.

Ari, his naked and writhing Ari, is right where he left her, sobbing out the agony of her desire. When Ben sees her, he starts struggling to get closer...and that's perfect. That's exactly what Caleb wants.

Kicking the door closed behind him, he sets Ben far enough away that he can't reach her. The question is, is Ben strong enough to crawl? Perhaps with the right persuasion.

Ari sees them then and wails with shame, trying to cover up and curling into the most adorable little ball. Ben looks at Caleb with wide, terrified eyes, as if he doesn't know what to do, but instinct is about to kick in, and it's about to kick in hard.

Protect.

Working his way closer, Caleb tries a soothing tone of voice, though it comes out strangled. "Shh, kitten. It will all be over soon." Getting down onto his knees, he grabs her shoulders and turns her over, exposing her breasts to the open air as she struggles to no avail.

"Caleb! No! Stop!" Ari tries, and Ben outright growls.

"What the fuck are you doing?!"

That's right, Benny. You can do it.

His wife fights him, as if she had a chance. "Why are you doing this?!"

Caleb looks at her gorgeous hazel eyes, red rimmed with exhaustion, humiliation, and sorrow. They glitter with tears like little stars as he chokes out, "Because I need you to hate me."

Her lower lip trembles perfectly. "Why?"

"Because that will make this next part easier."

Ben isn't even bothering to scream at him. He's just trying to crawl over, drag after drag, his teeth bared and his eyes wild. He'll make it...but there's still time.

Caleb kisses Ari good and deep, taking every last drop even as she writhes.

I love you. I fucking love you so much. I'm doing this for you. Please, be happy. Please get what I can't give you. Please love him with your whole heart because he deserves it.

Pulling back, he asks her, low and deep. "Who's your mate?"

She cries out, "YOU!"

But he shakes his head. Compelling her, commanding her, he pins her by the throat this time. "Don't fucking lie to me, Omega. *Who is your mate?!*"

Her heart shreds so deep he can feel it. Unable to resist him, she croaks, "Ben."

His brother snarls, just as he should, edging ever closer.

"But who mated you instead, kitten?"

She looks at him, lost. "You."

"That's right."

Ben's closer now. Near enough to almost reach. Caleb locks eyes with his wife again. "And who do you want to claim you? Who do you want to belong to?"

Her entire face crumbles. "Ben."

And it's the right answer.

With a single finger, he caresses her cheek, chasing a tear away. "How sad for me."

He kisses her again because he loves her. He'd wondered if he truly did, but this is the proof right here. It's twisted and wrong and always has been, but he'd do anything for her. Glaring at Ben, he asks one question. "Do you know how to claim a mated Omega?"

Ben halts immediately, his face falling into shock. Caleb knows in that moment that his brother understands. Anger snuffed out of him, Ben whispers. "Caleb, don't. Please."

But no, he needs to say the words. "How do you claim a MATED OMEGA?!"

Ben's voice trembles from the strain, and perhaps the hurt. "You...you bite her when she's in heat."

Caleb smiles, so soft, so sad. "That's right, Benny. That's right."

He looks at Ari again. She's still lost in her need and her body is begging for release, but she only weeps. She's so sensitive right now. He can feel her lust burning within his own body...just like she'll feel him very soon. He presses his forehead against hers, closing his eyes as his tears rain on her. "It's okay, kitten. You can do it. It will only hurt for a minute. I promise. Ben's going to take care of you."

With that, he whips around and bolts toward the open balcony.

Every time he's ever come out here and fed the crows, he's always wished he could fly. Caleb has no wings, but if he did, he knows they'd be black just like theirs.

He's strong, so a hand on the high railing is all it takes to launch himself up and over. As gravity takes him, he understands that a man like him was never meant to fly. He was fated for this from the very beginning. The wind tears at him as one last thought runs through his mind.

This was the right choice.

Ari *SCREECHES* as if everything in her body's been broken all at once. Cars squeal and honk below, slamming into one another, and she's curled on herself, screaming, screaming, screaming!

Ben has to move. His Alpha tells him that this is so much more than *Protect*. It's *SAVE!*

Ari sounds as though she's dying because Caleb...he can't think about it. All he can think about is the steady effort of pulling himself forward or he'll be lost.

Adrenaline fuels him as he tries to take her in his arms, but she's flailing and keening. Her wails rend his ears while he whispers against her, "Shhh. Be still. Please, please..." But he can't control her.

Because they're not truly mated.

Not yet.

Why like this? How could he do this?

It's cruel.

Ben's heart hurts more than his body as he opens his jaws, notches himself against the woman of his dreams...and bites down as hard as he can. Immediately, with one last shout, she goes limp in his arms as he clutches her. Lapping at her new wound, he tastes the blood on his tongue, reveling in it, feeling their new connection bloom, just as it was supposed to from the very beginning. Her physical pain ebbs and he can actually feel it go, but the overpowering sorrow remains. They share it even as he licks her, suckling her, needing her more than he's ever needed anything in his life. He's crushed—so absolutely, terribly destroyed—but still, now and for the rest of his life...

...Mate.

EPILOGUE

AT FIRST, neither of them spoke, lost and unable to take in the weight of what had happened...but then Ari's Omega called...and Ben's Alpha answered. He made love to her to stave off the pain, to take a moment of solace in each other before reality ruined them. Ari's heat ended as soon as that moment did, and a new kind of agony set in...for both of them. Just like with Caleb, their emotions ricocheted one to the other, compounding and drowning them both. But it was deeper somehow. More visceral. More inescapable.

Because they were true soulmates.

For an indeterminate amount of time, neither did anything other than tremble, listening to the scream of sirens. It was only when Ari's phone rang in the other room that she shattered, Ben along with her, each for their own reasons and each with enough regret to last a lifetime. But at least they had each other.

Sloane had offered to pay for Caleb's service. The best of the best, no expenses spared. The man smelled like someone who truly mourned, felt immense guilt, perhaps, but Ben lost his mind. Though Ari didn't know why, her soulmate nearly tore out Sloane's throat, weak as he was, and Sloane almost let him. In the end, only her fearful screams calmed her Alpha's feral rage, and Caleb's personal monster slinked away, becoming only a memory. Ari never understood why Caleb hated him so badly, he never talked about it, but Ben said there are some secrets he'll never tell.

Months went by and life found some normalcy. New faces, new spaces, and new definitions of what happiness looks like. It's not what Ari would have dreamed of for herself, not by a long shot, but that doesn't mean it can't have its joys. Some are so big, they're immeasurable. Ben feels the same.

He was top marks before the accident, studying to be a lawyer, and he's trying to pick up where he left off. It's hard for him to remember things like he used to, but he's working on it. Caleb had kept up immense life insurance policies specifically to take care of Ben in case he left this world. With that, they stay afloat, even with all the schooling and care Ben needs. He can walk with a cane now and smiles like an angel—though with a devilish, mischievous streak. Like his brother, he has a temper and swears like a sailor, but Ari loves it. She also loves the few silver strands heartbreak has woven into his hair.

No one has ever made Ari laugh so much or feel so enamored by just a shy smile or a hand scratching at the back of his neck as he concentrates. His anger never scares her because she can soothe him as soon as he riles up—and his fury is never pointed in her direction. He says he wants to work pro-bono like her, and it makes her burst with love. They joke that they're preparing for a life of poverty, but both of them are used to sacrificing themselves for the sake of others. It suits them. Like Ari, Ben wants to give others the chance for a happy future, as if he's trying to make up for the future his brother lost. There's a lot he does with his twin in mind.

Ben won't bite over any more of Caleb's marks. It's probably for the best. Ari already looks as though she has the most aggressive, possessive Alpha in the world. She wears her five visible bites with pride, though, refusing turtlenecks and long sleeves unless it's the dead of winter. Some still look at her with pity or disdain, but she's quick to put them in their place. She'd learned that particular skill from her first husband and is all the better for it. Working outside the city as she does now, no one knows her story, and that's exactly how she needs it to be. As far as anyone knows, Ben is her first and only. The only exception is Niles, who wept endlessly for her. And for Caleb.

Both she and Ben stare at the marks on her wrists sometimes, lost in their own world of memories. Ben rubs his fingers along them, just like Caleb used to. It's his way to say goodbye as much as it's his need to show her constantly how much he loves her.

He wouldn't let her claim him back at first. It was grief. But when they finally had their moment, it was beautiful and soft and filled with words of love. It was exactly what Ari wanted, when she wanted it, which mattered more to her than she could possibly say.

Ben tells her that Caleb had always been on the verge of letting go of life. Ben would have done anything and everything to stop it... so he did. He never told Caleb, but the truth is he never intended to survive the accident. Back then, he thought that the grief over his death would keep Caleb alive. That the rage and hurt over Ben's sacrifice would make Caleb fight on another day. He was right. And he hates himself for it.

Ben also tells her that, when Caleb was young, he would be selfish—taking and taking—but eventually something in him would click and he'd give Ben anything and everything for a while. Indulgent. Subservient. In those times, Caleb would tell him, "It's your turn, Benny." Ben thinks that's what Caleb had done this time, too. He'd taken his selfishness, turned it around, and given Ben what he wanted...part of it, anyway. Ben never wanted to lose his brother. Had almost given up his life specifically to save him. It was just like Caleb to leave a perfect wound to remember him by.

They talk about it a lot. They cry about it a lot. The "What if"s. What if Ben had just run away with Caleb when they were young? What if Ben had died? What if Ari had just seen out her heat with Paul? Or better yet, never tricked Caleb in the first place, though they both know in their hearts it wouldn't have mattered. As long as she faced him, Caleb would have tracked her down. After all, she was his soulmate...and he smelled almost perfect.

There's no scenario that has an entirely happily ever after. Just as Caleb said, "Everyone wants a fairy tale, but no one ever gets them." But that doesn't mean you can't find your own happiness, even through the pain. That's what Ari tells her pups, anyway. Hers and Ben's. Triplets, all with jet black hair. Two identical girls and one fraternal boy, named after his uncle, Caleb.

Secretly, oh so very secretly, Ari can't help but love that little one best. He's so much like his namesake, after all. A little moody and *very* protective of his siblings, he's the only one with the habit of getting into things he absolutely shouldn't, pushing every boundary with a smile on his face.

He's adorable. Affectionate to the point of needy.

And he smells like the purest of cinnamon.

END

AFTERWORD

First off, let me (sort of) apologize for the conclusion. I know that, in my advance readings, people hoped and prayed the story would end in a sexy throuple—or they wanted themselves to be inserted into the story to love Caleb with all their might—but the muse took me.

Originally, this story came from a prompt by my friend Sarah, and I wasn't sure how to end it. While driving, my brain told me that Caleb had to commit suicide. My heart broke then and there, making me weep in my car (and I spent several nights up late crying about it, too). That's how I knew it had to happen. I had to make you ride this pain train with me all the way to the bitter end. Partially because misery loves company. Also, because I may be a sadist. The jury is out on that one.

This story was very different for me. I'd never written A/B/O. I read it voraciously because it's so f*cking hot, but I'd never known how to write one. Welp, consider my cherry popped.

I'd also never written more than one sex scene in a book. I have a thing about making each sex scene different—virgins, emotionally edgy sex, bittersweet lovemaking—so it was really important to try and get the feelings different for each of the smut scenes. I dubbed them, "Sweetness," "Desperation," "Seduction," and "Devastation."

Also, I wrote this novel in two months, almost to the day... I'm impressed with myself. #ThisWillNeverHappenAgain

A special shout-out goes to my advance readers. This piece was originally a work of fanfiction (#Reylo forever) and I was humbled by the fandom's enthusiastic response to this work. They shared theories with me along the way on some alternative roads this story could have travelled on. Here are some of my favorites.

FAN THEORIES

- Caleb was saying "Ben" caused the accident, but that name was really just his alter ego. Caleb was the one who did everything... Dude, that's some next level deception right there!
- Sloane was keeping Ben in a coma to keep Caleb under his control... Wouldn't THAT have been just perfect. I love this damn idea.
- Sloane was the one who wrote Ben's "suicide note"... So, so twisted!
- All the different pairing options. Throuple. Ari has a secret twin. Caleb/Ben twincest. I loved it all!
- Death to Sloane... So many of you pictured all the delicious ways Caleb could off his boss. And I DO NOT blame you.
- ALL THE DIFFERENT ENDING OPTIONS! Caleb hooks up with the full-time nurse; Ben kills himself; Caleb kills himself; Ari kills herself; Caleb is slowly poisoning himself, that's why he smells wrong; Caleb runs away to leave Ben and Ari to themselves; Caleb kills Ari in a jealous rage; Caleb tries to knock up Ari before leaving;

Ari will realize she did love Caleb and Ben will never be good enough, regardless of chemistry; Ben will replace Caleb completely, assuming his identity at work, in his relationship, etc.; Caleb tries to kill himself and fails so Ari ends up having to take care of two invalids... SO MANY DEVASTATING OPTIONS!

THE TIMES I ALMOST MURDERED SLOANE

Let's be honest now. Sloane deserved a lot more than I gave him.

Another "I thought of this in the car" epiphany was, when Caleb quit, I was going to have him murder Sloane first. It would have been the straw that broke the camel's back. I had it all plotted in my head and it was horrifying and wonderful, but then I thought about Caleb's character. The one thing he prided himself on was that he "wasn't a murderer like his brother." Well, we all know how that turned out, but I felt like that sentiment would remain. Caleb wanted nothing more than to be better than who he was. He gave up in the end, but that was his dearest dream...besides Ari.

I also almost had Sloane commit suicide in the epilogue. Tristen, my magical beta reader, smacked me on the wrist and said it cheapened Caleb's moment. I agreed immediately. My thought behind it was that Sloane had built the crux of his business and his persona around Caleb, for better or for worse. Perhaps he'd thought that his treatment truly was making Caleb stronger because he saw no proof to the contrary. Caleb hid his sensitivity under a veneer of anger that Sloane perceived as strength. The minute Caleb showed any emotion other than rage, Sloane was disappointed. That's not the man he was honing to replace him. It's my opinion that, if Caleb "got with the program," Sloane would have given him back his bid for partner and much more. Sloane was a sick and twisted individual, but one who cared for Caleb in his own deranged way. Seeing someone he considered his successor, and potentially had paternal feelings for, kill himself probably opened Sloane's eyes to what he'd truly done to Caleb all those years. I wanted the guilt to take him down. I still do.

Unfortunately, he'll have to die offscreen. Without us to watch him, he will do it completely and utterly alone...just like Caleb said he would.

ABOUT ME

Nichol (Ashworth) Goldstein
Writer / Illustrator
www.nixcomix.com
Twitter: @Nixcomix | Facebook: Nixcomix
Tumblr: Nixcomix1 | Instagram: Nixcomix1

You know those people who quantify their self-worth by the amount of work they produce? That's me. I just described me.

I started writing novels on May 18th, 2020. As of June 2023, I've written seven books, several short stories, and have a litany of ideas in the pipeline—including a sequel to this story based on Niles! It will still be dark, and very, very spicy. I'd really love it if you followed me on social media as more published work comes out.

As an aside, I used to be a comic book writer/illustrator by trade, so I've also created over eighty fully illustrated art pieces to support my stories, as well as a whole damn comic strip and several chibi-comics. I need to calm the hell down. This is a bit much.

Because of this, please allow me to include some character designs for Caleb, Ari, and Ben. When this book was first serialized, one of my favorite things was illustrating every chapter, but these four were my favorite. I hope you enjoy them.

Be sure to follow me to see more of my doodles, paintings, and snarkasm™.

And thank you, every one of you, for reading.

When Niles, a rare male Omega, realizes a loveless life isn't for him, fate knocks on his door in the shape of an awkward coffeeshop encounter. Jason, a sweet Beta, falls head over heels for Niles at first sight, willing to be friends while holding his breath for something more. Could this brash blond be the one to fill the empty space in Niles's heart?

Or is it Tristan, Niles's volatile first love from high school? The sexy Alpha returns just in time to beg for a second chance, desperately wanting his Omega back in his life. With their chemistry and history together, how can Niles possibly say no?

It's Jason versus Tristan. Safety versus sultry. Which will Niles choose?

And which has a dark secret that goes way beyond sin?

ALSO BY NICHOL GOLDSTEIN

The war is never-ending. Morale is non-existent and magic stains the sky as dragon riders spiral, trying to take down the raging soldiers of the Dominion. The people are exhausted. The battles need to end. But how? The hate between the factions is just too strong. Unless...

When Reyanne, the White Mage of the Separatist movement, goes head-to-head with her arch nemesis Zanthrand, the Dark Moon of the Dominion, many choices abound. You, dear reader, hold their fates in your hand. Choose your path and choose wisely. Can you end the forever conflict? Can you bring these soul-bound sorcerers from enemies to lovers? Or will your choices doom them both?

Good luck, my friend. It's all up to you.

ALSO BY NICHOL GOLDSTEIN

Prepare to be surprised

THE RETELLING OF FAIRY TALES is a reimagining of some of our most beloved childhood stories for an adult audience, adding twists and turns that bring them into fantasy worlds, modern day settings, alien planets, and may even take the point of view of the villain.

Fully illustrated, this collection will make you laugh, pull your heartstrings, and let you fall in love. Come with us and enjoy the call of destiny, the sizzle of romance, the ache of tragedy, and the timelessness of magic, all wrapped together in this one unforgettable collection of short stories.